THE DANGER

"is expertly crafted, with enough action to keep the pages turning and enough intelligence to satisfy those readers who profess to scorn page-turners. . . . a thoroughly enjoyable, undemanding book . . . Francis creates believable characters, and doesn't forget the importance of seemingly minor ones. . . . Given the success of THE DANGER, the biggest danger to the reader is getting hooked on Francis and having to go buy his other twenty-two books."

The Atlanta Journal Constitution

THE
DANGER

DICK FRANCIS

FAWCETT CREST • NEW YORK

Liberty Market Ltd. is fictional,
though similar organizations exist.
No one who has helped me with the
background of this book wants to be
mentioned, but my thanks to them
just the same.
I acknowledge my debt also to
Kidnap and Ransom: The Response
by Richard Clutterbuck.

Contents

Kidnapping is a fact of life. Always has been, always will be. Extorting a ransom is an age-old pastime, less risky and more lucrative than robbing banks.

Kidnapping, twentieth-century style, has meant train loads and plane loads of hostages, athletes killed in company at Munich, men of substance dying lonely deaths. All kidnappers are unstable, but the political variety, hungry for power and publicity as much as money, make quicksand look like rock.

Give me the straightforward criminal any day, the villain who seizes and says pay up or else. One does more or less know where one is, with those.

Kidnapping, you see, is my business.

My job, that is to say, as a partner in the firm of Liberty Market Ltd., is both to advise people at risk how best not to be kidnapped and also to help negotiate with the kidnappers once a grab has taken place: to get the victim back alive for the least possible cost.

Every form of crime generates an opposing force, and to fraud, drugs, and murder one could add the Kidnap Squad, except that the kidnap squad is unofficial and highly discreet . . . and is often *us*.

Italy

One

There was a God-awful screw-up in Bologna.

I stood as still as possible while waves of cold rage and fiery anxiety jerked at my limbs and would have had me pacing.

Stood still . . . while a life which might depend on me was recklessly risked by others. Stood still among the ruins of a success nearly achieved, a freedom nearly won, safety within grasp.

The most dangerous, delicate stage of any kidnap is the actual handing over of the ransom, because it is then, at the moment of collection, that someone, somehow, must step out of the shadows . . . and a kidnapper comes to his waterhole with more caution than any beast in the jungle.

One suspicion, one sight or glint of a watcher is enough to send him scuttling away; and it is afterwards, seething with fright and in a turmoil of vengeful anger, that he can most easily kill. To bungle the drop is to escalate the threat to the victim a hundredfold.

Alessia Cenci, twenty-three years old, had by that time been in the hands of kidnappers for five weeks, three days, ten hours, and her life had never been closer to forfeit.

Enrico Pucinelli climbed grim-faced through the rear door of the ambulance in which I stood: a van, more accurately, which looked like an ambulance from the outside but whose darkly tinted windows concealed a bench, a chair, and a mass of electronic equipment within.

"I was off duty," he said. "I did not give those orders."

He spoke in Italian, but slowly, for my sake. As men, we got on very well. As linguists, speaking a little of each other's languages but understanding more, we had to take time. We spoke to each other carefully, each in our own tongue, and listened with attention, asking for repetition whenever necessary.

He was a carabinieri officer who had been leading the official investigations. He had agreed throughout on the need for extreme care and for the minimum of visible involvement. No emblazoned cars with busily flashing lights had driven to or from the Villa Francese, where Paolo Cenci waited with white face for news of his daughter. No uniformed men had been in evidence in any place where hostile eyes could watch. Not while Pucinelli himself had been able to prevent it.

He had agreed with me that the first priority was the girl's safety, and only the second priority the catching of the kidnappers. Not every policeman by any means saw things that way round, the hunting instincts of law enforcers everywhere being satisfied solely by the capture of their prey.

Pucinelli's colleague-on-duty on that devastating evening, suddenly learning that he could pounce with fair ease on the kidnappers at the moment they picked up the ransom, had seen no reason to hold back. Into the pregnant summer darkness, into the carefully negotiated, patiently damped-down moment of maximum quiet, he had sent a burst of men with batons waving, lights blazing, guns rising ominously against the night sky, voices shouting, cars racing, sirens wailing, uniforms running . . . all the moral aggression of a righteous army in full pursuit.

From the dark stationary ambulance a long way down the street I had watched it happen with sick disbelief and impotent fury. My driver, cursing steadily, had started the engine and crawled forward towards the melee, and we had both quite clearly heard the shots.

"It is regretted," Pucinelli said with formality, watching me.

I could bet it was. There had been so many carabinieri on the move in the poorly lit back street that, unsure where to look precisely, they had missed their target altogether. Two dark-clad men, carrying the suitcases which contained the equivalent of six hundred and fifty thousand pounds, had succeeded in reaching a hidden car, in starting it and driving off before the lawmen noticed; and certainly their attention had been more clearly focused, as was my own, on the sight of the young man spilling headfirst from the car which all along had been plainly in everyone's view, the car in which the ransom had been carried to this blown-open rendezvous.

The young man, son of a lawyer, had been shot. I could see the crimson flash on his shirt and the weak flutter of his hand, and I thought of him, alert and confident, as we'd talked before he set off. Yes, he'd said, he understood the risk, and yes, he would follow their instructions absolutely, and yes, he would keep me informed by radio direct from the car to the ambulance. Together we had activated the tiny transmitter sewn into the handle of the suitcase containing the ransom money and had checked that it was working properly as a homer, sending the messages back to the radar in the ambulance.

Inside the ambulance that same radar tracker was showing unmistakably that the suitcase was on the move and going rapidly away. I would without doubt have let the kidnappers escape, because that was safest for Alessia, but one of the carabinieri, passing and catching sight of the blip, ran urgently towards the bull-like man who with blowing whistle appeared to be chiefly in charge, shouting to him above the clamor and pointing a stabbing finger towards the van.

With wild and fearful doubt the officer looked agonizedly around him and then shambled towards me at a run. With his big head through the window of the cab he stared mutely at the radar screen, where he read the bad news unerringly with a pallid outbreak of sweat.

"Follow," he said hoarsely to my driver, and brushed away my attempt at telling him in Italian why he should do no such thing.

The driver shrugged resignedly and we were on our way with a jerk, accompanied, it seemed to me, by a veritable posse of wailing cars screaming through the empty streets of the industrial quarter, the factory workers long ago gone home.

"Since midnight," Pucinelli said, "I am on duty. I am again in charge."

I looked at him bleakly. The ambulance stood now in a wider street, its engine stilled, the tracker showing a steady trace, locating the suitcase inside a modern lower-income block of apartments. In front of the building, at an angle to the curb, stood a nondescript black car, its overheated engine slowly cooling. Around it, like a haphazard barrier, the police cars were parked at random angles, their doors open, headlights blazing, occupants in their fawn uniforms ducking into cover with ready pistols.

"As you see, the kidnappers are in the front apartment on the third floor," Pucinelli said. "They say they have taken hostage the people who live there, and will kill them, and also they say Alessia Cenci will surely die, if we do not give them safe passage."

I had heard them shouting from the open window, and had hardly needed the repetition.

"In a short time the listening bug will be in position," Pucinelli said, glancing uneasily at my rigid face. "And soon we will have a tap on the telephone. We have men on the staircase outside. They are fixing them."

I said nothing.

"My men say you would have let the kidnappers get away . . . taking the money with them."

"Of course."

We looked at each other unsmilingly, almost foes where recently we'd been allies. He was thin and about forty, give or take. Dark and intense and energetic. A communist in a communist city, disapproving of the capitalist whose daughter was at risk.

"They had shot the boy who drove the car," he said. "We could not possibly let them escape."

"The boy took his chances. The girl must still be saved."

"You English," he said. "So cold."

The anger inside me would have scorched asbestos. If his men hadn't tried their abortive ambush, the boy would not have been shot. He would have walked away unharmed and left the ransom in the car, as he'd been instructed.

Pucinelli turned his attention to the benchful of bolted-down radio receivers, turning a few knobs and pressing switches. "I am sending a man in here to receive messages," he said. "I will be here also. You can stay, if you wish."

I nodded. It was too late to do anything else.

It had been absolutely against my instincts and my training to be anywhere near the dropping point of the ransom, yet Pucinelli had demanded my presence there in return for a promise of his force's absence.

"You can go in our van," he had said. "Our radio van. Like an ambulance. Very discreet. You go. I'll send you a driver. When the kidnappers take the suitcase, you follow it. You can tell us where they're hiding. Then, when the girl is free, we'll arrest them. O.K.?"

"When the girl is free, I will tell you where they took the money."

He had narrowed his eyes slightly, but had clapped me on the shoulder and agreed to it, nodding. "The girl first."

Not knowing, as one never does, precisely when the kidnappers would set the handing-over procedure rolling, Pucinelli had stationed the van permanently in the garage at the Villa Francese, with the driver living in the house. Four days after we'd signaled to the kidnappers that the agreed money had been collected and was ready for them, they had sent their delivery instructions: and as promised between Pucinelli and myself, I had telephoned his office to tell him the drop was about to start.

Pucinelli had not been there, but we had planned for that contingency.

In basic Italian I had said, "I am Andrew Douglas. Tell Enrico Pucinelli immediately that the ambulance is moving."

The voice at the other end had said it understood.

I now wished with all my heart that I had not kept my promise to give Pucinelli that message; but cooperation with the local police was one of the firm's most basic policies.

Pucinelli's own trust in me, it now turned out, had not been so very great. Perhaps he had known I would rather have lost track of the suitcase than give away my presence near the drop. In any case, both the suitcase's homer, and a further homer in the van, had been trackable from Pucinelli's own official car. The colleague-on-duty, receiving my message, had not consulted Pucinelli but had simply set out with a maximum task force, taking Pucinelli's staff car and chasing personal glory. Stupid, swollen-headed, lethal human failing.

How in God's name was I going to tell Paolo Cenci? And who was going to break it to the lawyer that his bright student son had been shot?

"The boy who was driving," I said to Pucinelli. "Is he alive?"

"He's gone to hospital. He was alive when they took him. Beyond that, I don't know."

"His father must be told."

Pucinelli said grimly, "It's being done. I've sent a man."

This mess, I thought, was going to do nothing at all for the firm's reputation. It was positively my job to help to resolve a kidnap in the quietest way possible with the lowest of profiles and minimum action. My job to calm, to plan, to judge how little one could get a kidnapper to accept, to see that negotiations were kept on the coolest, most businesslike footing, to bargain without angering, to get the timing right. My brief, above all, to bring the victim home.

I had by that time been the advisor-on-the-spot in fifteen kidnaps, some lasting days, some weeks, some several months. Chiefly because kidnappers usually do release their victims unharmed once the ransom is in their hands, I hadn't so far been part of a disaster; but Alessia Cenci, reportedly one of the best woman jockeys in the world, looked set to be my first.

"Enrico," I said, "don't talk to these kidnappers yourself. Get someone else, who has to refer to you for decisions."

"Why?" he said.

"It calms things down. Takes time. The longer they go on talking the less likely they are to kill those people in the flat."

He considered me briefly. "Very well. Advise me. It's your job."

We were alone in the van and I guessed he was sorely ashamed of his force's calamity, otherwise he would never have admitted such a tacit loss of face. I had realized from shortly after my first arrival at the villa that as officer-in-charge he had never before had to deal with a real kidnap, though he had carefully informed me that all carabinieri were instructed in the theory of kidnap response, owing to the regrettable frequency of that crime in Italy. Between us, until that night, his theory and my experience had done well enough, and it seemed that he did still want the entente to go on.

I said, "Telephone that flat direct from here. Tell the kidnappers you are arranging negotiations. Tell them they must wait for a while. Tell them that if they tire of the waiting they may telephone to you. Give them a number . . . you have a line in this van?"

He nodded. "It's being connected."

"Once their pulses settle it will be safer, but if they are pressed too hard to start with they may shoot again."

"And my men would fire . . ." He blinked rapidly and went outside, and I could hear him speaking to his forces through a megaphone. "Do not return fire. I repeat, do not shoot. Await orders before firing."

He returned shortly, accompanied by a man unrolling a wire, and said briefly, "Engineer."

The engineer attached the wire to one of the switch boxes and passed Pucinelli an instrument which looked a cross between a microphone and a handset. It appeared to lead a direct line to the apartment's telephone because after a pause Pucinelli was clearly conversing with one of the kidnappers. The engineer, as a matter of course, was recording every word.

The Italian was too idiomatic for my ears, but I understood at least the tone. The near-hysterical shouting from the kidnapper slowly abated in response to Pucinelli's determined calmness and ended in a more manageable agitation. To a final forceful question Pucinelli, after a pause, answered slowly and distinctly, "I don't have that authority. I have to consult my superiors. Please wait for their reply."

The result was a menacing, grumbling agreement and a disconnecting click.

Pucinelli wiped his hand over his face and gave me the tiniest flicker of a smile. Sieges, as I supposed he knew, could go on for days, but at least he had established communication, taking the first vital step.

He glanced at the engineer and I guessed he was wanting to ask me what next, but couldn't because of the engineer and his recordings.

I said, "Of course you will be aiming searchlights at those windows soon so that the kidnappers will feel exposed."

"Of course."

"And if they don't surrender in an hour or two, naturally you'd bring someone here who's used to bargaining, to talk to them. Someone from a trades union, perhaps. And after that a psychiatrist to judge the kidnappers' state of mind and tell you when he thinks is the best time to apply most pressure, to make them come out." I shrugged deprecatingly. "Naturally you know that these methods have produced good results in other hostage situations."

"Naturally."

"And of course you could tell them that if Alessia Cenci dies, they will never get out of prison."

"The driver . . . they'll know they hit him . . ."

"If they ask, I am sure you would tell them he is alive. . . . Even if he dies, you would of course tell them he is still alive. One wouldn't want them to think they had nothing to lose."

A voice spluttered suddenly from one of the so far silent receivers, making both the engineer and Pucinelli whirl to listen. It was a woman's voice, gabbling, weeping, to me mostly unintelligible but in gist again plain enough.

The kidnapper's rough voice sliced in over hers, far too angry for safety, and then, in a rising wail, came a child's voice, crying, then another, calling Mama, Papa, Mama.

"God," Pucinelli said, "children! There are children, too, in that apartment." The thought appalled him. In one instant he cared more for them than he had in five weeks for the girl, and for the first time I saw real concern in his olive face. He listened intently to the now jumbled loud voices crowding through from the bug on the flat, a jumble finally resolving into a kidnapper yelling at the woman to give the children some biscuits to shut them up or he personally would throw them out of the window.

The threat worked. Comparative quietness fell. Pucinelli took the opportunity to begin issuing rapid orders by radio to his own base, mentioning searchlights, negotiator, psychiatrist. Half the time he looked upward to the third-floor windows, half the time down to the cluttered street outside: both, from our side of the van's darkly tinted glass, unrealistically dim. Not dark enough, however, for him not to catch sight of something which displeased him mightily and send him speeding out of the van at a shout. I followed the direction of his agitation and felt the same dismay: a photographer with flashlight had arrived, first contingent of the press.

For the next hour I listened to the voices from the apartment, sorting them gradually into father, mother, two children, a baby, and two kidnappers, one, the one who had talked on the telephone, with a growling bass voice, the other a more anxious tenor.

It was the tenor, I thought, who would more easily surrender: the bass the more likely killer. Both, it appeared, were holding guns. The engineer spoke rapidly with Pucinelli, who then repeated everything more slowly for my benefit: the kidnappers had locked the mother and three children in one of the bedrooms, and had mentioned ropes tying the father. The father moaned occasionally and was told violently to stop.

In the street the crowd multiplied by the minute, every apartment block in the neighborhood, it seemed, emptying its inhabitants to the free show on the doorstep. Even at two in the morning there were hordes of children oozing round every attempt of the carabinieri to keep them back, and everywhere, increasingly, sprouted the cameras, busy lenses pointing at the windows, now shut, where drama was the tenor kidnapper agreeing to warm the baby's bottle in the kitchen.

I ground my teeth and watched a television van pull up, its occupants leaping out with lights, cameras, microphones, setting up instant interviews, excitedly telling the world.

The kidnapping of Alessia Cenci had until that time been a piano affair, the first shock news of her disappearance having made the papers, but only briefly, for most editors all over the world acknowledged that reporters glued to such stories could be deadly. A siege in a public street, though, was everyone's fair game; and I wondered cynically how long it would be before one of the fawn-uniformed law-enforcers accepted a paper gift in exchange for the fact of just whose ransom was barricaded there three flights up.

I found myself automatically taking what one might call a memory snapshot, a clear frozen picture of the moving scene outside. It was a habit from boyhood, then consciously cultivated, a game to while away the boring times I'd been left in the car while my mother went into shops. From across the road from the bank I used to memorize the whole scene so that if any bank robbers had rushed out I would have been able to tell the police about all the cars which had been parked nearby, make, color, and numbers, and describe all the people in the street at the time. Getaway cars and drivers would never have got away unspotted by eagle-eyed ten-year-old Andrew D.

No bank robbers ever obliged me, nor smash-and-grabbers outside the jeweler's, nor baby snatchers from prams outside the baker's, nor muggers of the elderly collecting their pensions, nor even car thieves trying for unlocked doors. A great many innocent people had come under my sternly suspicious eye . . . and though I'd grown out of the hope of actually observing a crime, I'd never lost the ability of freeze-frame recall.

Thus it was that from behind the darkened glass, after a few moments' concentration, I had such a sharp mind's-eye picture that I could have described with certainty the number of windows in the block of

apartments facing, the position of each of the carabinieri cars, the clothes of the television crew, the
whereabouts of each civilian inside the police circle,
even the profile of the nearest press photographer,
who was hung with two cameras but not at that moment taking pictures. He had a roundish head with
smooth black hair, and a brown leather jacket with
gold buckles at the cuffs.

A buzzer sounded sharply inside the van and Pucinelli lifted the handset which connected with the
apartment's telephone. The bass-voiced kidnapper,
edgy with waiting, demanded action; demanded specifically a safe passage to the airport and a light aircraft to fly him, and his colleague and the ransom,
out.

Pucinelli told him to wait again, as only his superiors could arrange that. Tell them to bloody hurry,
said the bass. Otherwise they'd find Alessia Cenci's
dead body in the morning.

Pucinelli replaced the handset, tight-lipped.

"There will be no airplane," he said to me flatly.
"It's impossible."

"Do what they want," I urged. "You can catch
them again later, when the girl is free."

He shook his head. "I cannot make that decision.
Only the highest authority . . ."

"Get it, then."

The engineer looked up curiously at the fierceness
in my voice. Pucinelli, however, with calculation
was seeing that shuffling off the decision had seductive advantages, so that if the girl did die it
couldn't be held to be his fault. The thoughts ticked
visibly behind his eyes, coming to clarity, growing to
a nod.

I didn't know whether or not his superiors would let the kidnappers out; I only knew that Enrico couldn't. It was indeed a matter for the top brass.

"I think I'll go back to the Villa Francese," I said.

"But why?"

"I'm not needed here, but there . . . I might be." I paused fractionally. "But I came from there in this van. How, at this time of night, can I get a car to take me back there quietly?"

He looked vaguely at the official cars outside, and I shook my head. "Not one of those."

"Still the anonymity . . . ?"

"Yes," I said.

He wrote a card for me and gave me directions.

"All-night taxi, mostly for late drunks and unfaithful husbands. If he is not there, just wait."

I let myself out through the cab, through the door on the dark side, away from the noisy, brightly lit embroilment in the street, edging round behind the gawpers, disentangling myself from the public scene, heading for the unremarked shadows, my most normal sphere of work.

With one corner behind me the visible nightmare faded, and I walked fast through the sleeping summer streets, even my shoes, from long custom, making no clatter in the quiet. The taxi address lay beyond the far side of the old main square, and I found myself slowing briefly there, awed by the atmosphere of the place.

Somewhere in or near that aged city a helpless young woman faced her most dangerous night, and it seemed to me that the towering walls with their smooth closed faces embodied all the secrecy, the ill will and the implacability of those who held her.

The two kidnappers now besieged had been simply the collectors. There would be others. At the very least there would be guards still with her; but also, I thought, there was the man whose voice over five long weeks had delivered instructions, the man I thought of as HIM.

I wondered if he knew what had happened at the drop. I wondered if he knew yet about the siege, and where the ransom was.

Above all, I wondered if he would panic.

Alessia had no future, if he did.

Two

Paolo Cenci was doing the pacing I had stifled in myself: up and down his tiled and pillared central hall, driven by intolerable tension. He broke from his eyes-down automatic-looking measured stride and came hurrying across as soon as he saw me walking through from the kitchen passage.

"Andrew!" His face was gray in the electric light. "What in God's name has happened? Giorgio Traventi has telephoned me to say his son has been shot. He telephoned from the hospital. They are operating on Lorenzo at this minute."

"Haven't the carabinieri told you . . . ?"

"No one has told me anything. I am going mad with anxiety. It is five hours since you and Lorenzo set out. For five hours I've been waiting." His hoarse voice shook over the gracefully accented English, the emotion raw and unashamed. At fifty-six he was a strong man at the height of his business ability, but the past weeks had made appalling demands on his mental stamina, and even his hands now trembled often. I saw much of this distress in my job; and no matter how rich, no matter how powerful, the victim's family suffered in direct simple ratio to the depth of their love. Alessia's mother was dead: Alessia's father felt anguish enough for two.

With compassion I drew him into the library, where he sat most evenings, and with my own anger, I suppose, apparent, told him the details of the disaster. He sat with his head in his hands when I'd finished, as near to weeping as I'd seen him.

"They'll kill her . . ."

"No," I said.

"They are animals."

There had been enough bestial threats during the past weeks for me not to argue. The assaults on her body the kidnappers had promised should Cenci not obey their instructions had been brutally calculated to break any father's nerve, and my assurances that threats were more common than performance hadn't comforted him to any extent. His imagination was too active, his fear too relentlessly acute.

My relationship with victims' families was something like that of a doctor: called in in an emergency, consulted in a frightening and unsettling situation, looked to for miracles, leaned on for succor. I'd set off on my first solo advisory job without any clear idea of the iron I would need to grow in my own core, and still after four years could quake before the demands made on my strength. Never get emotionally involved, I'd been told over and over during my training, you'll crack up if you do.

I was thirty. I felt, at times, a hundred.

Paolo Cenci's numbness at the nature and extent

of the disaster began turning before my eyes to anger, and, not surprisingly, to resentment against me.

"If you hadn't told the carabinieri we were about to hand over the ransom, this wouldn't have happened. It's your fault. Yours. It's disgraceful. I should never have called you in. I shouldn't have listened to you. Those people warned me all along that if I brought in the carabinieri they would do unspeakable things to Alessia, and I let you persuade me, and I should not have done, I should have paid the ransom at once when they first demanded it, and Alessia would have been free weeks ago."

I didn't argue with him. He knew, but in his grief was choosing not to remember, that to raise the ransom at first demanded had been impossible. Rich though he was, the equivalent of six million pounds sterling represented the worth not only of his whole estate but in addition of a large part of his business. Nor, as I'd forcefully told him, had the kidnappers ever expected him to pay that much: they were simply bludgeoning him with a huge amount so that anything less would seem a relief.

"Everything that Alessia has suffered has been your fault."

Barring, presumably, the kidnap itself.

"Without you, I would have got her back. I would have paid. I would have paid anything . . ."

To pay too much too soon was to make kidnappers think they had underestimated the family's resources, and sometimes resulted in the extortion of a second ransom for the same victim. I had warned him of that, and he had understood.

"Alessia is worth more to me than everything I possess. I wanted to pay. . . . You wouldn't let me.

I should have done what I thought best. I would have given everything . . ."

His fury bubbled on, and I couldn't blame him. It often seemed to those who loved that literally no price was too great to pay for the safe return of the loved one, but I'd learned a great deal about the unexpected faces of stress over the past four years, and I'd seen that for the future health of the family's relationships it was essential that one member had not in fact cost the rest everything. After the first euphoria, and when the financial loss had begun to bite, the burden of guilt on the paid-for victim became too great, and the resentment of the payers too intense, and they too began to feel guilt for their resentment, and could eventually hate the victim for love of whom they had beggared themselves.

To save the victims' future equilibrium had gradually become to me as important as their actual physical freedom, but it was an aim I didn't expect Paolo Cenci at that moment to appreciate.

The telephone at his elbow started ringing, making him jump. He put out his hand towards it and then hesitated, and with a visible screwing up of courage lifted the receiver to his ear.

"Ricardo! . . . Yes. . . . Yes. . . . I understand. I will do that now, at once." He put down the receiver and rose galvanically to his feet.

"Ricardo Traventi?" I asked, standing also. "Lorenzo's brother?"

"I must go alone," he said, but without fire.

"You certainly must not. I will drive you."

I had been acting as his chauffeur since I had arrived, wearing his real chauffeur's cap and navy suit while that grateful man took a holiday. It gave me the sort of invisibility that the firm had found worked best: kidnappers always knew everything about a household they had attacked, and a newcomer too officiously visiting alarmed them. A kidnapper was as nervous as a stalking fox and tended to see dangers when they didn't exist, let alone when they did. I came and went at the villa through the servants' entrance, taking it for granted that everything else would be noted.

Cenci's fury had evaporated as quickly as it had grown, and I saw that we were back to some sort of trust. I was grateful both for my sake and his that he would still at all accept my presence, but it was with some diffidence that I asked, "What did Ricardo say?"

"They telephoned . . ." No need to ask who "they" were. "They" had been telephoning to Traventi's house with messages all along, taking it for granted that there was an official tap on the telephones to the Villa Francese. That the Traventis' telephone was tapped also, with that family's reluctant permission, seemed to be something "they" didn't know for certain.

"Ricardo says he must meet us at the usual place. He says he took the message because his parents are both at the hospital. He doesn't want to worry them. He says he will come on his scooter."

Cenci was already heading towards the door, sure that I would follow.

Ricardo, Lorenzo's younger brother, was only eighteen, and no one originally had intended the two boys to be involved. Giorgio Traventi had agreed, as a lawyer, to act as a negotiator between Paolo Cenci and the kidnappers. It was he who took messages, passed them on, and in due course delivered the replies. The kidnappers themselves had a negotiator . . . HIM . . . with whom Giorgio Traventi spoke.

At times Traventi had been required to pick up packages at a certain spot, usually but not always the same place, and it was to that place that we were now headed. It had become not just the post-box for proof of Alessia's still being alive, or for appeals from her, or demands from HIM, or finally, earlier that evening, for the instructions about where to take the ransom, but also the place where Giorgio Traventi met Paolo Cenci, so that they could consult together in private. Neither had been too happy about the carabinieri overhearing their every word on the telephone and I had to admit that their instincts had been right.

It was ironic that at the beginning Giorgio Traventi had been approached by Cenci and his own lawyer simply because Traventi did not know the Cenci family well, and could act calmly on their behalf. Since then the whole Traventi family had become determined on Alessia's release, until finally nothing could have dissuaded Lorenzo from carrying the ransom himself. I hadn't approved of their growing emotional involvement—exactly what I had been warned against myself—but had been unable to stop it, as all of the Traventis had proved strongwilled and resolute, staunch allies when Cenci needed them most.

Indeed, until the carabinieri's ambush, the progress of negotiations had been, as far as was possible in any kidnap, smooth. The demand for six million had been cooled to about a tenth of that, and Alessia, on that afternoon at least, had been alive, unmolested, and sane, reading aloud from that day's newspaper onto tape, and saying she was well.

The only comfort now, I thought, driving Cenci in his Mercedes to meet Ricardo, was that the kidnappers were still talking. Any message at all was better than an immediate dead body in a ditch.

The meeting place had been carefully chosen— by HIM—so that even if the carabinieri had had enough plainclothesmen to watch there day and night for weeks on end, they could have missed the actual delivery of the message: and indeed it was pretty clear that this had happened at least once. During the period of closest continual watch, to confuse things the messages had been delivered somewhere else.

We were heading for a highway restaurant several miles outside Bologna, where even at night people came and went anonymously, travelers unremembered, different every hour of every day. Carabinieri who sat for too long over a coffee could be easily picked out.

Messages from HIM were left in a pocket in a cheap, gray, thin, plastic raincoat, to be found hanging from a coatrack inside the restaurant. The row of pegs was passed by everyone who went in or out of the cafeteria-style dining room, and we guessed that the nondescript garment was in its place each time before the collect-the-message telephone call was made.

Traventi had taken the whole raincoat each time, but they had never been useful as clues. They were of a make sold throughout the region in flat pocket-sized envelopes as a handy insurance against sudden rainstorms. The carabinieri had been given the four

raincoats so far collected from the restaurant, and
the one from the airport and the one from the bus
station. All had been new, straight out of the packet,
wrinkled from being folded, and smelling of the
chemicals they were made from.

The messages had all been on tape. Regular issue
cassettes, sold everywhere. No fingerprints on anything. Everything exceedingly careful; everything, I
had come to think, professional.

Each tape had contained proof of Alessia's being
alive. Each tape contained threats. Each tape carried
a response to Traventi's latest offer. I had advised
him to offer only two hundred thousand at first, a
figure received by HIM with fury, faked or real.
Slowly, with hard bargaining, the gap between demand and credibility had been closed, until the ransom was big enough to be worth HIS trouble, and
manageable enough not to cripple Cenci entirely. At
the point where each felt comfortable if not content,
the amount had been agreed.

The money had been collected: Italian currency in
used everyday notes, fastened in bundles with rubber bands and packed in a suitcase. Upon its safe delivery, Alessia Cenci would be released.

Safe delivery . . . Ye gods.

The highway restaurant lay about equidistant
from Bologna and the Villa Francese, which stood in
turreted idyllic splendor on a small country hillside,
facing south. By day the road was busy with traffic
but at four in the morning only a few solitary pairs of
headlights flooded briefly into our car. Cenci sat silent beside me, his eyes on the road and his mind
heaven knew where.

Ricardo on his scooter arrived before us in the car

park, though if anything he had had farther to travel. Like his brother he was assertively intelligent, his eyes full now of the aggression brought on by the shooting, the narrow jaw jutting, the lips tight, the will to fight shouting from every muscle. He came across to the car as we arrived and climbed into the back seat.

"The bastards," he said intensely. "Lorenzo's state is critical, Papa says." He spoke Italian, but distinctly, like all his family, so that I could nearly always understand them.

Paolo Cenci made a distressed gesture with his hands, sparing a thought for someone else's child. "What is the message?" he said.

"To stand here by the telephones. He said I was to bring you, to speak to him yourself. No negotiator, he said. He sounded angry, very angry."

"Was it the same man?" I asked.

"I think so. I've heard his voice on the tapes, but I've never spoken to him before. Always Papa speaks to him. Before tonight he wouldn't speak to anyone but Papa, but I told him Papa was at the hospital with Lorenzo and would be there until morning. Too late, he said. I must take the message myself. He said that you, Signor Cenci, must be alone. If there were any more carabinieri, he said, you wouldn't see Alessia again. They wouldn't return even her body."

Cenci trembled beside me. "I'll stay in the car," I said. "In my cap. They'll accept that. Don't be afraid."

"I'll go with you," Ricardo said.

"No." I shook my head. "Ricardo too might be taken for carabinieri. Better stay here with me." I turned to Cenci. "We'll wait. Have you any *gettoni* if he asks you to call him back?"

He fished vaguely through his pockets, and Ricardo and I gave him some of the necessary tokens; then he fumbled with the door handle and stood up, as if disoriented, in the car park.

"The telephones are near the restaurant," Ricardo said. "In the hall just outside. I have telephoned from there often."

Cenci nodded, took a grip on the horrors, and walked with fair steadiness to the entrance.

"Do you think there will be someone watching?" Ricardo said.

"I don't know. We cannot take the risk." I used the Italian word for danger, not risk, but he nodded comprehension. It was the third time I'd worked in Italy: time I spoke the language better than I did.

We waited a long time, not speaking much. We waited so long that I began to fear either that no call would come to Cenci at all, that the message had been a retributive piece of cruelty, or even worse, that it had been a ruse to lure him away from his house while something dreadful took place in it. My heart thumped uncomfortably. Alessia's elder sister, Ilaria, and Paolo Cenci's sister, Luisa, were both upstairs in the villa, asleep.

Perhaps I should have stayed there . . . but Cenci had been in no state to drive. Perhaps I should have awoken his gardener in the village, who drove sometimes on the chauffeur's days off. . . . Perhaps, perhaps.

The sky was already lightening to dawn when he returned, the shakiness showing in his walk, his face rigid as he reached the car. I stretched over and

opened the door for him from the inside, and he sub-
sided heavily into the passenger seat.

"He rang twice." He spoke in Italian, automatically. "The first time, he said wait. I waited . . ."
He stopped and swallowed. Cleared his throat.
Started again with a better attempt at firmness. "I
waited a long time. An hour. More. Finally, he telephoned. He says Alessia is still alive but the price has
gone up. He says I must pay two thousand million
lire in two days."

His voice stopped, the despair sounding in it
clearly. Two thousand million lire was approaching
a million pounds.

"What else did he say?" I asked.

"He said that if anyone told the carabinieri of
the new demand, Alessia would die at once." He
seemed suddenly to remember that Ricardo was in
the car, and turned to him in alarm. "Don't speak of
this meeting, not to anyone. Promise me, Ricardo.
On your soul."

Ricardo, looking serious, promised. He also said
he would go now to the hospital, to join his parents
and get news of Lorenzo, and with a further passionate assurance of discretion he went over to his scooter
and putt-putted away.

I started the car and drove out of the car park.

Cenci said dully, "I can't raise that much. Not
again."

"Well," I said, "you should eventually get back
the money in the suitcase. With luck. That means
that the real extra is . . . um . . . seven hundred
million lire."

Three hundred thousand pounds. Said quickly, it
sounded less.

"But in two days . . ."

"The banks will lend it. You have the assets."

He didn't answer. So close on the other collection of random used notes, this would be technically more difficult. More money, much faster. The banks, however, would read the morning papers . . . and raising a ransom was hardly a process unknown to them.

"What are you to do, when you've collected it?" I asked.

Cenci shook his head. "He told me. . . . But this time I can't tell you. This time I take the money myself . . . alone."

"It's unwise."

"I must do it."

He sounded both despairing and determined, and I didn't argue. I said merely, "Will we have time to photograph the notes and put tracers on them?"

He shook his head impatiently. "What does it matter now? It is Alessia only that is important. I've been given a second chance. . . . This time I do what he says. This time I act alone."

Once Alessia was safe—if she were so lucky—he would regret he'd passed up the best chance of recovering at least part of the ransom and of catching the kidnappers. Emotion, as so often in kidnap situations, was stampeding common sense. But one couldn't, I supposed, blame him.

Pictures of Alessia Cenci, the girl I had never met, adorned most rooms in the Villa Francese.

Alessia Cenci on horses, riding in races round the world. Alessia the rich girl with the hands of silk and a temperament like the sun (a fanciful newspaper

report had said), bright, warm, and occasionally
scorching.

I knew little about racing, but I'd heard of her, the
glamour girl of the European tracks who nevertheless could really ride: one would have to have averted
one's eyes from the newspapers pretty thoroughly
not to. There seemed to be something about her that
captivated the daily scribblers, particularly in England, where she raced often; and in Italy I heard
genuine affection in every voice that spoke of her. In
every voice, that is to say, except for that of her sister, Ilaria, whose reaction to the kidnap had been
complex and revealing.

Alessia in close-up photographs wasn't particularly beautiful: thin, small-featured, dark-eyed, with
short head-hugging curls. It was her sister, by her
side in silver frames, who looked more feminine,
more friendly, and more pretty. Ilaria in life, however, was not particularly any of those things, at least
not in the present horrific family circumstances. One
couldn't tell what happiness might do.

She and her aunt Luisa still slept when Cenci and
I returned to the villa. All was quiet there, all safe.
Cenci walked straight into the library and poured a
large amount of brandy into a tumbler, indicating
that I should help myself to the same. I joined him,
reflecting that seven in the morning was as good a
time as any to get drunk.

"I'm sorry," he said. "I know it's not your fault.
The carabinieri . . . do what they want."

I gathered he was referring to the anger he'd
poured on me the last time we'd sat in those same
two chairs. I made a vague don't-think-about-it gesture and let the brandy sear a path to my stomach, a

shaft of vivid feeling going down through my chest.
It might not have been wise, but the oldest tranquilizer was still the most effective.

"Do you think we'll get her back?" Cenci asked.
"Do you really think so?"

"Yes." I nodded. "They wouldn't be starting
again more or less from scratch if they meant to kill
her. They don't want to harm her, as I've told you
all along. They only want you to believe they will
. . . and yes, I do think it's a good sign they still
have the nerve to bargain, with two of their number
besieged by the carabinieri."

Cenci looked blank. "I'd forgotten about those."

I hadn't; but then the ambush and the siege were
imprinted in my mind as memories, not reports. I
had wondered, through most of the night, whether
the two collectors had been carrying walkie-talkie ra-
dios, and whether HE had known of the debacle at
almost the moment it happened, not simply when
neither his colleagues nor the money turned up.

I thought that if I were HIM I'd be highly worried
about those two men, not necessarily for their own
sakes, but for what they knew. They might know
where Alessia was. They might know who had
planned the operation. They had to know where
they'd been expected to take the money. They might
be hired hands . . . but trusted enough to be collectors. They might be full equal partners, but I
doubted it. Kidnap gangs tended to have hierarch-
ies, like every other organization.

One way or another those two were going to fall
into the grasp of the carabinieri, either talking or
shot. They themselves had promised that if they
didn't go free, Alessia would die, but apparently HE

had said nothing like that to Cenci. Did that mean that HIS priority was money, that he was set on extorting only what he almost certainly could, money from Cenci, and not what he almost as certainly couldn't, the return of his friends? Or did it mean that he didn't have radio contact with his colleagues, who had made the threat in faith more than promise . . . or did it mean that by radio he had persuaded the colleagues to barricade themselves in and make the fiercest threats continually, staying out of the carabinieri's clutches long enough for HIM to spirit Alessia away to a new hideout, so that it wouldn't matter if the colleagues finally did talk, they wouldn't know the one thing worth telling . . . ?

"What are you thinking?" Cenci asked.

"Of hope," I said; and thought that the kidnappers in the apartment probably didn't have contact by radio after all, because they hadn't made any reference to it during the hour I'd listened to them via the bug. But then HE might guess about bugs . . . if HE was that clever . . . and have told them to switch off after his first burst of instructions.

If I'd been HIM, I'd have been in touch with those collectors from the moment they set out . . . but then there weren't so many radio frequencies as all that, and the possibility of being overheard was high. But there were codes and prearranged phrases. . . . And how did you prearrange a message which said the carabinieri have swarmed all over us and we've shot the man who brought the ransom?

If they hadn't taken the ransom with its homing transmitter, they would probably have escaped. If they hadn't been fanatical about taking the ransom, they wouldn't have shot the driver to get it.

If the carabinieri had acted stupidly, so had the kidnappers, and only as long as HE didn't decide after all to cut his losses was there any positive hope. I still thought that hope to be frail. One didn't, however, admit it to the victim's dad.

Cenci anyway had tears at last running down his cheeks, released, I guessed, by the brandy. He made no sound, nor tried to brush them away or hide them. Many a man would have come to that stage sooner, and in my own experience, most victims' parents did. Through outrage, anger, anxiety, and grief, through guilt and hope and pain, the steps they trod were the same. I'd seen so many people in despair that sometimes a laughing face would jolt me.

The Paolo Cenci I knew was the man sitting opposite, who hadn't smiled once in my sight. He had attempted at first to put up a civilized front, but the mask had soon crumbled as he got used to my presence, and it was the raw man whose feelings and strengths and blindnesses I knew. The urbane successful man-of-the-world looking out with genial wisdom from the portrait in the drawing room, he was the stranger.

For his part, after his first blink at my not being in his own age group, he had seemed to find me compatible on all counts. His cry for help had reached our office within a day of Alessia's disappearance, and I had been on his back-doorstep the next; but forty-eight hours could seem a lifetime in that sort of nightmare and his relief at my arrival had been undemanding. He would very likely have accepted a four-armed dwarf with blue skin, not just a five-ten thin frame with ordinary dark hair and washed-out gray eyes: but he was, after all, paying for my help, and if he really hadn't liked me he had an easy way out.

His original call to our office had been brief and direct. "My daughter has been kidnapped. I telephoned Tomasso Linardi, of the Milan Fine Leather Company, for advice. He gave me your name . . . he says it was your firm which got him safely home and helped the police trace the kidnappers. I need your help now myself. Please come."

Tomasso Linardi, owner of the Milan Fine Leather Company, had himself been held for ransom two years earlier, and it wasn't surprising that Paolo Cenci should have known him, as Cenci too was in the leather business, heading a corporation with worldwide trade. Half the Italian shoes imported into England, he had told me, had passed in the uncut leather stage through his firm.

The two men incidentally had proved to have a second and more tenuous factor in common, an interest in horses; Cenci of course because of Alessia's jockeyship, and Linardi because he had owned a majority share in a racetrack. This holding in a fashionable profit-making piece of flat land had been one of the things sold to raise his ransom, much to his sorrow when on his release he found it out. In his case, although some of the kidnappers had been arrested a month later, only a small part of the million-pound ransom had been recovered. The seven million which had at first been strongly demanded would have meant losing his business as well, so on the whole he had been relieved, resigned, and obviously content enough with Liberty Market to recommend us to the next guy in trouble.

I had shared the Linardi assignment with another

partner. We'd found Linardi's wife less than distraught about her husband and furious about the cost of getting him back. His mistress had wept buckets, his son had usurped his office chair, his cook had had hysterics, his sisters had squabbled and his dog had pined. The whole thing had been conducted with operatic histrionics fortissimo, leaving me finally feeling I'd been swamped by a tidal wave.

In the Villa Francese, a much quieter house, Paolo Cenci and I sat for a further half hour, letting the brandy settle and thinking of this and that. At length, his tears long dried, he sighed deeply and said that as the day had to be faced he would change his clothes, have breakfast, and go to his office. I would drive him no doubt, as usual. And I could photograph the new ransom money, as before. He had been thinking, and of course I was right, it was the best chance of getting any of it back.

Breakfast in that formal household was eaten in the dining room: coffee, fruit, and hot breads against murals of shepherdesses à la Marie Antoinette.

Ilaria joined us there, silently as usual, assembling her own preferences onto her plate. Her silences were a form of aggression; a positive refusal, for instance, to say good morning to her father even out of good manners. He seemed to be used to it, but I found it extraordinary, especially in the circumstances, and especially as it seemed there was no animosity or discord between them. Ilaria lived a privileged life which included no gainful occupation: mostly travel, tennis, singing lessons, shopping, and lunches, thanks to her father's money. He gave, she received. I wondered sometimes if it was resentment at this dependency that made her so insistently refuse to acknowledge it even to the extent of behaving sweetly, but she had apparently never wanted or sought a job. Her Aunt Luisa had told me so, with approval.

Ilaria was a fresh-looking twenty-four, curved, not skinny, with brown wavy hair superbly cut and frequently shampooed. She had a habit of raising her eyebrows and looking down her nose, as she was now doing at her coffee cup, which probably reflected her whole view of life and would undoubtedly set into creases before forty.

She didn't ask if there was any news of Alessia: she never did. She seemed if anything to be angry with her sister for being kidnapped, though she hadn't exactly said so. Her reaction, however, to my suggestion that she should not go so regularly at set times to the tennis court and in fact should go away altogether and stay with friends, because kidnappers if feeling frustrated by delays had been known to take a second speeding-up bite at the same family, had been not only negative but acid. "There wouldn't be the same agonized fuss over me."

Her father had looked aghast at her bitterness, but both she and I saw in his face that what she'd said was true, even if he had never admitted it to himself. It would in fact have been very much easier to abduct Ilaria, but even as a victim she had been passed over in favor of her famous little sister, her father's favorite. She had continued, with the same defiance as in her silences, to go at the same times to the same places, an open invitation to trouble. Cenci had begged her not to, to no avail.

I wondered if she even positively wanted to be taken, so that her father would have to prove his love for her, as for Alessia, by selling precious things to get her back.

Because she hadn't asked, we hadn't told her the evening before that that was the night for paying the ransom. Let her sleep, Cenci had said, contemplating his own wakeful ordeal and wishing to spare her. "Perhaps Alessia will be home for breakfast," he'd said.

He looked at Ilaria now and with great weariness told her that the hand-over had gone wrong, and that another and bigger ransom had to be collected for Alessia.

"Another . . ." She stared at him in disbelief, cup stopping halfway to her mouth.

"Andrew thinks we may get the first one back again, but meanwhile . . ." He made an almost beseeching gesture with his hand. "My dear, we are going to be poorer. Not just temporarily, but always. This extra demand is a grave setback. . . . I have decided to sell the house on Mikonos, but even that will not be enough. Your mother's jewels must go, also the collection of snuffboxes. The rest I must raise on the worth of this house and this estate, and if we do not recover the first ransom I will be paying interest on the loan out of the receipts from the olives, which will leave nothing over. The land I sold in Bologna to raise the first ransom will not now be providing us with any revenue, and we have to live on what I make in the business." He shrugged slightly. "We'll not starve. We'll continue to live here. But there are the pensions for our retired servants, and the allowances for my uncles' widows, which they live on. . . . It is going to be a struggle,

my dear, and I think you should know, and be prepared.''

She looked at him with absolute shock, and I
thought that until that moment she hadn't realized
that paying a ransom was a very cruel business.

Three

I drove Cenci to his office and left him there to his telephone and his grim task with the banks. Then, changing from chauffeur's uniform into nondescript trousers and sweater, I went by bus and foot to the street where the siege might still be taking place.

Nothing, it seemed, had changed there. The dark-windowed ambulance still stood against the curb on the far side of the road from the apartments, the carabinieri's cars were still parked helter-skelter in the same positions with fawn uniforms crouching around them, the television van still sprouted wires and aerials, and a commentator was still talking into a camera.

Daylight had subtracted drama. Familiarity had done the same to urgency. The scene now looked not frightening but peaceful, with figures moving at walking pace, not in scurrying little runs. A watching crowd stood and stared bovinely, growing bored.

The windows on the third floor were shut.

I hovered at the edge of things, hands in pockets,

hair tousled, local paper under arm, looking, I hoped, not too English. Some of the partners in Liberty Market were stunning at disguises, but I'd always found a slouch and vacant expression my best bet for not being noticed.

After a while during which nothing much happened I wandered off in search of a telephone, and rang the number of the switchboard inside the ambulance.

"Is Enrico Pucinelli there?" I asked.

"Wait." Some mumbling went on in the background, and then Pucinelli himself spoke, sounding exhausted.

"Andrew? Is it you?"

"Yes. How's it going?"

"Nothing has altered. I am off duty at ten o'clock for an hour."

I looked at my watch. Nine thirty-eight. "Where are you eating?" I said.

"Gino's."

"O.K.," I said, and disconnected.

I waited for him in the brightly lit glass-and-tile-lined restaurant that to my knowledge served fresh pasta at three in the morning with good grace. At eleven it was already busy with early lunchers, and I held a table for two by ordering loads of fettucine that I didn't want. Pucinelli, when he arrived, pushed away his cooling plateful with horror and ordered eggs.

He had come, as I knew he would, in civilian clothes, and the tiredness showed in black smudges under his eyes and in the droop of his shoulders.

"I hope you slept well," he said sarcastically.

I moved my head slightly, meaning neither yes nor no.

"I have had two of the top brass on my neck in the van all night," he said. "They can't make up their fat minds about the airplane. They are talking to Rome. Someone in the government must decide, they say, and no one in the government wanted to disturb his sleep to think about it. You would have gone quite crazy, my friend. Talk, talk, talk, and not enough action to shit."

I put on a sympathetic face and thought that the longer the siege lasted, the safer now for Alessia. Let it last, I thought, until she was free. Let HIM be a realist to the end.

"What are the kidnappers saying?" I asked.

"The same threats. The girl will die if they and the ransom money don't get away safely."

"Nothing new?"

He shook his head. His eggs came with rolls and coffee, and he ate without hurry. "The baby cried half the night," he said with his mouth full. "The deep-voiced kidnapper keeps telling the mother he'll strangle it if it doesn't shut up. It gets on his nerves." He lifted his eyes to my face. "You always tell me they threaten more than they do. I hope you're right."

I hoped so too. A crying baby could drive even a temperate man to fury. "Can't they feed it?" I said. "It has colic."

He spoke with the familiarity of experience, and I wondered vaguely about his private life. All our dealings had been essentially impersonal, and it was only in flashes, as now, that I heard the man behind the policeman.

"You have children?" I asked.

He smiled briefly, a glimmer in the eyes. "Three sons, two daughters, one . . . expected." He paused. "And you?"

I shook my head. "Not yet. Not married."

"Your loss. Your gain."

I laughed. He breathed deprecatingly down his nose as if to disclaim the disparagement of his lady. "Girls grow into mamas," he said. He shrugged. "It happens."

Wisdom, I thought, showed up in the most unexpected places. He finished his eggs as one at peace with himself, and drank his coffee. "Cigarette?" he asked, edging a packet out of his shirt pocket. "No. I forgot. You don't." He flicked his lighter and inhaled the first lungful with the deep relief of a dedicated smoker. Each to his own release: Cenci and I had found the same thing in brandy.

"During the night," I said. "Did the kidnappers talk to anyone else?"

"How do you mean?"

"By radio."

He lifted his thin face sharply, the family man retreating. "No. They spoke only to each other, to the hostage family, and to us. Do you think they have a radio? Why do you think that?"

"I wondered if they were in touch with their colleagues guarding Alessia."

He considered it with concentration and indecisively shook his head. "The two kidnappers spoke of what was happening, from time to time, but only as if they were talking to each other. If they were also transmitting on a radio and didn't want us to know, they are very clever. They would have to guess we are already listening to every word they say.'' He thought it over a bit longer and finally shook his head with more certainty. ''They are not clever. I've listened to them all night. They are violent, frightened, and . . .'' he searched for a word I would understand, ''. . . ordinary.''

''Average intelligence?''

''Yes. Average.''

''All the same, when you finally get them out, will you look around for a radio?''

''You personally want to know?''

''Yes.''

He looked at me assessingly with a good deal of professional dispassion. ''What are you not telling me?'' he said.

I was not telling him what Cenci passionately wished to keep private, and it was Cenci who was paying me. I might advise full consultation with the local law, but only that. Going against the customer's expressed wishes was at the very least bad for future business.

''I simply wonder,'' I said mildly, ''if the people guarding Alessia know exactly what's going on.''

He looked as if some sixth sense was busy doubting me, so to take his mind off it I said, ''I dare say you've thought of stun grenades as a last resort.''

''Stun?'' He didn't know the word. ''What's stun?''

''Grenades which more or less knock people out for a short while. They produce noise and shock waves, but do no permanent damage. While everyone is semiconscious, you walk into the flat and apply handcuffs where they're needed.''

''The army has them, I think.''

I nodded. "You are part of the army."

"Special units have them. We don't." He considered. "Would they hurt the children?"

I didn't know. I could see him discarding stun grenades rapidly. "We'll wait," he said. "The kidnappers cannot live there forever. In the end, they must come out."

Cenci stared morosely at a large cardboard carton standing on the desk in his office. The carton bore stick-on labels saying Fragile in white letters on red, but the contents would have survived any drop. Any drop, that is, except one to kidnappers.

"Fifteen hundred million lire," he said. "The banks arranged for it to come from Milan. They brought it straight to this office, with security guards."

"In that box?" I asked, surprised.

"No. They wanted their cases back . . . and this box was here." His voice sounded deathly tired. "The rest comes tomorrow. They've been understanding and quick, but the interest they're demanding will cripple me."

I made a mute gesture of sympathy, as no words seemed appropriate. Then I changed into my chauffeur's uniform, carried the heavy carton to the car, stowed it in the trunk, and presently drove Cenci home.

We ate dinner late in that house, though meals were often left unfinished according to the anxiety level of the day. Cenci would push his plate away in revulsion, and I sometimes thought my thinness resulted from never being able to eat heartily in the face of grief. My suggestions that Cenci might prefer my not living as family had been met with emphatic negatives. He needed company, he said, if he were to stay sane. I would please be with him as much as possible.

On that evening, however, he understood that I couldn't be. I carried the Fragile box upstairs to my room, closed the curtains, and started the lengthy task of photographing every note, flattening them in a frame of nonreflecting glass, four at a time of the same denomination. Even with the camera on a tripod, with bulk film, with cable release and with motor drive, the job always took ages. It was one that I did actually prefer not to leave to banks or the police, but even after all the practice I'd had I could shift only about fifteen hundred notes an hour. Large ransoms had me shuffling banknotes in my dreams.

It was Liberty Market routine to send the undeveloped films by express courier to the London office, where we had simple developing and printing equipment in the basement. The numbers of the notes were then typed into a computer, which sorted them into numerical order for each denomination and then printed out the lists. The lists were returned, again by courier, to the advisor in the field, who, after the victim had been freed, gave them to the police to circulate to all the country's banks, with a promise that any teller spotting one of the ransom notes would be rewarded.

It was a system which seemed to us best, principally because photography left no trace on the notes. The problem with physically marking them was that anything the banks could detect, so could the kidnappers. Banks had no monopoly, for instance, in scans to reveal fluorescence. Geiger counters for ra-

dioactive pin dots weren't hard to come by. Minute
perforations could be seen as easily by any eyes
against a bright light, and extra lines and marks
could be spotted by anyone's magnification. The
banks, through simple pressure of time, had to be
able to spot tracers easily, which put chemical invisible inks out of court. Kidnappers, far more thorough
and with fear always at their elbows, could test
obsessively for everything.

Kidnappers who found tracers on the ransom had
to be considered lethal. In Liberty Market, therefore, the markings we put on notes were so difficult
to find that we sometimes lost them ourselves, and
they were certainly unspottable by banks. They
consisted of transparent microdots (the size of the
full stops to which we applied them) which when sep-
arated and put under a microscope revealed a shadowy black logo of L and M, but through ordinary
magnifying glasses appeared simply black. We used
them only on larger denomination notes, and then
only as a back-up in case there should be any argu-
ment about the photographed numbers. To date we
had never had to reveal their existence, a state of affairs we hoped to maintain.

By morning, fairly dropping from fatigue, I'd
photographed barely half, the banks having taken
the "small denomination" instruction all too literally. Locking all that money into a wardrobe cupboard I showered and thought of bed, but after
breakfast drove Cenci to the office as usual. Three
nights I could go without sleep. After that, zonk.

"If the kidnappers get in touch with you," I said,
on the way, "you might tell them you can't drive.
Say you need your chauffeur. Say . . . um . . .

you've a bad heart, something like that. Then at least you'd have help, if you needed it."

There was such an intense silence from the back seat that at first I thought he hadn't heard, but eventually he said, "I suppose you don't know, then."

"Know what?"

"Why I have a chauffeur."

"General wealth, and all that," I said.

"No. I have no license."

I had seen him driving round the private roads on his estate in a jeep on one or two occasions, though not, I recalled, with much fervor. After a while he said, "I choose not to have a license, because I have epilepsy. I've had it most of my life. It is of course kept completely under control with pills, but I prefer not to drive on public roads."

"I'm sorry," I said.

"Forget it. I do. It's an inconvenience merely." He sounded as if the subject bored him, and I thought that regarding irregular brain patterns as no more than a nuisance was typical of what I'd gleaned of his normal business methods: routine fast and first, planning slow and thorough. I'd gathered from things his secretary had said in my hearing that he'd made few decisions lately, and trade was beginning to suffer.

When we reached the outskirts of Bologna he said, "I have to go back to those telephones at the highway restaurant tomorrow morning at eight. I have to take the money in my car. I have to wait for him . . . for his instructions. He'll be angry if I have a chauffeur."

"Explain. He'll know you always have a chauffeur. Tell him why."

"I can't risk it." His voice shook.

"Signor Cenci, he wants the money. Make him believe you can't drive safely. The last thing he wants is you crashing the ransom into a lamppost."

"Well . . . I'll try."

"And remember to ask for proof that Alessia is alive and unharmed."

"Yes."

I dropped him at the office and drove back to the Villa Francese, and because it was what the Cenci chauffeur always did when he wasn't needed during the morning, I washed the car. I'd washed the damn car so often I knew every inch intimately, but one couldn't trust kidnappers not to be watching; and the villa and its hillside, with its glorious views, could be observed closely by telescope from a mile away in most directions. Changes of routine from before to after a kidnap were of powerful significance to kidnappers, who were often better detectives than detectives, and better spies than spies. The people who'd taught me my job had been detectives and spies and more besides, so when I was a chauffeur, I washed cars.

That done I went upstairs and slept for a couple of hours and then set to again on the photography, stopping only to go and fetch Cenci at the usual hour. Reporting to his office I found another box on the desk, this time announcing it had been passed by customs at Genoa.

"Shall I carry it out?" I asked.

He nodded dully. "It is all there. Five hundred million lire."

We drove home more or less in silence, and I spent the evening and night as before, methodically click-

ing until I felt like a zombie. By morning it was
done, with the microdots applied to a few of the fifty-
thousand-lire notes, but not many, through lack of
time. I packed all the rubber-banded bundles into
the Fragile box and humped it down to the hall to
find Cenci already pacing up and down in the dining
room, white with strain.

"There you are!" he exclaimed. "I was just coming to wake you. It's getting late. Seven o'clock."

"Have you had breakfast?" I asked.

"I can't eat." He looked at his watch compulsively, something I guessed he'd been doing for
hours. "We'd better go. Suppose we were held up
on the way. Suppose there was an accident blocking
the road." His breathing was shallow and agitated,
and I said diffidently, "Signor Cenci, forgive me for
asking, but in the anxiety of this morning . . . have
you remembered your pills?"

He looked at me blankly. "Yes. Yes of course. Always with me."

"I'm sorry . . ."

He brushed it away. "Let's go. We must go."

The traffic on the road was normal: no accidents.
We reached the rendezvous half an hour early, but
Cenci sprang out of the car as soon as I switched off
the engine. From where I'd parked I had a view of
the entrance across a double row of cars, the doorway like the mouth of a beehive with people going in
and out continually.

Cenci walked with stiff legs to be lost among them,
and in the way of chauffeurs I slouched down in my
seat and tipped my cap forward over my nose. If I
wasn't careful, I thought, I'd go to sleep. . . .

Someone rapped on the window beside me. I

opened my eyes, squinted sideways, and saw a youngish man in a white open-necked shirt with a gold chain round his neck making gestures for me to open the window.

The car rather irritatingly had electric windows: I switched on the ignition and pressed the relevant button, sitting up slightly while I did it.

"Who are you waiting for?" he said.

"Signor Cenci."

"Not Count Rieti?"

"No. Sorry."

"Have you seen another chauffeur here?"

"Sorry, no."

He was carrying a magazine rolled into a cylinder and fastened by a rubber band. I thought fleetingly of one of the partners in Liberty Market who believed one should never trust a stranger carrying a paper cylinder because it was such a handy place to stow a knife . . . and I wondered, but not much.

"You're not Italian?" the man said.

"No. From Spain."

"Oh." His gaze wandered, as if seeking Count Rieti's chauffeur. Then he said absently in Spanish, "You're a long way from home."

"Yes," I said.

"Where do you come from?"

"Andalusia."

"Very hot, at this time of year."

"Yes."

I had spent countless school holidays in Andalusia, staying with my divorced half-Spanish father, who ran a hotel there. Spanish was my second tongue, learned on all levels from kitchen to penthouse: any time I didn't want to appear English, I became a Spaniard.

"Is your employer having breakfast?" he asked.

"I don't know." I shrugged. "He said wait, so I wait."

His Spanish had a clumsy accent and his sentences were grammatically simple, as careful as mine in Italian.

I yawned.

He could be a coincidence, I thought. Kidnappers were normally much too shy for such a direct approach, keeping their faces hidden at all costs. This man could be just what he seemed, a well-meaning citizen carrying a magazine, looking for Count Rieti's chauffeur and with time to spare for talking.

Could be. If not, I would tell him what he wanted to know: if he asked.

"Do you drive always for Signor . . . Cenci?" he said casually.

"Sure," I said. "It's a good job. Good pay. He's considerate. Never drives himself, of course."

"Why not?"

I shrugged. "Don't know. He hasn't a license. He has to have someone to drive him always."

I wasn't quite sure he had followed that, though I'd spoken pretty slowly and with a hint of drowsiness. I yawned again and thought that one way or another he'd had his ration of chat. I would memorize his face, just in case, but it was unlikely . . .

He turned away as if he too had found the conversation finished, and I looked at the shape of his round smooth head from the side, and felt most unwelcome tingles ripple all down my spine. I'd seen him before. . . . I'd seen him outside the ambulance, through the tinted glass, with cameras slung from his neck and gold buckles on the cuffs of his jacket. I could remember him clearly. He'd appeared at the siege . . . and he was here at the drop, asking questions.

No coincidence.

It was the first time I'd ever knowingly been physically near one of the shadowy brotherhood, those foes I opposed by proxy, whose trials I never attended, whose ears never heard of my existence. I slouched down again in my seat and tipped my cap over my nose and thought that my partners in London would emphatically disapprove of my being in that place at that time. The low profile was down the drain.

If I'd seen him, he'd seen me.

It might not matter: not if he believed in the Spanish chauffeur who was bored with waiting. If he believed in the bored Spanish chauffeur, he'd forget me. If he hadn't believed in the bored Spanish chauffeur I would quite likely be sitting there now with a knife through my ribs, growing cold.

In retrospect I felt distinctly shivery. I had not remotely expected such an encounter, and at first it had only been habit and instinct, reinforced by true tiredness, that had made me answer him as I had. I found it definitely scary to think that Alessia's life might have hung on a yawn.

Time passed. Eight o'clock came and went. I waited as if asleep. No one else came to my still-open window to ask me anything at all.

It was after nine before Cenci came back, half running, stumbling, sweating. I was out of the car as soon as I saw him, politely opening a rear door and helping him in as a chauffeur should.

"Oh, my God," he said. "I thought he wouldn't telephone. . . . It's been so long."

"Is Alessia all right?"

"Yes . . . yes . . ."

"Where to, then?"

"Oh . . ." He drew in some calming breaths while I got back behind the wheel and started the engine. "We have to go to Mazara, about twenty kilometers south. Another restaurant . . . another telephone. In twenty minutes."

"Um . . ." I said. "Which way from here?"

He said vaguely, "Umberto knows," which wasn't especially helpful, as Umberto was his real chauffeur, away on holiday. I grabbed the road map from the glove compartment and spread it on the passenger seat beside me, trying unsuccessfully to find Mazara while pulling in a normal fashion out of the car park.

The road we were on ran west to east. I took the first major-looking turn towards the south, and as soon as we were out of sight of the highway drew into the side and paused for an update on geography. One more turn, I thought, and there would be signposts: and in fact we made it to Mazara, which proved to be little more than a crossroads, with breathing time to spare.

On the way Cenci said, "Alessia was reading from today's paper . . . on tape, it must have been, because she just went on reading when I spoke to her . . . but to hear her voice . . ."

"You're sure it was her?"

"Oh, yes. She started as usual with one of those

memories of her childhood that you suggested . . . it was Alessia herself . . . my darling, darling daughter.''

Well, I thought. So far, so good.

"He said . . .'' Cenci gulped audibly. "He said if there are homers this time in the ransom he'll kill her. He says if there are marks on the notes, he'll kill her. He says if we are followed . . . if we don't do exactly as he says . . . if anything . . . anything . . . goes wrong, he'll kill her.''

I nodded. I believed it. A second chance was a partial miracle. We'd never get a third.

"You promise,'' he said, "that he'll find nothing on the notes.''

"I promise,'' I said.

At Mazara Cenci ran to the telephone, but again he was agonizingly kept waiting. I sat as before in the car, stolidly patient, as if the antics of my employer were of little interest, and surreptitiously read the map.

The restaurant at this place was simply a café next to a garage, a stop for coffee and gas. People came and went, but not many. The day warmed up under the summer sun, and as a good chauffeur should I started the purring engine and switched on the air-conditioning.

He returned with his jacket over his arm and flopped gratefully into the cool.

"Casteloro,'' he said. "Why is he doing this?''

"Standard procedure, to make sure we're not followed. He'll be doubly careful because of last time. We might be chasing about all morning.''

"I can't stand it,'' he said; but he could, of course, after the last six weeks.

I found the way to Casteloro and drove there: thirty-two kilometers, mostly of narrow, straight, exposed country roads. Open fields on both sides. Any car following us would have shown up like a rash.

"He made no trouble about you," Cenci said. "I said straight away that I'd brought my chauffeur because I have epilepsy, that it was impossible for me to drive, to come alone. He just said to give you instructions and not explain anything."

"Good," I said, and thought that if HE were me he'd check up with Alessia about the epilepsy, and be reassured.

At Casteloro, a small old town with a cobbled central square full of pigeons, the telephone Cenci sought was in a café, and this time there was no delay.

"Return to Mazara," Cenci said with exhaustion.

I reversed the car and headed back the way we had come, and Cenci said, "He asked me what I had brought the money in. I described the box."

"What did he say?"

"Nothing. Just to follow instructions or Alessia would be killed. He said they would kill her . . . horribly." His voice choked and came out as a sob.

"Listen," I said, "they don't want to kill her. Not now, not when they're so close. And did they say what 'horribly' meant? Were they . . . specific?"

On another sob he said, "No."

"They're frightening you," I said. "Using threats to make sure you'd elude the carabinieri, even if up to now you'd been letting them follow you."

"But I haven't!" he protested.

"They have to be convinced. Kidnappers are very nervous."

It was reassuring though, I thought, that they were still making threats, because it indicated they were serious about dealing. This was no cruel dummy run: this was the actual drop.

Back at the Mazara crossroads there was another lengthy wait. Cenci sat in the café, visible through the window, trembling over an undrunk cup of coffee. I got out of the car, stretched, ambled up and down a bit, got back in, and yawned. Three unexceptional cars filled with gas and the garage attendant scratched his armpits.

The sun was high, blazing out of the blue sky. An old woman in black cycled up to the crossroads, turned left, cycled away. Summer dust stirred and settled in the wake of passing vans, and I thought of Lorenzo Traventi, who had driven the last lot of ransom and now clung to life on machines.

Inside the café Cenci sprang to his feet, and after a while came back to the car in no better state than before. I opened the rear door for him as usual and helped him inside.

"He says . . ." He took a deep breath. "He says there is a sort of shrine by the roadside between here and Casteloro. He says we've passed it twice already . . . but I didn't notice . . ."

I nodded. "I saw it." I closed his door and resumed my own seat.

"Well, there," Cenci said. "He says to put the box behind the shrine, and drive away."

"Good," I said with relief. "That's it, then."

"But Alessia . . ." he wailed. "I asked him,

when will Alessia be free, and he didn't answer, he just put the telephone down . . ."

I started the car and drove again towards Casteloro.

"Be patient," I said gently. "They'll have to count the money. To examine it for tracers. Maybe, after last time, to leave it for a while in a place they can observe, to make sure no one is tracking it by a homer. They won't free Alessia until they're certain they're safe, so I'm afraid it means waiting. It means patience."

He groaned on a long breath. "But they'll let her go . . . when I've paid . . . they'll let her go, won't they?"

He was asking desperately for reassurance, and I said "Yes," robustly: and they would let her go, I thought, if they were satisfied, if they were sane, if something unforeseen didn't happen, and if Alessia hadn't seen their faces.

About ten miles from the crossroads, by a cornfield, stood a simple stone wayside shrine, a single piece of wall about five feet high by three across, with a weatherbeaten foot-high stone madonna offering blessings from a niche in front. Rain had washed away most of the blue paint of her mantle, and time or vandals had relieved her of the tip of her nose, but posies of wilting flowers lay on the ground before her, and someone had left some sweets beside her feet.

The road we were on seemed deserted, running straight in each direction. There were no woods, no cover, no obstructions. We could probably be seen for miles.

Cenci stood watching while I opened the trunk,

lugged out the box, and carried it to the back of the shrine. The box had just about been big enough to contain the whole ransom, and there it stood on the dusty earth, four-square, brown and ordinary, tied about with thick string to make carrying easier, and cheerfully labeled with red. Almost a million pounds. The house on Mikonos, the snuffbox collection, his dead wife's jewelry, the revenue forever from the olives.

Cenci stared at it blindly for a few moments, then we both returned to the car and I reversed and drove away.

Four

For the rest of that day, Saturday, and all Sunday, Cenci walked slowly round his estate, came heavily home, drank too much brandy and lost visible weight.

Ilaria, silently defiant, went to the tennis club as usual. Luisa, her aunt, drifted about in her usual wispy fashion, touching things as if to make sure they were still there.

I drove to Bologna, sent off the films, washed the car. Lorenzo still breathed precariously on his machines and in the meager suburban street the two kidnappers remained barricaded in the third-floor apartment, with talk going on from both sides, but no action, except a delivery of milk for the baby and bread and sausage for the others.

On the Sunday evening Ilaria came into the library where I was watching the news on television. The scene in the street looked almost exactly the same, except that there was no crowd, long discouraged from lack of excitement, and perhaps fewer fawn uniforms. The television coverage had become perfunctory: repetitive as-you-were sentences only.

"Do you think they'll release her?" Ilaria said, as the screen switched away to politicians.

"Yes, I think so."

"When?"

"Can't tell."

"Suppose they've told the carabinieri they'll keep her until those men in the flat go free. Suppose the ransom isn't enough."

I glanced at her. She'd spoken not with dread but as if the question didn't concern her beyond a certain morbid interest. Her face was unstudiedly calm. She appeared really not to care.

"I talked to Enrico Pucinelli this morning," I said. "By then they hadn't said anything like that."

She made a small noncommittal puffing noise through her nose and changed the television channel to a tennis match, settling to watch with concentration.

"I'm not a bitch, you know," she said suddenly. "I can't help it if I don't fall down and kiss the ground she walks on, like everyone else."

"And six weeks is a long time to keep up the hair-tearing?"

"God," she said, "you're on the ball. And don't think I'm not glad you're here. Otherwise he would have leaned on me for everything he gets from you, and I'd have ended up despising him."

"No," I said.

"Yes."

Her eyes had been on the tennis throughout.

"How would you behave," I said, "if you had a son, and he was kidnapped?"

The eyes came round to my face. "You're a right-eous sod," she said.

I smiled faintly. She went resolutely back to the tennis, but where her thoughts were, I couldn't tell.

Ilaria spoke perfect idiomatic English, as I'd been told Alessia did also, thanks to the British widow who had managed the Cenci household for many years after the mother's death. Luisa, Ilaria, and Alessia ran things between them nowadays, and the cook in exasperation had complained to me that nothing got done properly since dear Mrs. Blackett had retired to live with her brother in Eastbourne, England.

The next morning, during the drive to the office, Cenci said, "Turn round, Andrew. Take me home. It's no good, I can't work. I'll sit there staring at the walls. I hear people talk but I don't listen to what they say. Take me home."

I said neutrally, "It might be worse at home."

"No. Turn round. I can't face a new week in the office. Not today."

I turned the car and drove back to the villa, where he telephoned to his secretary not to expect him.

"I can't think," he said to me, "except of Alessia. I think of her as she was as a little girl, and at school, and learning to ride. She was always so neat, so small, so full of life . . ." He swallowed, turned away and walked into the library, and in a few seconds I heard bottle clink against glass.

After a while I went after him.

"Let's play backgammon," I said.

"I can't concentrate."

"Try." I got out the board and set up the pieces, but the moves he made were mechanical and without heart. He did nothing to capitalize on my shortcomings, and after a while simply fell to staring into space, as he'd done for hour after hour since we'd left the money.

At about eleven the telephone at his elbow brought him out of it, but sluggishly.

"Hello? . . . Yes, Cenci speaking . . ." He listened briefly and then looked at the receiver with an apathetic frown before putting it back in its cradle.

"What was it?" I said.

"I don't know. Nothing much. Something about my goods being ready, and to collect them. I don't know what goods . . . he rang off before I could ask."

I breathed deeply. "Your telephone's still tapped," I said.

"Yes, but what's that . . ." His voice died as his eyes widened. "Do you think . . . ? Do you really?"

"We could see," I said. "Don't bank on anything yet. What did he sound like?"

"A gruff voice." He was uncertain. "Not the usual one."

"Well . . . Let's try, anyway. Better than sitting here."

"But where? He didn't say where."

"Perhaps . . . where we left the ransom. Logical place."

Hope began swelling fast in his expression and I said hastily, "Don't expect anything. Don't believe. You'll never be able to stand it, if she isn't there. He may mean somewhere else . . . but I think we should try there first."

He tried to take a grip on things but was still hectically optimistic. He ran through the house to where the car stood waiting near the back door, where I'd parked it. Putting on my cap I followed him at a walk, to find him beckoning frantically and telling me to hurry. I climbed behind the wheel stolidly and thought that someone had known Cenci was at home when he was normally in the office. Perhaps his office had said so . . . or perhaps there was still a watcher. In any case, I reckoned that until Alessia was safely home, a chauffeur in all things was what I needed to be.

"Do hurry," Cenci said. I drove out of the gates without rush. "For God's sake, man . . ."

"We'll get there. Don't hope . . ."

"I can't help it."

I drove faster than usual, but it seemed an eternity to him; and when we pulled up by the shrine there was no sign of his daughter.

"Oh, no . . . Oh, no." His voice was cracking. "I can't . . . I can't . . ."

I looked at him anxiously, but it was normal crushing grief, not a heart attack, not a fit.

"Wait," I said, getting out of the car. "I'll make sure."

I walked round to the back of the shrine, to the spot where we'd left the ransom, and found her there, unconscious, curled like a fetus, wrapped in a gray plastic raincoat.

Fathers are odd. The paramount emotion filling Paolo Cenci's mind for the rest of that day was not joy that his beloved daughter was alive, safe, and emerging unharmed from a drugged sleep, but fear that the press would find out she had been more or less naked.

"Promise you won't say, Andrew. Not to anyone. Not at all."

"I promise."

He made me promise at least seven separate times, though in any case it wasn't necessary. If anyone told, it would be Alessia herself.

Her lack of clothes had disturbed him greatly, especially as he and I had discovered when we tried to pick her up that her arms weren't through the sleeves of the raincoat, and the buttons weren't buttoned. The thin gray covering had slid right off.

She had the body of a child, I thought. Smooth skin, slender limbs, breasts like buds. Cenci had strangely been too embarrassed to touch her, and it had been I, the all-purpose advisor, who'd steered her arms through the plastic and fastened her more discreetly inside the folds. She had been light to carry to the car, and I'd lain her on her side on the rear seat, her knees bent, her curly head resting on my rolled-up jacket.

Cenci sat beside me in front: and it was then that he'd started exacting the promise. When we reached the villa he hurried inside to reappear with a blanket, and I carried her up to her half-acre bedroom in woolly decency.

Ilaria and Luisa were nowhere to be found. Cenci discarded the cook as too talkative and finally asked in a stutter if I would mind very much substituting clothes for the raincoat while he called the doctor. As I'd seen her already once, he said. As I was sensible. Astonished but obliging I unearthed a shiftlike dress and made the exchange, Alessia sleeping peacefully throughout.

She was more awkward than anything else. I

pulled the blue knitted fabric over her head, fed her hands through the armholes, tugged the hem down to her knees and concentrated moderately successfully on my own nonarousal. Then I laid her on top of the bedclothes and covered her from the waist down with the blanket. Her pulse remained strong and regular, her skin cool, her breathing easy: sleeping pills, probably, I thought; nothing worse.

Her thin face was calm, without strain, long lashes lying in half-moon fringes on taut cheeks. Strong eyebrows, pale lips, hollows along the jaw. Hair tousled, clearly dirty. Let her sleep, I thought: she'd have little peace when she woke up.

I went downstairs and found Cenci again drinking brandy, standing up.

"Is she all right?" he said.

"Fine. Just fine."

"It's a miracle."

"Mm."

He put down the glass and began to weep. "Sorry. Can't help it," he said.

"It's natural."

He took out a handkerchief and blew his nose. "Do all parents weep?"

"Yes."

He put in some more work with the handkerchief, sniffed a bit, and said, "You lead a very odd life, don't you?"

"Not really."

"Don't say she had no clothes on. Promise me, Andrew."

"I promise."

I said I'd have to tell Pucinelli she was safe, and, immediately alarmed, he begged for the promise again. I gave it without impatience, because stress could come out in weird ways and the return of the victim was never the end of it.

Pucinelli was fortunately on duty in the ambulance, though presumably I could have spread the news directly via the wiretappers.

"She's home," I said laconically. "I'm in the villa. She's upstairs."

"Alessia?" Disbelief, relief, a shading of suspicion.

"Herself. Drugged but unharmed. Don't hurry, she'll probably sleep for hours. How's the siege going?"

"Andrew!" The beginnings of exasperation. "What's been going on?"

"Will you be coming here yourself?"

A short pause came down the line. He'd told me once that I always put suggestions into the form of questions, and I supposed that it was true that I did. Implant the thought, seek the decision. He knew the tap was on the telephone, he'd ordered it himself, with every word recorded. He would guess there were things I might tell him privately.

"Yes," he said. "I'll be coming."

"And of course you'll have a great lever now with those two kidnappers in the flat, won't you? And . . . um . . . will you bring the ransom money straight here when you lay your hands on it? It does of course belong to Signor Cenci."

"Of course," he said dryly. "But it may not be my decision."

"Mm. Well . . . I photographed all the notes, of course."

A pause. "You're wicked, you know that?"

"Things have disappeared out of police custody before now."

"You insult the carabinieri!" He sounded truly affronted, loyally angry.

"Certainly not. Police stations are not banks. I am sure the carabinieri would be pleased to be relieved of the responsibility of guarding so much money."

"It is evidence."

"The rest of the kidnappers, of course, are still free, and no doubt still greedy. The money could be held safe from them under an official seal in a bank of Signor Cenci's choosing."

A pause. "It's possible that I may arrange it," he said stiffly, not quite forgiving. "No doubt I will see you at the villa."

I put the telephone down with a rueful smile. Pucinelli himself I trusted, but not all law-enforcers automatically. In South American countries particularly, where I had worked several times, kidnappers regularly bribed or threatened policemen to look the wrong way, a custom scarcely unknown elsewhere. Kidnappers had no scruples and seldom any mercy, and many a policeman had had to choose between his duty and the safety of wife and children.

Within ten minutes Pucinelli was back on the line.

"Just to tell you . . . things are moving here. Come if you want. Come into the street from the west, on this side. I'll make sure you get through."

"Thanks."

The partners wouldn't have approved, but I went. I'd studied many case histories of sieges and been to lectures by people involved in some of them, but I'd never been on the spot before at first hand: too good a chance to miss. I changed from Spanish chauffeur to nondescript onlooker, borrowed the family's runabout, and was walking along the Bologna street in record time.

Pucinelli had been as good as his word: a pass awaiting me at the first barrier saw me easily through to the still-parked ambulance. I went into it as I'd left, through the nearside passenger door, and found Pucinelli there with his engineer and three men in city suits.

"You came," he said.

"You're kind."

He gave me a small smile and briefly introduced me to the civilians: negotiator, psychiatrist, psychiatrist.

"These two medical gentlemen have been advising us about the changing mental state of the kidnappers." Pucinelli spoke formally; they nodded gravely back.

"Mostly their mental state has been concerned with the baby," Pucinelli said. "The baby has cried a lot. Apparently the milk we sent in upset its stomach even worse."

As if on cue the bug on the apartment produced the accelerating wail of the infant getting newly into its stride, and from the faces of the five men in front of me it wasn't only the kidnappers who were finding the sound a frazzle.

"Forty minutes ago," Pucinelli said, turning down the baby's volume, "the deep-voiced kidnapper telephoned here and said they would come out if certain conditions were met. No airplane . . . they've abandoned that. They want only to be sure they aren't shot. In about twenty minutes . . . that's one hour from when they telephoned . . . they say the mother will leave with the baby. Then one of the kidnappers will come out. There are to be no carabinieri anywhere in the apartments. The stairs must be clear, also the front door and the pavement outside. The mother and baby will come out into the road, followed by the first kidnapper. He will have no gun. If he is taken peacefully, one of the children will leave, and after an interval, the father. If the second kidnapper is then sure he will be safe, he will come out with the second child in his arms. No gun. We are to arrest him quietly.''

I looked at him. ''Did they discuss all this between themselves? Did you hear them plan it, on the bug?''

He shook his head. ''Nothing.''

''They telephoned you very soon after Alessia was home.''

''Suspiciously soon.''

''You'll look for the radio?'' I said.

''Yes.'' He sighed. ''We have been monitoring radio frequencies these past few days. We've had no results, but I have thought once or twice before this that the kidnappers were being instructed.''

Instructed, I thought, by a very cool and bold intelligence. A pity such a brain was criminal.

''What do they plan to do with the money?'' I asked.

''Leave it in the apartment.''

I glanced at the screen which had shown the whereabouts of the homer in the ransom suitcase, but it was dark. I leaned over and flicked the on-off switch, and the trace obligingly appeared, efficient and steady. The suitcase, at least, was still there.

I said, "I'd like to go up there, as Signor Cenci's representative, to see that it's safely taken care of."

With suppressed irritation he said, "Very well."

"It's a great deal of money," I said reasonably.

"Yes . . . yes, I suppose it is." He spoke grudgingly, partly, I guessed, because he was himself honest, partly because he was a communist. So much wealth in one man's hands offended him, and he wouldn't care if Cenci lost it.

Across the street the apartment's windows were still closed. All the windows of all the apartments were closed, although the day was hot.

"Don't they ever open them?" I asked.

Pucinelli glanced across at the building. "The kidnappers open the windows sometimes for a short while when we switch off the searchlights at dawn. The blinds are always drawn, even then. There are no people now in any of the other apartments. We moved them for their own safety."

Down on the road there was little movement. Most of the official cars had been withdrawn, leaving a good deal of empty space. Four carabinieri crouched with guns behind the pair still parked, their bodies tense. Metal barriers down the street kept a few onlookers at bay, and the television van looked closed. One or two photographers sat on the ground in its shade, drinking beer from cans. On the bug the colicky crying had stopped, but no one seemed to be saying very much. It was siesta, after all.

Without any warning a young woman walked from the apartments carrying a baby and shielding her eyes against the brilliance of the sunlight. She was very disheveled and also heavily pregnant.

Pucinelli glanced as if stung at his wristwatch,

said, "They're early," and jumped out of the van. I watched him through the dark glass as he strode without hesitation towards her, taking her arm. Her head turned towards him and she began to fall, Pucinelli catching the baby and signaling furiously with his head to his men behind the cars.

One scurried forward, hauled the fainting woman unceremoniously to her feet and hustled her into one of the cars. Pucinelli gave the baby a sick look, carried it at arm's length in the wake of its mother, and, having delivered it, wiped his hands disgustedly on a handkerchief.

The photographers and the television van came to life as if electrified, and a young plump man walked three steps out of the apartments and slowly raised both hands.

Pucinelli, now sheltering behind the second car, stretched an arm through the window, removed a bullhorn, and spoke through it.

"Lie face down on the road. Legs apart. Arms outstretched."

The plump young man wavered a second, looked as if he would retreat, and finally did as he was bid.

Pucinelli spoke again. "Stay where you are. You will not be shot."

There was a long breath-holding hush. Then a boy came out; about six, in shorts, shirt, and bright blue and white training shoes. His mother frantically waved to him through the car window, and he ran across to her, looking back over his shoulder at the man on the ground.

I switched up the volume to full on the bug in the apartment, but there was still no talking, simply a few grunts and unidentifiable movements. After a while these ended, and shortly afterwards another man walked out into the street, a youngish man this time with his hands tied behind his back. He looked gaunt and tottery, with stubbled chin, and he stopped dead at the sight of the spreadeagled kidnapper.

"Come to the cars," Pucinelli said through the bull-horn. "You are safe."

The man seemed unable to move. Pucinelli, again exposing his whole body to the still-present threat of the guns in the apartment, walked calmly across the road, took him by the arm, and led him behind the car holding his wife.

The psychiatrists watching beside me shook their heads over Pucinelli, not approving such straightforward courage. I picked up a pair of binoculars which were lying on the bench and focused them on the opposite windows, but nothing stirred. Then I scanned the onlookers at the barriers down the street, and took in a close-up of the photographers, but there was no sign of the man from the highway car park.

I put down the glasses, and time gradually stretched out, hot and silent, making me wonder, making everyone wonder if by some desperate mischance at the last minute the surrender had gone wrong. There was no sound from the bug. There was stillness in the street. Forty-six minutes had passed since the mother and baby had emerged.

Pucinelli spoke through the bullhorn with firmness but not aggression. "Bring out the child. You will not be hurt."

Nothing happened.

Pucinelli repeated his instructions.

Nothing.

I thought of guns, of desperation, of suicide, murder, and spite.

Pucinelli's voice rang out. "Your only hope of ever being released from prison is to come out now as arranged."

No result.

Pucinelli's hand put the bullhorn through the car's window and reappeared holding a pistol. He pushed the pistol through his belt in the small of his back, and without more ado walked straight across the street and in through the door of the apartments.

The psychiatrists gasped and made agitated motions with their hands and I wondered if I would ever have had the nerve, in those circumstances, to do what Pucinelli was doing.

There were no shots: none that we could hear. No sounds at all, just more long-drawn-out quiet.

The carabinieri behind the cars began to grow dangerously restive for lack of their leader and to look at each other for guidance, waving their guns conspicuously. The engineer in the van was muttering ominously under his breath, and there was still silence from the bug. If nothing happened soon, I thought, there could be another excited, destructive, half-cocked raid.

Then, suddenly there was a figure in the doorway: a strong burly man carrying a little girl like a feather on one arm.

Behind him came Pucinelli, gun nowhere in sight. He pointed to the first kidnapper, still spreadeagled, and the big man with a sort of furious resignation walked over to him and put the small child on the ground. Then he lowered his bulk into the same outstretched attitude, and the little girl, only a toddler, stood looking at him for a moment and then lay down and copied him, as if it were a game.

The carabinieri burst like uncorked furies from behind the cars and bristling with guns and handcuffs descended on the prone figures with no signs of loving-kindness. Pucinelli watched while the kidnappers were marched to the empty car and the child returned to her parents, then came casually back to the open door of the ambulance as if he'd been out for a stroll.

He thanked the negotiator and the psychiatrists from there, and jerked his head to me to come out and follow him. I did: across the road, in through the door of the apartments and up the stone staircase beyond.

"The big man," Pucinelli said, "was up there," he pointed, "right at the top, sixth floor, where the stairs lead to the roof. It took me some time to find him. But we had barricaded that door, of course. He couldn't get out."

"Was he violent?" I asked.

Pucinelli laughed. "He was sitting on the stairs with the little girl on his knee, telling her a story."

"What?"

"When I went up the stairs with my pistol ready he said to put it away, the show was over, he knew it. I told him to go down into the street. He said he wanted to stay where he was for a while. He said he had a child of his own of that age and he'd never be able to hold her on his knee again."

Sob stuff, I thought. "What did you do?" I asked.

"Told him to go down at once."

The "at once," however, had taken quite a long

time. Pucinelli like all Italians liked children, and even carabinieri, I supposed, could be sentimental.

"That poor deprived father," I said, "abducted someone else's daughter and shot someone else's son."

"Your head," Pucinelli said, "is like ice."

He led the way into the apartment that had been besieged for four and a half days, and the heat and stink of it were indescribable. Squalor took on a new meaning. Apart from the stench of sweat and the decomposing remains of meals there were unmentionable heaps of cloth and rags and newspaper in two of the three small rooms: the baby, incontinent at both ends, had done more than cry.

"How did they stand it?" I wondered. "Why didn't they wash anything?"

"The mother wanted to. I heard her asking. They wouldn't let her."

We searched our way through the mess, finding the ransom suitcase almost immediately under a bed. As far as I could tell, the contents were untouched: good news for Cenci. Pucinelli gave the packets of notes a sour look and poked around for the radio.

The owners of the apartment had one themselves, standing openly on top of a television set, but Pucinelli shook his head over it, saying it was too elementary. He started a methodical search, coming across it eventually inside a box of Buitoni in a kitchen cupboard.

"Here we are," he said, brushing off pasta shells. "Complete with earplug for private listening." A smallish but elaborate walkie-talkie, aerial retracted.

"Don't disturb the frequency," I said.

"I wasn't born yesterday. Nor was the man giving the instructions, I shouldn't think."

"He might not have thought of everything."

"Maybe not. All criminals are fools sometimes, otherwise we'd never catch them." He wound the cord with its earpiece carefully around the radio and put it by the door.

"What range do you think that has?" I asked.

"Not more than a few miles. I'll find out. But too far, I would think, to help us."

There remained the pistols, and these were easy: Pucinelli found them on a windowsill when he let up one of the blinds to give us more light.

We both looked down from the window. The ambulance and the barriers were still there, though the drama had gone. I thought that the earlier host of official cars and of highly armed men crouching behind them must have been a fearsome sight. What with that threat ever present and the heat, the baby, the searchlights, and the stench, their nerves must have been near exploding point the whole time.

"He could have shot you any time," I said, "when you walked out across the street."

"I reckoned he wouldn't." He spoke unemotionally. "But when I was creeping up the stairs . . ." he smiled fractionally ". . . I did begin to wonder."

He gave me a cool and comradely nod and departed, saying he would arrange transit for the ransom and send his men to collect and label the pistols and radio.

"You'll stay here?" he asked.

I pinched my nose. "On the stairs outside."

He smiled and went away, and in due course people arrived. I accompanied the ransom to the bank of

Pucinelli's choosing, followed it to the vaults and accepted bank and carabinieri receipts. Then, on my way back to collect the Cenci runabout, I made a routine collect call to my firm in London. Reports from advisors-in-the-field were expected regularly, with wisdom from the collective office mind flowing helpfully back.

"The girl's home," I said. "The siege is over, the first ransom's safe, and how are my snaps doing of the second?"

"Lists with you tomorrow morning."

"Right."

They wanted to know how soon I'd be back.

"Two or three days," I said. "Depends on the girl."

Five

Alessia woke in the evening, feeling sick. Cenci rushed upstairs to embrace her, came down damp-eyed, said she was still sleepy and couldn't believe she was home.

I didn't see her. Ilaria slept all night on an extra bed in Alessia's room at her Aunt Luisa's sugges-tion, and did seem genuinely pleased at her sister's return. In the morning she came down with compo-sure to breakfast and said that Alessia felt ill and wouldn't get out of the bath.

"Why not?" Cenci said, bewildered.

"She says she's filthy. She's washed her hair twice. She says she smells."

"But she doesn't," he protested.

"No. I've told her that. It makes no difference."

"Take her some brandy and a bottle of scent," I said.

Cenci looked at me blankly but Ilaria said, "Well, why not?" and went off on the errand. She had talked more easily that morning than at any breakfast before, almost as if her sister's release had been also her own.

Pucinelli arrived mid-morning with a note-taking aide, and Alessia came downstairs to meet him. Standing there beside him in the hall I watched the tentative figure on the stairs and could clearly read her strong desire to retreat. She stopped four steps from the bottom and looked behind her, but Ilaria, who had gone up to fetch her, was nowhere to be seen.

Cenci went forward and put his arm round her shoulders, explaining briefly who I was, and saying Pucinelli wanted to know everything that had happened to her, hoping for clues to lead him to arrests.

She nodded slightly, looking pale.

I'd seen victims return with hectic jollity, with hysteria, with apathy; all with shock. Alessia's state looked fairly par for the circumstances: a mixture of shyness, strangeness, weakness, relief, and fear.

Her hair was still damp. She wore a T-shirt, jeans, and no lipstick. She looked a defenseless sixteen, recently ill; the girl I'd seen undressed. What she did not look was the glossy darling of the European racetracks.

Cenci led her to the library, and we scattered around on chairs.

"Tell us," Pucinelli said. "Please tell us what happened, from the beginning."

"I . . . it seems so long ago." She spoke mostly to her father, looking seldom at Pucinelli and not at all at me; and she used Italian throughout, though as she spoke slowly with many pauses, I could follow her with ease. Indeed it occurred to me fleetingly that I'd soaked in a good deal more of the language than I'd arrived with, and more than I'd noticed until then.

"I'd been racing here on our local track . . . but you know that."

Her father nodded.

"I won the six o'clock race, and there was an objection . . ."

More nods, both from Cenci and Pucinelli. The note-taking aide, eyes down to the task, kept his shorthand busily flowing.

"I drove home. I was thinking of England. Of riding Brunelleschi in the Derby . . ." She broke off. "Did he win?"

Her father looked blank. At the time, shortly after her disappearance, he'd have been unlikely to notice an invasion of Martians in the back yard.

"No," I said. "Fourth."

She said, "Oh," vaguely, and I didn't bother to explain that I knew where the horse had finished simply because it was she who had been going to ride it. Ordinary curiosity, nothing more.

"I was here . . . in sight of the house. Not far from the gate. I slowed down, to turn in . . ."

The classic spot for kidnaps; right outside the victim's house. She had a red sports car, besides, and had been driving it that day with the top down, as she always did in fine weather. Some people, I'd thought when I'd heard it, made abduction too simple for words.

"There was a car coming towards me . . . I waited for it to pass, so that I could turn . . . but it didn't pass, it stopped suddenly between me and the gate . . . blocking the way." She paused and looked anxiously at her father. "I couldn't help it, Papa. I really couldn't."

"My dear, my dear . . ." He looked surprised at the very thought. He didn't see, as I did, the iceberg tip of the burden of guilt, but then he hadn't seen it so often.

"I couldn't think what they were doing," she said. "Then all the car doors opened at once, and there were four men . . . all wearing horrid masks . . . truly horrible . . . devils and monsters. I thought they wanted to rob me. I threw my purse at them . . . and tried to reverse to get away backwards . . . and they sort of leaped into my car . . . just jumped right in . . ." She stopped with the beginnings of agitation and Pucinelli made small damping-down motions with his hands to settle her.

"They were so fast," she said, her voice full of apology. "I couldn't do anything . . ."

"Signorina," Pucinelli said calmly, "there is nothing to be ashamed of. If kidnappers wish to kidnap, they kidnap. Even all Aldo Moro's guards couldn't prevent it. And one girl alone, in an open car . . ." He shrugged expressively, finishing the sentence without words, and for the moment at least she seemed comforted.

A month earlier, to me in private, he had said that any rich girl who drove around in an open sports car was inviting everything from mugging to rape. "I'm not saying they wouldn't have taken her anyway, but she was stupid. She made it easy."

· "There's not much fun in life if you're twenty-three and successful and can't enjoy it by driving an open sports car on a sunny day. What would you ad-

vise her to do, go around in a middle-aged saloon
with the doors locked?"

"Yes," he said. "So would you, if your firm were
asked. That's the sort of advice you'd be paid for."

"True enough."

Alessia said, "They put a hood of cloth right over
my head . . . and then it smelled sweet . . ."

"Sweet?" Pucinelli said.

"You know. Ether. Chloroform. Something like
that. I simply went to sleep. I tried to struggle . . .
they had their hands on my arms . . . sort of lifting
me . . . nothing else."

"They lifted you out of the car?"

"I think so. I suppose so. They must have done."

Pucinelli nodded. Her car had been found a bare
mile away, parked on a farm track.

"I woke up in a tent," Alessia said.

"A tent?" echoed Cenci, bewildered.

"Yes . . . well . . . it was inside a room, but I
didn't realize that at first."

"What sort of tent?" Pucinelli asked. "Please describe it."

"Oh . . ." She moved a hand weakly. "I can describe every stitch of it. Green canvas. About two
and a half meters square . . . a bit less. It had walls
. . . I could stand up."

A frame tent.

"It had a floor. Very tough fabric. Gray. Water-
proof, I suppose, though of course that didn't matter . . ."

"When you woke up," Pucinelli asked, "what
happened?"

"One of the men was kneeling on the floor beside
me, slapping my face. Quite hard. Hurry up, he was

saying. Hurry up. When I opened my eyes he grunted and said I must just repeat a few words and I could go back to sleep.''

''Was he wearing a mask?''

''Yes . . . a devil face . . . orange . . . all warts.''

We all knew what the few words had been. We'd all listened to them, over and over, on the first of the tapes.

''This is Alessia. Please do as they say. They will kill me if you don't.'' A voice slurred with drugs, but alarmingly her own.

''I knew what I said,'' she said. ''I knew when I woke up properly . . . but when I said them, everything was fuzzy. I couldn't see the mask half the time . . . I kept switching off, then coming back.''

''Did you ever see any of them without masks?'' Pucinelli asked.

A flicker of a smile reached the pale mouth. ''I didn't see any of them again, even in masks. Not at all. No one. The first person I saw since that first day was Aunt Luisa . . . sitting by my own bed . . . sewing her tapestry, and I thought . . . I was dreaming.'' Tears unexpectedly appeared in her eyes and she blinked them slowly away. ''They said . . . if I saw their faces, they would kill me. They told me not to try to see them . . .'' She swallowed. ''So . . . I didn't . . . try.''

''You believed them?''

A pause. Then she said ''Yes'' with a conviction that brought understanding of what she'd been through vividly to life. Cenci, although he had believed the threats himself, looked shattered. Pucinelli gravely assured her that he was sure she had been right: and so, though I didn't mention it, was I.

"They said . . . I would go home safely . . . if I was quiet . . . and if you would pay for my release." She was still trying not to cry. "Papa . . ."

"My dearest . . . I would pay anything." He was himself close to tears.

"Yes," Pucinelli said matter-of-factly. "Your father paid."

I glanced at him. "He paid," he repeated, looking steadily at Cenci. "How much, and where he paid it, only he knows. In no other way would you be free."

Cenci said defensively, "I was lucky to get the chance, after your men . . ."

Pucinelli cleared his throat hurriedly and said, "Let's get on. Signorina, please describe how you have lived for the past six weeks."

"I didn't know how long it was, until Aunt Luisa told me. I lost count . . . there were so many days . . . I had no way of counting . . . and then it didn't seem to matter much. I asked why it was so long, but they didn't answer. They never answered any questions. It wasn't worth asking . . . but sometimes I did, just to hear my own voice." She paused. "It's odd to talk as much as this. I went days without saying anything at all."

"They talked to you, though, Signorina?"

"They gave me orders."

"What orders?"

"To take in the food. To put out the bucket . . ." She stopped, then said, "It sounds so awful, here in this room."

She looked round at the noble bookcases stretch-

ing to the high ceiling, at the silk brocaded chairs, at
the pale Chinese carpet on the marble-tiled floor.
Every room in the house had the same unself-
conscious atmosphere of wealth, of antique things
having stood in the same places for decades, of trea-
sures taken for granted. She must have been in many
a meager room in her racing career, but she was seeing her roots, I guessed, with fresh eyes.

"In the tent," she said resignedly, "there was a
piece of foam for me to lie on, and another small
piece for a pillow. There was a bucket . . . an ordinary bucket, like out of a stable. There was nothing
else." She paused, "There was a zip to open one
side of the tent. It would open only about fifty centi-
meters . . . it was jammed above that. They told me
to unzip it, and I would find food . . ."

"Could you see anything of the room outside the
tent?" Pucinelli asked.

She shook her head. "Beyond the zip there was
just more tent . . . but folded a bit, I think . . . I
mean, not properly put up like another room . . ."
She paused. "They told me not to try to get into it."
Another pause. "The food was always where I could
reach it easily, just by the zip."

"What was the food?" Cenci asked, deeply concerned.

"Pasta." A pause. "Sometimes warm, sometimes
cold. Mixed with sauce. Tinned, I think. Anyway . . ." she said tiredly, "it came twice a day . . .
and the second lot usually had sleeping pills in it."

Cenci exclaimed in protest, but Alessia said, "I
didn't mind . . . I just ate it . . . it was better really
than staying awake."

There was a silence, then Pucinelli said, "Was

there anything you could hear, which might help us to find where you were held?"

"Hear?" She glanced at him vaguely. "Only the music."

"What music?"

"Oh . . . tapes. Taped music. Over and over, always the same."

"What sort of music?"

"Verdi. Orchestral, no singing. Three quarters of that, then one quarter of pop music. Still no singing."

"Could you write down the tunes in order?"

She looked mildly surprised but said, "Yes, I should think so. All that I know the names of."

"If you do that today, I'll send a man for the list."

"All right."

"Is there anything else at all you can think of?"

She looked dully at the floor, her thin face tired with the mental efforts of freedom. Then she said, "About four times they gave me a few sentences to read aloud, and they told me each time to mention something that had happened in my childhood, which only my father would know about, so that he could be sure I was still . . . all right."

Pucinelli nodded. "You were reading from daily papers."

She shook her head. "They weren't newspapers. Just sentences typed on ordinary paper."

"Did you keep those papers?"

"No, they told me to put them out through the zip." She paused. "The only times they turned the music off was when I made the recordings."

"Did you see a microphone?"

"No . . . But I could hear them talk clearly

through the tent . . . so I suppose they recorded me from outside.''

"Would you remember their voices?"

An involuntary shudder shook her. "Two of them, yes. They spoke most . . . but there were others. The one who made the recordings . . . I'd remember him. He was just . . . cold. The other one was beastly . . . He seemed to enjoy it . . . but he was worse at the beginning . . . or at least perhaps I got used to him and didn't care. Then there was one sometimes who kept apologizing . . . 'Sorry, Signorina' . . . when he told me the food was there. And another who just grunted . . . None of them ever answered, if I spoke.''

"Signorina," Pucinelli said, "if we play you one of the tapes your father received, will you tell us if you recognize the man's voice?"

"Oh . . ." She swallowed. "Yes, of course."

He had brought a small recorder and copies of the tapes with him, and she watched apprehensively while he inserted a cassette and pressed a button. Cenci put out a hand to grasp one of Alessia's, almost as if he could shield her from what she would hear.

"Cenci," HIS voice said. "We have your daughter Alessia. We will return her on payment of one hundred and fifty thousand million lire. Listen to your daughter's voice." There was a click, and then Alessia's slurred words. Then, "Believe her. If you do not pay, we will kill her. Do not delay. Do not inform the carabinieri, or your daughter will be beaten. She will be beaten every day you delay, and also . . ." Pucinelli pressed the stop button decisively, abruptly and mercifully shutting off the worse, the bestial threats. Alessia anyway was shaking and could hardly speak. Her nods were small and emphatic. "Mm . . . yes . . ."

"You could swear to it?"

". . . Yes . . ."

Pucinelli methodically put away the recorder. "It is the same male voice on all the tapes. We have had a voiceprint made, to be sure."

Alessia worked saliva into her mouth. "They didn't beat me," she said. "They didn't even threaten it. They said nothing like that."

Pucinelli nodded. "The threats were for your father."

She said with intense anxiety, "Papa, you didn't pay that much? That's everything . . . you couldn't."

He shook his head reassuringly. "No, no, nothing like that. Don't fret . . . don't worry."

"Excuse me," I said in English.

All the heads turned in surprise, as if the wallpaper had spoken.

"Signorina," I said, "were you moved from place to place at all? Were you in particular moved four or five days ago?"

She shook her head. "No." Her certainty however began to waver, and with a frown she said, "I was in that tent all the time. But . . ."

"But what?"

"The last few days, there was a sort of smell of bread baking, sometimes, and the light seemed brighter . . . but I thought they had drawn a curtain perhaps . . . though I didn't think much at all. I mean, I slept so much . . . it was better . . ."

"The light," I said, "it was daylight?"

She nodded. "It was quite dim in the tent, but my eyes were so used to it . . . They never switched on any electric lights. At night it was dark, I suppose, but I slept all night, every night."

"Do you think you could have slept through a move, if they'd taken the tent from one room in one place and driven it to another place and set it up again?"

The frown returned while she thought it over. "There was one day not long ago I hardly woke up at all. When I did wake it was already getting dark and I felt sick . . . like I did when I woke here yesterday . . . and oh," she exclaimed intensely, "I'm so glad to be here, so desperately grateful . . . I can't tell you . . ." She buried her face on her father's shoulder and he stroked her hair with reddening eyes.

Pucinelli rose to his feet and took a formal leave of father and daughter, removing himself, his note-taker, and myself to the hall.

"I may have to come back, but that seems enough for now." He sighed. "She knows so little. Not much help. The kidnappers were too careful. If you learn any more, Andrew, you'll tell me?"

I nodded.

"How much was the ransom?" he said.

I smiled. "The list of the notes' numbers will come here today. I'll let you have them. Also, do you have the Identikit system, like in England?"

"Something like it, yes."

"I could build a picture of one of the other kidnappers, I think. Not the ones in the siege. If you like."

"If I like! Where did you see him? How do you know?"

"I've seen him twice. I'll tell you about it when I come in with the lists."

"How soon?" he demanded.

"When the messenger comes. Any time now."

The messenger obligingly arrived while Pucinelli was climbing into his car, so I borrowed the Fiat runabout again and followed him to his headquarters.

Fitting together pieces of head with eyes and mouth, chin and hairline, I related the two sightings. "You probably saw him yourself, outside the ambulance, the night the siege started," I said.

"I had too much to think of."

I nodded and added ears. "This man is young. Difficult to tell . . . not less than twenty-five, though. Lower thirties, probably."

I built a full face and a profile, but wasn't satisfied, and Pucinelli said he would get an artist in to draw what I wanted. "He works in the courts. Very fast."

A telephone call produced the artist within half an hour. He came, fat, grumbling, smelling of garlic and scratching, and saying that it was siesta, how could any sane man be expected to work at two in the afternoon? He stared with disillusion at my composite efforts, fished out a thin charcoal stick, and began performing rapid miracles on a sketch pad. Every few seconds he stopped to raise his eyebrows at me, inviting comment.

"Rounder head," I said, describing it with my hands. "A smooth round head."

The round head appeared. "What next?"

"The mouth . . . a fraction too thin. A slightly fuller lower lip."

He stopped when I could think of no more improvements and showed the results to Pucinelli. "This is the man as your English friend remembers him," he said, sniffing. "Memories are usually wrong, don't forget."

"Thanks," Pucinelli said. "Go back to sleep."

The artist grumbled and departed, and I said, "What's the latest on Lorenzo Traventi?"

"Today they say he'll live."

"Good," I said with relief. It was the first time anyone had been positive.

"We've charged the two kidnappers with intent to kill. They are protesting." He shrugged. "So far they are refusing to say anything about the kidnap, though naturally we are pointing out that if they lead us to other arrests their sentences will be shorter." He picked up the artist's drawings. "I'll show them these. It will shock them." A fleeting look of savage pleasure crossed his face: the look of a born police-man poised for a kill. I'd seen it on other faces above other uniforms, and never despised it: and he deserved his satisfaction, after the strains of the past week.

"The radio," Pucinelli said, pausing as he turned away.

"Yes?"

"It could transmit and receive on aircraft frequencies."

I blinked. "That's not usual, is it?"

"Not very. And it was tuned to the international emergency frequency . . . which is monitored all the time, and which certainly did not pick up any messages between kidnappers. We checked at the airport this morning."

I shook my head in frustration. Pucinelli went off

with eagerness to his interrogations, and I returned to the villa.

Alessia said, "Do you mind if I ask you something?"

"Fire away."

"I asked Papa but he won't answer, which I suppose anyway is an answer of sorts." She paused. "Did I have any clothes on, when you found me?"

"A gray plastic raincoat," I said matter-of-factly.

"Oh."

I couldn't tell whether the answer pleased her or not. She remained thoughtful for a while, and then said, "I woke up here in a dress I haven't worn for years. Aunt Luisa and Ilaria say they don't know how it happened. Did Papa dress me? Is that why he's so embarrassed?"

"Didn't you expect to have clothes on?" I asked curiously.

"Well . . ." She hesitated.

I lifted my head. "Were you naked . . . all the time?"

She moved her thin body restlessly in the armchair as if she would sink into it, out of sight. "I don't want . . ." she said; and broke off, swallowing, while in my mind I finished the sentence. Don't want everyone to know.

"It's all right," I said. "I won't say."

We were sitting in the library, the evening fading to dark, the heat of the day diminishing; freshly showered, casually dressed, waiting in the Cenci household routine to be joined by everyone for a drink or two before dinner. Alessia's hair was again damp, but she had progressed as far as lipstick.

She gave me short glances of inspection, not sure of me.

"Why are you here?" she said. "Papa says he couldn't have got through these weeks without you, but . . . I don't really understand."

I explained my job.

"An advisor?"

"That's right."

She thought for a while, her gaze wandering over my face and down to my hands and up again to my eyes. Her opinions were unreadable, but finally she sighed, as if making up her mind.

"Well . . . advise me, too," she said. "I feel very odd. Like jet lag, only much worse. Time lag. I feel as if I'm walking on tissue paper. As if nothing's real. I keep wanting to cry. I should be deliriously happy . . . why aren't I?"

"Reaction," I said.

"You don't know . . . you can't imagine . . . what it was like."

"I've heard from many people what it's like. From people like you, straight back from kidnap. They've told me. The first bludgeoning shock, the not being able to believe it's happening. The humiliations, forced on you precisely to make you afraid and defenseless. No bathrooms. Sometimes no clothes. Certainly no respect. No kindness or gentleness of any sort. Imprisonment, no one to talk to, nothing to fill the mind, just uncertainty and fear . . . and guilt . . . Guilt that you didn't escape in the beginning, guilt at the distress brought on your family, guilt at what a ransom will cost . . . and fear for your life . . . if the money can't be raised, or if something goes wrong . . . if the kidnappers panic.''

She listened intently, at first with surprise and then with relief. ''You do know. You do understand. I haven't been able to say . . . I don't want to upset them . . . and also . . . also . . .''

''Also you feel ashamed,'' I said.

''Oh.'' Her eyes widened. ''I . . . Why do I?''

''I don't know, but nearly everyone does.''

''Do they?''

''Yes.''

She sat quiet for a while, then she said, ''How long will it take . . . for me to get over it?''

To that there was no answer. ''Some people shake it off almost at once,'' I said. ''But it's like illness, or a death . . . you have to grow scar tissue.''

Some managed it in days, some in weeks, some in years; some bled forever. Some of the apparently strong disintegrated most. One couldn't tell, not on the day after liberation.

Ilaria came into the room in a stunning scarlet and gold toga and began switching on the lamps.

''It was on the radio news that you're free,'' she said to Alessia. ''I heard it upstairs. Make the most of the peace, the paparazzi will be storming up the drive before you can blink.''

Alessia shrank again into her chair and looked distressed. Ilaria, it occurred to me uncharitably, had dressed for such an event: another statement about not wanting to be eclipsed.

''Does your advice stretch to paparazzi?'' Alessia asked weakly, and I nodded, ''If you like.''

Ilaria patted the top of my head as she passed behind my chair. ''Our Mr. Fixit. Never at a loss.''

Paolo Cenci himself arrived with Luisa, the one looking anxious, the other fluttery, as usual.

"Someone telephoned from the television company," Cenci said. "They say a crew is on the way here. Alessia . . . you'd better stay in your room until they've gone."

I shook my head. "They'll just camp on your doorstep. Better, really, to get it over." I looked at Alessia. "If you could possibly . . . and I know it's hard . . . make some sort of joke, they'll go away quicker."

She said in bewilderment, "Why?"

"Because good news is brief news. If they think you had a really bad time, they'll keep on probing. Tell them the kidnappers treated you well, say you're glad to be home, say you'll be back on the racecourse very soon. If they ask you anything which it would really distress you to answer, blank the thoughts out and make a joke."

"I don't know . . . if I can."

"The world wants to hear that you're all right," I said. "They want to be reassured, to see you smile. If you can manage it now it will make your return to normal life much easier. The people you know will greet you with delight . . . they won't find meeting you uncomfortable, which they could if they'd seen you in hysterics."

Cenci said crossly, "She's not in hysterics."

"I know what he means," Alessia said. She smiled wanly at her father. "I hear you're paying for the advice, so we'd better take it."

Once mobilized, the family put on a remarkable show, like actors on stage. For Ilaria and Luisa it was least difficult, but for Cenci the affable host role must

have seemed bizarre, as he admitted the television
people with courtesy and was helpful about electric
plugs and moving furniture. A second television
crew arrived while the first was still setting up, and
after that several carsful of reporters, some from international news agencies, and a clatter of photographers. Ilaria moved like a scarlet bird among them,
gaily chatting, and even Luisa was appearing gracious, in her unfocused way.

I watched the circus assemble from behind the almost closed library door, while Alessia sat silent in
her armchair, developing shadows under her eyes.

"I can't do it," she said.

"They won't expect a song and dance act. Just be
. . . normal."

"And make a joke."

"Yes."

"I feel sick," she said.

"You're used to crowds," I said. "Used to people
staring at you. Think of being . . ." I groped,
". . . in the winner's circle. Lots of fuss. You're
used to it, which gives you a shield."

She merely swallowed, but when her father came
for her she walked out and faced the barrage of flash-
lights and questions without cracking. I watched
from the library door, listening to her slow, clear
Italian.

"I'm delighted to be home with my family. Yes,
I'm fine. Yes, I hope to be racing again very soon."

The brilliant lighting for the television cameras
made her look extra pale, especially near the glowing
Ilaria, but the calm half smile on her face never wavered.

"No, I never saw the kidnappers' faces. They were very . . . discreet."

The newsgatherers reacted to the word with a low growling rumble of appreciation.

"Yes, the food was excellent . . . if you like tinned pasta."

Her timing was marvellous: this time she reaped a full laugh.

"I've been living in the sort of tent people take on holiday. Size? A single bedroom . . . about that size. Yes . . . quite comfortable . . . I listened to music, most of the time."

Her voice was quiet, but rock-steady. The warmth of the newsmen towards her came over clearly now in their questions, and she told them an open sports car had proved a liability and she regretted having caused everyone so much trouble.

"How much ransom? I don't know. My father says it wasn't too much."

"What was the worst thing about being kidnapped?" She repeated the question as if herself wondering, and then, after a pause, said, "Missing the English Derby, I guess. Missing the ride on Brunelleschi."

It was the climax. To the next question she smiled and said she had a lot of things to catch up with, and she was a bit tired, and would they please excuse her?

They applauded her. I listened in amazement to the tribute from the most cynical bunch in the world, and she came into the library with a real laugh in her eyes. I saw in a flash what her fame was all about: not just talent, not just courage, but style.

England

Six

I spent two more days at the Villa Francese and then flew back to London; and Alessia came with me.

Cenci, crestfallen, wanted her to stay. He hadn't yet returned to his office, and her deliverance had not restored him to the man-of-the-world in the picture. He still wore a look of ingrained anxiety and was still making his way to the brandy at unusual hours. The front he had raised for the media had evaporated before their cars were out through the gate, and he seemed on the following day incapably lethargic.

"I can't understand him," Ilaria said impatiently. "You'd think he'd be striding about, booming away, taking charge. You'd think he'd be his bossy self again. Why isn't he?"

"He's had six terrible weeks."

"So what? They're over. Time for dancing, you'd think." She sketched a graceful ballet gesture with her arm, gold bracelets jangling. "Tell you the truth, I was goddam glad she's back, but the way Papa goes on, she might just as well not be.''

"Give him time," I said mildly.

"I want him the way he was," she said. "To be a man.''

When Alessia said at dinner that she was going to England in a day or two, everyone, including myself, was astonished.

"Why?'' Ilaria said forthrightly.

"To stay with Popsy.''

Everyone except myself knew who Popsy was, and why Alessia should stay with her, and I too learned afterwards. Popsy was a racehorse woman trainer, widowed, with whom Alessia usually lodged when in England.

"I'm unfit," Alessia said. "Muscles like jelly.''

"There are horses here," Cenci protested.

"Yes, but . . . Papa, I want to go away. It's fantastic to be home, but . . . I tried to drive my car out of the gate today and I was shaking . . . It was stupid. I meant to go to the hairdresser's. My hair needs cutting so badly. But I just couldn't. I came back to the house, and look at me, still curling onto my shoulders.'' She tried to laugh, but no one found it funny.

"If that's what you want," her father said worriedly.

"Yes . . . I'll go with Andrew, if he doesn't mind.''

I minded very little. She seemed relieved by her decision, and the next day Ilaria drove her in the Fiat to the hairdresser, and bought things for her because she couldn't face shops, and brought her cheerfully home. Alessia returned with a curly bob and a slight case of the trembles, and Ilaria helped her pack.

On that evening I tried to persuade Cenci that his family should still take precautions.

"The first ransom is still physically in one suitcase, and until the carabinieri or the courts, or whatever, free it and allow you to use it to replace some of the money you borrowed from Milan, I reckon it's still at risk. What if the kidnappers took you . . . or Ilaria? They don't often hit the same family twice, but this time . . . they might."

The horror was too much. He had crumbled almost too far.

"Just get Ilaria to be careful," I said hastily, having failed to do that myself. "Tell her to vary her life a bit. Get her to stay with friends, invite friends here. You yourself are much safer because of your chauffeur, but it wouldn't hurt to take the gardener along too for a while, he has the shoulders of an ox and he'd make a splendid bodyguard."

After a long pause, and in a low voice, he said, "I can't face things, you know."

"Yes, I do know," I agreed gently. "Best to start, though, as soon as you can."

A faint smile. "Professional advice?"

"Absolutely."

He sighed. "I can't bear to sell the house on Mikonos . . . my wife loved it."

"She loved Alessia too. She'd think it a fair swap."

He looked at me for a while. "You're a strange young man," he said. "You make things so clear." He paused. "Don't you ever get muddled by emotion?"

"Yes, sometimes," I said. "But when it happens . . . I try to sort myself out. To see some logic."

"And once you see some logic, you act on it?"

"Try to." I paused. "Yes."

"It sounds . . . cold."

I shook my head. "Logic doesn't stop you feeling. You can behave logically, and it can hurt like hell. Or it can comfort you. Or release you. Or all at the same time."

After a while he said, stating a fact, "Most people don't behave logically."

"No," I said.

"You seem to think everyone could, if they wanted to?"

I shook my head. "No." He waited, so I went on diffidently, "There's genetic memory against it, for one thing. And to be logical you have to dig up and face your own hidden motives and emotions, and of course they're hidden principally because you don't want to face them. So . . . um . . . it's easier to let your basement feelings run the upper stories, so to speak, and the result is rage, quarrels, love, jobs, opinions, anorexia, philanthropy . . . almost anything you can think of. I just like to know what's going on down there, to pick out why I truly want to do things, that's all. Then I can do them or not. Whichever."

He looked at me consideringly. "Self-analysis . . . did you study it?"

"No. Lived it. Like everyone does."

He smiled faintly. "At what age?"

"Well . . . from the beginning. I mean, I can't remember not doing it. Digging into my own true motives. Knowing in one's heart of hearts. Facing the shameful things . . . the discreditable impulses . . . Awful, really.''

He picked up his glass and drank some brandy. ''Did it result in sainthood?'' he said, smiling.

''Er . . . no. In sin, of course, from doing what I knew I shouldn't.''

The smile grew on his lips and stayed there. He began to describe to me the house on the Greek island that his wife had loved so, and for the first time since I'd met him I saw the uncertain beginnings of peace.

On the airplane Alessia said, ''Where do you live?''

''In Kensington. Near the office.''

''Popsy trains in Lambourn.'' She imparted it as if it were a casual piece of information. I waited, though, and after a while she said, ''I want to keep on seeing you.''

I nodded. ''Any time.'' I gave her one of my business cards, which had both office and home telephone numbers, scribbling my home address on the back.

''You don't mind?''

''Of course not. Delighted.''

''I need . . . just for now . . . I need a crutch.''

''Deluxe model at your service.''

Her lips curved. She was pretty, I thought, under all the strain, her face a mingling of small delicate bones and firm positive muscles, smooth on the surface, taut below, finely shaped under all. I had always been attracted by taller, softer, curvier girls, and there was nothing about Alessia to trigger the usual easy urge to the chase. All the same I liked her increasingly, and would have sought her out if she hadn't asked me first.

In bits and pieces over the past two days she had told me many more details of her captivity, gradually unburdening herself of what she'd suffered and felt and worried over; and I'd encouraged her, not only because sometimes in such accounts one got a helpful lead towards catching the kidnappers, but also very much for her own sake. Victim therapy, paragraph one: let her talk it all out and get rid of it.

At Heathrow we went through immigration, baggage claims, and customs in close proximity, Alessia keeping near to me nervously and trying to make it look natural.

"I won't leave you," I assured her, "until you meet Popsy. Don't worry."

Popsy was late. We stood and waited with Alessia apologizing twice every five minutes and me telling her not to, and finally, like a gust of wind, a large lady arrived with outstretched arms.

"My darling," she said, enveloping Alessia, "a bloody crunch on the motorway. Traffic crawling past like snails. Thought I'd never get here." She held Alessia away from her for an inspection. "You look marvellous. What an utterly drear thing to happen. When I heard you were safe I bawled, absolutely bawled."

Popsy was forty-fivish and wore trousers, shirt, and padded sleeveless waistcoat in navy, white, and olive green. She had disconcertingly green eyes, a mass of fluffy graying hair, and a personality as large as her frame.

"Popsy . . ." Alessia began.

"My darling, what you need is a large steak. Look

at your arms . . . matchsticks. The car's just outside, probably got some traffic cop writing a ticket, I
left it on double yellows, so come on, let's go.''

''Popsy, this is Andrew Douglas.''

''Who?'' She seemed to see me for the first time.
''How do you do.'' She thrust out a hand, which I
shook. ''Popsy Teddington. Glad to know you.''

''Andrew traveled with me . . .''

''Great,'' Popsy said. ''Well done.'' She had her
eyes on the exit, searching for trouble.

''Can we ask him to lunch on Sunday?'' Alessia
said.

''What?'' The eyes swiveled my way, gave me a
quick assessment, came up with assent. ''O.K., darling, anything you like.'' To me she said, ''Go to
Lambourn, ask anybody, they'll tell you where I
live.''

''All right,'' I said.

Alessia said ''Thank you'' half under her breath
and allowed herself to be swept away, and I reflected
bemusedly about irresistible forces in female form.

From Heathrow I went straight to the office,
where Friday afternoon was dawdling along as
usual.

The office, a nondescript collection of ground-
floor rooms along either side of a central corridor,
had been designed decades before the era of open-
plan, half-acre windows, and Kew Gardens ram-
pant. We stuck to the rabbit hutches with their strip
lighting because they were comparatively cheap; and
as most of us were partners, not employees, we each
had a sharp interest in low overheads. Besides, the
office was not where we mostly worked. The war

went on on distant fronts: headquarters was for discussing strategy and writing up reports.

I dumped my suitcase in the hutch I sometimes called my own and wandered along the row, both to announce my return and see who was in.

Gerry Clayton was in, making a complicated construction in folded paper.

"Hello," he said. "Bad boy. Tut-tut."

Gerry Clayton, tubby, asthmatic, fifty-three and bald, had appointed himself father-figure to many wayward sons. His specialty was insurance, and it was he who had recruited me from a firm at Lloyds, where I'd been a water-treading clerk looking for more purpose in life.

"Where's Twinkletoes?" I said. "I may as well get the lecture over."

"Twinkletoes, as you so disrespectfully call him, went to Venezuela this morning. The manager of Luca Oil was scooped."

"Luca Oil?" My eyebrows rose. "After all the work we did for them, setting up defenses?"

Gerry shrugged, carefully knifing a sharp crease in stiff white paper with his thumbnail. "That work was more than a year ago. You know what people are. Dead keen on precautions to start with, then perfunctory, then dead sloppy. Human nature. All any self-respecting dedicated kidnapper has to do is wait."

He was unconcerned about the personal fate of the abducted manager. He frequently said that if everyone took fortresslike precautions and never got themselves—in his word—scooped, we'd all be out of a job. One good kidnapping in a corporation encouraged twenty others to call us in to advise them how to avoid a similar embarrassment; and as he regularly pointed out, the how-not-to-get-scooped business was our bread and butter and also some of the jam.

Gerry inverted his apparently wrinkled heap of white paper and it fell miraculously into the shape of a cockatoo. When not advising antikidnap insurance policies to Liberty Market clients he sold origami patterns to a magazine, but no one grudged his paper-folding in the office. His mind seemed to coast along while he creased and tucked, and would come up often as if from nowhere with highly productive business ideas.

Liberty Market as a firm consisted at that time of thirty-one partners and five secretarial employees. Of the partners, all but Gerry and myself were ex-S.A.S., ex-police, or ex something ultrasecret in government departments. There were no particular rules about who did which job, though if possible everyone was allowed their preferences. Some opted for the lecture tour full time, giving seminars, pointing out dangers; all the how-to-stay-free bit. Some sank their teeth gratefully into the terrorist circuit; others, like myself, felt more useful against the simply criminal. Everyone in between times wrote their own reports, studied everyone else's, manned the office switchboard year round and polished up their techniques of coercive bargaining.

We had a chairman (the firm's founder) for our Monday morning state-of-the-nation meetings, a co-ordinator who kept track of everyone's whereabouts, and an adjuster—Twinkletoes—to whom partners addressed all complaints. If their complaints covered the behavior of any other partner, Twinkletoes passed the comments on. If enough partners disapproved of one partner's actions, Twinkletoes delivered the censure. I wasn't all that sorry he'd gone to Venezuela.

This apparently shapeless company scheme worked in a highly organized way, thanks mostly to the ingrained discipline of the ex-soldiers. They were lean, hard, proud, and quite amazingly cunning, most of them preferring to deal with the action of the after-kidnap affairs. They were in addition almost paranoid about secrecy, as also the ex-spies were, which to begin with I'd found oppressive but had soon grown to respect.

It was the ex-policemen who did most of the lecturing, not only advising on defenses but telling potential kidnap targets what to do and look for if they were taken, so that their captors could be in turn captured.

Many of us knew an extra like photography, languages, weaponry, and electronics, and everyone could use a word processor, because no one liked the rattle of typewriters all day long. No one was around the office long enough for serious feuds to develop, and the co-ordinator had a knack of keeping incompatibles apart. All in all it was a contented ship which everyone worked in from personal commitment, and, thanks to the kidnappers, business was healthy.

I finished my journey along the row of hutches, said a few hellos, saw I was penciled in with a question mark for Sunday midnight on the switchboard roster, and came at length to the big room across the far end, the only room with windows to the street. It just about seated the whole strength if we were ever there together, but on that afternoon the only person in it was Tony Vine.

" 'Lo," he said. "Hear you made an effing balls of it in Bologna."

"Yeah."

"Letting the effing carabinieri eff up the R.V."

"Have you tried giving orders to the Italian army?"

He sniffed as a reply. He himself was an ex-S.A.S. sergeant, now nearing forty, who would never in his service days have dreamed of obeying a civilian. He could move across any terrain in a way that made a chameleon look flamboyant, and he had three times tracked and liberated a victim before the ransom had been paid, though no one, not even the victim, was quite sure how. Tony Vine was the most secretive of the whole tight-lipped bunch, and anything he didn't want to tell didn't get told.

It was he who had warned me about knives inside rolled-up magazines, and I'd guessed he'd known because he'd carried one that way himself.

His humor consisted mostly of sarcasm, and he could hardly get a sentence out without an oiling of fuck, shit, and piss. He worked nearly always on political kidnaps because he, like Pucinelli, tended to despise personal and company wealth.

"If you're effing poor," he'd said to me once, "and you see some capitalist shitting around in a Roller, it's not so effing surprising you think of ways of leveling things up. If you're down to your last bit of goat cheese in Sardinia, maybe, or short of beans in Mexico, a little kidnap makes effing sense."

"You're romantic," I'd answered. "What about

the poor Sardinians who steal a child from a poor
Sardinian village, and grind all the poor people there
into poorer dust, forcing them all to pay out their pit-
iful savings for a ransom?''

''No one's effing perfect.''

For all that he'd been against me joining the firm
in the first place, and in spite of his feeling superior
in every way, whenever we'd worked together it had
been without friction. He could feel his way through
the psyches of kidnappers as through a minefield,
but preferred to have me deal with the families of the
victims.

''When you're with them, they stay in one effing
piece. If I tell them what to do, they fall to effing
bits.''

He was at his happiest cooperating with men in
uniform, among whom he seemed to command instant recognition and respect. Good sergeants ran
the army, it was said, and when he wanted to he had
the air about him still.

No one was allowed to serve in the S.A.S. for an
extended period, and once he'd been bounced out
because of age, he'd been bored. Then someone had
murmured in his ear about fighting terrorists a different way, and Liberty Market had never regretted
taking him.

''I put you in for Sunday midnight on the blower,
did you see, instead of me?'' he said.

I nodded.

''The wife's got this effing anniversary party organized, and like as not by midnight I'll be pissed.''

''All right,'' I said.

He was short for a soldier: useful for passing as a

woman, he'd told me once. Sandy-haired, blue-eyed, and light on his feet, he was a fanatic about fitness, and it was he who had persuaded everyone to furnish (and use) the iron-pumping room in the basement. He never said much about his origins: the tougher parts of London, from his accent.

"When did you get back?" I asked. "Last I heard you were in Colombia."

"End of the week."

"How was it?" I said.

He scowled. "We winkled the effing hostages out safe, and then the local strength got excited and shot the shit out of the terrorists, though they'd got their effing hands up and were coming out peaceful." He shook his head. "Never keep their bullets to themselves, those savages. Effing stupid, the whole shitting lot of them."

Shooting terrorists who'd surrendered was, as he'd said, effing stupid. The news would get around, and the next bunch of terrorists, knowing they'd be shot if they did and also shot if they didn't, would be more likely to kill their victims.

I had missed the Monday meeting where that debacle would have been discussed, but meanwhile there was my own report to write for the picking over of Bologna. I spent all Saturday on it and some of Sunday morning, and then drove seventy-five miles westward to Lambourn.

Popsy Teddington proved to live in a tall white house near the center of the village, a house seeming almost suburban but surprisingly fronting a great amount of stabling. I hadn't until that day realized that racing stables could occur actually inside villages, but when I remarked on it Popsy said with a smile that I should see Newmarket, they had horses where people in other towns had garages, greenhouses, and sheds.

She was standing outside when I arrived, looming over a five-foot man who seemed glad of the interruption.

"Just see to that, Sammy. Tell them I won't stand for it," she was saying forcefully as I opened the car door. Her head turned my way and a momentary "who-are-you?" frown crossed her forehead. "Oh, yes, Alessia's friend. She's around the back, somewhere. Come along." She led me past the house and behind a block of stabling, and we arrived suddenly in view of a small railed paddock, where a girl on a horse was slowly cantering, watched by another girl on foot.

The little paddock seemed to be surrounded by the backs of other stables and other houses, and the grass within it had seen better days.

"I hope you can help her," Popsy said straightly, as we approached. "I've never known her like this. Very worrying."

"How do you mean?" I asked.

"So insecure. She wouldn't ride out yesterday with the string, which she always does when she's here, and now look at her, she's supposed to be up on that horse, not watching my stable girl riding."

"Has she said much about what happened to her?" I asked.

"Not a thing. She just smiles cheerfully and says it's all over."

Alessia half turned as we drew near, and looked very relieved when she saw me.

"I was afraid you wouldn't come," she said.

"You shouldn't have been."

She was wearing jeans and a checked shirt and lipstick, and was still unnaturally pale from six weeks in dim light. Popsy shouted to the girl riding the horse to put it back in its stable. "Unless, darling, you'd like . . ." she said to Alessia. "After all?"

Alessia shook her head. "Tomorrow, I guess." She sounded as if she meant it, but I could see that Popsy doubted. She put a motherly arm around Alessia's shoulders and gave her a small hug. "Darling, do just what you like. How about a drink for your thirsty traveler?" To me she said, "Coffee? Whisky? Methylated spirits?"

"Wine," Alessia said. "I know he likes that."

We went into the house; antique dark furniture, worn Indian rugs, faded chintz, a vista of horses through every window.

Popsy poured Italian wine into cut crystal glasses with a casual hand and said she would cook steaks if we were patient. Alessia watched her disappear kitchenwards and said uncomfortably, "I'm a nuisance to her. I shouldn't have come."

"You're quite wrong on both counts," I said. "It's obvious she's glad to have you."

"I thought I'd be all right here . . . That I'd feel different. I mean, that I'd feel all right."

"You're sure to, in a while."

She glanced at me. "It bothers me that I just can't . . . shake it off."

"Like you could shake off double septic pneumonia?"

"That's different," she protested.

"Six weeks of no sunlight, no exercise, no decent food and a steady diet of heavy sleeping pills is hardly a recipe for physical health."

"But I . . . it's not just . . . physical."

"Still less can you just shake off the nonphysical." I drank some wine. "How are your dreams?"

She shuddered. "Half the time I can't sleep. Ilaria said I should keep on with sleeping pills for a while, but I don't want to, it revolts me to think of it . . . But when I do sleep . . . I have nightmares . . . and wake up sweating."

"Would you like me," I said neutrally, "to introduce you to a psychiatrist? I know quite a good one."

"No." The answer was instinctive. "I'm not mad, I'm just . . . not right."

"You don't need to be dying to go to a doctor."

She shook her head. "I don't want to."

She sat on a large sofa with her feet on a coffee table, looking worried.

"It's you that I want to talk to, not some shrink. You understand what happened, and to some strange doctor it would sound exaggerated. You know I'm telling the truth, but he'd be worrying half the time if I wasn't fantasizing or dramatizing or something and be looking for ways of putting me in the wrong. I had a friend who went to one . . . she told me it was weird, when she said she wanted to give up smoking he kept suggesting she was unhappy because she had repressed incestuous longings for her father." She ended with an attempt at a laugh, but I could see what she meant. Psychiatrists were accustomed to distortion and evasion, and looked for them in the simplest remark.

"I do think all the same that you'd be better off with expert help," I said.

"You're an expert."

"No."

"But it's you I want . . . Oh, dear," she broke off suddenly, looking most confused. "I'm sorry . . . You don't want to . . . . How stupid of me."

"I didn't say that. I said . . ." I too stopped. I stood up, walked over, and sat next to her on the sofa, not touching. "I'll untie any knots I can for you, and for as long as you want me to. That's a promise. Also a pleasure, not a chore. But you must promise me something too."

She said "What?" glancing at me and away.

"That if I'm doing you no good, you will try someone else."

"A shrink?"

"Yes."

She looked at her shoes. "All right," she said: and like any psychiatrist I wondered if she were lying.

Popsy's steaks came tender and juicy, and Alessia ate half of hers.

"You must build up your strength, my darling," Popsy said without censure. "You've worked so hard to get where you are. You don't want all those ambitious little jockey-boys elbowing you out, which they will if they've half a chance."

"I telephoned Mike," she said. "I said . . . I'd need time."

"Now my darling," Popsy protested. "You get straight back on the telephone and tell him you'll be fit a week today. Say you'll be ready to race tomorrow week, without fail."

Alessia looked at her in horror. "I'm too weak to stay in the saddle . . . let alone race."

"My darling, you've all the guts in the world. If you want to, you'll do it."

Alessia's face said plainly that she didn't know whether she wanted to or not.

"Who's Mike?" I asked.

"Mike Noland," Popsy said. "The trainer she often rides for in England. He lives here, in Lambourn, up the road."

"He said he understood," Alessia said weakly.

"Well of course he understands. Who wouldn't? But all the same, my darling, if you want those horses back, it's you that will have to get them."

She spoke with brisk, affectionate common sense, hallmark of the kind and healthy who had never been at cracking point. There was a sort of quiver from where Alessia sat, and I rose unhurriedly to my feet and asked if I could help carry the empty dishes to the kitchen.

"Of course you can," Popsy said, rising also, "and there's cheese, if you'd like some."

Alessia said horses slept on Sunday afternoons like everyone else, but after coffee we walked slowly round the yard anyway, patting one or two heads.

"I can't possibly get fit in a week," Alessia said. "Do you think I should?"

"I think you should try sitting on a horse."

"Suppose I've lost my nerve."

"You'd find out."

"That's not much comfort." She rubbed the nose of one of the horses absentmindedly, showing at least no fear of its teeth. "Do you ride?" she asked.

"No," I said. "And . . . er . . . I've never been to the races."

She was astonished. "Never?"

"I've watched them often on television."

"Not the same at all." She laid her own cheek briefly against the horse's. "Would you like to go?"

"With you, yes, very much."

Her eyes filled with sudden tears, which she blinked away impatiently. "You see," she said. "That's always happening. A kind word . . . and something inside me melts. I do try . . . I honestly do try to behave decently, but I know I'm putting on an act . . . and underneath there's an abyss . . . with things coming up from it, like crying for nothing, for no reason, like now."

"The act," I said, "is Oscar class."

She swallowed and sniffed and brushed the unspilled tears away with her fingers. "Popsy is so generous," she said. "I've stayed with her so often." She paused. "She doesn't exactly say 'Snap out of it' or 'Pull yourself together,' but I can see her thinking it. And I expect if I were someone looking at me, I'd think it too. I mean, she must be thinking that here I am, free and undamaged, and I should be grateful and getting on with life, and that far from moping I should be full of joy and bounce."

We wandered slowly along and peered into the shadowy interior of a box where the inmate dozed, its weight on one hip, its ears occasionally twitching.

"After Vietnam," I said, "when the prisoners came home, there were very many divorces. It wasn't just the sort of thing that happened after the war in Europe, when the wives grew apart from the husbands just by living, while for the men time stood still. After Vietnam it was different. Those prisoners had suffered dreadfully, and they came home to families who expected them to be joyful at their release."

Alessia leaned her arms on the half-door, and watched the unmoving horse.

"The wives tried to make allowances, but a lot of the men were impotent, and would burst into tears in public, and many of them took offense easily . . . and showed permanent symptoms of mental breakdown. Hamburgers and Coke couldn't cure them, nor going to the office nine to five." I fiddled with the bolt on the door. "Most of them recovered in time and lead normal lives, but even those will admit they had bad dreams for years and will never forget clear details of their imprisonment."

After a while she said, "I wasn't a prisoner of war."

"Oh, yes, just the same. Captured by an enemy through no fault of your own. Not knowing when— or whether—you would be free. Humiliated . . . deprived of free will . . . dependent on your enemy for food. All the same, but made worse by isolation . . . by being the only one."

She put the curly head down momentarily on the folded arms. "All they ever gave me, when I asked, were some tissues, and I begged . . . I begged . . . for those." She swallowed. "One's body doesn't stop counting the days, just because one's in a tent."

I put my arm silently round her shoulders. There were things no male prisoner ever had to face. She cried quietly, with gulps and small compulsive sniffs, and after a while simply said "Thank you," and I said "Any time," and we moved on down the line of boxes knowing there was a long way still to go.

Seven

Manning the office switchboard day and night was essential because kidnappers kept antisocial hours; and it was always a partner on duty, not an employee, for reasons both of reliability and of secrecy. The ex-spies feared "moles" under every secretarial desk and ran a security check on the janitor.

That particular Sunday night was quiet, with two calls only: one from a partner in Ecuador saying he'd discovered the local police were due to share in the ransom he was negotiating and asking for the firm's reactions, and the second from Twinkletoes, who wanted a copy of the set of precautions we'd drawn up for Luca Oil.

I made a note of it, saying, "Surely Luca Oil have one?"

"The kidnappers stole it," Twinkletoes said tersely. "Or bribed a secretary to steal it. Anyway, it's missing, and the manager was abducted at the weakest point of his daily schedule, which I reckon was no coincidence."

"I'll send it by courier straight away."

"And see who's free to join me out here. This will be a long one. It was very carefully planned. Send me Derek, if you can. And oh . . . consider yourself lucky I'm not there to blast you for Bologna."

"I do," I said, smiling.

"I'll be back," he said darkly. "Goodnight."

I took one more call, at nine in the morning, this time from the head of a syndicate at Lloyds which insured people and firms against kidnap. Much of our business came direct from him, as he was accustomed to make it a condition of insurance that his clients should call on our help before agreeing to pay a ransom. He reckoned we could bring the price down, which made his own liability less; and we in return recommended him to the firms asking our advice on defenses.

"Two English girls have been snatched in Sardinia," he said. "The husband of one of them insured her against kidnap for her two-weeks' holiday as he wasn't going to be with her, and he's been on to us. It seems to have been a fairly unplanned affair— the girls just happened to be in the wrong place, and were ambushed. Anyway, the husband is distraught and wants to pay what they're asking, straight away, so can you send someone immediately?"

"Yes," I said. "Er . . . what was the insurance?"

"I took a thousand pounds against two hundred thousand. For two weeks." He sighed. "Win some, lose some."

I took down names and details and checked on flights to Sardinia, where in many regions bandits took, ransomed, and released more or less as they pleased.

"Very hush hush," the Lloyds man had said. "Don't let it get to the papers. The husband has pressing reasons. If all goes well she'll be home in a week, won't she, and no one the wiser?"

"With a bit of luck," I agreed.

Bandits had nowhere to keep long-term prisoners and had been known to march their victims miles over mountainsides daily, simply abandoning them once they'd been paid. Alessia, I thought, would have preferred that to her tent.

The partners began arriving for the Monday conference and it was easy to find one with itchy feet ready to go instantly to Sardinia, and easy also to persuade Derek to join Twinkletoes at Luca Oil. The co-ordinator wrote them in on the new week's chart and I gave the request from the partner in Ecuador to the chairman.

After about an hour of coffee, gossip, and reading reports the meeting began, the bulk of it as usual being a review of work in progress.

"This business in Ecuador," the chairman said. "The victim's an American national, isn't he?"

A few heads nodded.

The chairman pursed his lips. "I think we'll have to advise that corporation to use local men and not send any more from the States. They've had three men captured in the last ten years, all Americans . . . you'd think they'd learn."

"It's an American-owned corporation," someone murmured.

"They've tried paying the police themselves," another said. "I was out there myself last time. The police took the money saying they would guard all the managers with their lives, but I reckon they also took a cut of the ransom then, too. And don't forget, the corporation paid a ransom of something like ten million dollars . . . plenty to spread around.''

There was a small gloomy silence.

''Right,'' the chairman said. ''Future advice, no Americans. Present advice?'' He looked around. ''Opinions, anyone?''

''The kidnappers know the corporation will pay in the end,'' Tony Vine said. ''The corporation can't afford not to.''

All corporations had to ransom their captured employees if they wanted anyone ever to work overseas for them in future. All corporations also had irate shareholders, whose dividends diminished as ransoms rose. Corporations tended to keep abductions out of the news, and to write the ransoms down as a ''trading loss'' in the annual accounts.

''We've got the demand down to ten million again,'' Tony Vine said. ''The kidnappers won't take less, they'd be losing face against last time, even if—especially if—they're a different gang.''

The chairman nodded. ''We'll advise the corporation to settle?''

Everyone agreed, and the meeting moved on.

The chairman, around sixty, had once been a soldier himself, and like Tony felt comfortable with other men whose lives had been structured, disciplined, and official. He had founded the firm because he'd seen the need for it; the action in his case of a practical man, not a visionary. It had been a friend of his, now dead, who had suggested partnerships rather than a hierarchy, advising the sweeping away of all former ranks in favor of one new one: equal.

The chairman was exceptionally good-looking, a distinctly marketable plus, and had an air of quiet confidence to go with it. He could maintain that manner in the face of total disaster, so that one always felt he would at any moment devise a brilliant victory-snatching solution, even if he didn't. It had taken me a while, when I was new there, to see that it was Gerry Clayton who had that sort of mind.

The chairman came finally to my report, photocopies of which most people had already read, and asked if any partners would like to ask questions. We gained always from what others had learned during a case, and I usually found question time very fruitful—though better when not doing the answering.

"This carabinieri officer . . . er . . . Pucinelli, what sort of a personal relationship could you have with him? What is your estimate of his capabilities?" It was a notoriously pompous partner asking: Tony would have said, "How did you get on with the sod? What's he like?"

"Pucinelli's a good policeman," I said. "Intelligent, bags of courage. He was helpful. More helpful, I found, than most, though never stepping out of the official line. He hasn't yet . . ." I paused. "He hasn't the clout to get any higher, I don't think. He's second-in-command in his region, and I'd say that's as far as he'll go. But as far as his chances of catching the kidnappers are concerned, he'll be competent and thorough."

"What was the latest, when you left?" someone asked. "I haven't yet had time to finish your last two pages."

"Pucinelli said that when he showed the drawings of the man I'd seen to the two kidnappers from the siege, they were both struck dumb. He showed them to them separately, of course, but in each case he said you could clearly see the shock. Neither of them would say anything at all and they both seemed scared. Pucinelli said he was going to circulate copies of the drawings and see if he could identify the man. He was very hopeful, when I left."

"Sooner the better," Tony said. "That million quid will be laundered within a week."

"They were a pretty cool lot," I said, not arguing. "They might hold it for a while."

"And they might have whisked it over a border and changed it into francs or schillings before they released the girl."

I nodded. "They could have set up something like that for the first ransom, and been ready."

Gerry Clayton's fingers as usual were busy with any sheet of paper within reach, this time the last page of my report. "You say Alessia Cenci came to England with you. Any chance she'll remember any more?" he asked.

"You cannot rule it out, but Pucinelli and I both went through it with her pretty thoroughly in Italy She knows so little. There were no church bells, no trains, no close airplanes, no dogs . . . she couldn't tell whether she was in city or country. She thought the faint smell she was conscious of during the last few days might have been someone baking bread. Apart from that . . . nothing."

A pause.

"Did you show the drawings to the girl?" someone asked. "Had she ever seen the man, before the kidnap?"

I turned to him. "I took a photostat to the villa, but she hadn't ever seen him that she could remember. There was absolutely no reaction. I asked if he could have been one of the four who abducted her, but she said she couldn't tell. None of her family or anyone in the household knew him. I asked them all."

"His voice . . . when he spoke to you outside the restaurant . . . was it the voice on the tapes?"

"I don't know," I admitted. "I'm not good enough at Italian. It wasn't totally different, that's all I could say."

"You brought copies of the drawings and the tapes back with you?" the chairman asked.

"Yes. If anyone would like . . . ?"

A few heads nodded.

"Anything you didn't put in the report?" the chairman asked. "Insignificant details?"

"Well . . . I didn't include the lists of the music. Alessia wrote what she knew, and Pucinelli said he would try to find out if they were tapes one could buy in shops, ready recorded. Very long shot, even if they were."

"Do you have the lists?"

"No, afraid not. I could ask Alessia to write them again, if you like."

One of the ex-policemen said you never knew. The other ex-policemen nodded.

"All right," I said. "I'll ask her."

"How is she?" Gerry asked.

"Just about coping."

There were a good many nods of understanding.

We'd all seen the devastation, the hurricane's path across the spirit. All of us, some oftener than others, had listened to the experiences of the recently returned: the debriefing, as the firm called it, in its military way.

The chairman looked around for more questions but none were ready. "All finished? Well, Andrew, we can't exactly sack you for coming up with pictures of an active kidnapper, but driving a car to the drop is not on the cards. Whether or not it turns out well this time, don't do it again. Right?"

"Right," I said neutrally; and that, to my surprise, was the full extent of the ticking-off.

A couple of days later the partner manning the switchboard called to me down the corridor, where I was wandering with a cup of coffee in search of anything new.

"Andrew? Call for you from Bologna. I'll put it through to your room."

I dumped the coffee and picked up the receiver, and a voice said, "Andrew? This is Enrico Pucinelli."

We exchanged hellos, and he began talking excitedly, the words running together in my ear.

"Enrico," I shouted. "Stop. Speak slowly. I can't understand you."

"Hah." He sighed audibly and began to speak clearly and distinctly, as to a child. "The young one of the kidnappers has been talking. He is afraid of being sent to prison for life, so he is trying to make bargains. He has told us where Signorina Cenci was taken after the kidnap."

"Terrific," I said warmly. "Well done."

Pucinelli coughed modestly, but I guessed it had been a triumph of interrogation.

"We have been to the house. It is in a suburb of Bologna, middle-class, very quiet. We have found it was rented by a father with three grown sons." He clicked his tongue disgustedly. "All of the neighbors saw men going in and out, but so far no one would know them again."

I smiled to myself. Putting the finger on a kidnapper was apt to be unhealthy anywhere.

"The house has furniture belonging to the owner, but we have looked carefully, and in one room on the upper floor all the marks where the furniture has stood on the carpet for a long time are in slightly different places." He stopped and said anxiously, "Do you understand, Andrew?"

"Yes," I said. "All the furniture had been moved."

"Correct." He was relieved. "The bed, a heavy chest, a wardrobe, a bookcase. All moved. The room is big, more than big enough for the tent, and there is nothing to see from the window except a garden and trees. No one could see into the room from the outside."

"And have you found anything useful . . . any clues . . . in the rest of the house?"

"We are looking. We went to the house for the first time yesterday. I thought you would like to know."

"You're quite right. Great news."

"Signorina Cenci," he said. "Has she thought of anything else?"

"Not yet."

"Give her my respects."

"Yes," I said. "I will indeed."

"I will telephone again," he said. "I will reverse the charges again, shall I, like you said? As this is private, between you and me, and I am telephoning from my own house?"

"Every time," I said.

He said goodbye with deserved satisfaction, and I added a note of what he'd said to my report.

By Thursday morning I was back in Lambourn, chiefly for the lists of music, and I found I had arrived just as a string of Popsy's horses were setting out for exercise. Over her jeans and shirt Popsy wore another padded waistcoat, bright pink this time, seeming not to notice that it was a warm day in July; and her fluffy gray-white hair haloed her big head like a private cumulus cloud.

She was on her feet in the stable yard surrounded by scrunching skittering quadrupeds, and she beckoned to me, when she saw me, with a huge sweep of the arm. Trying not to look nervous and obviously not succeeding, I dodged a few all-too-mobile half-tons of muscle and made it to her side.

The green eyes looked at me slantwise, smiling. "Not used to them, are you?"

"Er . . ." I said. "No."

"Want to see them on the gallops?"

"Yes, please." I looked round at the riders, hoping to see Alessia among them, but without result.

The apparently disorganized throng suddenly moved off towards the road in one orderly line, and Popsy jerked her head for me to follow her into the kitchen; and at the table in there, coffee cup in hand, sat Alessia.

She still looked pale, but perhaps now only in contrast to the outdoor health of Popsy, and she still looked thin, without strength. Her smile when she saw me started in the eyes and then curved to the pink lipstick; an uncomplicated welcome of friendship.

"Andrew's coming up on the Downs to see the schooling," Popsy said.

"Great."

"You're not riding?" I asked Alessia.

"No . . . I . . . anyway, Popsy's horses are jumpers."

Popsy made a face as if to say that wasn't a satisfactory reason for not riding them, but passed no other comment. She and I talked for a while about things in general and Alessia said not much.

We all three sat on the front seat of a dusty Land Rover while Popsy drove with more verve than caution out of Lambourn and along a side road and finally up a bumpy track to open stretches of grassland.

Away on the horizon the rolling terrain melted into blue haze, and under our feet, as we stepped from the Land Rover, the close turf had been mown to two inches. Except for a bird call or two in the distance there was a gentle enveloping silence, which was in itself extraordinary. No drone of airplanes, no clamor of voices, no hum of faraway traffic. Just wide air and warm sunlight and the faint rustle from one's own clothes.

"You like it, don't you?" observed Popsy, watching my face.

I nodded.

"You should be up here in January with the wind

howling across. Though mind you, it's beautiful even when you're freezing.''

She scanned a nearby valley with a hand shading her eyes. ''The horses will be coming up from there at a half-speed canter,'' she said. ''They'll pass us here. Then we'll follow them up in the Land Rover to the schooling fences.''

I nodded again, not reckoning I'd know a half-speed canter from a slow waltz, but in fact when the row of horses appeared like black dots from the valley I soon saw what speed she meant. She watched with concentration through large binoculars as the dots became shapes and the shapes flying horses, lowering the glasses only when the string of ten went past us, still one behind the other so that she had a clear view of each. She pursed her mouth but seemed otherwise not too displeased, and we were soon careering along in their wake, jerking to a stop over the brow of the hill and disembarking to find the horses circling with tossing heads and puffing breath.

''See those fences over there?'' said Popsy, pointing to isolated timber and brushwood obstacles looking like refugees from a racecourse. ''Those are schooling fences. To teach the horses how to jump.'' She peered into my face, and I nodded. ''The set on this side, they're hurdles. The far ones are . . . er . . . fences. For steeplechasers.'' I nodded again. ''From the start of the schooling ground up to here there are six hurdles—and six fences—so you can give a horse a good workout if you want to, but today I'm sending my lot over these top four only, as they're not fully fit.''

She left us abruptly and strode over to her excited four-legged family, and Alessia with affection said,

"She's a good trainer. She can see when a horse isn't feeling right, even if there's nothing obviously wrong. When she walks into the yard all the horses instantly know she's there . . . You see all the heads come out, like a chorus."

Popsy was dispatching three of the horses towards the lower end of the schooling ground. "Those three will come up over the hurdles," Alessia said. "Then those riders will change onto three more horses and start again."

I was surprised. "Don't all of the riders jump?" I asked.

"Most of them don't ride well enough to teach. Of those three doing the schooling, two are professional jockeys and the third is Popsy's best lad."

Popsy stood beside us, binoculars ready, as the three horses came up over the hurdles. Except for a ratatatat at the hurdles themselves it was all very quiet, mostly, I realized, because there was no broadcast commentary as on television, but partly also because of the Doppler effect. The horses seemed to be making far more noise once they were past and going away.

Popsy muttered unintelligibly under her breath and Alessia said "Borodino jumped well" in the sort of encouraging voice which meant the other two hadn't.

We all waited while the three schooling riders changed horses and set off again down the incline to the starting point, and I felt Alessia suddenly stir beside me and take a bottomless breath, moving from there into a small, restless, aimless circle. Popsy glanced at her but said nothing, and after a while Alessia stopped her circling and said, "To-morrow . . ."

"Today, here and now," Popsy interrupted firmly, and yelled to a certain Bob to come over to her at once.

Bob proved to be a middle-aged lad riding a chest-nut which peeled off from the group and ambled over in what looked to me a sloppy walk.

"Hop off, will you," Popsy said, and when Bob complied she said to Alessia, "O.K., just walk round a bit. You've no helmet, so I don't want you break-ing the speed limit, and besides old Paperbag here isn't as fit as the others."

She made a cradle for Alessia's knee and threw her casually up into the saddle, where the lady jockey landed with all the thump of a feather. Her feet slid into the stirrups and her hands gathered the reins, and she looked down at me for a second as if be-mused at the speed with which things were happen-ing. Then as if impelled she wheeled her mount and trotted away, following the other three horses down the schooling ground.

"At last," Popsy said. "And I'd begun to think she never would."

"She's a brave girl."

"Oh, yes." She nodded. "One of the best."

"She had an appalling time."

Popsy gave me five seconds of the direct green eyes. "So I gather," she said, "from her refusal to talk about it. Let it all hang out, I told her, but she just shook her head and blinked a couple of tears away, so these past few days I've stopped trying to jolly her along, it was obviously doing no good." She raised the binoculars to watch her three horses coming up over the hurdles and then swung them back down the hill, focusing on Alessia.

"Hands like silk," Popsy said. "God knows where she got it from, no one else in the family knows a spavin from a splint."

"She'll be better now," I said, smiling, "but don't expect . . ."

"Instant full recovery?" she asked, as I paused.

I nodded. "It's like convalescence. Gradual."

Popsy lowered the glasses and glanced at me briefly. "She told me about your job. What you've done for her father. She says she feels safe with you." She paused. "I've never heard of a job like yours. I didn't know people like you existed."

"There are quite a few of us . . . round the world."

"What do you call yourself, if people ask?"

"Safety consultant, usually. Or insurance consultant. Depends how I feel."

She smiled. "They both sound dull and worthy."

"Yes . . . er . . . that's the aim."

We watched Alessia come back up the hill, cantering now, but slowly, and standing in the stirrups. Though of course I'd seen them do it, I'd never consciously noted before then that that was how jockeys rode, not sitting in the saddle but tipped right forward so their weight could be carried over the horse's shoulder, not on the lower spine. Alessia stopped beside Bob, who took hold of the horse's reins, and she dismounted by lifting her right leg forward over the horse's neck and dropping lightly, feet together, to the ground: a movement as graceful and springy as ballet.

A different dimension, I thought. The expertise of

the professional. Amazing to the non-able, like seeing an artist drawing.

She patted the horse's neck, thanked Bob and came over to us, slight in shirt and jeans, smiling.

"Thanks," she said to Popsy.

"Tomorrow?" Popsy said. "With the string?"

Alessia nodded, rubbing the backs of her thighs. "I'm as unfit as marshmallow."

With calmness she watched the final trio of horses school, and then Popsy drove us again erratically back to her house, while the horses walked, to cool down.

Over coffee in the kitchen Alessia rewrote the lists of the music she'd listened to so often, a job she repeated out of generosity, and disliked.

"I could hum all the other tunes that I don't know the titles of," she said. "But frankly I don't want to hear them ever again." She pushed the list across: Verdi, as before, and modern gentle songs like "Yesterday" and "Send in the Clowns," more British and American in origin than Italian.

"I did think of something else," she said hesitantly. "I dreamed it, the night before last. You know how muddled things are in dreams . . . I was dreaming I was walking out to a race. I had silks on, pink and green checks, and I know I was supposed to be going to ride, but I couldn't find the parade ring, and I asked people, but they didn't know, they were all catching trains or something and then someone said, 'At least an hour to Viralto' and I woke up. I was sweating and my heart was thumping, but it hadn't been a nightmare, not a bad one anyway. Then I thought that I'd actually heard someone say 'at least an hour to Viralto' at that minute, and I was afraid there was someone in the room . . . It was horrible, really.'' She put a hand on her forehead, as if the clamminess still stood there. ''But of course, when I woke up properly, there I was in Popsy's spare bedroom, perfectly safe. But my heart was still thumping.'' She paused, then said, ''I think I must have heard one of them say that, when I was almost asleep.''

''This dream,'' I asked slowly, considering. ''Was it in English . . . or Italian?''

''Oh.'' Her eyes widened. ''I was riding in England. Pink and green checks . . . one of Mike Noland's horses. I asked the way to the parade ring in English . . . they were English people, but that voice saying 'at least an hour to Viralto,' that was Italian.'' She frowned. ''How awfully odd. I translated it into English in my mind, when I woke up.''

''Do you often go to Viralto?'' I asked.

''No. I don't even know where it is.''

''I'll tell Pucinelli,'' I said, and she nodded consent.

''He found the house you were kept in most of the time,'' I said neutrally.

''Did he?'' It troubled her. ''I . . . I don't want . . .''

''You don't want to hear about it?''

''No.''

''All right.''

She sighed with relief. ''You never make me face things. I'm very grateful. I feel . . . I still feel I could be pushed over a cliff . . . break down, I suppose . . . if too much is forced on me. And it's absolutely ridiculous—I didn't cry at all, not once, when I was . . . in that tent.''

''That's thoroughly normal, and you're doing fine,'' I said. ''And you look fabulous on a horse.''

She laughed. ''God knows why it took me so long. But up on the Downs . . . such a gorgeous morning . . . I just felt . . .'' She paused. ''I love horses, you know. Most of them, anyway. They're like friends . . . but they live internal lives, secret, with amazing instincts. They're telepathic . . . I suppose I'm boring you.''

''No,'' I said truthfully, and thought that it was horses, not I, who would lead her finally back to firm ground.

She came out to the car with me when I left and kissed me goodbye, cheek to cheek, as if I'd known her for years.

Eight

"Viralto?" Pucinelli said doubtfully. "It's a village off one of the roads into the mountains. Very small. No roads in the village, just alleyways between houses. Are you sure she said Viralto?"

"Yes," I said. "Is it one of those hilltop villages with houses all stuck together with red tiled roofs and blinding white walls without windows? All on slopes, shut in and secret?"

"Like that, yes."

"Would it be an hour's drive from Bologna? From the house where Alessia was kept?"

"I suppose so . . . If you knew the way. It is not on a main road."

"And . . . er . . . would it have a bakery?"

After the faintest of pauses he said smoothly, "My men will be up there at once, searching thoroughly. But Andrew . . . it would not be usual to take a kidnapped person there. In these villages everyone knows everyone. There is no room to hide a stranger."

"Try Viralto on the kidnapper who told you about the first house," I said.

"You can be sure I will," he said happily. "He has now confessed that he was one of the four people in masks who abducted Alessia. He also sometimes sat in the house at night to guard her, but he says he never spoke to her, she was always asleep." He paused. "I have asked him several times every day for the name of the man in the drawings. He says the man's name is Giuseppe. He says that's what he called him and he doesn't know any other name for him. This may be true. Maybe not. I keep asking. Perhaps one day he will tell me different."

"Enrico," I said diffidently. "You are an expert investigator. I hesitate to make a suggestion . . ."

A small laugh traveled by wire from Bologna. "You don't hesitate very often."

"Then . . . Before you go to Viralto, shall we get Paolo Cenci to offer a reward for the recovery of any of the ransom money? Then you could take that promise and also the drawings of 'Giuseppe' with you . . . perhaps."

"I will also take photographs of our kidnappers and of Alessia," he said. "Signor Cenci will surely agree to the reward. But . . ." he paused, "Viralto . . . was only a word in a dream."

"A word which caused sweating and an accelerated heartbeat," I said. "It frightened her."

"Did it? Hm. Then don't worry, we'll sweep through the village like the sirocco."

"Ask the children," I said.

He laughed. "Andrew Machiavelli Douglas . . . every child's mother would prevent us."

"Pity."

When we'd finished talking I telephoned to Paolo Cenci, who said "willingly" to the reward, and then again to Pucinelli to confirm it.

"I am making a leaflet for photocopying," he said. "The reward offer and all the pictures. I'll call you if there are any results."

"Call me anyway."

"Yes, all right."

He called me again on the following day, Friday, in the evening, while I happened to be on duty at the switchboard.

"I've been up in that damned village all day," he said exhaustedly. "Those people . . . they shut their doors and their faces and their minds."

"Nothing?" I asked with disappointment.

"There's something," he said, "but I don't know what. The name of Viralto was a shock to the kidnapper who talks, but he swears it means nothing to him. He swears it on his dead mother's soul, but he sweats while he swears. He is lying." He paused. "But in Viralto . . . we found nothing. We went into the bakery. We threatened the baker, who also keeps the very small grocery store. There is nowhere near his bakehouse that Alessia could have been hidden, and we searched everywhere. He gave us permission. He said he had nothing to hide. He said he would have known if Alessia had been brought to the village; he says he knows everything. He says she was never there."

"Did you believe him?" I asked.

"I'm afraid so. We asked at every single house. We did even ask one or two children. We found nothing; we heard nothing. But . . ."

"But . . . ?" I prompted.

"I have looked at a map," he said, yawning. "Viralto is up a side road which goes nowhere else. But if when one gets to the turn to Viralto one drives past it, straight on, that road goes on up into the mountains, and although it is not a good road it crosses the Apennines altogether and then descends towards Firenze. Above Viralto there is a place which used to be a castle but is now a hotel . . . People go there to walk and enjoy the mountains. Perhaps the Signorina didn't hear enough . . . perhaps it was at least an hour to Viralto, and longer still to wherever they planned to go. Tomorrow," he paused, sighing, "tomorrow I am off duty. Tomorrow I expect I will however be on duty after all. I'll go up to the hotel and blow the sirocco through that."

"Send some of your men," I suggested.

After a definite pause he said levelly, "I have given instructions that no one is to act again in this case in any way without my being there in person."

"Ah."

"So I will telephone again tomorrow, if you like."

"Tomorrow I'll be here from four until midnight," I said gratefully. "After that, at home."

In the morning, Saturday, Popsy telephoned while I was pottering round my apartment trying to shut my eyes to undone chores.

"Something the matter?" I asked, interpreting the tone of her hello.

"Sort of. I want your help. Can you come?"

"This instant, or will tomorrow do? I have to be in the office, really, by four."

"On Saturday afternoon?" she sounded surprised.

" 'Fraid so."

She hesitated. "Alessia didn't ride out with the string yesterday because of a headache."

"Oh . . . and today?"

"Today she didn't feel like it . . . Look," she said abruptly, "I'd say the idea scared her, but how can it, you saw how she rode?" The faint exasperation in her voice came over clearly, accompanying the genuine concern. When I didn't answer immediately she demanded, "Are you there?"

"Yes. Just thinking." I paused. "She wasn't scared of the horses or of riding, that's for sure. So perhaps she's scared . . . and I don't think that's the right word, but it'll do for now . . . of being closed in . . . of being unable to escape . . . of being in the string. Like a sort of claustrophobia, even though it's out in the open air. Perhaps that's why she wouldn't go in the string before, but felt all right on her own, up on the Downs."

She thought it over, then said, "Perhaps you're right. She certainly wasn't happy yesterday . . . she spent most of the day in her room, avoiding me."

"Popsy . . . don't press her. She needs you very badly, but just as someone there . . . and undemanding. Tell her not to try to go out with the string until she can't bear not to. Say it's fine with you, you're glad to have her, she can do what she likes. Would that be O.K.? Could you say that? And I'll come down tomorrow morning."

"Yes, yes, and yes," she said sighing. "I'm very fond of her. Come to lunch and wave your wand."

* * *

Pucinelli telephoned late in the evening with the news: good, bad, and inconclusive.

"The Signorina was right," he said first, sounding satisfied. "She was taken past Viralto, up to the hotel. We consulted the manager. He said he knew nothing, but we could search all the outbuildings, of which there are very many, most used for storage, but once living quarters for servants and carriage horses and farm animals. In one of the old animal feed lofts we found a tent!" He broke off for dramatic effect, and I congratulated him.

"It was folded," he said. "But when we opened it, it was the right size. Green canvas walls, gray floor-covering, just as she said. The floor of the loft itself was of wood, with hooks screwed into it, for the tent ropes." He paused. "In the house in the suburbs, we think they tied the tent ropes to the furniture."

"Mm," I said encouragingly.

"The loft is in a disused stable yard which is a small distance behind the hotel kitchens. It is perhaps possible she could smell baking . . . the hotel bakes its own bread."

"Terrific," I said.

"No, not terrific. No one there saw her. No one is saying anything. The stores of the hotel are kept in the outbuildings and there are great stocks of household items there, also cold stores for vegetables and meat, and a huge freezer room . . . vans make deliveries to these storerooms every day. I think the Signorina could have been taken to the hotel in a van, and no one would have paid much attention. There are so many outbuildings and courtyards at the back . . . garages, garden equipment stores, furniture stores for things not in use, barns full of useless objects which used to be in the old castle, ancient cooking stoves, old baths, enough rubbish to fill a town dump. You could hide for a month there. No one would find you.''

''No luck, then, with the pictures of the kidnappers?'' I said.

''No. No one knew him. No one knew the two we have in jail. No one knew anything.'' He sounded tired and discouraged.

''All the same,'' I said, ''you do have the tent. And it's pretty certain that one of the kidnappers knew the hotel fairly well, because that loft doesn't sound like a place you'd find by accident.''

''No.'' He paused. ''Unfortunately the Vistaclara has many people staying there and working there. One of the kidnappers might have stayed there, or worked there, in the past.''

''Vistaclara . . . is that the name of the hotel?'' I asked.

''Yes. In the past there were horses in the stable yard, but the manager says they no longer have them, not enough people want to ride in the hills, they prefer now to play tennis.''

Horses, I thought vaguely.

''How long ago did they have horses?'' I asked.

''Before the manager came. I could ask him, if you like. He said the stable yard was empty when he started, about five years ago. It has been empty ever since. Nothing has been stored there in case one day it would again be profitable to offer riding for holidays.''

''Pony trekking,'' I said.

''What?''

"Riding over hills on ponies. Very popular in some parts of Britain."

"Oh," he said without enthusiasm. "Anyway, there were grooms once and a riding instructor, but now they have a tennis pro instead . . . and he didn't know any of the kidnappers in our pictures."

"It's a big hotel, then?" I said.

"Yes, quite. People go there in the summer, it is cooler than on the plains or on the coast. Just now there are thirty-eight on the staff besides the manager, and there are rooms for a hundred guests. Also a restaurant with views of the mountains."

"Expensive?" I suggested.

"Not for the poor," he said. "But also not for princes. For people who have money, but not for the jet set. A few of the guests live there always . . . old people, mostly." He sighed. "I asked a great many questions, as you see. No one at all, however long they had lived there, or been employed there, showed any interest in our pictures."

We talked it over for a while longer but without reaching any conclusion except that he would try "Vistaclara" on the talkative kidnapper the next day: and on that next day, Sunday, I drove down again to Lambourn.

Alessia had by that time been free for nearly two weeks and had progressed to pink varnish on her nails. A lifting of the spirits, I thought.

"Did you buy the varnish?" I asked.

"No . . . Popsy did."

"Have you been shopping yet on your own?"

She shook her head. I made no comment, but she said, "I suppose you think I ought to."

"No. Just wondered."

"Don't press me."

"No."

"You're as bad as Popsy." She was looking at me almost with antagonism, something wholly new.

"I thought the varnish looked pretty," I said equably.

She turned her head away with a frown, and I drank the coffee Popsy had poured before she'd walked out round her yard.

"Did Popsy ask you to come?" Alessia said sharply.

"She asked me to lunch, yes."

"Did she complain that I've been acting like a cow?"

"No," I said. "Have you?"

"I don't know. I expect so. All I know is that I want to scream. To throw things. To hit someone." She spoke indeed as if a head of steam was being held in by slightly precarious will power.

"I'll drive you up to the Downs."

"Why?"

"To scream. Kick the tires. So on."

She stood up restlessly, walked aimlessly round the kitchen and then went out of the door. I followed in a moment and found her standing halfway to the Land Rover, irresolute.

"Go on, then," I said. "Get in." I made a questioning gesture to where Popsy stood, pointing to the Land Rover, and from the distance collected a nod.

The keys were in the ignition. I sat in the driver's seat and waited, and Alessia presently climbed in beside me.

"This is stupid," she said.

I shook my head, started the engine, and drove the

way we'd gone three days earlier, up to the silence and the wide sky and the calling birds.

When I braked to a stop and switched off, Alessia said defensively, "Now what? I can't just . . . scream."

"If you care to walk off along there on your own and see if you want to, I'll wait here."

Without looking at me directly she did exactly as I'd said, sliding down from the Land Rover and walking away. Her narrow figure diminished in the distance but stayed in sight, and after a fair while she came slowly back. She stopped with dry eyes at the open window beside me and said calmly, "I can't scream. It's pointless."

I got out of the Land Rover and stood on the grass near her. I said, "What is it about riding in the string which makes you feel trapped?"

"Did Popsy say that?"

"No, she just said you didn't want to."

She leaned against the front fender of the Land Rover, not looking at me.

"It's nonsense," she said. "I don't know why. On Friday I got dressed to go. I wanted to go . . . but I felt all churned up. Breathless. Worse than before my first big race . . . but the same sort of feeling. I went downstairs, and it got much worse. Stifling. So I told Popsy I had a headache . . . which was nearly true . . . and yesterday it was just the same. I didn't even go downstairs . . . I felt so wretched, but I just couldn't . . ."

I pondered, then said, "Start from getting up. Think of riding clothes. Think of the horses. Think of riding through the street. Think of everything separately, one by one, and then say at what thought you begin to feel . . . churned up.''

She looked at me dubiously, but blinked a few times as she went through the process and then shook her head. ''I don't feel churned now. I don't know what it is . . . I've thought of everything. *It's the boys.*'' The last three words came out as if impelled; as if unpremeditated and from the depths.

''The boys?''

''The lads.''

''What about them?''

''Their eyes.'' The same erupting force.

''If you rode at the back they wouldn't see you,'' I said.

''I'd think of their eyes.''

I glanced at her very troubled face. She was taking me out of my depth, I thought. She needed professional help, not my amateur common sense.

''Why their eyes?'' I said.

''Eyes . . .'' She spoke loudly, as if the words themselves demanded violence. ''They watched me. I knew they did. When I was asleep. They came in and watched.''

She turned suddenly towards the Land Rover and did actually kick the tire.

''They came in. I know they did. I hate . . . I hate . . . I can't bear . . . their eyes.''

I stretched out, put my arms round her and pulled her against my chest. ''Alessia . . . Alessia . . . It doesn't matter. What if they did?''

''I feel . . . filthy . . . dirty.''

''A kind of rape?'' I said.

''Yes.''

''But not . . . ?''

She shook her head silently and conclusively.

"How do you know they came in?" I said.

"The zip," she said. "I told you I knew every stitch of the tent . . . I knew how many teeth in the zip. And some days, it would open higher than others. They undid the zip . . . and came in . . . and fastened it at a different level . . . six or seven teeth higher, ten lower . . . I dreaded it."

I stood holding her, not knowing what to say.

"I try not to care," she said. "But I dream . . ." She stopped for a while, then said, "I dream about eyes."

I rubbed one of my hands over her back, trying to comfort.

"Tell me what else," I said. "What else is unbearable?"

She stood quiet for so long with her nose against my chest that I thought there might be nothing, but finally, with a hard sort of coldness, she said, "I wanted him to like me. I wanted to please him. I told Papa and Pucinelli that his voice was cold . . . but that was . . . at the beginning. When he came each time with the microphone, to make the tapes, I was . . . ingratiating." She paused. "I . . . loathe . . . myself. I am . . . hateful . . . and dreadfully . . . unbearably . . . ashamed."

She stopped talking and simply stood there, and after a while I said, "Very often people who are kidnapped grow to like their kidnappers. It isn't even unusual. It's as if a normal human being can't live without some sort of friendly contact. In ordinary criminal prisons, the prisoners and warders grow into definitely friendly relationships. When a lot of hostages are taken, some of them always make

friends with one or more of the terrorists holding
them. Hostages sometimes beg the police who are
rescuing them not to harm their kidnappers. You
mustn't, you shouldn't, blame yourself for trying to
make the man with the microphone like you. It's
normal. Usual. And . . . how did he respond?''

She swallowed. ''He called me . . . dear girl.''

''Dear girl,'' I said myself, meaning it. ''Don't
feel guilty. You are normal. Everyone tries to be-
friend their kidnappers to some extent, and it's better that they should.''

''Why?'' The word was muffled, but passionate.

''Because antagonism begets antagonism. A kidnapped person who can make the kidnappers like
her is much safer. They'll be less likely to harm her
. . . and more careful, for her own sake, not to let
her see their faces. They wouldn't want to kill someone they'd grown to like.''

She shivered.

''And as for coming in to see you when you were
asleep . . . maybe they looked on you with friendship . . . maybe they wanted to be sure you were all
right, as they couldn't see you when you were
awake.''

I wasn't sure whether I believed that last bit myself, but it was at least possible: and the rest was all
true.

''The lads are not the kidnappers,'' I said.

''No, of course not.''

''Just other men.''

She nodded her smothered head.

''It's not the lads' eyes you dream about.''

''No.'' She sighed deeply.

''Don't ride with the string until you feel O.K.

about it. Popsy will arrange a horse for you up on the Downs." I paused. "Don't worry if tomorrow you still feel churned up. Knowing the reason for the feelings doesn't necessarily stop them coming back."

She stood quiet for a while and then disconnected herself slowly from my embrace, and without looking at my face said, "I don't know where I'd be without you. In the nut-house, for sure."

"One day," I said mildly, "I'll come to the Derby and cheer you home."

She smiled and climbed into the Land Rover, but instead of pointing its nose homewards I drove on over the hill to the schooling ground.

"Where are you going?" she said.

"Nowhere. Just here." I stopped the engine and put on the brakes. The flights of hurdles and fences lay neat and deserted on the grassy slope, and I made no move to get out of the car.

"I've been talking to Pucinelli," I said.

"Oh."

"He's found the second place, where you were kept those last few days."

"Oh." A small voice, but not panic-stricken.

"Does the Hotel Vistaclara mean anything to you?"

She frowned, thought, and shook her head.

"It's up in the mountains," I said. "Above the place called Viralto, that you told me about. Pucinelli found the green tent there, folded, not set up, in a loft over a disused stable yard."

"Stables?" She was surprised.

"Mm."

She wrinkled her nose. "There was no smell of horses."

"They've been gone five years," I said. "But you said you could smell bread. The hotel makes its own, in the kitchens. The only thing is . . ." I paused, ". . . why just bread? Why not all cooking smells?"

She looked forward through the windscreen to the peaceful rolling terrain and breathed deeply of the sweet fresh air, and calmly, without strain or tears, explained.

"At night when I had eaten the meal one of them would come and tell me to put the dish and the bucket out through the zip. I could never hear them coming because of the music. I only knew they were there when they spoke." She paused. "Anyway, in the morning when I woke they would come and tell me to take the bucket in again . . . and at that point it would be clean and empty." She stopped again. "It was then that I could smell the bread, those last few days. Early . . . When the bucket was empty." She fell silent and then turned her head to look at me, seeking my reaction.

"Pretty miserable for you," I said.

"Mm." She half-smiled. "It's incredible . . . but I got used to it. One wouldn't think one could. But it was one's own smell, after all . . . and after the first few days I hardly noticed it." She paused again. "Those first days I thought I'd go mad. Not just from anxiety and guilt and fury . . . but from boredom. Hour after hour of nothing but that damned music . . . no one to talk to, nothing to see . . . I tried exercises, but day after day I grew less fit and more dopey, and after maybe two or three weeks I just stopped. The days seemed to run into each other, then. I just lay on the foam mattress and let the music wash in and out, and I thought about things that had happened in my life, but they seemed far away and hardly real. Reality was the bucket and pasta and a polystyrene cup of water twice a day . . . and hoping that the man with the microphone would think I was behaving well . . . and like me."

"Mm," I said. "He liked you."

"Why do you think so?" she asked, and I saw that curiously she seemed glad at the idea, that she still wanted her kidnapper to approve of her, even though she was free.

"I think," I said, "that if you and he had felt hate for each other he wouldn't have risked the second ransom. He would have been very much inclined to cut his losses. I'd guess he couldn't face the thought of killing you . . . because he liked you." I saw the deep smile in her eyes and decided to straighten things up in her perspective. No good would come of her falling in love with her captor in fantasy or in retrospect. "Mind you," I said, "he gave your father an appalling time and stole nearly a million pounds from your family. We may thank God he liked you, but it doesn't make him an angel."

"Oh . . ." She made a frustrated, very Italian gesture with her hands. "Why are you always so . . . so sensible?"

"Scottish ancestors," I said. "The dour sort, not the firebrands. They seem to take over and spoil the fun when the quarter of me that's Spanish aches for flamenco."

She put her head on one side, half laughing. "That's the most I've ever heard you say about yourself."

"Stick around," I said.

''I don't suppose you believe it,'' she said, sighing deeply and stretching her limbs to relax them, ''but I am after all beginning to feel fairly sane.''

Nine

July crept out in a drizzle and August swept in with a storm in a week of little activity in the London office but a good deal in Italy.

Pucinelli telephoned twice to report no progress and a third time, ecstatically, to say that Cenci's offer of a reward had borne results. The offer, along with the kidnappers' pictures, had been posted in every possible public place throughout Bologna and the whole province around; and an anonymous woman had telephoned to Paolo Cenci himself to say she knew where a part of the ransom could be found.

"Signor Cenci said she sounded spiteful. A woman scorned. She told him it would serve 'him' right to lose his money. She wouldn't say who 'he' was. In any case, tomorrow Signor Cenci and I go to where she says the money can be found, and if she is right, Signor Cenci will post a reward to her. The address to send the reward is a small hotel, not high class. Perhaps we will be able to find the woman and question her."

On the following evening he sounded more moderately elated.

"It was true we found some of the money," he said. "But unfortunately not very much, when you think of the whole amount."

"How much?" I asked.

"Fifty million lire."

"That's . . . er . . .," I did rapid sums, "nearly twenty-five thousand pounds. Hm . . . The loot of a gang member, not a principal, wouldn't you say?"

"I agree."

"Where did you find it?" I asked.

"In a luggage locker at the railway station. The woman told Signor Cenci the number of the locker, but we had no key. We had a specialist to open the lock for us."

"So whoever left the money thinks it's still there?"

"Yes. It is indeed still there, but we have had the lock altered. If anyone tries to open it, he will have to ask for another key. Then we catch him. We've set a good trap. The money is in a soft travel bag, with a zip. The numbers on the notes match the photographs. There is no doubt it is part of the ransom. Signor Cenci has sent a reward of five million lire and we will try to catch the woman when she collects it. He is disappointed, though, as I am, that we didn't find more."

"Better than nothing," I said. "Tell me how you get on."

There were two usual ways to deal with "hot" money, of which the simplest was to park the loot somewhere safe until the fiercest phase of investigation was over. Crooks estimated the safety margin variously from a month to several years, and were then fairly careful to spend the money far from home, usually on something which could instantly be resold.

The second, more sophisticated method, most used for large amounts, was to sell the hot money to a sort of fence, a professional who would buy it for about two thirds of its face value, making his profit by floating it in batches onto the unsuspecting public via the operators of casinos, markets, fairgrounds, racecourses or anywhere else where large amounts of cash changed hands quickly. By the time the hot money percolated back to far-flung banks the source of it couldn't be traced.

Some of Paolo Cenci's million quid could have been lopped by a third in such laundering, some could have been split between an unknown number of gang members, and some could have been spent in advance on outgoings, such as renting the suburban house. The expenses of a successful kidnapping were high, the ransom never wholly profit. All the same, despite its risks, it was the fastest way to a fortune yet devised, and in Italy particularly the chances of being detected and caught were approximately five percent. In a country where no woman could walk in the streets of Rome with a handbag over her arm for fear of having it razored off by thieves on motorcycles, kidnapping was regarded as a fact of life, like ulcers.

Pucinelli telephoned two days later in a good mood to report that the woman who had collected the reward had been followed home without challenge and had proved to be the wife of a man who had served two terms in jail for raids on liquor stores.

Neighbors said the man was known for chasing girls, his wife hot-bloodedly jealous. Pucinelli thought that an arrest and search of the man on suspicion would present no problems, and the next evening reported that the search had revealed the luggage locker ticket in the man's wallet. The man, identified as Giovanni Santo, was now in a cell and pouring out information like lava from a volcano.

"He is stupid," Pucinelli said disparagingly. "We've told him he will spend his whole life in jail if he doesn't cooperate, and he's shit scared. He has told us the names of all the kidnappers. There were seven of them altogether. Two we already have, of course, and now Santo. At this minute we have men picking up three others."

"And Giuseppe?" I asked, as he stopped.

"Giuseppe," he said reluctantly, "is not one of them. Giuseppe is the seventh. He was the leader. He recruited the others, who were all criminals before. Santo doesn't know Giuseppe's real name, nor where he came from, nor where he's gone. I'm afraid in this instance Santo speaks the truth."

"You've done marvels," I said.

He coughed modestly. "I've been lucky. And Andrew . . . between us privately I will admit it . . . it has been most helpful to talk to you. It clears things in my mind to tell them to you. Very odd."

"Carry right on," I said.

"Yes. It's a pleasure," he said; and he telephoned three days later to say they now had all six gang members in custody and had recovered a further hundred million lire of Cenci's money.

"We have also taken recordings of all six men and had voiceprints made and analyzed, but none of them is the voice on the tapes. And none of them is the man you saw, of whom we have the picture.''

"Giuseppe," I said. "On the tapes."

"Yes," he agreed gloomily. "None of them knew him before. He recruited one as a stranger in a bar, and that one recruited the other five. We will convict the six, there's no doubt, but it's hollow without Giuseppe."

"Mm." I hesitated. "Enrico, isn't it true that some of the students who joined the Red Brigades in their hot-headed youth grew out of it and became ordinary blameless citizens?"

"I've heard so, but of course they keep the past secret."

"Well . . . it just struck me a day or two ago that Giuseppe might have learned the techniques of kidnapping from the Red Brigades, when he was a student, perhaps, or even as a member."

Pucinelli said doubtfully, "Your Identikit pictures don't match anyone with a criminal record."

"I just wondered if it might be worthwhile to show those pictures to ex-students of about the same age, say twenty-five to forty, at perhaps some sort of students' reunion. It's a faint chance, anyway."

"I'll try," he said. "But the Red Brigades, as I'm sure you know, are organized in small cells. People in one cell can't identify people in other cells because they never meet them."

"I know it's a long shot and involves a lot of probably fruitless work," I agreed.

"I'll think about it."

"O.K."

"All the universities are closed for summer vacations."

"So they are," I said. "But in the autumn . . ."

"I will think about it," he said again. "Goodnight, friend. Sleep well."

Alessia heard from her father about the recovery of some of the ransom and from me of the capture of six of the kidnappers.

"Oh," she said blankly.

"Your man with the microphone isn't among them."

"Oh." She looked at me guiltily, hearing, as I did, the faint relief in her voice. We were sitting in Popsy's minute tree-shrouded garden where four lounging chairs squeezed onto a square of grass and low stone surrounding walls failed to obscure views of stable yard on three sides. We were drinking iced coffee in the heat wave which had followed the storms, clinking the cubes and being watched politely by equine heads peering in rows over half-doors.

I had invited myself down on my day off, a move neither Alessia nor Popsy had objected to, and I'd found Popsy alone when I arrived, as usual out in her yard.

"Hello," she said, as I drew up. "Sorry about the wet." She was standing in green gumboots, hose in hand, watering the lower hind leg of a large chestnut horse. Bob held its head. Its eyes blinked at me as if bored. The water ran in a stream across the yard to a drain. "It's got a leg," Popsy said, as if that explained things.

I stifled a desire to say that as far as I could see it had four.

"Alessia walked along to the shops," she said.

"She won't be long." She squelched away and turned off a tap, flinging the hose in loose coils beside it. "That'll do for now, Bob," she said. "Get Jamie to roll up that hose." She dried her hands on the seat of her pants and gave me a bright blaze from the green eyes.

"She rides, you know," she said as Bob led the watered horse off to an empty box, "but only up on the Downs. She goes up and down with me in the Land Rover. We don't discuss it. It's routine."

"How is she otherwise?"

"Much happier, I'd say." She grinned hugely and clapped me lightly on the shoulder. "Don't know how anyone so cold can bring someone else to life."

"I'm not cold," I protested.

"No?" She considered me quizzically. "There's a feeling of iron about you. Like a rod. You don't smile much. You're not intimidating . . . but I'm sure you could be, if you tried."

I shook my head.

"Do you ever get drunk?" she said.

"Not often."

"Never, more like." She waved a hand towards the kitchen. "Like a drink? It's so bloody hot."

We went into a cool interior with her shaking off her gumboots on the doorstep, and she brought white wine from the refrigerator to the kitchen in fawn socks.

"I'll bet for instance," she said, pouring, "that you never get helpless giggles or sing vulgar songs or generally make an ass of yourself."

"Often."

She gave me an "oh, yeah" look and settled her

large self comfortably onto a kitchen chair, putting her heels up on the table.

"Well, sometimes," I said.

She drank some wine cheerfully. "What makes you giggle, then?" she asked.

"Oh . . . one time I was with an Italian family during a kidnap and they all behaved like a comic soap opera at the top of their voices, and it was painful. I had to go upstairs sometimes to stop myself laughing . . . awful giggles over and over, when really the whole thing was deadly dangerous. I had terrible trouble. My face was aching with the effort of keeping it straight."

"Like wanting to explode in church," Popsy said, nodding.

"Just like that."

We sipped the cold wine and regarded each other with friendliness, and in a moment or two Alessia appeared with a bag of groceries and a welcoming smile. There was color in her cheeks at last, and a sort of rebirth taking place of the girl she must have been before. I could see a great difference in even the carriage of her head; self-respect returning to straighten the spine.

I got up at the sight of her and kissed her cheek in greeting and she put the groceries on the table and gave me a positive hug.

"Hi," she said. "Please note, I've been shopping. That's the third time. We are now back in business . . . no nerves, not to speak of."

"Terrific."

She poured herself some wine and the three of us amicably ate lunch, and it was afterwards, when Popsy had gone off to her office to do paperwork, that I told Alessia in the garden about the new arrests.

"Do you think they'll catch him . . . the man with the microphone?" she asked.

"He called himself Giuseppe," I said, "though that's almost certainly not his name. The six captured kidnappers knew him just as Giuseppe, and none of them knows anything else. I think he's cool and intelligent, and I'm afraid Pucinelli won't find him . . . or the bulk of your ransom."

She was quiet for a while and then said, "Poor Papa. Poor all of us. I love the house on Mikonos . . . so full of brilliant light, right by the sapphire sea . . . Papa says the money so far recovered won't be enough to save it. He says he keeps postponing putting it up for sale, just hoping . . . but it's not just its value, there's the upkeep, and the fares there two or three times a year. It was always a luxury, even before." She paused. "Part of my childhood. Part of my life."

"Giuseppe took it," I said.

She stirred slightly and finally nodded. "Yes, you are right."

We drank the iced coffee. Time passed tranquilly.

"I thought of going to the races next week," she said. "To Brighton. Mike Noland runs a lot of horses there, because he used to train in Sussex, and many of his owners still live there. I may as well go and talk to them . . . show them I'm still alive."

"If I went," I said, "would I be in your way?"

She smiled over at the still-watching horses. "No, you wouldn't."

"Which day?"

"Wednesday."

I thought of switchboard schedules. "I'll fix it," I said.

Gerry Clayton having agreed with a thoroughly false martyred expression to sit in for me from four to midnight, I drove early to Lambourn to collect Alessia, pausing only for coffee and encouragement from Popsy before setting off on the three-hour trek to Brighton.

"I could have got a lift," Alessia said. "You didn't have to come all this huge way round."

"Sure," I said.

She sighed, but not apparently with regret. "Half a dozen trainers or jockeys will be driving from here to Brighton."

"Bully for them."

"So I could always get a lift back."

I looked at her sideways. "I'll drive you unless you definitely prefer not."

She didn't answer; just smiled. We drove to Brighton and talked of many things for which there had never been peace enough before; of likes and dislikes, places, books, people; cabbages and kings.

It was the first time, I thought, that I had seen her in a skirt: if one excepted, of course, the dress I had pulled over her unconscious head. A vision of her lean nakedness rose unbidden; an agreeable memory, to be honest. For Brighton she had covered the basics with a neat pale-coffee-colored dress, and wore big gold earrings under her short curls.

Her reappearance on a racecourse was greeted with a warmth that almost overwhelmed her, with everyone who saw her seemingly intent on hugging her until her bones cracked. She introduced me vaguely many times but no one took any notice. The eyes were only for her, devouring her with curiosity, but also with love.

"Alessia! How super!"

"Alessia! Fantastic!"

"Alessia! Marvellous . . . smashing . . . delirious . . . terrific . . ."

She need not have doubted that Mike Noland's owners would notice her reemergence. At least four widely-grinning couples assured her that as soon as she was fit they would be thrilled to have her back in their saddles. Mike Noland himself, big and fifty, told her it was time to leave Popsy's jumpers and come to ride work on the two-year-olds; and passing bright-silked jockeys, I was interested to see, greeted her with genuine pleasure under more casual greetings.

"Hello, Alessia, how's it going?"

"How ya doing?"

"Well done; glad you're back."

"Get your boots on, Cenci."

Their direct camaraderie meant a lot to her. I could see the faint apprehension of the outward journey vanishing minute by minute, replaced by the confidence of being at home. She kept me beside her all the same, glancing at me frequently to check I was still there and never moving a step without being sure I followed. One might have thought of it as a courtesy except for what had gone before.

I saw little enough of the races themselves, and nor did she, from the press of people wanting to talk; and the afternoon was cut short, as far as I was concerned, by a message broadcast over the loud-speakers after the fourth event.

"Would Mr. Andrew Douglas please go to the Clerk of the Course's office. Mr. Andrew Douglas, please, go to the Clerk of the Course's office."

Alessia, looking worried, said she'd show me where the office was, and told me that messages of that sort nearly always meant bad news. "I hope it's not . . . Papa," she said. "Popsy would ask for you . . . so as not to frighten me."

We went quickly to the Clerk's office, brushing away the nonstop clutching greetings with quick smiles. Alessia's anxiety deepened with every step, but when we arrived at the office the Clerk of the Course himself put her fears to rest.

"I'm so sorry, Mr. Douglas," he said to me, "but we have a distressing message for you. Please would you ring this number . . ." He handed me a slip of paper. "Your sister has had a bad accident . . . I'm so sorry."

Alessia said "Oh!" faintly, as if not sure whether to be glad or horrified, and I put a hand comfortingly on her arm.

"There's a more private telephone just over there," the Clerk said, pointing to a small alcove at the rear. "Do use it. How splendid, Miss Cenci, to see you back."

She nodded vaguely and followed me across the room. "I'm so sorry . . ." she said.

I shook my head. I had no sister. The number on the slip of paper was that of the office. I dialed the number and was answered by Gerry Clayton.

"It's Andrew," I said.

"Thank God. I had to tell all sorts of lies before they'd put out a call for you."

"What happened?" I said with an amount of agitation appropriate to the circumstances.

He paused, then said, "Can you be overheard?"

"Yes."

The Clerk himself was listening with half an ear and Alessia with both. Two or three other people were looking my way.

"Right. I won't expect comments. There's been a boy kidnapped from the beach at West Wittering. That's about an hour's drive along the coast from Brighton, I'd guess. Go over there pronto and talk to the mother, will you?"

"Where is she?" I said.

"In the Breakwater Hotel, Beach Road, climbing the walls. I promised her we'd have someone with her in two hours, and to hang on. She's incoherent, most unhelpful. We had a telephone call from Hoppy at Lloyds, the father got in touch with his insurers and got passed along a chain to us. The father's had instructions to stay by his home telephone. Tony Vine's on his way to him now. Can you take down the number?"

"Yes, hang on." I fumbled for pen and paper. "Fire away."

He read out the father's number. "His name is John Nerrity." He spelled it. "The child's name is Dominic. Mother's, Miranda. Mother and son were alone in the hotel on holiday, father busy at home. Got all that?"

"Yes."

"Get her to agree to the police."

"Yes."

"Hear from you later? Sorry about your day at the races."

"I'll go at once," I said.

"Break a leg."

I thanked the Clerk of the Course and left his office with Alessia still looking distressed on my behalf.

"I'll have to go," I said apologetically. "Can you possibly get a lift back to Lambourn? With Mike Noland, perhaps?"

Even though she had herself earlier suggested it, she looked appalled at the idea and vigorously shook her head. Panic stood quite clearly in her eyes.

"No," she said. "Can't I come with you? Please . . . I won't be a nuisance. I promise. I could help . . . with your sister."

"You're never a nuisance, but I can't take you." I looked down at her beseeching face, at the insecurity still so close to the surface. "Come out to the car with me, away from these crowds, and I'll explain."

We walked through the gates and along to the car park, and I said, "I haven't any sisters. There was no crash. I have to go on a job . . . a child's been kidnapped, and I have to go to his mother, so dearest Alessia . . . we must find Mike Noland. You'll be safe with him. You know him well."

She was horrified and apologetic and also shaking. "Couldn't I comfort the mother?" she said. "I could tell her . . . her child will come back . . . as I did?"

I hesitated, knowing the suggestion stemmed from her not wanting to go home with Mike Noland but also thinking that perhaps it made sense. Perhaps Alessia would indeed be good for Miranda Nerrity.

I looked at my watch. "Mrs. Nerrity's expecting me," I said indecisively, and she interrupted sharply, "Who? Who did you say?"

"Nerrity. Miranda Nerrity. But . . ."

Her mouth had literally fallen open. "But I know her," she said. "Or at least, I've met her . . . Her husband is John Nerrity, isn't he?"

I nodded, nonplussed.

"Their horse won the Derby," Alessia said.

I lifted my head.

Horses.

So many horses.

"What is it," Alessia said. "Why do you look so . . . bleak?"

"Right," I said, not directly answering. "Get in the car. I'd be glad for you to come, if you really mean it. But there's a good chance we won't be going back to Lambourn tonight. Would you mind that?"

For answer she slid into the front passenger seat and closed the door, and I walked round to climb in beside her.

As I started the engine and drove out of the gate she said, "The Nerritys' horse won the Derby last year. Ordinand. Don't you remember?"

"Um . . ." No, actually, I didn't.

"It wasn't one of the really greats," she said assessingly, "or at least no one thought so . . . He was an outsider. Thirty-three to one. But he's been winning this year quite well . . ." She stopped. "I can't bear to think of that child."

"His name's Dominic," I said. "Haul the map out of the glove compartment and find the fastest route to Chichester."

She reached for the map. "How old is he?"

"Don't know."

We sped westwards through Sussex in the golden

afternoon and came eventually to the Breakwater
Hotel, right on the pebbly beach at West Wittering.

"Look," I said, putting on brakes and pulling off
my tie. "Behave like a holidaymaker. Walk into
the hotel slowly. Smile. Talk to me. Don't seem
worried. O.K.?"

She looked at me with puzzlement turning to comprehension. "Do you think . . . someone's watching?"

"Someone usually is," I said astringently. "Always take it for granted that someone is. Kidnappers
post watchers to make sure the police don't arrive in
huge numbers."

"Oh."

"So we're on holiday."

"Yes," she said.

"Let's go in."

We climbed, stretching, out of the car, and Alessia
wandered a few steps away from the hotel to look out
to the English Channel, shading her eyes and speaking to me over her shoulder. "I'm going in for a
swim."

I put my arm round her shoulders and stood beside her for a few seconds, then with me saying teas-
ingly "Mind the jellyfish" we walked through the
hotel's glass entrance doors into a wide armchair-
scattered lounge. A few people sat around drinking
tea, and a girl in a black dress was moving to and fro
behind a polished brown counter labeled "Reception."

"Hello," I said, smiling. "We think a friend of
ours is staying here. A Mrs. Nerrity?"

"And Dominic," Alessia said.

"That's right," the girl said calmly. She looked at

a guest list. "Room sixty-three . . . but they're probably still on the beach. Lovely day, isn't it?"

"Gorgeous," Alessia agreed.

"Could you give their room a ring?" I asked. "Just in case."

The girl obligingly turned to the switchboard and was surprised at receiving an answer. "Pick up the phone," she said, pointing to a handset on the counter, and I lifted the receiver with an appropriate smile.

"Miranda?" I said. "This is Andrew Douglas."

"Where are you?" a small voice said tearfully.

"Downstairs, here in the hotel."

"Oh . . . Come up . . . I can't bear . . ."

"On my way," I said.

The girl gave us directions which we followed to a room with twin beds, private bathroom, view of the sea. Miranda Nerrity opened her door to us with swollen eyes and a clutched, soaking handkerchief and said between gulps, "They said . . . the man in London said . . . you would get Dominic back . . . he promised me . . . Andrew Douglas will get him back . . . he always does, he said . . . don't worry . . . but how can I not worry? Oh, my God . . . my baby . . . Get him back for me. Get him back."

"Yes," I said gently. "Come and sit down." I put my arm round her shoulders this time, not Alessia's, and guided her over to one of the armchairs. "Tell us what happened. Then we'll make a plan to get him back."

Miranda took a very small grip on things, recognizing Alessia with surprise and pointing to a piece of paper which lay on one of the beds.

"A little girl gave it to me," she said, the tears

rolling. "She said a man had asked her. Oh, dear . . . oh, dear . . ."

"How old was the little girl?" I asked.

"What? Oh . . . eight . . . something like that . . . I don't know."

Alessia knelt beside Miranda to comfort her, her own face pale again and taut with strain, and I picked up the sheet of paper and unfolded it, and read its brutal block-lettered message.

WE'VE TAKEN YOUR KID. GIVE YOUR HUBBY A BELL. TELL HIM TO GO HOME. WE'LL TELL YOUR HUBBY WHAT WE WANT. DON'T GO SQUAWK-ING TO NO ONE. NO ONE AT ALL, SEE. IF YOU WANT TO SEE YOUR KID AGAIN DON'T GO TO NO POLICE. WE'LL TIE A PLASTIC BAG OVER HIS HEAD IF YOU GET THE POLICE. SAVVY?

I lowered the page. "How old is Dominic?" I asked.

"Three and a half," Miranda said.

Ten

Miranda, twenty-six, had long blond hair falling from a center parting and on other occasions might have been pretty. She still wore a bathing suit with a toweling robe over, and there was still sand on her legs from the beach. Her eyes were glazed behind the puffed eyelids as if too much devastated emotion had put a film over them to repel reality, and she made vague pointless movements with her hands as if total inactivity was impossible.

Out of habit I carried with me always a flat container like a cigarette case, which contained among other things a small collection of pills. I took out the case, opened it, and sorted out a strip of white tablets in foil.

"Take one of these," I said, fetching water in a toothmug and sliding a pill from its wrapper.

Miranda simply swallowed as instructed. It was Alessia who said, "What are you giving her?"

"Tranquilizer."

"Do you carry those round with you always?" she asked incredulously.

"Mostly," I nodded. "Tranquilizers, sleeping pills, aspirins, things for heart attacks. First aid, that's all."

Miranda drank all the water.

"Do they have room service in this hotel?" I asked.

"What?" she said vaguely. "Yes . . . I suppose so . . . They'll be bringing Dominic's supper soon . . ." The idea of it reduced her to fresh deep sobs, and Alessia put her arm round her and looked shattered.

I telephoned to room service for tea, strong, as soon as possible, for three. Biscuits? Certainly biscuits. Coming right away, they said: and with very little delay the tray arrived, with me meeting the maid at the door and thanking her for her trouble.

"Mrs. Nerrity, drink this," I said, putting down the tray and pouring tea for her. "And eat the biscuits." I poured another cup for Alessia. "You too," I said.

They each drank and ate like automatons, and slowly in Miranda the combined simple remedies of tranquilizer, caffeine and carbohydrate took the worst edge off the pain so that she could bear to describe what had happened.

"We were on the sand . . . with his bucket and spade, making a sandcastle. He loves making sandcastles . . ." She stopped and swallowed, tears trickling down her cheeks. "A lot of the sand was wet, and I'd left our things up on the shingle . . . towels, a beach chair, our lunch box, packed by the hotel, Dominic's toys . . . it was a lovely hot day,

not windy like usual . . . I went up to sit on the chair
. . . I was watching him all the time . . . he was
only thirty yards away . . . less, less . . . squatting,
playing with his bucket and spade . . . patting the
sandcastle . . . I was watching him all the time, I
really was." Her voice tapered off into a wail, the
dreadful searing guilt sounding jagged and raw.

"Were there a lot of people on the beach?" I
asked.

"Yes, yes there were . . . it was so warm . . .
but I was watching him, I could see him all the
time . . ."

"And what happened?" I said.

"It was the boat . . ."

"What boat?"

"The boat on fire. I was watching it. Everyone
was watching it. And then . . . when I looked back
. . . he wasn't there. I wasn't scared. It was less
than a minute . . . I thought he'd be going over to
look at the boat . . . I was looking for him . . . and
then the little girl gave me the note . . . and I read
it . . ."

The awfulness of that moment swept over her
again like a tidal wave. The cup and saucer rattled
and Alessia took them from her.

"I shouted for him everywhere . . . I ran up and
down . . . I couldn't believe it . . . I couldn't . . .
I'd seen him such a short time ago . . . just a minute
. . . and then I came up here . . . I don't know how
I got up here . . . I telephoned John . . . and I've
left all our things . . . on the beach."

"When is high tide?" I said.

She looked at me vaguely. "This morning . . .

the tide had just gone out . . . the sand was all wet . . .''

"And the boat? Where was the boat?"

"On the sand."

"What sort of boat?" I asked.

She looked bewildered. "A sailing dinghy. What does it matter? There are millions of sailing dinghies round here."

But millions of sailing dinghies didn't go on fire at the exact moment that a small child was kidnapped. A highly untrustworthy coincidence of timing.

"Both of you drink some more tea," I said. "I'll go down and fetch the things from the beach. Then I'll ring Mr. Nerrity—"

"No," Miranda interrupted compulsively. "Don't. Don't."

"But we must."

"He's so angry," she said piteously. "He's . . . livid. He says it's my fault . . . he's so angry . . . you don't know what he's like . . . I don't want to talk to him . . . I can't . . ."

"Well," I said. "I'll telephone from another place. Not this room. I'll be as quick as I can . . . will you both be all right?"

Alessia nodded although she was herself shaking, and I went downstairs and found a public telephone tucked into a private corner of the entrance hall.

Tony Vine answered from John Nerrity's number.

"Are you alone?" I asked.

"No. Are you?"

"Yes. What's the score?"

"The pinchers have told him he'll get his boy back safe . . . on conditions."

"Such as?"

"Five million."

"For God's sake," I said, "has he got five million?" The Breakwater Hotel, nice enough, wasn't a millionaire's playground.

"He's got a horse," Tony said baldly.

A horse.

Ordinand, winner of the Derby.

"Ordinand?" I said.

"No slouch, are you? Yeah, Ordinand. The pinchers want him to sell it at once."

"How did they tell him?" I asked.

"On the telephone. No tap, of course, at that point. He says it was a rough voice full of slang. Aggressive. A lot of threats."

I told Tony about the block-lettered note. "Same level of language?"

"Yeah." Tony's occasional restraint in the matter of eff this and eff that was always a source of wonder, but in fact he seldom let rip in front of clients. "Mr. Nerrity's chief, not to say sole, asset, as I understand it, is the horse. He is . . . er . . ."

"Spitting mad?" I suggested.

"Yeah."

I half smiled. "Mrs. Nerrity is faintly scared of him."

"Not in the least surprising."

I told Tony how the kidnap had been worked and said I thought the police ought to investigate the dinghy very fast.

"Have you told the local fuzz anything yet?"

"No. Miranda will take a bit of persuading. I'll do it next. What have you told them from your end?"

"Nothing so far. I tell Mr. Nerrity we can't help

him without the police, but you know what it's like . . ."

"Mm. I'll call you again, shortly."

"Yeah." He put his receiver down and I ambled out of the hotel and rolled my trouser legs up to the knees on the edge of the shingle, sliding down the banks of pebbles in great strides towards the sand. Once there I took off shoes and socks and strolled along carrying them, enjoying the evening sun.

There were a few breakwaters at intervals along the beach, black fingers stretching stumpily seawards, rotten in places and overgrown with molluscs and seaweed. Miranda's chair, towels, and paraphernalia were alone on the shingle, most other people having packed up for the day; and not far away there was still a red plastic bucket and a blue plastic spade on the ground beside a half-trampled sandcastle. The British seaside public, I reflected, were still remarkably honest.

The burnt remains of the dinghy were the focal point for the few people still on the sand, the returning tide already swirling an inch deep around the hull. I walked over there as if drawn like everyone else, and took the closest possible look, paddling, like others, to see inside the shell.

The boat had been fiberglass and had melted as it burned. There were no discernible registration numbers on what was left of the exterior, and although the mast, which was aluminum, had survived the blaze and still pointed heavenward like an exclamation mark, the sail which would have borne identification lay in ashes round its foot. Something in the scorched mess might tell a tale—but the tide was inexorable.

"Shouldn't we try to haul it up to the shingle?" I suggested to a man paddling like myself.

He shrugged. "Not our business."

"Has anyone told the police?" I said.

He shrugged again. "Search me."

I paddled round to the other side of the remains and tried another more responsible-looking citizen but he too shook his head and muttered about being late already, and it was two fourteen-sized boys, overhearing, who said they would give me a hand, if I liked.

They were strong and cheerful. They lifted, strained, staggered willingly. The keel slid up the sand leaving a deep single track and between us we manhandled it up the shingle to where the boys said the tide wouldn't reach it to whisk it away.

"Thanks," I said.

They beamed. We all stood hands on hips admiring the result of our labors and then they too said they had to be off home to supper. They loped away, vaulting a breakwater, and I collected the bucket and spade and all Miranda's belongings and carried them up to her room.

Neither she nor Alessia was in good shape, and Alessia, if anything, seemed the more relieved at my return. I gave her a reassuring hug, and to Miranda I said, "We're going to have to get the police."

"No." She was terrified. "No . . . no . . ."

"Mm." I nodded. "Believe me, it's best. The people who've taken Dominic don't want to kill him, they want to sell him back to you safe and sound. Hold on to that. The police will be very helpful and we can arrange things so that the kidnappers won't know we've told them. I'll do that. The police will want to know what Dominic was wearing . . . on the beach . . . and if you have a photograph, that would be great.''

She wavered helplessly. "John said . . . keep quiet, I'd done enough damage . . .''

I picked up the telephone casually and got through again to her husband's number. Tony again answered.

"Andrew," I said.

"Oh." His voice lost its tension; he'd been expecting the kidnappers.

"Mrs. Nerrity will agree to informing the police on her husband's say-so."

"Go ahead, then. He understands we can't act for him without . . . He . . . er . . . doesn't want us to leave him. He's just this minute decided, when he heard the phone ring.''

"Good. Hang on . . ." I turned to Miranda. "Your husband says we can tell the police. Do you want to talk to him?"

She shook her head violently. "O.K.," I said to Tony. "Let's get started and I'll call you later.''

"What was the kid wearing?" he asked.

I repeated the question to Miranda and between new sobs she said red bathing trunks. Tiny toweling trunks. No shoes, no shirt . . . it had been hot.

Tony grunted and rang off, and as unhurriedly as I could I asked Miranda to put some clothes on and come out driving with me in my car. Questioning, hesitant, and fearful, she nevertheless did what was needed, and presently, having walked out of the hotel in scarf and sunglasses between Alessia and myself, sat with Alessia in the rear seats as I drove all three of us in the direction of Chichester.

Checks on our tail and an unnecessary detour showed no one following, and with one pause to ask directions I stopped the car near the main police station but out of sight of it, round a corner. Inside the station I asked for the senior officers on duty, and presently explained to a chief inspector and a C.I.D. man how things stood.

I showed them my own identification and credentials, and one of them, fortunately, knew something of Liberty Market's work. They looked at the kidnappers' threatening note with the blankness of shock, and rapidly paid attention to the account of the death of the dinghy.

"We'll be on to that straight away," said the chief inspector, stretching a hand to the telephone. "No one's reported it yet, as far as I know."

"Er . . ." I said. "Send someone dressed as a seaman. Gumboots. Seaman's sweater. Don't let them behave like policemen, it would be very dangerous for the child."

The chief inspector drew back from the telephone, frowning. Kidnapping in England was so comparatively rare that very few local forces had any experience of it. I repeated that the death threat to Dominic was real and should be a prime consideration in all procedure.

"Kidnappers are full of adrenaline and easily frightened," I said. "It's when they think they're in danger of being caught that they kill . . . and bury . . . the victim. Dominic really is in deadly danger, but we'll get him back safe if we're careful."

After a silence the C.I.D. officer, who was roughly my own age, said they would have to call in his super.

"How long will that take?" I asked. "Mrs. Nerrity is outside in my car with a woman friend, and I don't think she can stand very much waiting. She's highly distressed."

They nodded. Telephoned. Guardedly explained. The super, it transpired to their relief, would speed back to his office within ten minutes.

Detective Superintendent Eagler could have been born to be a plainclothes cop. Even though I was expecting him I gave the thin harmless-looking creature who came into the room no more than a first cursory glance. He had wispy balding hair and a scrawny neck rising from an ill-fitting shirt. His suit looked old and saggy and his manner seemed faintly apologetic. It was only when the other two men straightened at his arrival that with surprise I realized who he was.

He shook my hand, not very firmly, perched a thin rump on one corner of the large official desk, and asked me to identify myself. I gave him one of the firm's business cards with my name on. With neither haste nor comment he dialed the office number and spoke, I supposed, to Gerry Clayton. He made no remark about whatever answers Gerry gave him, but merely said "Thanks" and put down the receiver.

"I've studied other cases," he said directly to me and without more preamble. "Lesley Whittle . . . and others that went wrong. I want no such disasters on my patch. I'll listen to your advice, and if it seems good to me, I'll act on it. Can't say more than that."

I nodded and again suggested seamen-lookalikes to collect the dinghy, to which he instantly agreed, telling his junior to doll himself up and take a partner, without delay.

"Next?" he asked.

I said, "Would you talk to Mrs. Nerrity in my car, not in here? I don't think she should be seen in a police station. I don't think even that I should walk you directly to her. I could meet you somewhere. One may be taking precautions quite unnecessarily, but some kidnappers are very thorough and suspicious, and one's never quite sure."

He agreed and left before me, warning his two colleagues to say nothing whatever yet to anyone else.

"Especially not before a press black-out has been arranged," I added. "You could kill the child. Seriously; I mean it."

They gave earnest assurances, and I walked back to the car to find both girls too near collapse. "We're going to pick someone up," I said. "He's a policeman, but he doesn't look like it. He'll help to get Dominic back safely and to arrest the kidnappers." I sighed inwardly at my positive voice, but if I couldn't give Miranda even a shred of confidence, I could give her nothing. We stopped for Eagler at a crossroads near the cathedral, and he slid without comment into the front passenger seat.

Again I drove awhile on the lookout for company, but as far as I could see no kidnappers had risked it. After a few miles I stopped in a parking place on the side of a rural road, and Eagler got Miranda again to describe her dreadful day.

"What time was it?" he said.

"I'm not sure . . . After lunch. We'd eaten our lunch."

"Where was your husband, when you telephoned him?"

"In his office. He's always there by two."

Miranda was exhausted as well as tearful. Eagler, who was having to ask his questions over the clumsy barrier of the front seats, made a sketchy stab at patting her hand in a fatherly way. She interpreted the intention behind the gesture and wept the harder, choking over the details of red swimming trunks, no shoes, blue eyes, fair hair, no scars, suntanned skin . . . they'd been at the seaside for nearly two weeks . . . they were going home on Saturday.

"She ought to go home to her husband tonight," I said to Eagler, and although he nodded, Miranda vehemently protested.

"He's so angry with me . . ." she wailed.

"You couldn't help it," I said. "The kidnappers have probably been waiting their chance for a week or more. Once your husband realizes . . ."

But Miranda shook her head and said I didn't understand.

"That dinghy," Eagler said thoughtfully, "the one which burnt . . . had you seen it on the beach on any other day?"

Miranda glanced at him vaguely as if the question were unimportant. "The last few days have been so windy . . . We haven't sat on the beach much. Not since the weekend, until today. We've mostly been by the pool, but Dominic doesn't like that so much because there's no sand."

"The hotel has a pool?" Eagler asked.

"Yes, but last week we were always on the beach . . . everything was so simple, just Dominic and me.'' She spoke between sobs, her whole body shaking.

Eagler glanced at me briefly, ''Mr. Douglas, here,'' he said to Miranda, ''he says you'll get him back safe. We all have to act calmly, Mrs. Nerrity. Calm and patience, that's the thing. You've had a terrible shock, I'm not trying to minimize it, but what we have to think of now is the boy. To think calmly for the boy's sake.''

Alessia looked from Eagler to me and back again. ''You're both the same,'' she said blankly. ''You've both seen so much suffering . . . so much distress. You both know how to make it so that people can hold on . . . It makes the unbearable . . . possible.''

Eagler gave her a look of mild surprise, and in a totally unconnected thought I concluded that his clothes hung loosely about him because he'd recently lost weight.

''Alessia herself was kidnapped,'' I explained to him. ''She knows too much about it.'' I outlined briefly what had happened in Italy, and mentioned the coincidence of the horses.

His attention focused in a thoroughly Sherlockian manner.

''Are you saying there's a positive significance?''

I said, ''Before Alessia I worked on another case in Italy in which the family sold their shares in a racecourse to raise the ransom.''

He stared. ''You do, then, see a . . . a thread?''

''I fear there's one, yes.''

''Why fear?'' Alessia asked.

''He means,'' Eagler said, ''that the three kidnaps have been organized by the same perpetrator. Someone normally operating within the racing world and consequently knowing which targets to hit. Am I right?''

''On the button,'' I agreed, talking chiefly to Alessia. ''The choice of target is often a prime clue to the identity of the kidnappers. I mean . . . to make the risks worthwhile, most kidnappers make sure in advance that the family or business actually can pay a hefty ransom. Of course every family will pay what they can, but the risks are just as high for a small ransom as a large, so it makes more sense to aim for the large. To know, for instance, that your father is much richer than the fathers of most other jockeys, women or not.''

Alessia's gaze seemed glued to my face. ''To know . . . that the man who owns Ordinand has a son . . . ?'' She stopped, the sentence unfinished, the thought trotting on.

''Yes,'' I said.

She swallowed. ''It costs just as much to keep a bad horse in training as a good one . . . I mean, I do clearly understand what you're saying.''

Miranda seemed not to have been listening but the tears had begun to dry up, like a storm passing.

''I don't want to go home tonight,'' she said in a small voice. ''But if I go . . . Alessia, will you come with me?''

Alessia looked as if it were the last thing she could face and I answered on her behalf, ''No, Mrs. Nerrity, it wouldn't be a good idea. Have you a mother, or a sister . . . someone you like? Someone your husband likes.''

Her mordant look said as much as words about the

current state of her marriage, but after a moment or two she said faintly, "I suppose . . . my mother."

"That's right," Eagler said paternally. "Now would you two ladies just wait a few minutes while I walk a little way with Mr. Douglas?"

"We won't be out of sight," I said.

All the same they both looked as insecure as ever as we opened the front doors and climbed out. I looked back as we walked away and waggled a reassuring hand at their two anxious heads showing together from the rear seat.

"Very upsetting," Eagler observed as we strolled away. "But she'll get her kid back, with a bit of luck, not like some I've dealt with. Little kids snatched at random by psychos and murdered . . . sexual, often. Those mothers . . . Heartbreaking. Rotten. And quite often we know the psychos. Know they'll probably do something violent one day. Kill someone. We can often arrest them within a day of the body being found. But we can't prevent them. We can't keep them locked up forever, just in case. Nightmare, those people. We've got one round here now. Time bomb waiting to go off. And some poor kid, somewhere, will be cycling along, or walking, at just the wrong time, just the wrong place. Some woman's kid. Something triggers the psycho. You never know what it is. Something small. Tips them over. After, they don't know why they've done it, like as not."

"Mm," I said. "Worse than kidnappers. With them there's always hope."

During his dissertation he'd given me several sideways glances: reinforcing his impressions, I thought. And I too had been doing the same, getting to know what to expect of him, good or bad. Occasionally someone from Liberty Market came across a policeman who thought of us as an unnecessary nuisance encroaching on their jealously guarded preserves, but on the whole they accepted us along the lines of if you want to understand a wreck, consult a diver.

"What can you tell me that you wouldn't want those two girls to hear?" he asked.

I gave him a small smile; got reserved judgment back.

"The man who kidnapped Alessia," I said. "Recruited local talent. He recruited one, who roped in another five. The carabinieri have arrested those six, but the leader vanished. He called himself Giuseppe, which will do for now. We produced a drawing of him and flooded the province with it, with no results. I'll let you have a copy of it, if you like." I paused. "I know it's a long shot. This horse thing may be truly and simply a coincidence."

Eagler put his head on one side. "File it under fifty-fifty, then."

"Right. And there's today's note . . ."

"Nothing Italian about that, eh?" Eagler looked genial. "But local talent? Just the right style for local talent, wouldn't you say?"

"Yes, I would."

"Just right for an Italian leaning over the local talent's shoulder saying in broken English 'tell her to telephone her husband, tell her not to inform the police.' " He smiled fleetingly. "But that's all conjecture, as they say."

We turned as of one accord and began to stroll back to the car.

"The lady jockey's a bit jumpy still," he said.

"It does that to them. Some are jumpy with strangers forever."

"Poor thing," he said, as if he hadn't thought of freedom having problems; victims naturally being vastly less interesting than villains to the strong arm of the law.

I explained about Tony Vine being at that moment with John Nerrity, and said that Nerrity's local force would also by now know about Dominic. Eagler noted the address and said he would "liaise."

"I expect Tony Vine will be in charge from our point of view," I said. "He's very bright, if you have any dealings with him."

"All right."

We arranged that I would send the photostats of Giuseppe and a report on Alessia's kidnapping down to him on the first morning train; and at that point we were back at the car.

"Right then, Mr. Douglas." He shook my hand limply as if sealing a bargain, as different from Pucinelli as a tortoise from a hare: one wily, one sharp; one wrinkled in his carapace, one leanly taut in his uniform; one always on the edge of his nerves, one avuncularly relaxed.

I thought that I would rather be hunted by Pucinelli, any day.

Eleven

John Nerrity was a heavily built man of medium height with graying hair cut neat and short; clipped moustache to match. On good days I could imagine him generating a fair amount of charm, but on that evening I saw only a man accustomed to power who had married a girl less than half his age and looked like regretting it.

They lived in a large detached house on the edge of a golf course near Sutton, Surrey, south of London, only about three miles distant from where their four-legged wonder had made a fortune on Epsom Downs.

The exterior of the house, in the dusk of our arrival, had revealed itself as thirties-developed Tudor, but on a restrained and successful scale. Inside, the carpets wall-to-wall looked untrodden, the brocade chairs un-sat-on, the silk cushions unwrinkled, the paper and paint unscuffed. Unfaded velvet curtains hung in stiff regular folds from beneath elaborate pelmets, and upon several glass and chromium coffee tables lay large glossy books, unthumbed. There were no photographs and no flowers, and the pictures had been chosen to occupy wall space, not the mind; the whole thing more like a shop window than the home of a little boy.

John Nerrity was holding a gin and tonic with ice clinking and lemon slice floating, a statement in itself of his resistance to crisis. I couldn't imagine Paolo Cenci organizing ice and lemon six hours after the first ransom demand: it had been almost beyond him to pour without spilling.

With Nerrity were Tony Vine wearing his most enigmatic expression and another man, sour of mouth and bitter of eye, who spoke with Tony's accent and looked vaguely, in his flannels and casual sweater, as if he'd been out for a stroll with his dog.

"Detective Superintendent Rightsworth," Tony said, introducing him deadpan. "Waiting to talk to Mrs. Nerrity."

Rightsworth gave me barely a nod, and that more of repression than of acknowledgement. One of those, I thought. A civilian-hater. One who thought of the police as "us" and the public as "them," the "them" being naturally inferior. It always surprised me that policemen of that kind got promoted, but Rightsworth was proof enough that they did.

Alessia and Miranda had come into the sitting room close together and a step behind me, as if using me as a riot shield: and it was clear from John Nerrity's face that the first sight of his wife prompted few loving, comforting, or supportive feelings.

He gave her no kiss. No greeting. He merely said, as if in a continuing conversation, "Do you realize that Ordinand isn't mine to sell? Do you realize we're in hock to the limit? No, you don't. You can't do anything. Not even something simple like looking after a kid.''

Miranda crumpled behind me and knelt on the floor. Alessia and I bent to help her up, and I said to Miranda's ear, ''People who are frightened are often angry and say things that hurt. He's as frightened as you are. Hang on to that.''

''What are you mumbling about?'' Nerrity demanded. ''Miranda, for Christ's sake get up, you look a wreck.'' He stared with disfavor at the ravaged face and untidy hair of his son's mother, and with only the faintest flicker of overdue compassion said impatiently, ''Get up, get up, they say it wasn't your fault.''

She would always think it had been, though; and so would he. Few people understood how persistent, patient, ingenious, and fast committed kidnappers could be. Whomever they planned to take, they took.

Rightsworth said he wanted to ask Mrs. Nerrity some questions and guided her off to a distant sofa, followed by her bullish husband with his tinkling glass.

Alessia sat in an armchair as if her legs were giving way, and Tony and I retreated to a window seat to exchange quiet notes.

''He . . .'' Tony jerked his head towards Nerrity, ''has been striding up and down here wearing holes in the effing carpet and calling his wife an effing cow. All sorts of names. Didn't know some of them myself.'' He grinned wolfishly. ''Takes them like that, sometimes, of course.''

"Pour the anger on someone that won't kick back?"

"Poor little bitch."

"Any more demands?" I asked.

"Zilch. All pianissimo. That ray of sunshine Rightsworth brought a suitcase full of bugging gear with him from the telephone blokes but he didn't know how to use half of it, I ask you. I fixed the tap on the phone myself. Can't bear to see effing amateurs mucking about."

"I gather he doesn't like us," I said.

"Rightsworth? Despises the ground we walk on."

"Is it true John Nerrity can't raise anything on the horse?"

I'd asked very quietly, but Tony looked round to make sure neither the Nerritys nor Rightsworth could hear the answer. "He was blurting it all out, when I got here. Seems his effing business is dicky and he's pledged bits of that horse to bail him out. Borrowed on it, you might say. All this bluster, I reckon it's because he hasn't a hope of raising the wherewithal to get his nipper back, he's in a blue funk and sending his effing underpants to the laundry."

"What did he say about our fee?"

"Yeah." Tony looked at me sideways. "Took him in the gut. He says he can't afford us. Then he begs me not to go. He's not getting on too effing well with Rightsworth, who would? So there he is, knackered every which way and taking it out on the lady wife." He glanced over at Miranda, who was again in tears. "Seems she was his secretary. That's her photo, here on this table. She was a knockout, right enough."

I looked at the glamorous studio-lit portrait: a divinely pretty face with fine bones, wide eyes and a hint of a smile. A likeness taken just before marriage, I guessed, at the point of her maximum attraction: before life rolled on and trampled over the heady dreams.

"Did you tell him we'd help him for nothing?" I asked.

"No, I effing didn't. I don't like him, to be honest."

We sometimes did, as a firm, work for no pay: it depended on circumstances. All the partners agreed that a family in need should get help regardless, and none of us begrudged it. We never charged enough anyway to make ourselves rich, being in existence on the whole to defeat extortion, not to practice it. A flat fee, plus expenses: no percentages. Our clients knew for sure that the size of the ransom in no way affected our own reward.

The telephone rang suddenly, making everyone in the room jump. Both Tony and Rightsworth gestured to Nerrity to answer it and he walked towards it as if it were hot. I noticed that he pulled his stomach in as the muscles tightened and saw his breath become shallow. If the room had been silent I guessed we would actually have heard his heart thump. By the time he stretched out an unsteady hand to pick up the receiver Tony had the recorder running and the amplifier set so that everyone in the room could hear the caller's words.

"Hello," Nerrity said hoarsely.

"Is that you, John?" It was a woman's voice, high and anxious. "Are you expecting me?"

"Oh." Miranda jumped to her feet in confusion.

"It's Mother. I asked her . . ." Her voice trailed off as her husband held out the receiver with the murderous glare of a too suddenly released tension, and she managed to take it from him without touching him skin to skin.

"Mother?" she said, waveringly. "Yes, please do come. I thought you were coming . . ."

"My dear girl, you sounded so flustered when you telephoned earlier. Saying you wouldn't tell me what was wrong! I was worried. I don't like to interfere between you and John, you know that."

"Mother, just come."

"No, I . . ."

John Nerrity snatched the telephone out of his wife's grasp and practically shouted, "Rosemary, just come. Miranda needs you. Don't argue. Get here as fast as you can. Right?" He crashed the receiver down in annoyance, and I wondered whether or not the masterfully bossy tone would indeed fetch the parent. The telephone rang again almost immediately and Nerrity snatched it up in fury, saying, "Rosemary, I told you . . ."

"John Nerrity, is it?" a voice said. Male, loud, aggressive, threatening. Not Rosemary. My own spine tingled. Tony hovered over the recording equipment, checking the quivering needles.

"Yes," Nerrity said breathlessly, his lungs deflating.

"Listen once. Listen good. You'll find a tape in a box by your front gate. Do what it says." There was a sharp click followed by the dialing tone, and then Tony, pressing buttons, was speaking to people who were evidently telephone engineers.

"Did you get the origin of the second call?" he

asked. We read the answer on his face. "O.K.," he said resignedly. "Thanks." To Nerrity he said, "They need fifteen seconds. Better than the old days. Trouble is, the crooks know it too."

Nerrity was on his way to the front door and could presently be heard crunching across his gravel.

Alessia was looking very frail indeed. I went down on my knees by her chair and put my arms protectively around her.

"You could wait in another room," I said. "Watch television. Read a book."

"You know I can't."

"I'm sorry about all this."

She gave me a rapid glance. "You tried to get me to go home to Popsy. It's my own fault I'm here. I'm all right. I won't be a nuisance, I promise." She swallowed. "It's all so odd . . . to see it from the other side."

"You're a great girl," I said. "Popsy told me so, and she's right."

She looked a small shade less fraught and rested her head briefly on my shoulder. "You're my foundations, you know," she said. "Without you the whole thing would collapse."

"I'll be here," I said. "But seriously it would be best if you and Miranda went into the kitchen and found some food. Get her to eat. Eat something yourself. Carbohydrate. Biscuits, cake . . . something like that."

"Fattening," she said automatically: the jockey talking.

"Best for your bodies just now though. Carbohydrates are a natural tranquilizer. It's why unhappy people eat and eat."

"You do know the most extraordinary things."

"And also," I said, "I don't want Miranda to hear what's on the tape."

"Oh." Her eyes widened as she remembered. "Pucinelli switched off that tape . . . so I couldn't hear."

"Yes. It was horrid. So will this be. The first demands are always the most frightening. The threats will be designed to pulverize. To goad Nerrity into paying anything, everything, very quickly, to save his little son. So dearest Alessia, take Miranda into the kitchen and eat cake."

She smiled a shade apprehensively and walked over to Miranda, who was sobbing periodically in isolated gulps, like hiccups, but who agreed listlessly to making a cup of tea. The two went off to their haven, and Nerrity crunched back with a brown cardboard box.

Rightsworth importantly took charge of opening it, telling everyone else to stand back. Tony's eyebrows were sardonic. Rightsworth produced a pair of clear plastic gloves and methodically put them on before carefully slitting with a penknife the heavy adhesive tape fastening the lid.

Opening the box Rightsworth first peered inside, then put an arm in and brought out the contents: one cassette tape, in plastic case, as expected.

Nerrity looked at it as if it would bite and waved vaguely at an ornate stretch of gilt and padded wall unit, some of whose doors proved to be screening a bank of expensive stereo. Rightsworth found a slot for the cassette, which he handled carefully with the plastic gloves, and Nerrity pushed the relevant buttons.

The voice filled the room, harsh, thunderous, uncompromising.

"Now, you, Nerrity, you listen good."

I took three quick strides and turned down the volume, on the grounds that threats fortissimo would sound even worse than threats should. Tony nodded appreciatively, but Rightsworth was irritated. The voice went on, more moderate in decibels, immoderate in content.

"We nicked your kid, Nerrity, and if you want your heir back in one piece you do what you're told like a good boy. Otherwise we'll take our knife out, Nerrity, and slash off something to persuade you. Not his hair, Nerrity. A finger maybe. Or his little privates. Those for sure. Understand, Nerrity? No messing about. This is for real.

"Now you got a horse, Nerrity. Worth a bit, we reckon. Six million. Seven. Sell it, Nerrity. Like we said, we want five million. Otherwise your kid suffers. Nice little kid, too. You don't want him screaming, do you? He'll scream with what we'll do to him.

"You get a bloodstock agent busy. We'll wait a week. One week, seven days. Seven days from now, you get that money ready in used notes, nothing bigger than twenty. We'll tell you where to leave it. You do what we tell you, or it's the castration. We'll send you a tape of what it sounds like. Slash. Rip. Scream.

"And you keep away from the police. If we think you've called in the Force, your kid's for the plastic bag. Final. You won't get his body back. Nothing. Think about it.

"Right, Nerrity. That's the message."

The voice stopped abruptly and there was a numb

minute of silence before anyone moved. I'd heard a score of ransom demands, but always, every time, found them shocking. Nerrity, like many a parent before him, was poleaxed to his roots.

"They can't . . ." he said, his mouth dry, the words gagging.

"They can," Tony said flatly. "But not if we manage it right."

"What did they say to you this afternoon?" I asked. "What's different?"

Nerrity swallowed. "The . . . the knife. That part. Before, he just said 'five million for your kid.' And I said I hadn't got five million . . . He said 'you've got a horse, so sell it.' That was all. And no police, he said that too. Five million, no police, or the boy would die. He said he'd be getting in touch. I began to shout at him . . . he just rang off."

Rightsworth took the cassette out of the recorder and put it in its box, putting that in its turn in the cardboard carton, all with exaggerated care in the plastic gloves. He would be taking the tape, he said. They would maintain the tap on Mr. Nerrity's telephone, he said. They would be working on the case, he said.

Nerrity, highly alarmed, begged him to be careful; and begging didn't come easy, I thought, to one accustomed to bully. Rightsworth said with superiority that every care would be taken, and I could see Tony thinking, as I was, that Rightsworth was treating the threats too pompously and was not, in consequence, a brilliant detective.

When he had gone, Nerrity, his first fears subsiding, poured himself another stiff gin and tonic, again with ice and lemon. He picked the ice out of a bucket with a pair of tongs. Tony watched with incredulity.

"Drink?" he said to us as an afterthought.

We shook our heads.

"I'm not paying that ransom," he said defensively. "For one thing, I can't. The horse is due to be sold in any case. It's four years old, and going to stud. I don't need to get a bloodstock agent, it's being handled already. Some of the shares have already been sold, but I'll hardly see a penny. Like I said, I've got business debts." He took a deep drink. "You may as well know, that horse is the difference to me between being solvent and bankrupt. Biggest stroke of luck ever, the day I bought it as a yearling." He swelled slightly, giving himself a mental pat on the back, and we could both see an echo of the expansiveness with which he must have waved many a gin and tonic while he recounted his good fortune.

"Isn't your business," I said, "a limited company? If you'll excuse my asking."

"No, it isn't."

"What is your business?" Tony asked him casually.

"Importer. Wholesale. One or two wrong decisions . . ." He shrugged. "Bad debts. Firms going bankrupt, owing me money. On my scale of operations it doesn't take much of a recession to do a damned lot of damage. Ordinand will clear everything. Set me to rights. Fund me for future trading. Ordinand is a bloody miracle." He made a furious chopping gesture with his free hand. "I'm damned if I'm going to throw away my entire life for those bloody kidnappers."

He'd said it, I thought. He'd said aloud what had

been festering in his mind ever since Miranda's phone call. He didn't love his son enough for the sacrifice.

"How much is Ordinand worth?" Tony said unemotionally.

"They got it right. Six million, with luck. Forty shares at a hundred and fifty thousand each." He drank, the ice clinking.

"And how much do you need to straighten your business?"

"That's a bloody personal question."

Tony said patiently, "If we're going to negotiate for you, we have to know just what is or isn't possible."

Nerrity frowned at his lemon slice, but then said, "Four and a half, thereabouts, will keep me solvent. Five would clear all debts. Six will see me soundly based for the future."

Tony glanced about him at the overplush room. "What about this house?"

Nerrity looked at him as if he were a financial baby. "Every brick mortgaged," he said shortly.

"Any other assets?"

"If I had any other bloody assets I'd have cashed them by now."

Tony and I exchanged glances, then Tony said, "I reckon we might get your kid back for less than half a million. We'll aim lower, of course. First offer a hundred thousand. Then take it from there."

"But they won't . . . they said . . ." Nerrity stopped, floundering.

"The best thing," I said, "would be to get yourself onto the City pages of the newspapers. Go into print telling the world there's nothing like a Derby winner for keeping the bailiffs out."

"But . . ."

"Yes," I interrupted. "Maybe not in the normal way good for business. But your creditors will be sure they'll be paid, and the kidnappers will be sure they won't. Next time they get in touch, they'll demand less. Once they acknowledge to themselves that the proceeds will be relatively small compared with their first demand, that's what they'll settle for. Better than nothing, sort of thing."

"But they'll harm Dominic . . ."

I shook my head. "It's pretty doubtful, not if they're sure they'll make a profit in the end. Dominic's their only guarantee of that profit. Dominic, alive and whole. They won't destroy or damage their asset in any way if they're convinced you'll pay what you can. So when you talk to the press, make sure they understand—and print—that there'll be a margin over, when Ordinand is sold. Say that the horse will wipe out all your debts and then some."

"But . . ." he said again.

"If you have any difficulty approaching the City editors, we can do that for you," I said.

He looked from Tony to me with the uncertainty of a commander no longer in charge.

"Would you?" he said.

We nodded. "Straight away."

"Andrew will do it," Tony said. "He knows the City. Cut his teeth in Lloyds, our lad here." Neither he nor I explained how lowly my job there had been. "Very smooth, our Andrew, in his city suit," Tony said.

Nerrity looked me up and down. I hadn't replaced

my tie, although I'd long unrolled my trousers. "He's young," he said disparagingly.

Tony silently laughed. "As old as the pyramids," he said. "We'll get your nipper back, don't you fret."

Nerrity said uncomfortably, "It's not that I don't like the boy. Of course I do." He paused. "I don't see much of him. Five minutes in the morning. He's in bed when I get home. Weekends . . . I work, go to the races, go out with business friends. Don't have much time for lolling about."

Not much inclination, either, I diagnosed.

"Miranda dotes on him," Nerrity said, as if that were no virtue. "You'd have thought she could keep her eyes on him for five minutes, wouldn't you? I don't see how she could have been so bloody stupid."

I tried explaining about the determination of kidnappers, but it seemed to have no effect.

"It was her idea to have the kid in the first place," Nerrity grumbled. "I told her it would spoil her figure. She went on and on about being lonely. She knew what my life was like before she married me, didn't she?"

From the other side, I thought. From the office side, where his life was most intense, where hers was busy and fulfilled.

"Anyway, we had the kid." He made another sharply frustrated gesture. "And now . . . this."

Miranda's mother arrived conveniently at that point, and shortly afterwards I put Alessia in my car and talked to Tony quietly in the garden.

"Thursday, tomorrow," I said. "Wittering's a sea-

side place. Good chance the same people will be on the
beach tomorrow as today, wouldn't you think?''

"The super in Chichester, would he buy that?"
Tony asked.

"Yes, I'm sure."

"I wouldn't mind a day myself of sitting on the
effing pebbles."

"The tide's going out in the mornings," I said.
"How about if you take the stuff down to Eagler on
the train, and I'll join you for a paddle when I've
buzzed up the City?"

He nodded. "See you at the Breakwater Hotel,
then?"

"Yeah. Tell them at Reception that we're taking
over Miranda's room. She's booked in until Saturday. Tell them the boy's ill, she's had to take him
home, we're her brothers, we've come down to collect her clothes and her car . . . and pay her bill."

"I don't know that sitting around in the Breakwater too long will do much good."

I grinned in the darkness. "Make a change from
the switchboard, though."

"You're an effing rogue, I always knew it."

He vanished into the shadows without noise, de-
parting on foot to his distantly parked car, and I
climbed in beside Alessia and pointed our nose towards Lambourn.

I asked if she were hungry and would like to stop
somewhere for a late dinner, but she shook her head.
"Miranda and I ate cornflakes and toast until our
eyes crossed. And you were right, she seemed a bit
calmer by the time we left. But oh . . . when I think
of that little boy . . . so alone, without his mother
. . . I can't bear it."

* * *

I spent the next morning in Fleet Street swearing various business-page editors to secrecy and enlisting their aid, and then drove back to West Wittering, reflecting that I'd spent at least twelve of the past thirty hours with my feet on the pedals.

Arriving at the Breakwater in jeans and sports shirt, I found Tony had checked in and left a message that he was out on the beach. I went down there and came across him sitting on a gaudy towel, wearing swimming trunks and displaying a lot of impressive keep-fit muscle. I dropped down beside him on a towel of my own and watched the life of the beach ebb and flow.

"Your Eagler already had the same idea," Tony said. "Half the holidaymakers on this patch of sand are effing plainclothesmen quizzing the other half. They've been out here since breakfast."

It appeared that Tony had got on very well with Eagler. Tony considered he had "constructive effing ideas," which was Tony's highest mark of approval. "Eagler's already sorted out what arson device was used to fire the dinghy. The dinghy was stolen, what a surprise."

Some small children were digging a new sand-castle where Dominic's had been wiped out by the tide.

"A little girl of about eight gave Miranda the kidnapper's note," I said. "What do you bet she's still here?"

Without directly answering Tony rose to his feet and loped down onto the sand, where he was presently passing the time of day with two agile people kicking a football.

"They'll look for her," he said, returning. "They've found plenty who saw the boat. Some who saw who left it. The one with the green shorts has a stat of Giuseppe in his pocket, but no luck with that, so far."

The two boys who had helped me carry the boat up from the grasp of the tide came by and said hello, recognizing me.

"Hi," I said. "I see the boat's gone, what was left of it."

One of them nodded. "We came back along here after supper and there were two fisherman types winching it onto a pickup truck. They didn't know whose it was. They said the coastguards had sent them to fetch it into a yard in Itchenor."

"Do you live here?" I asked.

They shook their heads. "We rent a house along there for August." One of them pointed eastwards, along the beach. "We come every year. Mum and Dad like it."

"You're brothers?" I asked.

"Twins, actually. But fraternal, as you see."

They picked up some pebbles and threw them at an empty Coke can for target practice, and presently moved off.

"Gives you a thought or two, doesn't it?" Tony said.

"Yes."

"Eagler wanted to see us anyway at about five," he said. "In the Silver Sail Café in that place the boy mentioned. Itchenor. Sounds like some disgusting effing disease."

The football-kicker in green shorts was presently

talking to a little girl whose mother bustled up in alarm and protectively shepherded her nestling away.

"Never mind," Tony said. "That smashing bit of goods in the pink bikini over there is a policewoman. What'll you bet green shorts will be talking to her in two effing ticks?"

"Not a pebble," I said.

We watched while green shorts got into conversation with pink bikini. "Nicely done," Tony said approvingly. "Very natural."

The pink-bikini girl stopped looking for shells exclusively and started looking for small girls as well, and I took my shirt off and began turning a delicate shade of lobster.

No dramas occurred on the beach. The hot afternoon warmed to teatime. The football-kickers went off across the breakwaters and the pink bikini went in for a swim. Tony and I stood up, stretched, shook and folded our towels, and in good holidaymaker fashion got into my car and drove westwards to Itchenor.

Eagler, inconspicuous in an open-necked shirt, baggy gray flannels and grubby tennis shoes, was drinking tea in the Silver Sail and writing a picture postcard.

"May we join you?" I asked politely.

"Sit down, laddie, sit down."

It was an ordinary sort of café; sauce bottles on the tables, murals of sailing boats round the walls, brown tiled floor, plastic stacking chairs in blue. A notice by a cash desk stated "The best chips on the coast" and a certain warm oiliness in the atmosphere tended to prove their popularity.

"My W.P.C. found your girl child," Eagler said, sticking a stamp on his postcard. "Name of Sharon

Wellor, seven years old, staying in a guest house until Saturday. She couldn't describe the man who asked her to deliver the note. She says he gave her a roll of fruit pastilles, and she's scared now because her mother's always told her never to take sweets from strangers.''

"Did she know whether he was old or young?" I asked.

"Everyone over twenty is old to a seven-year-old," Eagler said. "She told my W.P.C. where she's staying, though, so perhaps we'll ask again." He glanced at us. "Come up with any more ideas, have you?"

"Yeah," Tony said. "Kidnappers often don't transport their victims very far from their snatching point. Lowers the risk."

"In holiday resorts," I said mildly. "Half the houses are for rent."

Eagler fiddled aimlessly with his teaspoon. "Thousands of them," he said dryly.

"But one of them might have been rented sometime last week."

We waited, and after a while he nodded. "We'll do the legwork. Ask the travel agents, estate agents, local papers." He paused, then said without emphasis, "The kid may have been taken off in a boat."

Tony and I paid fast attention.

"There was a motorboat there," Eagler said. "One of those putt-putt things for hire by the hour. My detective constables were told that when the dinghy went on fire the other boat was bobbing round in the shallows with no one in it, but a man in swimming trunks standing knee-deep in the water holding on to it by the bows. Then, our informants said, the dinghy suddenly went up in flames, very fast, with a whoosh, and everyone ran towards it, naturally. Our informants said that afterwards the motorboat had gone, which they thought perfectly normal as its time was probably up.'' He stopped, looking at us neutrally but with a smile of satisfaction plainly hovering.

''Who were your informants?'' I asked.

The smile almost surfaced. ''A ten-year-old canal digger and his grandmother.''

''Very reliable,'' I said.

''The boat was blue, clinker built, with a number seventeen in white on its bow and stern.''

''And the man?''

''The man was a man. They found the boat more interesting.'' He paused again. ''There's a yard here in Itchenor with boats like that for hire. The trouble is they've got only ten. They've never had one with seventeen on it, ever.''

''But who's to know?'' Tony said.

''Look for a house with a boat shed,'' I murmured.

Eagler said benignly, ''It wouldn't hurt, would it, to find the kid?''

''If they spot anyone looking they'll be off in a flash,'' I said, ''and it would be dangerous for the boy.''

Eagler narrowed his eyes slightly at our alarm. ''We'll go round the agencies,'' he said. ''If we turn up anything likely on paper we won't surround it without telling you first. How's that?''

We both shook our heads.

''Better to avoid raids and sieges if possible,'' I said.

Tony said to Eagler, ''If you find a likely house on paper, let me suss it out. I've had all sorts of experience at this sort of thing. I'll tell you if the kid's there. And if he is, I'll get him out.''

Twelve

There was an urgent message from the office at the Breakwater Hotel for me to telephone Alessia, which I did.

"Miranda's distracted . . . she's in pieces," she said, sounding strung up herself beyond sympathy to near snapping point. "It's awful . . . She's telephoned me three times, crying terribly, begging me to get you to do something . . ."

"Sweet Alessia," I said. "Take three deep breaths and sit down if you're standing up."

"Oh . . ." Her cough of surprise had humor in it, and after a pause she said, "All right. I'm sitting. Miranda's dreadfully frightened. Is that better?"

"Yes," I said, half smiling. "What's happened?"

"Superintendent Rightsworth and John Nerrity are making a plan and won't listen to Miranda, and she's desperate to stop them. She wants you to make them see they mustn't." Her voice was still high and anxious, the sentences coming fast.

"What's the plan?" I asked.

"John is going to pretend to do what the kidnappers tell him. Pretend to collect the money. Then when the pretend money is handed over, Superintendent Rightsworth will jump on the kidnappers and make them say where Dominic is." She gulped audibly. "That's what went wrong . . . with me . . . in Bologna . . . isn't it?"

"Yes," I said, "an ambush at the R.V. is to my mind too high a risk."

"What's the R.V.?"

"Sorry. Rendezvous. The place where the ransom is handed over."

"Miranda says John doesn't want to pay the ransom and Superintendent Rightsworth is telling him not to worry, he doesn't need to."

"Mm," I said, "well, I can see why Miranda's upset. Did she talk to you from the telephone in her own house?"

"What? Oh, my goodness, it's tapped, isn't it, with the police listening to every word?"

"It is indeed," I said dryly.

"She was up in her bedroom. I suppose she didn't think. And . . . heavens . . . she said John was regretting calling in Liberty Market, because you were advising him to pay. Superintendent Rightsworth has assured him the police can take care of everything, there's no need to have outsiders putting their oar in."

The phrase had an authentic Rightsworth ring.

"Miranda says John is going to tell Liberty Market he doesn't want their help anymore. He says it's a waste of money . . . and Miranda's frantic."

"Mm," I said. "If she telephones you again, try to remind her the phone's tapped. If she has any

sense she'll ring you back from somewhere else.
Then reassure her that we'll do our best to change
her husband's mind.''

"But how?" Alessia said, despairing.

"Get our chairman to frighten him silly, I
daresay," I said. "And I never said that. It's for
your ears only."

"Will it work?" Alessia said doubtfully.

"There are also people who can overrule Rightsworth."

"I suppose there are." She sounded happier with
that. "Shall I tell Miranda to telephone directly to
you, in your office?"

"No," I said. "I'll be moving about. When
you've heard from her, leave a message again for me
to call you, and I will."

"All right." She sounded tired. "I haven't been
able to think of anything else all day. Poor Miranda.
Poor, poor little boy. I never really understood until
now what Papa went through because of me."

"Because of your kidnappers," I said, "and for
love of you, yes."

After a pause she said, "You're telling me again
. . . I must feel no guilt."

"That's right," I said. "No more guilt than
Dominic."

"It's not easy . . ."

"No," I agreed. "But essential."

She asked if I would come to lunch on Sunday,
and I said yes if possible but not to count on it.

"You will get him back alive, won't you?" she
said finally, none of the worry dissipated; and I said
"Yes," and meant it.

"Goodbye, then . . ."

"Goodbye," I said. "And love to Popsy."

Liberty Market, I reflected, putting down the receiver, might have an overall success rate as high as ninety-five percent, but John Nerrity seemed to be heading himself perilously towards the other tragic five. Perhaps he truly believed, perhaps even Rightsworth believed, that an ambush at the drop produced the best results. And so they did, if capturing some of the kidnappers was the overriding aim.

There had been a case in Florida, however, when the police had ambushed the man who picked up the ransom and shot him down as he ran to escape, and only because the wounded man relented and told where his victim was a few seconds before he slid into a final coma had they ever found the boy alive. He had been left in the trunk of a parked car, and would slowly have suffocated if the police had fired a fraction straighter.

I told Tony of Nerrity's plans and he said disgustedly, "What is he, an effing optimist?" He bit his thumbnail. "Have to find that little nipper, won't we?"

"Hope to God."

"Better chance in this country than anywhere else, of course."

I nodded. Among well-meaning peoples, like the British, kidnappers were disadvantaged. Their crime was reviled, not tolerated, and the population not afraid of informing. Once the victim was safely home, the trace-and-capture machinery had proved excellent.

Finding the hideout before the payoff was easier in Britain than in Italy, but still dauntingly difficult: and most successes along that line had come from coincidence, from nosy neighbors, and from guessing who had done the kidnap because of the close knowledge inadvertently revealed of the victim's private life.

"No one knew my daughter was going to be at that dance except her boyfriend," one grief-stricken father had told us: and sure enough her apparently shattered boyfriend had organized the extortion—that time without the girl's knowledge, which wasn't always so. Collusion with the "victim" had to be considered every time, human greed being what it was. The girl in that case had been found and freed without a ransom being paid, but she'd had a worse time in captivity than Alessia and the last I'd heard she was being treated for deep prolonged depression.

"I think I'll just mosey around a bit where the boats are," Tony said. "Can I borrow your car? You can use Miranda's if you're desperate. Do you mind if I go home later for some gear? I'll see you at effing breakfast."

"Don't crunch it," I said, giving him the keys.

"As if I would."

I spent the evening eating the hotel's very reasonable dinner and packing Miranda's belongings. Dominic's clothes, quiet and folded, filled a neat small suitcase. I put his cuddly toys, a teddy and a Snoopy, in beside them, and shut the lid: and thought of him, so defenseless, so frightened, and knew that it was because of people like him and Alessia that what I was doing was a job for life.

In view of John Nerrity's change of heart I guessed he wouldn't be too pleased with the morning newspapers' money columns, where the financial editors had done him proud. The word "Nerrity" sprang out in large black letters from every paper I'd visited, which were mostly of the sort that I guessed the writer of the kidnap note would read.

"Nerrity Home and Dried," "Nerrity's Nag to the Rescue," "Nerrity Floats on Stud," they said: and "Nerrity Solvent by Short Head." To kidnappers nervously scanning the press for signs of police activity, the bad news couldn't be missed. Creditors were zeroing in on the Ordinand proceeds, and there would be precious little left for other sharks.

Eagler telephoned me in Miranda's room while I was still reading. "These papers . . . Is this your doing?" he asked.

"Er, yes."

He chuckled. "I thought I detected the fine hand. Well, laddie, we're doing a spot of rummaging around the classifieds in the local rags of a week to two weeks ago, and we're checking through all the properties to rent. We'll have a partial list for you anytime today." He paused. "Now I'm putting a lot of faith in your friend Tony Vine, and I want to be sure it's not misplaced."

"He's an ex-S.A.S.," I said. "A sergeant."

"Ah." He sounded relieved.

"He prefers working at night."

"Does he now." Eagler was almost purring. "I should have a fairly complete list for you by late this afternoon. Will you fetch it?"

We arranged time and place, and rang off; and when I went downstairs to breakfast Tony was walking in through the front door, yawning.

Over bacon, eggs, and kippers he recounted what he'd found. "Did you know there's a whole internal water system behind the coast here? Itchenor Creek goes all the way to Chichester. But there's a lock some way up, and our fellows didn't go through it." He chewed. "I hired a rowing boat. Sneaked around a bit. Reckon it's an effing needle in a haystack we're after. There's dozens, hundreds of likely houses. Holiday flats. Chalets. You name it. And on top of that the water goes clear to somewhere called Hayling Island, with thousands more little bungalows, and there are uncountable places where a car could have met the boat and taken the nipper anywhere."

I gloomily ate some toast and told him about Eagler's impending list.

"O.K. then," Tony said. "I'll swim this morning, sleep this afternoon, work tonight, O.K.?"

I nodded and passed him one of the newspapers. Tony read the financial news over the rim of his cup of tea. "You hit the effing bull's-eye. No one could miss it," he said.

Nerrity himself certainly hadn't missed it. Gerry Clayton telephoned to say that Nerrity was furious and insisting we drop the case. He wanted nothing more to do with Liberty Market.

"He admitted he'd agreed to your getting the story into the papers," Gerry said. "But he didn't think it would happen so quickly, and he had intended to cancel it."

"Too bad."

"Yes. So officially you and Tony can break off and come home."

"No," I said. "We're working for Mrs. Nerrity now. She specifically asked for us to continue."

Gerry's voice had a smile in it. "I thought you

might, but it makes it all a damn sight more tricky. Both of you . . . take care.''

"Yeah,'' I said. ''Fold some nice paper. Try a boat.''

"Boat?''

"A boat to thrust a small boy into so that you can put a tarpaulin or some such over him, a boat to chug noisily away over the breaking waves so that no one can hear him crying out.''

"Is that how it was done?'' Gerry asked soberly.

"We think so, yes.''

"Poor little blighter,'' Gerry said.

Tony and I in true holiday-making fashion spent the morning in or out of water, although the day was not so warm nor the beach so fruitfully crowded. The policewoman, now in a white bikini, came to splash with us in the shallows but said she hadn't been able to find anyone who had seen Dominic carried off. "Every single person seems to have been looking at the dinghy,'' she said disgustedly. "And all we know about that is that it was stranded on the sand when the tide went out, and it had a large piece of paper taped to the seat saying 'Don't touch the boat, we'll be back for it soon.' ''

"Didn't someone say they'd seen who left it?'' I asked.

"Well, yes, but that was a boy playing up on the shingle, and all he could say was that they were two men in shorts and bright orange rainproof sailing jackets, who had pulled the dinghy up the sand a bit and been busy round it for a while and then had walked off northwest along the beach. The boy went down to the dinghy soon afterwards and read the note, and after that he went off to get an ice cream.

He wasn't here in the afternoon when it went up in flames, much to his disgust. When he came back it was burnt and black.''

The policewoman was shivering in the rising breeze and turning a pale shade of blue. ''Time for a sweater and thick socks,'' she said cheerfully. ''And I might as well chat up the ancient ladies living in the Haven Rest Home along there.'' She pointed. ''They've nothing to do but look out of the windows.''

Tony and I picked up our belongings and moved to the shelter of the hotel, and in the afternoon while the clouds thickened overhead he slept undisturbed in Miranda's bed.

At five I drove to Chichester to collect the list of rentals from Eagler: he came to meet me himself, looking insignificant and slow, and climbed into the passenger seat at my side.

''These top eleven are the most promising,'' he said, pointing. ''They are collected from all the agencies we could think of. They are all holiday homes on or near the water and they were all rented at the last minute. The weather was so bad in July and at the beginning of August that there were more properties than usual available, and then when it turned warmer there was a rush.''

I nodded. ''Miranda herself decided to come here only a few days in advance. The hotel had had cancellations because of the weather, and could take her.''

''I wonder what would have happened if she hadn't come,'' Eagler said thoughtfully.

''They'd have grabbed him at home.''

"You'd have thought they'd have found it easier to wait until he was back there."

"Kidnappers don't try to make things easy for themselves," I said mildly. "They plan to the last inch. They spend money. They're obsessional. There's never anything casual about a kidnap. Kidnappers would see a good chance of success while the child was in charge of his mother alone down here, and I bet once they'd done the planning they waited day after day for the right minute. If it hadn't presented itself they would have followed Miranda home and thought up a new plan. Or perhaps have reverted to a former plan which hadn't so far borne fruit. You never can tell. But if they'd wanted him, they would have got him in the end."

"How would they have known she was coming here?" Eagler asked.

"Kidnappers watch," I said. "They're obsessional about that, too. What conclusion would you come to if you saw Miranda load suitcases and a beach chair into her car, strap Dominic into his seat, and drive away waving?"

"Hm."

"You'd follow," I said.

"I expect so."

"Miranda in her nice red car, driving at a moderate speed, as mothers do with their children in the back."

"True," he said. He stirred. "Anyway, the next bunch of houses on the list are all at least one street away from the water, and the last lot are further inland, but still in the coastline villages. Beyond that . . ." he stopped, looking doubtful. "This whole section of Sussex is one big holiday area."

"We'll try these," I said.

"I've some good men," Eagler suggested. "They could help."

I shook my head. "They might just possibly inquire of one of the kidnappers themselves if they'd heard a child crying. That's happened before. The kidnapper said no, and the child turned up dead on some waste ground a week later. It happened in Italy. The police caught the kidnappers in the end, and the kidnappers said they'd panicked when they found the police were so close to their hideout."

Eagler stroked thumb and forefinger down his nose. "All right," he said. "We'll do it your way." He glanced at me sideways. "But to be honest, I don't think you'll succeed."

Tony, back at the hotel, wasn't particularly hopeful either. He looked judiciously at the first eleven addresses and said he would first locate them by land and then approach by rowing boat, and those eleven alone would take him all night. He said he would take my car, which still had his gear stowed in it, and he'd be back in the morning.

"Sleep tomorrow, try again tomorrow night," he said. "That brings us to Sunday. Hope those effing kidnappers meant it about giving Nerrity a week to collect the dough. They might be twitchy after the newspapers. Might advance the time of the drop. Hope effing not."

He ate little for dinner and drove away when it was getting dark. I telephoned Alessia for news of Miranda, but except for her having come out of the house to call Alessia, nothing much had happened. Miranda continued distraught. The kidnappers had not been in touch again. John Nerrity still appeared

to have faith in the ambush plan and had said he
thought Miranda's near-collapse excessive.

"I wonder how he would have reacted if it had
been Ordinand who'd been kidnapped," I said.

Alessia nearly laughed. "Don't talk of it. And it's
been done."

"Without success," I agreed. "Enough to put the
horsenappers off for life."

"Would your firm work to free a horse?" she
asked curiously.

"Sure. Extortion is extortion, however many legs
the victim has. Ransoms can be negotiated for anything."

"Paintings?"

"Anything anyone cares about."

"Like 'I'll give you your ball back if you pay me a
penny'?"

"Exactly like that."

"Where are you?" she said. "Not at home . . . I
tried there."

"An evening off," I said. "I'll tell you when I see
you."

"Do come on Sunday."

"Yes, I'll try."

We spent more time than necessary saying
goodbye. I thought that I could easily have talked to
her all evening, and wished vaguely that she felt secure enough to travel and drive alone.

Tony came back soon after dawn, waking me from
a shallow sleep.

"There are two possibles out of those eleven
places," he said, stripping off for a shower. "Nine of
them are occupied by bona-fide effing holiday-

makers. I went into four to make absolutely sure, but there they were, tucked up nice and unsuspecting, dads, mums, grannies, and kids, all regular law-abiding citizens.''

Tony's skill, as he immodestly said, would make any professional night burglar look like a herd of elephants. ''A creeper as good as me,'' I'd heard him say, ''can touch a person in bed and get them to turn over to stop them snoring. I could take the polish off their nails, let alone the wallets from under the pillows. Good thing I'm effing honest.''

I waited while he stepped into the shower and sluiced lavishly about. ''There's two of those places,'' he said, reappearing eventually and toweling his sandy-brown hair, ''that gave me bad vibes. One of them's got some sort of electronic gadget guarding the door: it sent my detection gear into a tizzy. I'd guess it's one of those do-it-yourself alarms you can buy anywhere to stop hotel creepers fitting you up while you're sleeping off the mickey the barman slipped you.'' He dried his neck. ''So I left a couple of bugs on that one, and we'll go back soon and listen in.''

He wrapped the towel round his body like a sarong and sat on Miranda's bed. ''The other one's got no electronic gadgets that I could see, but it's three stories high. Boat shed on the ground floor. Empty. Just water and effing fish. Above that, rooms overlooking the creek. Above that, more rooms. There's a sort of scrubby paved garden on two sides. Not much cover. I didn't fancy going in. Anyway I stuck two bugs on it, one on each of the two upper floors. So we'll listen to them as well.''

''Cars?'' I said.

"Can't tell." He shook his head. "Neither place has a garage. There were cars along the streets." He stood up and began to dress. "Come on then," he said. "Get out of the effing pit, and let's go fishing."

He meant it literally, it seemed. By eight-thirty we were out on Itchenor Creek in the chilly morning in his rented rowing boat, throwing lines with maggots on hooks over the side.

"Are you sure this is the right bait?" I said.

"Who cares? Bass swallow bare hooks sometimes, silly buggers."

He paddled the boat along like a born waterman with one oar in a loop of rope over the stern. No creaking rowlocks, he explained. Ultra-silent travel: high on the S.A.S. curriculum.

"The tide was low at five this morning," he said. "You can't get a boat ashore at low tide in a lot of places, so if they landed the kid from that motorboat it was probably somewhere where there's water at half tide. Both our possibles qualify, just."

Our rowing boat drifted along on slowly flooding water. The fish disdained the maggots and there was a salty smell of seaweed.

"We're just coming to the place with the electronic bulldog," Tony said. "Hold this aerial so it looks like a fishing rod." He untelescoped about six feet of thin silvery rod and handed it over, and I found there was a line tied to the end of it with a small weight. "Chuck the weight in the water," he said, bending down to fiddle with the radio receiver in what looked like a fishing-gear box. "Keep your eyes on the briny and pin back the lugs."

I did all of those things but nothing much happened. Tony grunted and did some fine tuning, but in the end he said, "The lazy so-and-so's aren't awake. The bugs are working. We'll come back when we've checked the other house."

I nodded and he paddled a good way northwards before stopping again to deploy the lines. Again we drifted on the tide, apparently intent on catching our breakfast, and Tony bent to his knobs.

The voice when it came nearly tipped me out of the boat.

"Give the little bleeder his breakfast and tape off his noise if he starts whining."

The voice—unmistakably the voice—which we had heard on the tape in John Nerrity's house. Not overloud, but crystal clear.

"My God," I said numbly, not believing it.

"Bingo," Tony said with awe. "Holy effing hell."

A different voice on the tape said, "He won't eat it. What's the point of taking it up there?"

"Son," said the first voice with exaggerated patience, "do we want our little gold mine to starve to death? No we don't. Take him his bread and jam, and shut up."

"I don't like this job," the second voice complained. "Straight up, I don't."

"You were keen enough when I put you up for it. Good work, you said; those were your words."

"I didn't reckon on the kid being so . . ."

"So what?"

"So stubborn."

"He's not that bad. Pining, most like. You concentrate on the payola and get up the bleeding stairs."

Tony flipped a couple of switches and for a while

we sat in silence listening to the faint slap of the water against our own drifting boat; and then the second voice, sounding much more distant, said, "Here you are kid, eat this."

There was no audible reply.

"Eat it," the voice said with irritation, and then, after a pause, "I'd stuff it down your throat if you were mine, you snotty little sod."

Tony said "Charming" under his breath and began to pull in the lines. "Heard enough, haven't we? That second bug is on the top floor, facing the street."

I nodded. Tony reversed his switches and the second voice, downstairs again, said, "He's just lying there staring, same as usual. Gives me the willies. Sooner we're shot of him, the better."

"Patience," the first voice said, as if humoring an idiot. "You got to let the man sell his horse. Stands to reason. One week we gave him. One week is what he'll get."

"We're not collecting the five million, though, are we?" He sounded aggrieved. "Not a chance."

"We were never going to get five million, stupid. Like Peter said, you demand five to frighten the dads and take half a million nice and easy, no bones broken."

"What if Nerrity calls in the Force, and they jump us?"

"No sign of them, is there? Be your age. Terry and Kevin, they'd spot the law the minute it put its size twelves over the doorstep. Those two, they got antennae where you've got eyes. No one at the hotel. No one at the house in Sutton. Right?"

The second voice gave an indistinguishable grumble, and the first voice answered, "Peter knows what he's doing. He's done it before. He's an expert. You just do what you're bleeding told and we'll all get rich, and I've had a bellyful of your grousing, I have, straight up."

Tony put the single oar over the stern of the boat and without fuss or hurry paddled us off towards where we'd set out, against the swirling incoming tide. I rolled up the fishing lines and unbaited the hooks, my fingers absentminded while my thoughts positively galloped.

"Don't let's tell Eagler until . . ." I said.

"No," Tony answered.

He looked across at me, half smiling. "And let's not tell the chairman either," I said. "Or Gerry Clayton."

Tony's smile came out like the sun. "I was afraid you'd insist."

"No." I paused. "You watch from the water and I'll watch from the land. O.K.? And this evening we'll tell Eagler. On our terms."

"And the low profile can rest in effing peace."

"You just get that vacuum pump purring like a cat and don't fall off any high walls."

"In our report," Tony said, "we will write that the police found the hideout."

"Which they did," I said reasonably.

"Which they did," he repeated with satisfaction.

Neither Tony nor I were totally committed to the advice-only policy of the firm, though we both adhered to it more or less and agreed that in most circumstances it was prudent. Tony with his exceptional skills tended always to be more actively involved than I, and his reports were peppered with phrases like "it was discovered" and "as it happened" and never with the more truthful "I planted a dozen illegal bugs and heard . . ." or "I let off a smoke canister and under its cover . . ."

Tony steered the boat back to where we'd left the car and rapidly set up a duplicate receiver to work through the car's aerial.

"There you are," he said, pointing. "Left switch for the lower floor bug, middle switch for the top floor. Don't touch the dials. Right switch, up for me to talk to you, down for you to talk to me. O.K.?"

He dug around in the amazing stores he called his gear and with a nod of pleasure took out a plastic lunch box. "Long-term subsistence supplies," he said, showing me the contents. "Nut bars, beef jerky, vitamin pills . . . keep you fighting fit for weeks."

"This isn't the South American outback," I said mildly.

"Saves a lot of shopping, though." He grinned and stowed the lunch box in the rowing boat along with a plastic bottle of water. "If the worst should happen and they decide to move the kid, we're in dead trouble."

I nodded. Trouble with the law, with Liberty Market and with our own inescapable guilt.

"And let's not forget," he added slowly, "that somewhere around we have Terry and Kevin and Peter, all with their antennae quivering like effing mad, and you never know whether that crass bastard Rightsworth won't drive up to Nerrity's house with his blue light flashing."

"He's not that crazy."

"He's smug. Self-satisfied. Just as dangerous."

He put his head on one side, considering. "Anything else?"

"I'll go back to the hotel, pay the bill, collect the cases."

"Right. Give me a buzz when you're on station." He stepped into the boat and untied its painter. "And, by the way, do you have a dark sweater? Black, high neck?"

"Yes, I brought one."

"Good. See you tonight."

I watched him paddle away, a shortish figure of great physical economy, every movement deft and sure. He waved goodbye briefly, and I turned the car and got on with the day.

Thirteen

The hours passed slowly with the mixture of tension and boredom that I imagined soldiers felt when waiting before battle. Half of the time my pulse rate was up in the stratosphere, half the time I felt like sleep. At only one point did the watch jerk from standby to nerve-racking, and that was at midday.

For most of the morning I had been listening to the bug on the lower of the two floors, not parking the whole time in one place but moving about and stopping for a while in any of the streets within range. The two kidnappers had repeated a good deal of what we'd already heard; grouse, grouse, shut up.

Dominic at one point had been crying.

"The kid's whining," the first voice said.

I switched to the top floor bug and heard the lonely heartbreaking grizzle, the keening of a child who'd lost hope of being given what he wanted. No one came to talk to him, but presently his voice was obliterated by pop music.

I switched to the lower bug again and felt my muscles go into knots.

A new voice was speaking, ". . . a bloke sitting in a car a couple of streets away, just sitting there. I don't like it. And he's a bit like one of the people staying in the hotel."

The first-voice kidnapper said decisively, "You go and check him out, Kev. If he's still there, come right back. We're taking no bleeding risks. The kid goes down the chute."

The second-voice kidnapper said, "I've been sitting at this ruddy window all morning. There's been no one in sight here, sussing us out. Just people walking, not looking."

"Where did you leave the car?" Kevin demanded. "You've moved it."

"It's in Turtle Street."

"That's where this bloke is sitting."

There was silence among the kidnappers. The bloke sitting in the car in Turtle Street, his heart lurching, started his engine and removed himself fast.

A red light on Tony's radio equipment began flashing, and I pressed the switch to talk to him. "I heard," I said. "Don't worry, I'm on my way. Talk to you when I can."

I drove a mile and pulled up in the car park of a busy pub, and beat my ears to catch the much fainter transmissions.

"The bloke's gone," a voice eventually said.

"What do you reckon, Kev?"

The reply was indistinguishable.

"There hasn't been a smell of the Force. Not a flicker." The first-voice kidnapper sounded as if he were trying to reassure himself as much as anyone else. "Like Peter said, they can't surround this place without us seeing, and it takes eight seconds, that's all, to put the kid down the chute. You know it, I know it, we practiced. There's no way the police would find anything here but three blokes having a bleeding holiday and a little gamble on the cards."

There were some more indecipherable words, then the same voice. "We'll both watch, then. I'll go upstairs, ready. You, Kev, you walk round the bleeding town and see if you can spot that bloke hanging about. If you see him, give us a bell, then we'll decide. Peter won't thank us if we panic. We got to give the goods back breathing, that's what he said. Otherwise we get nothing, savvy, and I don't want to have gone through all this aggravation for a hole in the bleeding pocket."

I couldn't hear the replies, but first-voice seemed to have prevailed. "Right then. Off you go, Kev. See you later."

I went inside the pub where I was parked and ate a sandwich with fingers not far from trembling. The low profile, I judged, had never been more justified or more essential, and I'd risked Dominic's life by not sticking to the rules.

The problem with dodging Kevin was that I didn't know what he looked like while he could spot me easily, and probably he knew the color, make, and number of my car. Itchenor was too small for handy hiding places like multi-story parks. I concluded that as I couldn't risk being seen I would have to give the place a miss altogether, and drove by a roundabout route to reach Itchenor Creek at a much higher point, nearer Chichester. I could no longer hear the bugs, but hoped to reach Tony down the water; and he responded to my first inquiry with a faint voice full of relief.

"Where are you?" he demanded.

"Up the creek."

"You've said it."

"What's happened in the house?"

"Nothing. Whatever that chute is, the goods have not yet gone down it. But they're still quivering like effing jellyfish." He paused. "Effing bad luck, them having their car in that street."

He was excusing me. I was grateful. I said, "I'd been there only ten minutes."

"Way it goes. Kev is back with them, incidentally."

"I'll be here, if you need me."

"O.K.," he said. "And by the way, it was the one called Peter who picked the goods up. Sweet as a daisy, they said. Peter phones them every day and apparently might go there himself tomorrow or the day after. Pity we can't wait."

"Too risky."

"Yeah."

We agreed on a time and place for me to meet him, and switched off to conserve the power packs he had with him in the boat. Listening to the bugs was far more important, and, besides, drained the batteries less.

There was always the slight chance with radio that someone somewhere would be casually listening on the same channel, but I reviewed what we'd said and thought it wouldn't have enlightened or alarmed anyone except the kidnappers themselves, even if we had, on the whole, sounded like a couple of thieves.

I stayed by the water all afternoon, in or near the car, but heard no more from Tony, which was in itself a sign that the status was still quo. At a few minutes to five I drove inland to the nearest telephone box and put a call through to Eagler.

He was off duty, the station said. What was my name?

Andrew Douglas.

In that case, would I ring the following number?

I would, and did, and he answered immediately. What a terrific change, I thought fleetingly, from my disaster with Pucinelli's second-in-command.

"Can your men work at night?" I said.

"Of course."

"Tony found the kidnappers," I said.

"I don't believe it!"

"It should be possible for you to arrest them."

"Where are they?"

"Er," I said. "They are extremely alert, watching for any sign of police activity. If you turn up there too soon it would be curtains for the boy. So would you . . . um . . . act on our suggestions, without questioning them, and positively, absolutely not altering the plan in any way?"

There was a fair pause, then he said, "Am I allowed to approve this plan, or not?"

"Er . . . not."

Another pause. "Take it or leave it?"

"I'm afraid so."

"Hm." He deliberated. "The kidnappers on your terms, or not at all?"

"Yes," I said.

"I hope you know what you're doing, laddie."

"Mm," I said.

A final pause, then he said, "You're on. All right. What's the plan?"

"You need enough men to arrest at least three people," I said. "Can you get them to your Chichester main police station by one in the morning?"

"Certainly." He sounded almost affronted. "Plainclothes or in uniform?"

"I don't think it will matter."

"Armed or not?"

"It's up to you. We don't know if the kidnappers have guns."

"Right. And where are my men to go?"

"I'll call you with directions after one o'clock."

He snorted. "Not very trusting, are you?"

"I do trust you," I said. "Otherwise I wouldn't be setting this up for you at all."

"Well, well," he said. "The iron man in the kid glove, just as I rather suspected. All right, laddie, your trust won't be misplaced, and I'll play fair with you. And I'll tear the both of you to shreds if you bungle it."

"It's a deal," I said thankfully. "I'll call you at the station."

I went back to the water to wait but heard no squeak from Tony; and long after it had grown dark I drove to where we'd agreed to meet, and transferred him and his equipment from boat to car.

"They simmered down a bit in the house," he said. "They had a phone call from Peter, whoever he is, and that seemed to steady them a bit. Pity I couldn't have fixed a tap on the telephone. Anyway,

Peter apparently told them to carry on with the look-out and not dump the boy unless they could see the police outside.'' He grinned. ''Which I hope they won't effing do.''

''No.'' I stowed the power packs in the boat beside a large amorphous canvas bag. ''Our friend Eagler promised. Also . . .'' I hesitated, ''I've thought of another safeguard.''

''Tricky, aren't we?'' Tony said, when I told him. ''But yes, we can't afford a balls-up. Want a nut bar? Good as dinner.''

I ate a nut bar and we sat quietly and waited, and a good while after one o'clock I telephoned to Eagler and told him when and where to bring—and conceal—his men.

''Tell them to be silent,'' I said. ''Not just quiet. Silent. No talking. No noisy feet. Absolutely silent.''

''All right.''

''Wait for us, for Tony and me. We will come to meet you. We may be a long time after you get there, we're not sure. But please wait. Wait in silence.''

''That's all you're telling me?'' he said doubt-fully.

''We'll tell you the rest when we meet you. But it's essential to get the timing right . . . so will you wait?''

''Yes,'' he said, making up his mind.

''Good. We'll see you, then.''

I put the receiver down and Tony nodded with satisfaction.

''All right, then,'' he said. ''How are your nerves?''

''Lousy. How are yours?''

"To be honest," he said, "when I'm doing this sort of thing I feel twice as alive as usual."

I drove us gently back to Itchenor and parked in a row of cars round the corner from the kidnappers' house. There was only one street lamp, weak and away on a corner, which pleased Tony particularly, as he wanted time for us to develop night vision. He produced a tube of makeup and blacked his face and hands, and I tuned into the bugs again for a final checkup.

There was no noise from either of them.

I looked at my watch. Two-fifteen. Eagler's men were due to be in position by two-thirty. With luck the kidnappers would be asleep.

"Black your face," Tony said, giving me the tube. "Don't forget your eyelids. If you hear anyone walking along the street, squat in a corner and close your eyes. It's almost impossible to see anyone in the shadows who's doing that. Standing up and moving with your eyes open and gleaming, that's playing silly buggers."

"All right."

"And be patient. Silence takes time."

"Yes."

He grinned suddenly, the white teeth satanic in the darkened face. "What's the good of years of training if you never put them to effing use?"

We got out of the car into the quiet deserted street, and from the large shapeless canvas bag in the trunk Tony extracted his intricate and lovingly tended harness. I held the supple black material for him while he slid his arms through the armholes and fastened the front from waist to neck with a zip. It changed his shape from lithe normality to imitation hunchback, the power packs on his shoulders lumpy and grotesque.

The harness itself was a mass of pockets, both patched on and hanging, each containing something essential for Tony's purpose. Everything was in pockets because things which were merely clipped on, as in a climber's harness, clinked and jingled and also threw off gleams of light. Everything Tony used was matt black and if possible covered in slightly tacky binding, for a good grip. I'd been utterly fascinated the first time he'd shown me his kit, and had also felt privileged, as he kept its very existence private from most of the partners, for fear they would ban its use.

"O.K.?" he said.

I nodded. He seemed to have no trouble breathing, but my own lungs appeared to have stopped. He had gone in, though, with his bare hands in many a land where to be discovered was death, and I daresay a caper in an English seaside village seemed a picnic beside those.

He pressed an invisible knob somewhere up by his neck, and there was a small muffled whine as the power came on, steadying to a faint hiss inaudible at two paces.

"Fine, then," he said. "Bring the bag."

I took the canvas bag out of the trunk and quietly shut and locked the car. Then without any fuss we walked in our black clothes as far as the corner, where Tony seemed to melt suddenly into shadow and disappear. I counted ten as agreed, slid to my knees, and with caution and thumping heart took my first dim view of the target.

"Always kneel," Tony had said. "Lookouts look at head height, not near the ground."

The house's paved garden, weed-grown, was in front of me, but dimly perceived, even with night-accustomed eyes. "Move to the house wall, on the righthand side," Tony had said. "Bend double, head down. When you get there, stand up, face the wall, stay in any deep shadow you can find."

"Right."

I followed his instructions, and no one shouted, no one set up a clamor in the house.

Above me on the wall I could see, looking up, a dark irregular shadow where no one would expect a man to be. No one except people like Tony, who was climbing the bare walls with sucker clamps fastened on by a battery-powered vacuum pump. Tony who could go up a tower block, for whom two stories were a doddle.

I seemed all the same to wait for several centuries, my heart thudding in my chest. No one walked along the road; no insomniacs, no people humoring importunate dogs. Sussex-by-the-Sea was fast asleep and dreaming, with only policemen, Liberty Market and perhaps kidnappers wide awake.

Something hit me gently in the face. I put my hand up to catch it and fastened my fingers round the dangling length of black nylon rope.

"Tie the bag on, give the rope two tugs, I'll pull it up," Tony had said.

I obeyed his instructions, and the canvas holdall disappeared into the darkness above.

I waited, heart racing worse than ever. Then suddenly the bag was down with me again, but heavy, not empty. I took it into my arms and gave two more tugs on the rope. The rope itself dropped down into the shadows round my feet, and I began to pull it in awkwardly, my arms full of bag.

I didn't hear Tony come down. His skill was truly amazing. One second he wasn't there, the next moment he was, stowing the last of the released clamps into voluminous pockets. He felt for the rope I was trying to wind in and had it collected into the holdall in a flash. Then he touched me on the arm, and we both left the scrubby garden, me hunched double over my burden and Tony already sliding out of his harness. Once in the road and out of any possible sight of the house I stood upright and grasped the bag by both handles, carrying it in one hand as one normally would.

"Here," Tony said quietly. "Rub this over your face." He gave me something moist and cold, a sort of sponge, with which I wiped away a good deal of the blacking, and I could see that he too was doing the same.

We reached the car on silent feet.

"Don't slam the doors," Tony said, dumping his harness onto the front passenger seat. "We'll close them properly later."

"O.K."

I took the bag with me into the rear seats and removed its precious contents: one very small boy, knees bent to his chest, lying on his back, with coils of black nylon rope falling over his legs. He was more than normally asleep but not totally unconscious: unwakably drowsy. Uncombed blond-brown curls outlined his head, and across his mouth there was a wide band of medicated sticky tape. I wrapped him in the rug I always kept in the car, and laid him along the back seat.

"Here," Tony said, passing me a bottle and a tiny cloth over from the front seats, "this'll clean the adhesive off."

"Did they do this?" I said.

"No, I did. Couldn't risk the kid waking up and bawling." He started the car and drove off in one fluid movement, and I pulled the plaster off gently and cleaned the stickiness away.

"He was asleep," Tony said, "but I gave him a whiff of ether. Not enough to put him right out. How does he look?"

"Dopey."

"Fair enough."

He drove quietly to where I'd told Eagler to take his men, which was to another of the eleven houses on his list; to the one which had had the electronic antiburglar device, a good half mile away.

Tony stopped the car short of the place, then got out and walked off, and presently returned with Eagler himself, alone. When I saw them coming I got out of the car myself, and for a moment in the dim light Eagler looked bitterly disappointed.

"Don't worry," I said. "He's here, in the car."

Eagler bent to look as I opened a rear door gently, and then, relieved, straightened up. "We're taking him straight to his mother," I said. "She can get her own doctor. One the boy knows."

"But . . ."

"No buts," I said. "What he absolutely doesn't want is a police station full of bright lights, loud voices, and assorted officials. Fair's fair, we got the boy, you get the kidnappers. You also get the media coverage, if you don't mind. We want our two selves and Liberty Market left out of it completely. We're useful only as long as we're unknown, both to the general public and especially to all prospective kidnappers."

"All right, laddie," he said, listening and capitulating paternally. "I'll stick to the bargain. Where do we go?"

Tony gave him directions.

"I left a canister of tear-gas there," he said cheerfully. "I took it as a precaution, but I didn't need it myself. It had a timer on it." He looked at his watch. "I set it to go off seven minutes from now. There's enough in it to fill the house, more or less, so if you wait another five to ten minutes you should have a nice easy task. The air will be O.K. to breathe about then, but their eyes will be steaming . . . that is, if they haven't already come out."

Eagler listened enigmatically, neither objecting nor commending.

"The kid was on the top floor," Tony said. "He was wearing one of those harness things they put in prams. He was tied to the bed with it. I cut it off him, it's still there. Also there's some floor boards up. Mind your P.C.s don't fall down the hole. God knows where they'd get to." He fished into the car and brought five cassette tapes out of the glove compartment. "These make good listening. You play them to our friends when you have them in the nick. No one's going to confess where they came from. Bugging other people's conversations ain't gentlemanly. Andrew and I never saw these recordings before."

Eagler took the tapes, looking faintly bemused.

"That's about all then," Tony said. "Happy hunting."

He slid into the car behind the steering wheel, and before I followed him, I said to Eagler, "The kidnappers' leader is due to join them tomorrow or the day after. I don't suppose he'll come, now, but he might telephone . . . if the news doesn't break too soon."

Eagler bent down as I maneuvered myself into the rear seat. "Thanks, laddie," he said.

"And to you," I answered. "You're the best."

Tony started the car and waved to Eagler as he closed the rear door, and without more fuss we were away and on the road, taking a direction opposite to the kidnappers' house, set fair for safety.

"Wow," Tony said, relaxing five miles on. "Not a bad bit of liberating, though I say it myself."

"Fantastic," I said, "and if you go round any more corners at that speed Dominic will fall off the seat."

Tony glanced back to where I was awkwardly jammed sideways to let Dominic lie stretched out, and decided to stop the car for rearrangements, which included removing more thoroughly the black from our faces and stowing Tony's gear tidily in the trunk. When we set off again I had Dominic on my lap with his head cradled against my shoulder, and he was half grasping the cuddly teddy which I'd taken from his suitcase.

His eyes opened and fell shut occasionally, but even when it was clear the ether had worn off, he didn't wake. I wondered for a while if he'd been given sleeping pills like Alessia, but later concluded it was only the middle-of-the-night effect on the extremely young, because towards the end of the journey I suddenly found his eyes wide open, staring up at my face.

"Hello, Dominic," I said.

Tony looked over briefly. "He's awake?"

"Yes."

"Good."

I interpreted the "good" to be satisfaction that the patient had survived the anesthetic. Dominic's eyes slid slowly in Tony's direction and then came back to watch mine.

"We're taking you to your mother," I said.

"Try mummy," Tony said dryly.

"We're taking you to your mummy," I said.

Dominic's eyes watched my face, unblinking.

"We're taking you home," I said. "Here's your teddy. You'll soon be back with your mummy."

Dominic showed no reaction. The big eyes went on watching.

"You're safe," I said. "No one will hurt you. We're taking you home to your mummy."

Dominic watched.

"Talkative kid," Tony said.

"Frightened out of his wits."

"Yeah, poor little bugger."

Dominic was still wearing the red swimming trunks in which he'd been stolen away. The kidnappers had added a blue jersey, considerably too large, but no socks or shoes. He had been cold to the touch when I'd taken him out of the holdall, but his little body had warmed in the rug to the point where I could feel his heat coming through.

"We're taking you home," I said again.

He made no reply but after about five minutes sat

upright on my lap and looked out of the car window. Then his eyes came round again to look at mine, and he slowly relaxed back into his former position in my arms.

"Nearly there," Tony said. "What'll we do? It's only four. She'll pass effing out if we give her a shock at this time of night."

"She might be awake," I said.

"Yeah," he said. "Worrying about the kid. I suppose she might. Here we are, just down this road."

He turned in through the Nerrity gates, the wheels crunching on the gravel: stopped right beside the front door, and got out and rang the bell.

A light went on upstairs and after a considerable wait the front door opened four inches on a chain.

"Who is it?" John Nerrity's voice said. "What on earth do you want at this hour?"

Tony stepped closer into the light coming through the crack.

"Tony Vine . . ."

"Go away." Nerrity was angry. "I've told you . . ."

"We brought your kid back," Tony said flatly. "Do you want him?"

"What?"

"Dominic," Tony said with mock patience. "Your son."

"I . . ." He floundered.

"Tell Mrs. Nerrity," Tony said.

I imagined he must have seen her behind her husband, because very shortly the front door opened wide and Miranda stood there in a nightgown, looking gaunt. For a moment she hovered as if terrified, not daring to believe it, and I climbed out of the car with Dominic hanging on tight.

"Here he is," I said. "Safe and sound."

She stretched out her arms and Dominic slid from my embrace to hers, the rug dropping away. He wrapped his little arms round her neck and clung with his legs like a limpet, and it was as if two incomplete bodies had fused into one whole.

Neither of them spoke a word. It was Nerrity who did all the talking.

"You'd better come in, then," he said.

Tony gave me a sardonic look and we stepped through into the hall.

"Where did you find him?" Nerrity demanded. "I haven't paid the ransom . . ."

"The police found him," Tony said. "In Sussex."

"Oh."

"In conjunction with Liberty Market," I added smoothly.

"Oh." He was nonplussed, not knowing how to be grateful or how to apologize or how to say he might have been wrong in giving us the sack. Neither of us helped him. Tony said to Miranda, "Your car's still at the hotel, but we brought all your gear . . . your clothes, chair, and so on . . . back with us."

She looked at him vaguely, her whole consciousness attuned to the limpet.

"Tell Superintendent Rightsworth the boy's back," I said to Nerrity.

"Oh . . . Yes."

Dominic, seen by electric light, was a nice-looking child with a well-shaped head on a slender stalk of a neck. He had seemed light in my arms but Miranda leaned away from his weight as he sat on her hip, the two of them still entwined as if with glue.

"Good luck," I said to her. "He's a great kid."

She looked at me speechlessly, like her son.

Tony and I unloaded their seaside stuff into the hall and said we would telephone in the morning to check if everything was all right; but later, when Nerrity had finally come up with a strangled thank you and shut his door on us, Tony said, "What do you think we'd better do now?"

"Stay here," I said decisively. "Roughly on guard. There's still Terry and Peter unaccounted for, and maybe others. We'd look right idiots if they walked straight in and took the whole family hostage."

Tony nodded. "Never think the enemy have ceased hostilities, even though they've effing surrendered. Vigilance is the best defense against attack." He grinned. "I'll make a soldier of you yet."

Fourteen

For one day there was peace and quiet. Tony and I went to the office for a few hours and wrote a joint report, which we hoped would be acceptable to the assembled partners on the following morning. Apart from being misleading about the order in which Dominic's escape and the entry of the gladiators had occurred, we stuck fairly closely to the truth: as always it was in the wording itself that the less orthodox activities were glossed over.

"We deduced that the child was being held in the upper story," he wrote, without saying how the deduction had been made. "After the child had been freed, Superintendent Eagler was of the opinion that he (the child) should be reunited with his parents as soon as possible, and consequently we performed the service."

On the telephone Eagler had allayed our slightly anxious inquiries.

"Don't you fret. We took them without a fight. They were coughing and crying all over the place."

His voice smiled. "There were three of them. Two were on the top story running about, absolutely frantic, looking for the kid and not being able to see for tears. They kept saying he'd fallen down the chute."

"Did you find the chute?" I asked curiously.

"Yes. It was a circular canvas thing like they have for escapes from aircraft. It slanted from the hole in the floorboards into a small cupboard on the floor below. The door of the cupboard had been bricked up and wallpapered and there was a wardrobe standing in front of it. All freshly done, the cement wasn't thoroughly dried. Anyway, they could have slid the boy down the chute and replaced the chunk of floorboards and put a rug over the trap door, and no ordinary search would have found him."

"Would he have survived?" I asked.

"I should think so, yes, as long as they'd taken him out again, but to do that they'd have to have unbricked the doorway."

"All rather nasty," I said soberly.

"Yes, very."

Tony and I put Eagler's account of the chute into our report and decided not to tell Miranda.

Eagler also said that none of the kidnappers was talking; that they were tough, sullen, and murderously angry. None of them would give his name, address, or any other information. None of them had said a single word that could with propriety be taken down and used in evidence. All their utterances had been of the four-letter variety, and they had been sparing even with those.

"We've sent their prints to the central registry, of course, but with no results so far." He paused. "I've been listening to your tapes. Red-hot stuff. I'll pry open these fine oysters with what's on them, never fear.''

"Hope they utter pearls," I said.

"They will, laddie."

Towards midday I telephoned to Alessia to postpone the lunch invitation and was forgiven instantly.

"Miranda telephoned," she said. "She told me you brought Dominic home. She can't speak for tears, but at least this time they're mostly happy."

"Mostly?" I said.

"John and that policeman, Superintendent Rightsworth, both insisted on Dominic being examined by a doctor, and of course Miranda didn't disagree, but she says they are talking now of treatment for him, not because of his physical state, which isn't bad, but simply because he won't talk."

"What sort of treatment?"

"In hospital."

"They can't be serious!" I said with alarm.

"They say Miranda can go with him, but she doesn't like it. She's trying to persuade everyone to let Dominic stay at home with her in peace for a few days. She says she's sure he'll talk to her, if they're alone."

I reflected that once the news of his kidnap and return hit the public consciousness there would be little enough peace for a while, but that otherwise her instincts were right on the button.

I said, "Do you think you could persuade John Nerrity, referring to your own experiences, that to be carted off to hospital among strangers would be desperately disturbing for Dominic now, even if Miranda went with him, and could make him worse, not better?"

There was a silence. Then she said slowly, "If Papa had sent me to a hospital, I would have gone truly mad."

"People sometimes do awful things with the best intentions."

"Yes," she said faintly. "Are you at home?"

"No. In the office. And . . . about lunch . . . I'm very sorry . . ."

"Another day will do fine," she said absently. "I'll talk to John and ring you back."

She telephoned back when Tony and I had finished the report and he'd gone home to a well-earned sleep.

"John was very subdued, you'd be surprised," she said. "All that self-importance was in abeyance. Anyway, he's agreed to give Dominic more time, and I've asked Miranda and Dominic down to Lambourn tomorrow. Popsy's such a darling. She says it's open house for kidnap victims. She also suggested you should come as well, if you could, and I think . . . I do think it would be the best ever thing . . . if you could."

"Yes, I could," I said. "I'd like to, very much."

"Great," she said; then, reflectively, "John sounded pleased, you know, that Miranda and Dominic would be out of the house. He's so odd. You'd think he'd be delirious with joy, having his son back, and he almost seemed . . . annoyed."

"Think of your own father's state after you got home."

"Yes, but . . ." She broke off. "How very strange."

"John Nerrity," I said neutrally, "is like one of those snowstorm paperweights, all shaken up, with bits of guilt and fear and relief and meanness all floating around in a turmoil. It takes a while after something as traumatic as the last few days for everything in someone's character to settle, like the snowstorm, so to speak, and for all the old pattern to reassert."

"I'd never thought of it like that."

"Did he realize," I asked, "that the press will descend on him, as they did on you?"

"No, I don't think so. Will they?"

" 'Fraid so. Sure to. Someone down in Sussex will have tipped them off."

"Poor Miranda."

"She'll be fine. If you ring her again, tell her to hold on to Dominic tight through all the interviews and keep telling him in his ear that he's safe and that all the people will go away soon."

"Yes."

"See you tomorrow," I said.

Dominic was a big news item on breakfast television and near-headlines in the newspapers. Miranda, I was glad to see, had met the cameras with control and happiness, the wordless child seeming merely shy. John Nerrity, head back, moustache bristling, had confirmed that the sale of his Derby winner would go through as planned, though he insisted he was nowhere near bankruptcy; that the story had been merely a ploy to confound the kidnappers.

They all asked who rescued his son.

The police, John Nerrity said. No praise was too high.

Most people in the office, having seen the cover-

age, read Tony's and my report with interest, and
we both answered questions at the Monday session.
Gerry Clayton's eyebrows rose a couple of times, but
on the whole no one seemed to want to inquire too
closely into what we had done besides advise. The
chairman concluded that even if Nerrity stuck to his
guns and refused to pay a fee it shouldn't worry us.
The deliverance of Dominic, he said contentedly,
had been tidily and rapidly carried out at little cost to
the firm. Liaison with the police had been excellent.
Well done, you two chaps. Any more business? If
not, we'll adjourn.

Tony adjourned to the nearest pub and I to Lambourn, arriving later than I would have liked.

"Thank goodness," Alessia said, coming out of
the house to meet me. "We thought you'd got lost."

"Held up in the office." I hugged her with affection.

"No excuse."

There was a new lightness about her: most encouraging. She led me through the kitchen to the
more formal drawing room where Dominic sat
watchfully on Miranda's lap and Popsy was pouring
wine.

"Hello," Popsy said, giving me a welcoming kiss,
bottle in one hand, glass in the other. "Out with the
wand, it's badly needed."

I smiled at her green eyes and took the filled glass.
"Pity I'm not twenty years younger," she said. I
gave her an "oh, yeah" glance and turned to Miranda.

"Hello," I said.

"Hello." She was quiet and shaky, as if ill.

"Hello, Dominic."

The child stared at me gravely with the big wide eyes. Blue eyes, I saw by daylight. Deep blue eyes.

"You looked terrific on the box," I said to Miranda. "Just right."

"Alessia told me . . . what to do."

"Alessia told her to dress well, to look calm, and to pretend everything was normal," Popsy said. "I heard her. She said it was a good lesson she'd learned from you, and Miranda might as well benefit."

Popsy had made an informal lunch in the kitchen, of which Miranda ate little and Dominic nothing, and afterwards she drove us all up to the Downs in her Land Rover, thinking instinctively, I reckoned, that as it was there that Alessia felt most released, so would Dominic also.

"Has Dominic eaten anything at all since we brought him back?" I asked on the way.

"Only milk," Miranda said. "He wouldn't touch even that until I tried him with one of his old bottles." She kissed him gently. "He always used to have his bedtime milk in a bottle, didn't you, poppet? He only gave it up six months ago."

We all in silence contemplated Dominic's regression to babyhood, and Popsy put the brakes on up by the schooling fences.

"I brought a rug," she said. "Let's sit on the grass."

The three sat, with Dominic still clinging to his mother, and I leaned against the Land Rover and thought that Popsy was probably right: the peace of the rolling hills was so potent it almost stretched out and touched you.

Miranda had brought a toy car, and Alessia

played with it, wheeling it across the rug, up Miranda's leg and onto Dominic's. He watched her gravely for a while without smiling and finally hid his face in his mother's neck.

Miranda said, her mouth trembling, "Did they . . . did they hurt him? He hasn't any bad bruises, just little ones . . . but . . . what did they do, what did they do to make him like this?"

I squatted beside her and put an arm round her shoulder, embracing Dominic also. He looked at me with one eye from under his mother's ear, but didn't try to squirm away.

"They apparently kept him fastened to a bed with the sort of harness you get in prams. I didn't see it, but I was told. I don't think the harness itself would have hurt him. He would have been able to move a little—sit up, kneel, lie down. He refused to eat any food and he cried sometimes because he was lonely." I paused. "It's possible they deliberately frightened him more than they had to, to keep him quiet." I paused again. "There was a hole in the floorboards. A big hole, big enough for a child to fall through." I paused again. "They might have told Dominic that if he made a lot of noise they'd put him down that hole."

Miranda's whole body shuddered and Dominic let out a wail and clung to his mother with frenzy. It was the first sound I'd heard him utter, and I wasn't going to waste it.

"Dominic," I said firmly. "Some nice policemen have filled up that hole so that no little boys can fall down it. The three men who took you away in a boat are not coming back. The policemen have locked them up in prison. No one is going to take you to the seaside." I paused. "No one is going to stick any more tape on your mouth. No one is going to be angry with you and call you horrid names."

"Oh, darling," Miranda said in distress, hugging him.

"The hole is all filled in," I said. "There is no hole anymore in the floor. Nobody can fall down it."

The poor little wretch would have nightmares about it perhaps all his life. Any person who could find a prevention for nightmares, I often thought, would deserve a Nobel prize.

I stood up and said to Alessia and Popsy, "Let's go for a stroll," and when they stood up I said to Dominic, "Give your mummy lots of kisses. She cried all the time, when those horrid men took you. She needs a lot of kisses."

She needed the kisses her husband hadn't given her, I thought. She needed the comfort of strong adult arms. She was having to generate strength enough to see herself and Dominic through alone, and it still seemed to me a tossup whether she'd survive triumphantly or end in breakdown.

Popsy, Alessia, and I walked slowly over to one of the schooling fences and stood there talking.

"Do you think you did right, reminding him of the hole in the floor?" Popsy asked.

"Splinters have to come out," I said.

"Or the wound festers?"

"Yes."

"How did you know what they threatened?"

"I didn't know. I just guessed. It was so likely, wasn't it? The hole was there. He was crying. Shut up you little bleeder or we'll put you down it."

Popsy blinked. Alessia swallowed. "Tell Miranda," I said to her, "that it takes a long time to get over something as awful as being kidnapped. Don't let her worry if Dominic wets the bed and clings to her. Tell her how it's been with you. How insecure it made you feel. Then she'll be patient with Dominic once the first joy of having him back has cooled down."

"Yes, I'll tell her."

Popsy looked from Alessia to me and back again, but said nothing, and it was Alessia herself who half smiled and gave voice to Popsy's thought.

"I've clung to you all right," she said to me, looking briefly over to Miranda and then back. "When you aren't here, and I feel panicky, I think of you, and it's a support. I'll tell Miranda that too. She needs someone to cling to, herself, poor girl."

"You make Andrew sound like a sort of trellis for climbing plants," Popsy said. We walked again, as far as the next schooling fence, and stopped, looking out across the hills. High cirrus clouds curled in feathery fronds near the sun, omen of bad weather to come. We'd never have found Dominic, I thought, if it had rained the day after he was taken and there had been no canal digger with his grandmother on the beach.

"You know," Alessia said, suddenly stirring, "it's time for me to go back to racing." The words came out as if unpremeditated and seemed to surprise her.

"My darling!" Popsy exclaimed. "Do you mean it?"

"I think I mean it at this moment," Alessia said hesitantly, smiling nervously. "Whether I mean it tomorrow morning is anyone's guess."

We all saw, however, that it was the first trickle through the dike. I put my arms round Alessia and kissed her: and in an instant it wasn't just a gesture of congratulation but something much fiercer, something wholly different. I felt the fire run through her in return and then drain away, and I let go of her thinking that the basement had taken charge of me right and proper.

I smiled. Shrugged my shoulders. Made no comment.

"Did you mean that?" Alessia demanded.

"Not exactly," I said. "It was a surprise."

"It sure was." She looked at me assessingly and then wandered away on her own, not looking back.

"You've pruned her off the trellis," Popsy said, amused. "The doctor kissed the patient; most unprofessional."

"I'll kiss Dominic too if it will make you feel better."

She took my arm and we strolled in comradely fashion back to the Land Rover and the rug. Miranda was lying on her back, dozing, with Dominic loosely sprawled over her stomach. His eyes, too, were shut, his small face relaxed, the contours rounded and appealing.

"Poor little sweetheart," Popsy murmured. "Pity to wake them."

Miranda woke naturally when Alessia returned, and with Dominic still asleep we set off on the short drive home. One of the bumps in the rutted Downs track must have roused him, though, because I saw him half sit up in Miranda's arms and then lie back, with Miranda's head bent over him as if to listen.

Alessia gave me a wild look and she too bent her

head to listen, but I could hear nothing above the sound of the engine, and anyway it didn't seem to me that Dominic's lips were moving.

"Stop the car," Alessia said to Popsy, and Popsy, hearing the urgency, obeyed.

Dominic was humming.

For a few seconds the low noise went on: randomly, I thought at first, though certainly not on one note.

"Do you know what that is?" Alessia said incredulously, when the child stopped. "I simply don't believe it."

"What, then?" I said.

For answer she hummed the phrase again, exactly as Dominic had done. He sat up in Miranda's arms and looked at her, clearly responding.

"He knows it!" Alessia exclaimed. "Dominic knows it."

"Yes, darling," Popsy said patiently. "We can see he does. Can we drive on now?"

"You don't understand," Alessia said breathlessly. "That's out of *Il Trovatore*. 'The Soldiers' Chorus.' "

My gaze sharpened on her face. "Do you mean . . ." I began.

She nodded. "I heard it five times a day for six weeks."

"What are you talking about?" Miranda asked. "Dominic doesn't know any opera. Neither John nor I like it. Dominic only knows nursery rhymes. He picks those up like lightning. I play them to him on cassettes."

"Holy hell," I said in awe. "Popsy, drive home. All is fine."

With good humor Popsy restarted the car and took us back to the house, and once there I went over to my car to fetch my briefcase and carry it into the kitchen.

"Miranda," I said, "I'd like Dominic to look at a picture."

She was apprehensive but didn't object. She sat at the kitchen table with Dominic on her lap, and I took out one of the photostats of Giuseppe and laid it face up on the table. Miranda watched Dominic anxiously for a frightened reaction, but none came. Dominic looked at the face calmly for a while and then turned away and leaned against Miranda, his face to her neck.

With a small sigh I put the picture back in the case and accepted Popsy's offer of a universal cup of tea.

"*Ciao bambino,*" Dominic said.

My head and Alessia's snapped round as if jerked by strings.

"What did you say?" Alessia asked him, and Dominic snuggled his face deeper into Miranda's neck.

"He said *ciao bambino,*" I said.

"Yes . . . that's what I thought."

"Does he know any Italian?" I asked Miranda.

"Of course not."

"Goodbye baby," Popsy said. "Isn't that what he said?"

I took the picture of Giuseppe out of the case again and laid it on the table.

"Dominic, dear little one," I said, "what was the man called?"

The great eyes swiveled my way, but he said nothing.

"Was his name . . . Michael?" I asked.

Dominic shook his head: a fraction only, but a definite negative.

"Was his name David?"

Dominic shook his head.

"Was his name Giuseppe?"

Dominic's eyes didn't waver. He shook his head.

I thought a bit. "Was his name Peter?"

Dominic did nothing except look at me.

"Was his name Dominic?" I said.

Dominic almost smiled. He shook his head.

"Was his name John?"

He shook his head.

"Was his name Peter?"

Dominic was still for a long time; then, slowly, very slightly, he nodded.

"Who's Peter?" Alessia asked.

"The man who took him for a ride in a boat."

Dominic stretched out a hand and briefly touched the pictured face with one finger before drawing back.

"Ciao bambino," he said again, and tucked his head against his mother.

One thing was crystal clear, I thought. It wasn't Giuseppe-Peter who had most frightened Dominic. The baby, like Alessia herself, had liked him.

Eagler said, "I thought the boy wouldn't talk. Superintendent Rightsworth told me he'd tried, but the child was in shock, and the mother was being obstructive about treatment."

"Mm," I said. "Still, that was yesterday. Today Dominic has positively identified the photostat as being one of the kidnappers, known to him as Peter.''

"How reliable do you think the kid is?"

"Very. He certainly knew him."

"All right. And this Peter—and I suppose he's the one the kidnappers are talking about on those tapes—he's Italian?"

"Yes. Dominic had learned two words from him: *ciao bambino*.''

"Luv-a-duck," Eagler said quaintly.

"It seems also," I said, "as if Giuseppe-Peter has a fondness for Verdi. Alessia Cenci said her kidnappers played three of Verdi's operas to her, over and over. Dominic is humming 'The Soldiers' Chorus' from *Il Trovatore*, which was one of them. Did you by any chance find a cassette player in that house?"

"Yes, we did." He sounded as if nothing ever again would surprise him. "It was up in the room where the kid was kept. There were two tapes there, and yes, laddie, one was Verdi. *Il Trovatore*.''

"It's conclusive, then, isn't it?" I said. "We have a practitioner."

"A what?"

"Practitioner. Sorry; it's what in Liberty Market we call a man who kidnaps on a regular basis. Like a safe-breaker or a con-man. His work."

"Yes," Eagler agreed. "We have a practitioner; and we have you. I wonder if Giuseppe-Peter knows of the existence of Liberty Market."

"His constant enemy," I said.

Eagler almost chuckled. "I daresay you made things too hot for him in his part of Italy, flooding the place with what is obviously a recognizable portrait. It would be ironic if he'd decided to move to

England and came slap up against you all over again. He'd be speechless if he knew.''

''I daresay he'll find out,'' I said. ''The existence of Liberty Market isn't a total secret, even though we don't advertise. Any kidnapper of experience would hear of us sometime. Perhaps one of these days there'll be a ransom demand saying no police and no Liberty Market, either.''

''I meant you, personally, laddie.''

''Oh.'' I paused. ''No, he wouldn't know that. He saw me once, in Italy, but not here. He didn't know then who I worked for. He didn't even know I was British.''

''He'll have a fit when he finds his picture all over England too.'' Eagler sounded cheerfully smug. ''Even if we don't catch him, we'll chase him back where he came from in no time.''

''You know,'' I said tentatively, ''you and Pucinelli might both flash that picture about among horse people, not just put it up in police stations. Many crooks are ostensibly sober citizens, aren't they? Both of the kidnaps that we're sure are his work are to do with racing. They're the people who'd know him. Someone, somewhere, would know him. Perhaps the racing papers would print it.''

''It's a pity I càn't compare notes with your friend Pucinelli,'' Eagler said. ''I sometimes think police procedures do more to prevent the exchange of information than to spread it. Even in England it's hard enough for one county to get information from another county, let alone talk to regional coppers in Europe.''

''I don't see why you can't. I can tell you his

phone number. You could have an interpreter this end, standing by."

"Ring Italy? It's expensive, laddie."

"Ah." I detected also in his voice the reluctance of many of the British to make overseas calls: almost as if the process itself was a dangerous and difficult adventure, not just a matter of pressing buttons.

"If I want to know anything particular," Eagler said, "I'll ask you to ask him. Things I learn from you come under the heading of information received, origin unspecified."

"So glad."

He chuckled. "We had our three kidnappers in court this morning: remanded in custody for a week. They're still saying nothing. I've been letting them stew while I listened to all the tapes, but now, tonight, and with what you've just told me, I'll bounce them out of their socks."

Fifteen

Eagler opened his oysters, but they were barren of pearls. He concluded, as Pucinelli had done, that none of the arrested men had known Giuseppe-Peter before the day he recruited one of them in a pub.

"Does Giuseppe-Peter speak English?" I asked.

"Yes, apparently, enough to get by. Hewlitt understood him, right enough."

"Who's Hewlitt?"

"Kidnapper. The voice on the ransom tape. Voiceprints made and matched. Hewlitt has a record as long as your arm, but for burglary, not anything like this. The other two are in the same trade; housebreaking, nicking silver and antiques. They finally gave their names, once they saw we'd got them to rights. Now they're busy shoving all the blame onto Peter, but they don't know much about him."

"Were they paid at all?" I asked.

"They say not, but they're lying. They got some on account, must have. Stands to reason."

"I suppose Giuseppe-Peter didn't telephone the house in Itchenor, did he?"

There was dead silence from Eagler. Embarrassment, I diagnosed.

"He did," I suggested, "and got a policeman?"

"Well . . . there was one call from someone unknown."

"But you got a recording?"

"All he said," said Eagler resignedly, "was 'Hello.' My young P.C. thought it was someone from the station and answered accordingly, and the caller rang off."

"Can't be helped," I said.

"No."

"Did Hewlitt say how Giuseppe-Peter knew of him? I mean, you can't go up to a perfect stranger in a British pub and proposition him to kidnap."

"On that subject Hewlitt is your proverbial silent stone. There's no way he's going to say who put him up. There's some things, laddie, one just can't find out. Let's just say that there are a lot of Italians in London, where Hewlitt lives, and there's no way he's going to point the finger at any of them."

"Mm," I said. "I do see that."

I telephoned Alessia to ask how she was feeling and found her full of two concerns: the first, her own plans for a comeback race, and second, the predicament of Miranda and Dominic.

"Miranda's so miserable and I don't know how to help her," she said. "John Nerrity's being thoroughly unreasonable in every way, and he and Miranda are now sleeping in different rooms, because he won't have Dominic sleeping in the room with them, and Dominic won't sleep by himself.''

"Quite a problem," I agreed.

"Mind you, I suppose it's difficult for both of them. Dominic wakes up crying about five times every night, and won't go to sleep again unless Miranda strokes him and talks to him, and she says she's getting absolutely exhausted by it, and John is going on and on about sending Dominic to hospital." She paused. "I can't ask Popsy to have her here to stay. I simply don't know what to do."

"Hm . . . How much do you like Miranda?"

"Quite a lot. More than I expected, to be honest."

"And Dominic?"

"He's a sweetheart. Those terrific eyes. I love him."

I paused, considering, and she said, "What are you thinking? What should Miranda do?"

"Is her mother still with her?"

"No. Her mother has a job and doesn't seem to be much help."

"Does Miranda have any money except what John gives her?"

"I don't know. But she was his secretary."

"Yeah. Well . . . Miranda should take Dominic to a doctor I know of, and she should go and stay for a week near someone supportive like you that she can be with for a good deal of every day. And I don't know how much of that is possible."

"I'll make it possible," Alessia said simply.

I smiled at the telephone. She sounded so whole, her own problems submerged under the tidal wave of Dominic's.

"Don't let Miranda mention my name to her husband in connection with any plan she makes," I said. "I'm not in favor with him, and if he knew I'd suggested anything he'd turn it down flat."

"But you brought Dominic back!"

"Much to his embarrassment. He'd sacked us two days earlier."

She laughed. "All right. What's the name of the doctor?"

I told her, and also told her I'd telephone the doctor myself, to explain the background and verify Dominic's need.

"You're a poppet," Alessia said.

"Oh, sure. What was it you said about going racing?"

"I rode out with the string today and yesterday, and I can't understand why I didn't do it sooner. I'm riding work for Mike Noland tomorrow and he says if I'm fit and O.K. he'll give me a ride next week at Salisbury."

"Salisbury . . . races?" I said.

"Yes, of course."

"And, um, do you want an audience?"

"Yes, I do."

"You've got it."

She said goodbye happily and in the evening rang me at home in my apartment.

"It's all fixed," she said. "Miranda said your doctor sounded a darling, and she's taking Dominic there first thing tomorrow. Then she's coming straight down here to Lambourn. I've got her a room in a cottage owned by a retired nanny, who I went to see, and who's pleased with the whole idea, and John raised no objections, absolutely the contrary, he's paying for everything."

"Terrific," I said, with admiration.

"And Popsy wants you down again. And so does Miranda. And so do I."

"I give in, then. When?"

"Soon as you can."

I went on the following day and also twice more during the following week. Dominic slept better because of a mild liquid sleeping draught in his nightly bottle of milk and progressed to eating chocolate drops and, later, mashed bananas. The ex-nanny patiently took away rejected scrambled eggs and fussed over Miranda in a way which would have worn my nerves thin but in that love-deprived girl produced a grateful dependency.

Alessia spent much of every day with them, going for walks, shopping in the village, all of them lunching most days with Popsy, sunbathing in the cottage garden.

"You're a clever clogs, aren't you?" Popsy said to me on my third visit.

"How do you mean?"

"Giving Alessia something so worthwhile to do."

"It was accidental, really."

"And encouraged."

I grinned at her. "She looks great, doesn't she?"

"Marvellous. I keep thinking about those first days when she was so deathly pale and shaky. She's just about back to her old self now."

"Has she driven anywhere yet, on her own?"

Popsy glanced at me. "No. Not yet."

"One day she will."

"And then?"

"Then she'll fly . . . away."

I heard in my voice what I hadn't intended or expected to be there: a raw sense of loss. It was all very well mending birds' broken wings. They could take your heart off with them when you set them free.

She wouldn't need me, I'd always known it, once her own snowstorm had settled. I could have tried, I supposed, to turn her dependence on me into a love affair, but it would have been stupid: cruel to her, unsatisfactory to me. She needed to grow safely back to independence and I to find a strong and equal partner. The clinging with the clung-to wasn't a good proposition for long-term success.

We were all at that moment out in Popsy's yard, with Alessia taking Miranda slowly round and telling her about each horse as they came to it. Dominic by then had developed enough confidence to stand on the ground, though he hung on to Miranda's clothes permanently with one hand and needed lifting to her hip at the approach of any stranger. He had still not said anything else, but day by day, as the fright level slowly declined, it became more likely that he soon would.

Popsy and I strolled behind the two girls and on an impulse I squatted down to Dominic's height and said, "Would you like a ride on my shoulders?"

Miranda encouragingly swept up Dominic and perched him on me with one leg past each ear.

"Hold on to Andrew's hair," Alessia said, and I felt the little fingers gripping as I stood upright.

I couldn't see Dominic's face, but everyone else was smiling, so I simply set off very slowly past the boxes, so he could see the inmates over the half-doors.

"Lovely horses," Miranda said, half anxiously. "Big horses, darling, look."

We finished the tour of the yard in that fashion and when I lifted Dominic down he stretched up his arms to go up again. I hoisted him onto my left arm, my face level with his. "You're a good little boy," I said.

He tucked his head down to my neck as he'd done so often with Miranda, and into my receptive ear he breathed one very quiet word, "Andrew."

"That's right," I said, equally quietly, "and who's that?" I pointed at Miranda.

"Mummy." The syllables weren't much more than a whisper, but quite clear.

"And that?" I said.

"Lessia."

"And that?"

"Popsy."

"Very good." I walked a few steps with him away from the others. He seemed unalarmed. I said in a normal voice, "What would you like for tea?"

There was a fairly long pause; then he said, "Chocolate," still quietly.

"Good. You shall have some. You're a very good boy."

I carried him further away. He looked back only once or twice to check that Miranda was still in sight, and I reckoned that the worst of his troubles were over. Nightmares he would have, and bouts of desperate insecurity, but the big first steps had been taken, and my job there too was almost done.

"How old are you, Dominic?" I asked.

He thought a bit. "Three," he said, more audibly.

"What do you like to play with?"

A pause. "Car."

"What sort of car?"

He sang "Dee-dah dee-dah dee-dah" into my ear very clearly on two notes, an exact imitation of a police car's siren.

I laughed and hugged him. "You'll do," I said.

Alessia's return to race-riding was in some respects unpromising as she came back white-faced after finishing last.

The race itself, a five-furlong sprint for two-year-olds, had seemed to me to be over in a flash. Hardly had she cantered down to the start, a bent figure in shining red silks, than the field of eighteen were loaded into the stalls and set running. The red silks had shown briefly and been swamped, smothered by a rainbow wave which left them slowing in the wake. The jockey sat back onto her saddle the moment she passed the winning post, stopping her mount to a walk in very few strides.

I went to where all except the first four finishers were being dismounted, where glum-faced little groups of owners and trainers listened to tale after tale of woe and disaster from impersonal jockeys whose minds were already on the future. I heard snatches of what they were saying while I waited unobtrusively for Alessia.

"Wouldn't quicken when I asked him . . ."

"Couldn't act on the going . . ."

"Got bumped . . . shut in . . . squeezed out."

"Still a baby . . ."

"Hanging to the left . . ."

Mike Noland, without accompanying owners, noncommittally watched Alessia approaching, then patted his horse's neck and critically inspected its

legs. Alessia struggled to undo the buckles on the
girths, a service Noland finally performed for her,
and all I heard her say to him was "Thanks . . .
Sorry," which he received with a nod and a pat on
the shoulder: and that seemed to be that.

Alessia didn't spot me standing there and hurried
away towards the weighing room; and it was a good
twenty minutes before she emerged. She still looked
pale. Also strained, thin, shaky, and miserable.

"Hi," I said.

She turned her head and stopped walking. Managed a smile. "Hello."

"What's the matter?" I said.

"You saw."

"I saw that the horse wasn't fast enough."

"You saw that every talent I used to have isn't
there anymore."

I shook my head. "You wouldn't expect a prima
ballerina to give the performance of a lifetime if
she'd been away from dancing for three months."

"This is different."

"No. You expected too much. Don't be so . . . so
cruel to yourself."

She gazed at me for a while and then looked away,
searching for another face. "Have you seen Mike
Noland anywhere?" she said.

"Not since just after the race."

"He'll be furious." She sounded desolate. "He'll
never give me another chance."

"Did he expect his horse to win?" I asked. "It
started at about twelve to one. Nowhere near favorite."

Her attention came back to my face with another
flickering smile. "I didn't know you betted."

"I didn't. I don't. I just looked at the bookies' boards, out of interest."

She had come from Lambourn with Mike Noland, and I had driven from London. When I'd talked to her before she went to change for the race she'd been nervously expectant: eyes wide, cheeks pink, full of small movements and half smiles, wanting a miracle.

"I felt sick in the parade ring," she said. "I've never been like that before."

"But you didn't actually vomit . . ."

"Well, no."

"How about a drink?" I suggested. "Or a huge sandwich?"

"Fattening," she said automatically, and I nodded and took her arm.

"Jockeys whose talents have vanished into thin air can eat all the sandwiches they want," I said.

She pulled her arm away and said in exasperation, "You . . . You always make people see things straight. All right. I'll admit it. Not every vestige of talent is missing, but I made a rotten showing. And we'll go and have a . . . a small sandwich, if you like."

Some of the blues were dispersed over the food, but not all, and I knew too little about racing to judge whether her opinion of herself was fair. She'd looked fine to me, but then so would almost anyone have done who could stand in the stirrups while half a ton of thoroughbred thundered forward at over thirty miles an hour.

"Mike did say something on the way here about giving me a ride at Sandown next week if everything was O.K. today, and I don't suppose he will, now."

"Would you mind very much?"

"Yes, of course," she said passionately. "Of course I'd mind." She heard both the conviction and the commitment in her voice, and so did I. Her head grew still, her eyes became more peaceful, and her voice, when she spoke again, was lower in pitch. "Yes, I'd mind. And that means I still want to be a jockey more than anything on earth. It means that I've got to work harder to get back. It means that I must put these last three months behind me, and get on with living." She finished the remains of a not very good chicken sandwich and sat back in her chair and smiled at me. "If you come to Sandown, I'll do better."

We went eventually in search, Alessia said, of an honest opinion from Mike Noland; and with the forthrightness I was coming to see as normal among the racing professionals he said, "No, you were no good. Bloody bad. Sagging all over the place like a sponge. But what did you expect, first time back, after what you've been through? I knew you wouldn't win. I doubt if that horse could have won today anyway, with Fred Archer incarnate in the saddle. He might have been third . . . fourth." He shrugged. "On the form book he couldn't have touched the winner. You'll do better next time. Sure to. Sandown, right?"

"Right," Alessia said faintly.

The big man smiled kindly from the height of his fifty years and patted her again on the shoulder. "Best girl jockey in Europe," he said to me. "Give or take a dozen or two."

"Thanks so much," Alessia said.

* * *

I went to Sandown the following week and to two more race meetings the week after, and on the third of those days Alessia won two races.

I watched the applause and the acclaim and saw her quick bright smiles as she unsaddled her winners, saw the light in her eyes and the certainty and speed of her movements, saw the rebirth of the skills and the quality of spirit which had taken her before to the heights. The golden girl filled to new stature visibly day by day and on the morning after her winners the newspapers printed her picture with rapturous captions.

She still seemed to want me to be there; to see me, specifically, waiting. She would search the surrounding crowds with her eyes and stop and smile when she saw me. She came and went from Lambourn every time with Mike Noland and spent her free minutes on the racecourse with me, but she no longer grasped me physically to save herself from drowning. She was afloat and skimming the waves, her mind on far horizons. She had begun to be, in the way she most needed to be, happy.

"I'm going home," she said one day.

"Home?"

"To Italy. To see Papa. I've been away so long."

I looked at the fine-boned face, so healthy now, so brown, so full of poise, so intimately known.

"I'll miss you," I said.

"Will you?" She smiled into my eyes. "I owe you a debt I can't pay."

"No debt," I said.

"Oh, yes." Her voice took it for granted. "Anyway, it's not goodbye forever, or anything dramatic like that. I'll be back. The Flat season will be finished here in a few weeks, but I'll definitely be riding here some of the time next summer.''

Next summer seemed a long way away.

''Alessia,'' I said.

''No.'' She shook her head. ''Don't say whatever's in your mind. You carry on giving a brilliant imitation of a rock, because my foundations are still shaky. I'm going home to Papa . . . but I want to know you're only a telephone call away . . . some days I wake up sweating . . .'' She broke off. ''I'm not making sense.''

''You are indeed,'' I assured her.

She gave me a brief but searching inspection. ''You never need telling twice, do you? Sometimes you don't need telling once. Don't forget me, will you?''

''No,'' I said.

She went to Italy and my days seemed remarkably empty even though my time was busily filled.

Nerrity's near-loss of Ordinand had caused a huge flutter in the dovecotes of owners of good-as-gold horses, and I in conjunction with our chummy insurance syndicate at Lloyds was busy raising defenses against copycat kidnaps.

Some owners preferred to insure the animals themselves against abduction, but many saw the point of insuring their wives and children. I found myself invited to ring the front door bell of many an imposing pile and to pass on the chairman's considered judgments, the chairman in some erroneous way having come to consider me an expert on racing matters.

The Lloyds syndicate did huge new business, and into every contract they wrote as usual a stipulation that in the case of "an event," the advice of Liberty Market should be instantly sought. You scratch my back, I'll scratch yours: both the syndicate and Liberty Market were purring.

The Jockey Club showed some interest. I was dispatched to their offices in Portman Square in London to discuss the problems of extortion with the senior steward, who shook my hand firmly and asked whether Liberty Market considered the danger a real one.

"Yes," I said moderately. "There have been three kidnaps in the racing world recently: a man in Italy who owned a racecourse, Alessia Cenci, the jockey, whom you must know about, and John Nerrity's son."

He frowned. "You think they're connected?"

I told him how positively the latter two were connected and his frown deepened.

"No one can tell whether this particular man will try again now that the Nerrity venture has ended in failure," I said, "but the idea of forcing someone to sell a valuable horse may be seductive enough to attract imitators. So yes, we do think owners would be prudent to insure against any sort of extortion involving their horses."

The senior steward watched my face unsmilingly. He was a thick-set man, maybe sixty, with the same natural assumption of authority as our chairman, though not with the same overpowering good looks. Morgan Freemantle, senior steward, top authority of the huge racing industry, came across as a force of more power than charm, more intelligence than kindness, more resolution than patience. I guessed that in general people respected him rather than liked him, and also that he was probably good news for the health of the racing world.

He had said he had heard of our existence from a friend of his who was an underwriter at Lloyds, and that he had since made several inquiries.

"It seems your firm is well-regarded," he told me austerely. "I must say I would have seen no need for such an organization, but I now learn there are approximately two hundred kidnaps for ransom in the world each year, not counting tribal disturbances in Africa, or political upheavals in Central and South America."

"Er . . ." I said.

He swept on. "I am told there may be many more occurrences than those actually reported. Cases where families or firms settle in private and don't inform the police."

"Probably," I agreed.

"Foolish," he said shortly.

"Most often, yes."

"I understand from the police commissioners that they are willing to work with your firm whenever appropriate." He paused, and added almost grudgingly, "They have no adverse criticisms."

Bully for them, I thought.

"I think we can say, therefore," Morgan Freemantle went on judiciously, "that if anything further should happen to anyone connected with racing, you may call upon the Jockey Club for any help it is within our power to give."

"Thank you very much," I said, surprised.

He nodded. "We have an excellent security service. They'll be happy to work with you also. We in the Jockey Club," he informed me regretfully, "spend a great deal of time confounding dishonesty, because unfortunately racing breeds fraud."

There didn't seem to be an answer to that, so I gave none.

"Let me know, then, Mr. . . . er . . . Douglas," he said, rising, "if your firm should be engaged by anyone in racing to deal with a future circumstance which might come within our province. Anything, that is to say, which might affect the stability of racing as a whole. As extortion by means of horses most certainly does."

I stood also. "My firm could only advise a client that the Jockey Club should be informed," I said neutrally. "We couldn't insist."

He gave me a straight considering stare. "We like to know what's going on in our own back yard," he said. "We like to know what to defend ourselves against."

"Liberty Market will always cooperate as fully as possible," I assured him.

He smiled briefly, almost sardonically. "But you, like us, don't know where an enemy may strike, or in what way, and we find ourselves wishing for defenses we never envisaged."

"Mm," I said. "Life's like that."

He shook my hand again firmly and came with me from his desk to the door of his office.

"Let's hope we've seen an end to the whole thing. But if not, come to see me."

"Yes," I said.

I telephoned to the Villa Francese one evening and my call was answered by Ilaria.

"Hello, Mr. Fixit," she said with amusement. "How's it going?"

"Every which way," I said. "And how are you?"

"Bored, wouldn't you know?"

"Is Alessia there?" I asked.

"The precious girl is out visiting with Papa."

"Oh . . ."

"However," Ilaria said carefully, "she should be back by ten. Try again later."

"Yes. Thank you."

"Don't thank me. She is out visiting Lorenzo Traventi, who has made a great recovery from his bullets and is now looking particularly ravishing and romantic and is kissing her hand at every opportunity."

"Dear Ilaria," I said. "Always so kind."

"Shit," she said cheerfully. "I might tell her you called."

She did tell her. When I rang again, Alessia answered almost immediately.

"Sorry I was out," she said. "How's things?"

"How are they with you?" I asked.

"Oh . . . fine. Really fine. I mean it. I've ridden in several races since I've been back. Two winners. Not bad. Do you remember Brunelleschi?"

I thought back. "The horse you didn't ride in the Derby?"

"That's right. Spot on. Well . . . he was one of my winners last week, and they're sending him to Washington to run in the International, and believe it or not but they've asked me to go too, to ride him." Her voice held both triumph and apprehension in roughly equal amounts.

"Are you going?" I said.

"I . . . don't know."

"Washington, D.C.?" I asked. "America?"

"Yes. They have an international race every year there at Laurel racecourse. They invite some really super horses from Europe to go there . . . pay all their expenses, and those of the trainers and jockeys. I've never been, but I've heard it's great. So what do you think?"

"Go, if you can," I said.

There was a small silence. "That's the whole thing, isn't it? If I can. I almost can. But I have to decide by tomorrow at the latest. Give them time to find someone else."

"Take Ilaria with you," I suggested.

"She wouldn't go," she said positively, and then more doubtfully, "would she?"

"You can but ask."

"Yes. Perhaps I will. I do wish, though, that you could go, yourself. I'd sail through the whole thing if I knew you were there."

"Not a chance," I said regretfully. "But you will be all right."

We talked for a while longer and disconnected, and I spent some time wondering if I could, after all, wangle a week off and blow the fare: but we were all at that time very shorthanded in the office, Tony Vine having been called away urgently to Brazil and four or five partners tied up in a multiple mess in Sardinia. I was constantly taking messages from them on the switchboard in between the advisory trips to racehorse owners, and even Gerry Clayton's folded birds of paradise had given way to more orthodox paperwork.

Nothing happens the way one expects.

Morgan Freemantle, senior steward of the Jockey Club, went to Laurel for a week to be the guest of honor of the president of the racecourse, a courtesy between racing fraternities.

On the second day of his visit he was kidnapped.

Washington, D. C.

Sixteen

The chairman sent me round to the Jockey Club, where shock had produced suspended animation akin to the waxworks.

For a start there were very few people in the place and no one was quite sure who was in charge; a flock without its leader. When I asked which individual had received the first demand from the kidnappers I was steered to the office of a stiff-backed middle-aged woman in silk shirt and tweed skirt who looked at me numbly and told me I had come at a bad time.

"Mrs. Berkeley?" I inquired.

She nodded, her eyes vague, her thoughts elsewhere, her spine rigid.

"I've come about Mr. Freemantle," I said. It sounded rather as if I'd said "I've come about the plumbing," and I had difficulty in stifling a laugh. Mrs. Berkeley paid more attention and said, "You're not the man from Liberty Market, are you?"

"That's right."

"Oh." She inspected me. "Are you the person who saw Mr. Freemantle last week?"

"Yes."

"What are you going to do about it?"

"Do you mind if I sit down?" I asked, indicating the chair nearest to me, beside her large polished desk.

"By all means," she said faintly, her voice civilized upper class, her manner an echo of country house hostess. "I'm afraid you find us . . . disarranged."

"Could you tell me what messages you have actually received?" I said.

She looked broodingly at her telephone as if it were itself guilty of the crime. "I am taking all incoming calls to the senior steward's private number on this telephone during his absence. I answered . . . There was an American voice, very loud, telling me to listen carefully . . . I felt disembodied, you know. It was quite unreal."

"The words," I said without impatience. "Do you remember the words?"

"Of course I do. He said the senior steward had been kidnapped. He said he would be freed on payment of ten million English pounds sterling. He said the ransom would have to be paid by the Jockey Club." She stared at me with the shocked glaze still in her eyes. "It's impossible, you know. The Jockey Club doesn't have any money. The Jockey Club are administrators. There are no . . . assets."

I looked at her in silence.

"Do you understand?" she said. "The Jockey Club are just people. Members. Of a club."

"Rich members?" I asked.

Her mouth, half open, stopped moving.

"I'm afraid," I said neutrally, "that kidnappers usually couldn't care less where the money comes from or who it hurts. We'll get the demand down to far below ten million pounds, but it may still mean that contributions will be sought from racing people." I paused. "You didn't mention any threats. Were there any threats?"

She nodded slowly. "If the ransom wasn't paid, Mr. Freemantle would be killed."

"Straight and simple?"

"He said . . . there would be another message later."

"Which you haven't yet received?"

She glanced at a round-faced clock on a wall where the hands pointed to four-fifty.

"The call came through just after two," she said. "I told Colonel Tansing. He thought it might have been a hoax, so we telephoned to Washington. Mr. Freemantle wasn't in his hotel. We got through to the public relations people who are looking after his trip and they said he hadn't turned up yesterday evening at a reception and they didn't know where he'd gone. Colonel Tansing explained about the ransom demand and they said they would tell Eric Rickenbacker . . . that's the president of the racecourse . . . and Mr. Rickenbacker would get the police onto it straight away."

"Was there any mention of not going to the police, on your ransom-demand call?"

She shook her head slowly. "No."

She had a firm, tidy-looking face with brown wavy hair graying at the sides: the sort of face that launched a thousand pony clubs and church bazaars, worthy, well-intentioned, socially secure. Only something of the present enormity could have produced her current rudderlessness, and even that, I judged, would probably transform to brisk competence very soon.

"Has anyone told the British police?" I asked.

"Colonel Tansing thought it best to contact your chairman first," she said. "Colonel Tansing, you see, is . . ." She paused as if seeking for acceptable words. "Colonel Tansing is the deputy licensing officer, whose job is mainly the registration of racehorse owners. No one of any seniority is here this afternoon, though they were this morning. No one here now really has the power to make top-level decisions. We're trying to find the stewards . . . they're all out." She stopped rather blankly. "No one expects this sort of thing, you know."

"No," I agreed. "Well, the first thing to do is to tell the police here and get them to put a tap on all the Jockey Club's telephones, and after that to get on with living, and wait."

"Wait?"

I nodded. "While the ransom negotiations go on. I don't want to alarm you, but it may be some time before Mr. Freemantle comes home . . . and what about his family? His wife? Has she been told?"

She said glumly, "He's a widower."

"Children?"

"He has a daughter," she said dubiously, "but I don't think they get on well. I believe she lives abroad . . . Mr. Freemantle never mentions her."

"And, excuse me," I said. "Is Mr. Freemantle himself . . . er . . . rich?"

She looked as if the question were in ultra-poor

taste but finally answered, "I have no idea. But anyone who becomes senior steward must be considered to have personal funds of some sort."

"Ten million?" I asked.

"Certainly not," she said positively. "By many standards he is moderate in his expenditure." Her voice approved of this. "He dislikes waste."

Moderate spending habits and a dislike of waste turned up often enough in the most multi of millionaires, but I let it go. I thanked her instead and went in search of Colonel Tansing, who proved to be a male version of Mrs. Berkeley, courteous, charming, and shocked to near immobility.

In his office I telephoned to the police and got things moving there and then asked him who was the top authority at the Jockey Club in Mr. Freemantle's absence.

"Sir Owen Higgs," he said. "He was here this morning. We've been trying to reach him . . ." He looked slightly apprehensive. "I'm sure he will agree we had to call you in."

"Yes," I said reassuringly. "Can you arrange to record all calls on all your telephones? Separately from and in addition to the police?"

"Shall be done," he said.

"We have a twenty-four-hour service at Liberty Market, if you want us."

He clasped my hand. "The Jockey Club is one of the most effective organizations in Britain," he said apologetically. "This business has just caught us on the hop. Tomorrow everything will swing into action."

I nodded and departed, and went back to the Liberty Market offices reflecting that neither the colonel nor Mrs. Berkeley had speculated about the victim's present personal sufferings.

Stunned disbelief, yes. Tearful sympathetic devotion, no.

Sir Owen Higgs having formally engaged Liberty Market services I set off to Washington the following morning, and by early afternoon, their time, was driving a rented car towards Laurel racecourse to talk to Eric Rickenbacker, its president.

The racecourse lay an hour's drive away from the capital city along roads ablaze with brilliant trees, golden, red, orange, tan, nature's last great flourish of trumpets before winter. The first few days of November: warm, sunny, and windless under a high blue sky. The sort of day to lift the spirits and sing to. I felt liberated, as always in America, a feeling which I thought had something to do with the country's own vastness, as if the wide-apartness of everything flooded into the mind and put spaces between everyday problems.

Mr. Rickenbacker had left instructions about me at the raceclub entrance: I was to be conveyed immediately to his presence. Not so immediately, it transpired, as to exempt me from being stamped on the back of the hand with an ultraviolet dye, normally invisible to the eye but transformed to a glowing purple circular pattern under special lamps. My pass into the club, it was explained: without it I would be stopped at certain doorways. A ticket one couldn't lose or surreptitiously pass to a friend, I thought. It would wash off, they said.

Mr. Rickenbacker was in the president's domain, a retreat at the top of the grandstand, reached by ele-

vator, hand-checks, a trudge through the members'
lounges, more checks, an inconspicuous doorway
and a narrow stair. At the top of the stair, a guardian
sitting at a table. I gave my name. The guardian
checked it against a list, found it, ticked it, and let
me through. I went round one more corner and finished the journey. The president's private dining
room, built on three levels, looked out across the
course through acres of glass, with tables for about a
hundred people; but it was almost empty.

The only people in the place were sitting round
one of the furthest tables on the lowest level. I walked
over and down, and they looked up inquiringly at
my approach. Six men, four women, dressed for tidy
racing.

"Mr. Rickenbacker?" I said generally.

"Yes?"

He was a big man with thick white hair, quite
clearly tall even though sitting down. His eyes had
the reflecting brilliance of contact lenses and his skin
was pale and smooth, immensely well-shaven.

"I'm Andrew Douglas," I said briefly.

"Ah." He stood up and clasped my hand, topping
me by a good six inches. "These are friends of
mine." He indicated them with a small gesture but
made none of the usual detailed introductions, and
to them he said, "Excuse me, everyone, I have some
business with Mr. Douglas." He waved to me to follow him and led the way up deep-carpeted steps to a
yet more private aerie, a small room beyond, above,
behind his more public dining room.

"This is a goddam mess," he said forcefully,
pointing me to an armchair. "One minute Morgan
was telling me about John Nerrity's troubles, and

the next . . ." He moved his arms frustratedly. "We've heard nothing ourselves from any kidnappers. We've told the police both here and in Washington of the ransom demand received in London, and they've been looking into Morgan's disappearance. How much do you know about that?"

"Nothing," I said. "Please tell me."

"Do you want a drink?" he said. "Scotch? Champagne?"

"No, thank you."

"We have a public relations firm that handles a lot of things here for us. This is a social week, you follow me? We have a lot of overseas visitors. There are receptions, press conferences, sponsors' parties. We have guests of honor—Morgan was one of those—for whom we arrange transport from the hotel to the racecourse, and to the various receptions, you follow?"

I nodded.

"The public relations firm hires the cars from a limousine service. The cars come with drivers, of course. The public relations firm tells the limousine service who to pick up from where, and where to take them, and the limousine service instructs its drivers, you follow me?"

"Yes," I said.

"Morgan was staying at the Ritz Carlton, you follow? We put him in there, it's a nice place. The racecourse is picking up his tab. Morgan was supposed to join us at a reception in Baltimore the evening before last. The reception was for the press . . . many overseas sportswriters come over for our big race, and I guess we do everything we can to make them feel welcome."

"Mm," I said, understanding. "World coverage of a sports event is good for the gate."

He paused a fraction before nodding. Maybe I shouldn't have put it so badly; but the public-relations-promotions bandwagon generated business and business generated jobs, and the artificial roundabout bought real groceries down the line.

"Morgan didn't arrive at the reception," Rickenbacker said. "He was expected . . . He had assured me he would be there. I know he intended to say he was glad to be representing British racing, and to tell the press of some of the plans the English Jockey Club is making for the coming year."

"He was going to speak?" I said. "I mean, make a speech?"

"Yes, didn't I make that clear? We always have three or four speakers at the press party, but very short and informal, you follow, just a few words of appreciation, that sort of thing. We were surprised when Morgan didn't show, but not disturbed. I was myself surprised he hadn't sent a message, but I don't know him well. We met just three days ago. I wouldn't know if he would be careful about courtesies, you follow?"

"Yes," I said. "I follow."

He smoothed a muscular hand over the white hair. "Our public relations firm told the limousine service to pick Morgan up from the Ritz Carlton and take him to the Harbor Room in Baltimore." He paused. "Baltimore is nearer to this racetrack than Washington is, you follow me, so a majority of the press stay in Baltimore." He paused again, giving me time for understanding. "The Ritz Carlton report a chauffeur coming to the front desk, saying he had been assigned to collect Morgan. The front desk called Morgan, who came down, left his key, and went out with the chauffeur. And that's all. That's all anyone knows.''

"Could the front desk describe the chauffeur?'' I asked.

"All they could positively remember was that he wore a chauffeur's uniform and a cap. He didn't say much. They think he may have spoken with some sort of non-American accent, but this is a polyglot city and no one took much notice.''

"Mm,'' I said. "What happened to the real chauffeur?''

"The real . . . ? Oh, no, nothing. The Ritz Carlton report a second chauffeur appeared. They told him Morgan had already been collected. The chauffeur was surprised, but not too much. With an operation of this size going on there are always mixups. He reported back to his service, who directed him to another assignment. The limousine service thought Morgan must have taken a ride with a friend and not told them. They were philosophical. They would charge the racetrack for their trouble. They wouldn't lose.''

"So no one was alarmed,'' I said.

"Of course not. The public relations firm called the Ritz Carlton in the morning—that was yesterday—and the front desk said Morgan's key was there, he must already have gone out. No one was alarmed until we had the call from your Colonel Tansing asking about a hoax.'' He paused. "I was at home eating breakfast.''

"Rather a shock,'' I said. "Have all these pressmen woken up yet to the story under their noses?''

With the first faint glimmer of humor he said that things were at the unconfirmed rumor stage, the whole hive buzzing.

"It'll put your race on the world map like nothing else will," I said.

"I'm afraid so." He looked undecided about the worth of that sort of publicity, or more probably about the impropriety of dancing up and down with commercial glee.

"You told the police," I said.

"Sure. Both here in Laurel and in Washington. The people in Washington are handling it."

I nodded and asked which police, specifically: there were about five separate forces in the capital.

"The Metropolitan Police," he said. "Sure, the F.B.I. and the Missing Persons Bureau have taken an interest, but they've sorted it out that it's the Metropolitan Police's baby. The man in charge is a Captain Kent Wagner. I told him you were coming. He said I could send you along, if you wanted."

"Yes, please."

He took a wallet from an inner pocket and removed a small white card. "Here you are," he said, handing it over. "And also . . ." he sorted out another card, "this is my home number. If I've left the racetrack, you can call me there."

"Right."

"Tomorrow morning we have the press breakfast," he said. "That's when all the overseas owners and trainers and jockeys meet downstairs here in the club." He paused. "We have a press breakfast before most big races in America . . . have you been to one before?"

"No," I said.

"Come tomorrow. You'll be interested. I'll arrange passes for you."

I thanked him, not sure whether I could manage it. He nodded genially. A small thing like the abduction of Britain's top racing executive was not, it seemed, going to dent the onward steamrollering of the week's serious pleasures.

I asked him if I could make a call to Liberty Market before I went to the police in Washington, and he waved me generously to the telephone.

"Sure. Go right ahead. It's a private line. I'll do everything possible to help, you know that, don't you? I didn't know Morgan himself real well, and I guess it couldn't be thought this racetrack's fault he was kidnapped, but anything we can do . . . we'll give it our best shot."

I thanked him and got through to London, and Gerry Clayton answered.

"Don't you ever go home?" I said.

"Someone has to mind the store," he said plaintively; but we all knew he lived alone and was lonely away from the office.

"Any news from the Jockey Club?" I asked.

"Yeah, and how. Want me to play you the tape they got by Express Mail?"

"Fire away."

"Hang on." There was a pause and a few clicks, and then an American voice, punchy and hard.

"If you Brits in the Jockey Club want Freemantle back, listen good. It's going to cost you ten million English pounds sterling. Don't collect the money in notes. You're going to pay in certified banker's checks. You won't get Freemantle back until the checks are cleared. You've got one week to collect the bread. In one week you'll get more instructions. If you fool around, Freemantle will lose his fingers. You'll get one every day, Express Mail, starting two weeks from now.

"No tricks. You in the Jockey Club, you've got money. Either you buy Freemantle back, or we kill him. That's a promise. We'll take him out. And if you don't come up with the bread, you won't even get his corpse. If we kill him, we'll kill him real slow. Make him curse. Make him scream. You hear us? He gets no tidy single shot. He dies hard. If we kill him, you'll get his screams on tape. If you don't want that, you're going to have to pay.

"Freemantle wants to talk to you. You listen."

There was a pause on the line, then Freemantle's own voice, sounding strong and tough and incredibly cultured after the other.

"If you do not pay the ransom, I will be killed. I am told this is so, and I believe it."

Click.

"Did you get all that?" Gerry Clayton's voice said immediately.

"Yeah."

"What do you think?"

"I think it's our man again," I said. "For sure."

"Right. Same feel."

"How long will you be on the switchboard?" I asked.

"Until midnight. Seven P.M., your time."

"I'll probably ring again."

"O.K. Happy hunting."

I thanked Rickenbacker and drove off to Washington, and after a few false trails found Captain of Detectives Kent Wagner in his precinct.

The captain was a walking crime deterrent, big of body, hard of eye, a man who spoke softly and reminded one of cobras. He was perhaps fifty with flat-brushed dark hair, his chin tucked back like a fighting man; and I had a powerful impression of facing a wary, decisive intelligence. He shook my hand perfunctorily, looking me over from heat to foot, summing up my soul.

"Kidnappers never get away with it in the United States," he said. "This time will be no exception."

I agreed with him in principle. The American record against kidnappers was second to none.

"What can you tell me?" he asked flatly, from his look not hoping much.

"Quite a lot, I think," I said mildly.

He eyed me for a moment, then opened the door of his glasswalled office and called across an expanse of desks, "Ask Lieutenant Stavoski to step in here, if you please."

One of the many blue-uniformed men rose to his feet and went on the errand, and through the windows I watched the busy, orderly scene, many people moving, telephones ringing, voices talking, typewriters clacking, computer screens flicking, cups of coffee on the march. Lieutenant Stavoski, when he came, was a pudgy man in the late thirties with a large drooping moustache and no visible doubts about himself. He gave me a disillusioned stare; probably out of habit.

The captain explained who I was. Stavoski looked unimpressed. The captain invited me to give. I obligingly opened my briefcase and brought out a few assorted articles, which I laid on his desk.

"We think this is definitely the third, and probably the fourth, of a series of kidnappings instigated by one particular person,'' I said. ''The Jockey Club in England has today received a tape from the kidnappers of Morgan Freemantle, which I've arranged for you to hear now on the telephone, if you like. I've also brought with me the ransom-demand tapes from two of the other kidnaps.'' I pointed to them as they lay on the desk. ''You might be interested to hear the similarities.'' I paused slightly. ''One of the tapes is in Italian.''

''Italian?''

''The kidnapper himself is Italian.''

Neither of them particularly liked it.

''He speaks English,'' I said, ''but in England he recruited an English national to utter his threats, and on today's tape the voice is American.''

Wagner pursed his lips. ''Let's hear today's tape then.'' He gave me the receiver from his telephone and pressed a few preliminary buttons. ''This call will be recorded,'' he said. ''Also all our conversations from now on.''

I nodded and got through to Gerry Clayton, who gave the kidnapper a repeat performance. The aggressive voice rasped out loudly through the amplifier in Captain Wagner's office, both the policemen listening with concentrated disgust.

I thanked Gerry and disconnected, and without a word Wagner held out a hand to me, his eyes on the tapes I'd brought. I gave him the Nerrity one, which he fitted into a player and set going. The sour threats to Dominic, the cutting off of fingers, the screams, the nonreturn of the body, all thundered into the office like an echo. The faces of Wagner and Stavoski both grew still and then judicious and finally convinced.

"The same guy," Wagner said, switching off. "Different voice, same brain."

"Yes," I said.

"Get Patrolman Rossellini in here," he told the lieutenant and it was Stavoski, this time, who put his head out of the door and yelled for the help. Patrolman Rossellini, large-nosed, young, black-haired, very American, brought his Italian grandparentage to bear on the third of the tapes and translated fluently as it went along. When it came to the last of the series of threats to Alessia's body his voice faltered and stopped, and he glanced uneasily around, as if for escape.

"What is it?" Wagner demanded.

"The guy says," Rossellini said, squaring his shoulders to the requirement, "well to be honest, Captain, I'd rather not say."

"The guy roughly said," I murmured, coming to the rescue, "that bitches were accustomed to dogs and that all women were bitches."

Wagner stared. "You mean . . . ?"

"I mean," I said, "that that threat was issued to reduce her father to pulp. There seems to have been no intention whatsoever of carrying it out. The kidnappers never threatened anything like it to the girl herself, nor anything indeed about daily beatings. They left her completely alone."

Patrolman Rossellini went away looking grateful, and I told Wagner and Stavoski most of what had happened in Italy and England and in what ways the similarities of the two kidnappings might be of use to them now. They listened silently, faces impassive, reserving comments and judgment to the end.

"Let's get this straight," Wagner said eventually, stirring. "One; this Giuseppe-Peter is likely to have rented a house in Washington, reasonably near the Ritz Carlton, within the last eight weeks. That, as I understand it, is when Morgan Freemantle accepted Eric Rickenbacker's invitation."

I nodded. "That was the date given us by the Jockey Club."

"Two; there are likely to be at least five or six kidnappers involved, all of them American except Giuseppe-Peter. Three; Giuseppe-Peter has an inside edge on racecourse information and therefore must be known to people in that world. And four," with a touch of grim humor, "at this moment Morgan Freemantle may be getting his ears blasted off by Verdi."

He picked up the photocopy likeness of Giuseppe-Peter.

"We'll paper the city with this," he said. "If the Nerrity kid recognized him, anyone can." He gave me a look in which, if there wasn't positive friendship, one could at least read a sheathing of poison fangs.

"Only a matter of time," he said.

"But . . . er . . ." I said diffidently. "You won't of course forget that if he sees you getting close, he'll kill Morgan Freemantle. I'd never doubt he means that part. Kill him and bury him. He'd built a tomb for little Dominic that might not have been found for years."

Wagner looked at me with speculation. "Does this man Giuseppe-Peter frighten you?"

"As a professional adversary, yes."

Both men were silent.

"He keeps his nerve," I said. "He thinks. He plans. He's bold. I don't believe a man like that would turn to this particular crime if he were not prepared to kill. Most kidnappers will kill. I'd reckon Giuseppe-Peter would expect to kill and get away with it, if killing were necessary. I don't think he would do it inch by inch, as the tape threatened. But a fast kill to cut his losses, to escape, yes, I'd bet on it."

Kent Wagner looked at his hands. "Has it occurred to you, Andrew, that this Giuseppe-Peter may not like you personally one little bit?"

I was surprised by his use of my first name but took it thankfully as a sign of a working relationship about to begin; and I answered similarly, "Kent, I don't think he knows I exist."

He nodded, a smile hovering, the connection made, the common ground acknowledged.

Seventeen

Silence from the kidnappers, indignation from the about-to-be-dunned members of the Jockey Club and furor from the world's sporting press: hours of horrified talk vibrating the airwaves, but on the ground overnight a total absence of action. I went to the press breakfast in consequence with a quiet conscience and a light heart, hoping to see Alessia.

The raceclub lounges were packed when I arrived, the decibel count high. Glasses of orange juice sprouted from many a fist, long-lensed cameras swinging from many a shoulder. The sportswriters were on their feet, moving, mingling, agog for exclusives, ears stretching to hear conversations behind them. The majority, knowing each other, clapped shoulders in passing. Trainers held small circular conferences, the press heads bending to catch vital words. Owners stood around looking either smug or bemused according to how often they'd attended this sort of shindig; and here and there, like gazelles among the herd, like a variation of the species, stood short light-boned creatures, heads thrown back, being deferred to like stars.

"Orange juice?" someone said, handing me a glass.

"Thanks."

I couldn't see Rickenbacker, nor anyone I knew. No Alessia. The gazelles I saw were all male.

I wandered about, knowing that without her my presence there was pointless; but it had seemed unlikely that she would miss taking her place among her peers.

I knew she'd accepted Laurel's invitation, and her name was plainly there at the breakfast, on a list pinned to a notice board on an easel, as the rider of Brunelleschi. I read through the list, sipping orange juice. Fourteen runners; three from Britain, one from France, one from Italy, two from Canada, two from Argentina, all the rest home grown. Alessia seemed to be the only female jockey.

Presumably at some sort of signal the whole crowd began moving into a large side room, in which many oblong tables were formally laid with flowers, tablecloths, plates, and cutlery. I had vaguely assumed the room to be made ready for lunch, but I'd been wrong. Breakfast meant apparently not orange juice on the wing, but bacon and eggs, waitresses, and hot breads.

I hung back, thinking I wouldn't stay, and heard a breathless voice by my left ear saying incredulously, "Andrew?" I turned. She was there after all, the thin face strong now and vivid, the tilt of the head confident. The dark curls shone with health, the eyes below them gleaming.

I hadn't been sure what I felt for her, not until that

moment. I hadn't seen her for six weeks and before that I'd been accustomed to thinking of her as part of my job; a rewarding pleasure, a victim I much liked, but transient, like all the others. The sight of her that morning came as almost a physical shock, an intoxicant racing in the bloodstream. I put out my arms and hugged her, and felt her cling to me momentarily with savagery.

"Well . . ." I looked into her brown eyes. "Want a lover?"

She gasped a bit and laughed, and didn't answer. "We're at a table over there," she said, pointing deep into the room. "We were sitting there waiting. I couldn't believe it when I saw you come in. There's room for you at our table. A spare place. Do join us."

I nodded and she led the way: and it wasn't Ilaria who had come with her from Italy, but Paolo Cenci himself. He stood up at my approach and gave me not a handshake but an immoderate Italian embrace, head to head, his face full of welcome.

Perhaps I wouldn't have recognized him, this assured, solid, pearl-gray-suited businessman, if I'd met him unexpectedly in an American street. He was again the man I hadn't known, the competent manager in the portrait. The shaky wreckage of five months earlier had retreated, become a memory, an illness obliterated by recovery. I was glad for him and felt a stranger with him, and would not in any way have referred to the anxieties we had shared.

He himself had no such reservations. "This is the man who brought Alessia back safely," he said cheerfully in Italian to the three other people at the table, and Alessia, glancing briefly at my face, said, "Papa, he doesn't like us to talk about it."

"My darling girl, we don't often, do we?" He smiled at me with intense friendship. "Meet Bruno and Beatrice Goldoni," he said in English. "They are the owners of Brunelleschi."

I shook hands with a withdrawn-looking man of about sixty and a strained-looking woman a few years younger, both of whom nodded pleasantly enough but didn't speak.

"And Silvio Lucchese, Brunelleschi's trainer," Paolo Cenci said, introducing the last of the three.

We shook hands quickly, politely. He was dark and thin and reminded me of Pucinelli; a man used to power but finding himself at a disadvantage, as he spoke very little English very awkwardly, with an almost unintelligible accent.

Paolo Cenci waved me to the one empty chair, between Alessia and Beatrice Goldoni, and when all in the room were seated a hush fell on the noisy general chatter and Rickenbacker, followed by a few friends, made a heralded entrance, walking in a modest procession down the whole room, heading for a top table facing everyone else.

"Welcome to Laurel racecourse," he said genially, reaching his center chair, his white hair crowning his height like a cloud. "Glad to see so many overseas friends here this morning. As I expect most of you have now heard, one of our good friends is missing. I speak of course of Morgan Freemantle, senior steward of the British Jockey Club, who was distressfully abducted here two days ago. Everything possible is being done to secure his early release and of course we'll keep you all informed as we go along.

Meanwhile, have a good breakfast, and we'll all talk later.''

A flurry of waitresses erupted all over the place, and I suppose I ate, but I was conscious only of my stirred feelings for Alessia, and of her nearness, and of the question she hadn't answered. She behaved to me, and I daresay I to her, with civil calm. In any case, since everyone at the table was talking in Italian, my own utterances were few, careful, and limited in content.

It seemed that the Goldonis were enjoying their trip, though one wouldn't have guessed it from their expressions.

''We are worried about the race tomorrow,'' Beatrice said. ''We always worry, we can't help it.'' She broke off. ''Do you understand what I'm saying?''

''I understand much more than I speak.''

She seemed relieved and immediately began talking copiously, ignoring repressive looks from her gloomier husband. ''We haven't been to Washington before. Such a spacious, gracious city. We've been here two days . . . we leave on Sunday for New York. Do you know New York? What should one see in New York?''

I answered her as best I could, paying minimal attention. Her husband was sporadically discussing Brunelleschi's prospects with Lucchese as if it were their fiftieth reiteration, rather like the chorus of a Greek play six weeks into its run. Paolo Cenci told me five times he was delighted to see me, and Alessia ate an egg but nothing else.

An ocean of coffee later the day's real business began, proving to be short interviews with all the trainers and jockeys and many of the owners of the following day's runners. Sportswriters asked questions, Rickenbacker introduced the contestants effusively, and everyone learned more about the foreign horses than they'd known before or were likely to remember after.

Alessia interpreted for Lucchese, translating the questions, slightly editing the answers, explaining in one reply that Brunelleschi didn't actually mean anything, it was the name of the architect who'd designed a good deal of the city of Florence; like Wren in London, she said. The sportswriters wrote it down. They wrote every word she uttered, looking indulgent.

On her own account she said straightforwardly that the horse needed to see where he was going in a race and hated to be shut in.

"What was it like being kidnapped?" someone asked, transferring the thought.

"Horrible." She smiled, hesitated, said finally that she felt great sympathy for Morgan Freemantle and hoped sincerely that he would soon be free.

Then she sat down and said abruptly, "When I heard about Morgan Freemantle I thought of you, of course . . . wondered if your firm would be involved. That's why you're here, isn't it? Not to see me race."

"Both," I said.

She shook her head. "One's work, one's luck." She sounded merely practical. "Will you find him, like Dominic?"

"A bit unlikely," I said.

"It brings it all back," she said, her eyes dark. "Don't . . ."

"I can't help it. Ever since I heard . . . when we

got to the track this morning . . . I've been thinking of him.''

Beatrice Goldoni was talking again like a rolling stream, telling me and also Alessia, who must have heard it often before, what a terrible shock it had been when dear Alessia had been kidnapped, and now this poor man, and what a blessing that I had been able to help get dear Alessia back . . . and I thought it colossally lucky she was speaking in her own tongue, which I hoped wouldn't be understood by the newspaper ears all around.

I stopped her by wishing her firmly the best of luck in the big race, and by saying my farewells to the whole party. Alessia came with me out of the dining room and we walked slowly across the bright club lounge to look out across the racecourse.

"Tomorrow," I said, "they'll be cheering you."

She looked apprehensive more than gratified. "It depends how Brunelleschi's traveled."

"Isn't he here?" I asked, surprised.

"Oh, yes, but no one knows how he feels. He might be homesick . . . and don't laugh, the tap water here tastes vile to me, God knows what the horse thinks of it. Horses have their own likes and dislikes, don't forget, and all sorts of unimaginable factors can put them off."

I put my arm round her tentatively.

"Not here," she said.

I let the arm fall away. "Anywhere?" I asked.

"Are you sure . . . ?"

"Don't be silly. Why else would I ask?"

The curve of her lips was echoed in her cheekbones and in her eyes, but she was looking at the track, not at me.

"I'm staying at the Sherryatt," I said. "Where are you?"

"The Regency. We're all there . . . the Goldonis, Silvio Lucchese, Papa and I. All guests of the racecourse. They're so generous, it's amazing."

"How about dinner?" I said.

"I can't. We've been invited by the Italian ambassador. Papa knows him . . . I have to be there."

I nodded.

"Still," she said, "we might go for a drive or something this afternoon. I don't truthfully want to spend all day here on the racecourse. We were here yesterday . . . all the foreign riders were shown what we'll be doing. Today is free."

"I'll wait for you here, then, on this spot."

She went to explain to her father but returned immediately saying that everyone was about to go round to the barns and she couldn't get out of that either, but they'd all said I was very welcome to go with them, if I'd like.

"Barns?" I said.

She looked at me with amusement. "Where they stable the horses on American racecourses."

In consequence I shortly found myself, along with half the attendance from the breakfast, watching the morning routines on the private side of the tracks; the feeding, the mucking-out, the grooming, the saddling-up and mounting, the breezes (short sharp canters), the hot-walking (for cooling off from exercise), the sand-pit rolling, and all around, but constantly shifting, the tiny individual press conferences where trainers spoke prophecies like Moses.

I heard the trainer of the home-based horse that

was favorite saying confidently, "We'll have the speed all the way to the wire."

"What about the foreign horses?" one of the reporters asked. "Is there one to beat you?"

The trainer's eye wandered and lit on Alessia, by my side. He knew her. He smiled. He said gallantly, "Brunelleschi is the danger."

Brunelleschi himself, in his stall, seemed unimpressed. Silvio Lucchese, it appeared, had brought the champion's own food from Italy so that the choosy appetite should be unimpaired. And Brunelleschi had, it seemed, "eaten up" the evening before (a good sign), and hadn't kicked his stable-lad, as he did occasionally from displeasure. Everyone patted his head with circumspection, keeping their fingers away from his strong white teeth. He looked imperious to me, like a bad-tempered despot. No one asked what he thought of the water.

"He's nobody's darling," Alessia said out of the owners' earshot. "The Goldonis are afraid of him, I often think."

"So am I," I said.

"He puts all his meanness into winning." She looked across with rueful affection at the dark tossing head. "I tell him he's a bastard, and we get on fine."

Paolo Cenci seemed pleased that Alessia would be spending most of the day with me. He, Lucchese, and Bruno Goldoni intended to stay for the races. Beatrice, with a secret, sinful smile of pleasure, said she was going to the hotel's hairdresser, and, after that, shopping. Slightly to my dismay Paolo Cenci suggested Alessia and I should give her a lift back to Washington to save the limousine service doubling the journey, and accordingly we passed the first hour of our day with the voluble lady saying nothing much at great length. I had an overall impression that separation, even temporary, from her husband, had caused an excited rise in her spirits, and when we dropped her at the Regency she had twin spots of bright red on her sallow middle-aged cheeks and guilt in every line of her heavy face.

"Poor Beatrice, you'd almost think she was meeting a lover," Alessia said smiling, as we drove away, "not just going shopping."

"You, on the other hand," I observed, "are not blushing a bit."

"Ah," she said. "I haven't promised a thing."

"True." I stopped the car presently in a side street and unfolded a detailed map of the city. "Anything you'd like to see?" I asked. "Lincoln Monument, White House, all that?"

"I was here three years ago, visiting. Did all the tours."

"Good . . . Do you mind then, if we just drive around a bit? I want to put . . . faces . . . onto some of these street names."

She agreed looking slightly puzzled but after a while said, "You're looking for Morgan Freemantle."

"For possible districts, yes."

"What are possible?"

"Well . . . Not industrial areas. Not decayed housing. Not all-black neighborhoods. Not parks, museums, or government offices. Not diplomatic residential areas . . . embassies and their offices. Not blocks of flats with janitors. Not central shopping areas, nor banking areas, nor schools or colleges, nowhere with students."

"What's left?"

"Private housing. Suburbs. Anywhere without prying neighbors. And at a guess, somewhere north or west of the center, because the Ritz Carlton is there."

We drove for a good long while, methodically sectioning the sprawling city according to the map, but concentrating most and finally on the north and west. There were beauties to the place one couldn't guess from the tourist round, and miles and hosts of residential streets where Morgan Freemantle could be swallowed without trace.

"I wonder if we've actually been past him," Alessia said at one point. "Gives one the shivers, not knowing. I can't bear to think of him. Alone . . . dreadfully alone . . . somewhere close."

"He might be further out," I said. "But kidnappers don't usually go for deserted farmhouses or places like that. They choose more populated places, where their comings and goings aren't noticeable."

The scale of it all, however, was daunting, even within the radius I thought most likely. Analysis of recent rentals wouldn't come up this time with just eleven probables: there would be hundreds, maybe one or two thousand. Kent Wagner's task was impossible, and we would have to rely on negotiation, not a second miracle, to get Morgan Freemantle safe home.

We were driving up and down some streets near Washington Cathedral, simply admiring the houses for their architecture: large old sprawling houses with frostings of white railings, lived-in houses with signs of young families. On every porch, clusters of Halloween pumpkins.

"What are those?" Alessia said, pointing at the grinning orange faces of the huge round fruits on the steps outside every front door.

"It was Halloween four days ago," I said.

"Oh, yes, so it was. You don't see those at home."

We passed the Ritz Carlton on Massachusetts Avenue and paused there, looking at the peaceful human-scaled hotel with its blue awnings from where Morgan had been so unceremoniously snatched, and then coasted round Dupont Circle and made our way back to the more central part. Much of the city was built in radii from circles, like Paris, which may have made for elegance but was a great recipe for getting lost: we'd chased our tails several times in the course of the day.

"It's so vast," Alessia said, sighing. "So confusing. I'd no idea."

"We've done enough," I agreed. "Hungry?"

It was three-thirty by then, but time meant nothing to the Sherryatt Hotel. We went up to my room on the twelfth floor of the anonymous, enormous, bustling pile and we ordered wine and avocado shrimp salad from room service. Alessia stretched lazily on one of the armchairs and listened while I telephoned Kent Wagner.

Did I realize, he asked trenchantly, that the whole goddam population of North America was on the move through Washington, D.C., and that a list of rentals would bridge the Potomac?

"Look for a house without pumpkins," I said.

"What?"

"Well, if you were a kidnapper, would you solemnly carve Halloween faces on pumpkins and put them on the front steps?''

"No, I guess not." He breathed out in the ghost of a chuckle. "Takes a Brit to come up with a suggestion as dumb as that."

"Yeah," I said. "I'll be at the Sherryatt this evening and at the races tomorrow, if you should want me."

"Got it."

I telephoned next to Liberty Market, but nothing much had developed in London. The collective fury of the members of the Jockey Club was hanging over Portman Square in a blue haze and Sir Owen Higgs had retreated for the weekend to Gloucestershire. Hoppy at Lloyds was reported to be smiling cheerfully as in spite of advising everyone else to insure against extortion the Jockey Club hadn't done so itself. Apart from that, nix.

The food arrived and we ate roughly jockey-sized amounts. Then Alessia pushed her plate away and, looking at her wine glass, said, "Decision time, I suppose."

"Only for you," I said mildly. "Yes or no."

Still looking down she said, "Would no . . . be acceptable?"

"Yes, it would," I said seriously.

"I . . ." She took a deep breath. "I want to say yes, but I feel . . ." She broke off, then started again. "I don't seem to want . . . since the kidnap . . . I've thought of kissing . . . of love . . . and I'm dead . . . I went out with Lorenzo once or twice and he wanted to kiss me . . . his mouth felt like rubber to me." She looked at me anxiously, willing me to understand. "I did love someone passionately once, years ago, when I was eighteen. It didn't last beyond summer . . . We both simply grew up . . . but I know what it's like, what I should feel, what I should want . . . and I don't.''

''Darling Alessia.'' I stood up and walked to the window, thinking that for this battle I wasn't strong enough, that there was a limit to controlled behavior, that what I myself longed for now was warmth. ''I do truly love you in many ways,'' I said, and found the words coming out an octave lower than in my normal voice.

''Andrew!'' She came to her feet and walked towards me, searching my face and no doubt seeing there the vulnerability she wasn't accustomed to.

''Well . . .'' I said, struggling for lightness; for a smile; for Andrew the unfailing prop. ''There's always time. You ride races now. Go shopping. Drive your car?''

She nodded.

''It all took time,'' I said. I wrapped my arms around her lightly and kissed her forehead. ''When rubber begins feeling like lips, let me know.''

She put her head against my shoulder and clung to me for help as she had often clung before; and it was I, really, who wanted to be enfolded and cherished and loved.

She rode in the race the next day, a star in her own firmament.

The racecourse had come alive, crowds pressing, shouting, betting, cheering. The grandstands were packed. One had to slide round strangers to reach any goal. I had my hand stamped and checked and my name taken and ticked, and Eric Rickenbacker welcomed me busily to the biggest day of his year.

The president's dining room, so echoingly empty previously, spilled over now with chattering guests all having a wow of a time. Ice clinked and waitresses passed with small silver trays and a large buffet table offered crab cakes to afficionados.

Paolo Cenci was there with the Goldonis and Lucchese, all of them looking nervous as they sat together at one of the tables. I collected a glass of wine from an offered trayful and went over to see them, wishing them well.

"Brunelleschi kicked his groom," Paolo Cenci said.

"Is that good or bad?"

"No one knows," he said.

I kept the giggle in my stomach. "How's Alessia?" I asked.

"Less worried than anyone else."

I glanced at the other faces; at Lucchese, fiercely intense, at Bruno Goldoni, frowning, and at Beatrice, yesterday's glow extinguished.

"It's her job," I said.

They offered me a place at their table but I thanked them and wandered away, too restless to want to be with them.

"Any news from London?" Eric Rickenbacker said in my ear, passing close.

"None this morning."

He clicked his tongue, indicating sympathy "Poor Morgan. Should have been here. Instead . . ." He shrugged resignedly, moving away, greeting new guests, kissing cheeks, clapping shoulders, welcoming a hundred friends.

The Washington International was making the world's news. Poor Morgan, had he been there, wouldn't have caused a ripple.

They saved the big race until ninth of the ten on the card, the whole afternoon a titillation, a preparation, with dollars flooding meanwhile into the pari-mutuel and losing tickets filling the trashcans.

The whole of the front of the main stands was filled in with glass, keeping out the weather, rain or shine. To one slowly growing used to the rigors of English courses the luxury was extraordinary, but, when I commented on it, one of Rickenbacker's guests said reasonably that warm betters betted, cold betters stayed at home. A proportion of the day's take at the pari-mutuel went to the racecourse: racegoer comfort was essential.

For me the afternoon passed interminably, but in due course all the foreign owners and trainers left the president's dining room to go down nearer the action and speed their horses on their way.

I stayed in the aerie, belonging nowhere, watching the girl I knew so well come out onto the track; a tiny gold and white figure far below, one in a procession, each contestant led and accompanied by a liveried outrider. No loose horses on the way to the post, I thought. No runaways, no bolters.

A trumpet sounded a fanfare to announce the race. A frenzy of punters fluttered fistfuls of notes. The runners walked in procession across in front of the stands and cantered thereafter to the start, each still with an escort. Alessia looked from that distance identical with the other jockeys: I wouldn't have known her except for the colors.

I felt, far more disturbingly than on the English

tracks, a sense of being no part of her real life. She lived most intensely there, on a horse, where her skill filled her. All I could ever be to her as a lover, I thought, was a support: and I would settle for that, if she would come to it.

The runners circled on the grass, because the one-and-a-half-mile International was run on living green turf, not on dirt. They were fed into the stalls on the far side of the track. Lights still flickered on the pari-mutuel, changing the odds: races in America tended to start when the punters had finished, not to any rigid clock.

They were off, they were running, the gold and white figure with them, going faster than the wind and to my mind crawling like slow motion.

Brunelleschi, the brute who kicked, put his bad moods to good use, shouldering his way robustly round the first bunched-up bend, forcing himself through until there was a clear view ahead. Doesn't like to be shut in, Alessia had said. She gave him room and she held him straight: they came past the stands for the first time in fourth place, the whole field close together. Round the top bend left-handed, down the backstretch, round the last corner towards home.

Two of the leaders dropped back: Brunelleschi kept on going. Alessia swung her stick twice, aimed the black beast straight at the target and rode like a white and gold arrow to the bull.

She won the race and was cheered as she came to the winner's enclosure in front of the stands. She was photographed and filmed, her head back, her mouth laughing. As Brunelleschi stamped around in his winner's garland of laurels (what else?) she reached forward and gave his dark sweating neck a wide-armed exultant pat, and the crowd again cheered.

I wholeheartedly shared in her joy: and felt lonely.

They all came up to the dining room for champagne, winners, losers, and Eric Rickenbacker looking ecstatic.

"Well done," I said to her.

"Did you see?" She was high, high with achievement.

"Yes, I did."

"Isn't it fantastic?"

"The day of a lifetime."

"Oh, I do love you," she said, laughing, and turned away immediately, and talked with animation to a throng of admirers. Ah, Andrew, I thought wryly, how do you like it? And I answered myself: better than nothing.

When I finally got back to the hotel the message button was flashing on my telephone. My office in England had called when I was out. Please would I get through to them straight away.

Gerry Clayton was on the switchboard.

"Your Italian friend rang from Bologna," he said. "The policeman, Pucinelli."

"Yes?"

"He wants you to telephone. I couldn't understand him very well, but I think he said he had found Giuseppe-Peter."

Eighteen

By the time I got the message it was three in the morning, Italian time. On the premise, however, that the law neither slumbered nor slept I put the call through straight away to the carabinieri, and was answered by a yawning Italian who spoke no English.

Pucinelli was not there.

It was not known when Pucinelli would be there next.

It was not known if Pucinelli was in his own house.

I gave my name, spelling it carefully letter by letter but knowing it would look unpronounceable to most Italians.

I will telephone again, I said: and he said "Good."

At one in the morning, Washington time, I telephoned to Pucinelli's own home, reckoning his family would be shaping to breakfast. His wife answered, children's voices in the background, and I asked for her husband, in Italian.

"Enrico is in Milan," she said, speaking slowly

for my sake. "He told me to give you a message." A short pause with paper noises, then, "Telephone this house at fourteen hours today. He will return by that time. He says it is very important, he has found your friend."

"In Milan?" I asked.

"I don't know. Enrico said only to ask you to telephone."

I thanked her and disconnected, and slept fitfully while four thousand miles away Pucinelli traveled home. At fourteen hours, two P.M. his time, eight A.M. in Washington, I got through again to his house and found he had been called out on duty the minute he returned.

"He is sorry. Telephone his office at seventeen hours."

By that time, I reckoned, my fingernails would be bitten to the knuckle. My stomach positively hurt with impatience. I ordered breakfast from room service to quieten it and read the Washington Sunday papers and fidgeted, and finally at eleven I got him.

"Andrew, how are you?" he said.

"Dying of suspense."

"What?"

"Never mind."

"Where are you?" he said. "Your office said America."

"Yes. Washington. Have you really found Giuseppe-Peter?"

"Yes and no."

"What do you mean?"

"You remember," he said, "that we have been inquiring all the time among horse people, and also

that we were going to try some students' reunions, to
see if anyone recognized him from the drawing.''

"Yes, of course,'' I said. We had drifted automatically into our normal habit of speaking in two languages, and it seemed just as satisfactory as ever.

"We have succeeded in both places. In both
worlds.'' He paused for effect and sounded undeni-
ably smug. "He lives near Milan. He is thirty-four
now. He went to Milan University as a student and
joined radical political groups. It is believed he was
an activist, a member of the Red Brigades, but no
one knows for sure. I was told it was a fact, but there
was no true evidence. Anyway, he did not continue
in political life after he left university. He left without sitting his final examinations. The university
asked him to leave, but not because of his radical
opinions. They made him leave because he forged
checks. He was not prosecuted, which I think is a
mistake.''

"Mm,'' I agreed, riveted.

"So then I had his name. And almost immediately, the same day that I learned it, we had the information from the horse people. They say he is not
well known in the horse world, he never goes to the
races, he is the black sheep of a well-regarded family,
and is banished from their house. No one seems to be
absolutely certain in detail why this is, but again
there are many rumors that it is to do with fraud and
forging checks. Everyone believes the father repaid
every penny to keep the family name out of the dis-
grace.''

"But the horse world told you this?''

"Yes. In the end, someone recognized him. Our
men were very diligent, very persistent.''

"They're to be congratulated," I said sincerely.

"Yes, I agree."

"What is his name?" I asked. It hardly seemed to matter, but it would be tidier to give him the proper label.

"His father owns racehorses," Pucinelli said. "His father owns the great horse Brunelleschi. Giuseppe-Peter's real name is Pietro Goldoni."

Washington, D.C., seemed to stand still. Suspended animation. I actually for a while stopped breathing. I felt stifled.

"Are you there, Andrew?" Pucinelli said.

I let out a long breath. "Yes . . ."

"No one has seen Pietro Goldoni since the summer. Everyone thinks he went abroad and hasn't come back." He sounded pleased. "It fits the timetable, doesn't it? We chased him out of Italy and he went to England."

"Er . . ." I said faintly. "Have you heard about Morgan Freemantle? Did you read anything in the papers yesterday or today, see anything on television?"

"Who? I have been so busy in Milan. Who is Morgan Freemantle?"

I told him. I also said, "Bruno and Beatrice Goldoni have been here all this week in Washington. I have talked to them. Brunelleschi won the big International race here yesterday afternoon. Alessia Cenci rode it."

There was the same sort of stunned breathless silence from his end as there had been from mine.

"He is there," he said finally. "Pietro Goldoni is in Washington."

"Yeah."

"You of course knew that."

"I assumed that Giuseppe-Peter was here, yes."

He paused, considering. "In what way is it best that I inform the American police of his identity? It may be that my superiors would want to consult . . ."

"If you like," I said politely, "I myself will first tell the police captain in charge of things here. The captain might be pleased to talk to you then direct. There's an Italian-speaker in his force who could translate for you both."

Pucinelli was grateful and careful not to sound it. "That would be excellent. If you would arrange it, I am sure it would be helpful."

"I'll do it at once," I said.

"It is Sunday," he said, almost doubtfully.

"But you yourself are working," I pointed out. "And I'll reach him, somehow."

He gave me his schedule of times on and off duty, which I wrote down.

"You've done marvels, Enrico," I said warmly, near the end. "I do congratulate you. It must be worth promotion."

He laughed shortly, both pleased and unhopeful. "This Goldoni has still to be caught." A thought struck him. "In which country, do you think, will he be brought to trial?"

"On his past record," I said dryly, "nowhere. He'll skip to South America as soon as the police get near him here, and next year maybe a polo player will be snatched from out of a chukka."

"What?"

"Untranslatable," I said. "Goodbye for just now."

I telephoned immediately to Kent Wagner's headquarters and by dint of threats and persuasion finally tracked him to the home of his niece, who was celebrating her birthday with a brunch.

"Sorry," I said; and explained at some length.

"Jesus Christ," he said. "Who is this guy Pucinelli?"

"A good cop. Very brave. Talk to him."

"Yeah."

I gave him the telephone numbers and Enrico's schedule. "And the Goldonis are going to New York," I said. "Mrs. Goldoni told me. I think they're going today. They've been staying here at the Regency."

"I'll get onto it right away. Will you be at the Sherryatt still?"

"Yes, I'm there now."

"Stay by the phone."

"O.K."

He grunted. "Thanks, Andrew."

"A pleasure, Kent," I said, meaning it. "Just catch him. He's all yours."

As soon as I put the receiver down there was a knock on the door, and I was already opening it before it occurred to me that perhaps I should start to be careful. It was only the maid, however, on my doorstep; short, dumpy, middle-aged and harmless, wanting to clean the room.

"How long will you be?" I said, looking at the cart of fresh linen and the large vacuum cleaner.

She said in Central-American Spanish that she didn't understand. I asked her the same question in Spanish. Twenty minutes, she said stolidly. Accordingly I lifted the telephone, asked the switchboard to put any calls through to me in the lobby temporarily, and went downstairs to wait.

To wait—and to think.

I thought chiefly about Beatrice Goldoni and her excited guilt. I thought of her son, banished from his father's house. I thought it highly likely that it wasn't a lover Beatrice had been sneaking off to meet in Washington that Friday, but a still beloved black sheep. He would have set it up himself, knowing she was there for the race, and still feeling, on his part, affection.

For a certainty she didn't know he was the kidnapper of Alessia and Freemantle. She hadn't that sort of guile. She did know, however, that it had been I who'd negotiated Alessia's ransom, because at that Friday breakfast Paolo Cenci had told her. What else he had told her, heaven knew. Maybe he had told her also about Dominic: it wouldn't have been unreasonable. Many people didn't understand why Liberty Market liked to keep quiet about its work, and saw no great harm in telling.

I had myself driven Beatrice into Washington; and she talked, always, a lot. Chatter, chatter, we're here with the Cencis, you remember Alessia who was kidnapped . . . and there's a young man with her, the one who came to Italy to get her back safely . . . he's here because of this other kidnapping . . . and Paolo Cenci told us he rescued a little boy called Dominic in England . . . Alessia was there too . . . chatter, chatter, chatter.

I stood up from the lobby sofa, went to the desk, and said I was checking out; would they please prepare my bill. Then I got through again to Kent Wagner, who said I'd just caught him, he was leaving the brunch.

"You sure as hell broke up my day," he said, though sounding philosophical. "Thought of something else?"

I said I was leaving the Sherryatt, and why.

"Jee-sus," he said. "Come down to headquarters; I'll put you into a good place where Goldoni would never find you . . . it's sure prudent to assume that he does now know you exist."

"Might be safer," I agreed. "I'm on my way."

The desk said my account would be ready when I came down with my gear. The twenty minutes was barely up, but when I stepped out of the lift I saw the maid pushing her cart away down the passage. I unlocked my door and went in.

There were three men in there, all in high-domed peaked caps and white overalls, with International Rug Co. Inc. on chests and backs. They had pushed some of the furniture to the walls and were unrolling a large Indian-type rug in the cleared free center.

"What . . ." I began. And I thought: it's Sunday.

I spun on my heel to retreat, but it was already too late.

A fourth man, International Rug Co. Inc. on his chest, was blocking the doorway; advancing, stretching out his arms, thrusting me forcefully backwards into the room.

I looked into his eyes . . . and knew him.

I thought in lightning flashes.

I thought: I've lost.

I thought: I'm dead.

I thought: I meant to win. I thought I would win. I

thought I'd find him and get him arrested and stop him, and it never seriously occurred to me it could be this way round.

I thought: I'm a fool . . . and I've lost . . . I thought I would win, and Brunelleschi . . . the danger . . . has beaten me.

Everything happened very fast, in a blur. A sort of canvas bag came down over my head, blocking out sight. I was tripped and tossed by many hands to the floor. There was a sharp sting in my thigh, like a wasp. I was conscious of being turned over and over . . . realized dimly that I was being rolled up like a sausage in the Indian rug.

It was the last thing I thought for quite a long while.

I woke up out of doors, feeling cold.

I was relieved to wake up at all, but that said, could find little else of comfort.

For a start, I had nothing on.

Sod it, I thought furiously. True to bloody form. Just like Alessia. Morgan Freemantle . . . he too, I dared say, was currently starkers.

Liberty Market's own private unofficial training manual, issued to each partner on joining, spelled it out: "immediate and effective domination and demoralization of the victim is achieved by depriving him/her of clothes."

Dominic had had clothes: they'd even added a jersey to his tiny shorts. Dominic, on the other hand, was too little to find anything humiliating in nakedness. There would have been no point.

The only thing to do was to try to think of myself as dressed.

I was sitting on the ground; ground being loamy earth covered with fallen leaves. I was leaning against the tree from which most of the said leaves appeared to have descended: a small tree with a smooth hard trunk no more than four inches in diameter.

The view was limited on every side by growths of evergreen; mostly, it seemed to me ironically, of laurel. I was in a small clearing, with only one other youthful tree for company. Beech trees, perhaps, I thought.

The main and most depressing problem was the fact of being unable to walk away on account of having something that felt like handcuffs on my wrists, on the wrong side of the tree trunk, behind my back.

It was quiet in the clearing, but beyond I could hear the muffled constant roar which announced itself as city. Wherever I was, it wasn't far out. Not nearly as far, for instance, as Laurel. More like a mile or two . . . in a suburb.

I opened my mouth and yelled at the top of my lungs the corny old word "Help." I yelled it many times. Consistently negative results.

The sky, so blue for the race-week, was clouding over: gray, like my thoughts.

I had no idea what time it was. My fingers, exploring, discovered I had no watch.

I could stand up.

I stood.

I could kneel down: didn't bother.

I could circle round the tree.

I did that. The surrounding greenery was similar from all angles.

The branches of the tree spread from just above

my head, narrow hard arms ending in smaller off-shoots and twigs. A good many tan-colored leaves still clung there. I tried shaking them off, but my efforts hardly wobbled them and they stubbornly remained.

I sat down again and thought a good many further unwelcome thoughts, chief among them being that in the Liberty Market office I would never live this day down . . . if ever I lived to tell.

Getting myself kidnapped . . . bloody stupid.

Embarrassing to a degree.

I thought back . . . If Pucinelli had been easier to reach I would have learned about the Goldoni family sooner, and I would have been long gone by the time the International Rug Co. Inc. arrived at the Sherry-att with their rug.

If I hadn't gone back upstairs to fetch my things . . .

If, if, if.

I thought of the face of Giuseppe-Peter-Pietro Goldoni coming through my bedroom door; intent, determined, a soldier in action, reminding me in his speed and neatness of Tony Vine. He had himself taken Dominic from the beach, and in a mask had been there personally to seize Alessia. It was possible to imagine that it had been he who had announced himself as the chauffeur to collect Morgan Freemantle; and if so the actual act of successful abduction could be almost as potent a satisfaction to him as the money it brought.

If I understood him, I wondered, would I be better equipped? I'd never negotiated face to face with a kidnapper before: always through proxies. The art of coercive bargaining, Liberty Market training manual, chapter six. Hard to be coercive while at the present disadvantage.

Time passed. Airliners flew at intervals overhead and a couple of birds came crossly to inspect the stranger in their territory. I sat, not uncomfortably, trying to shape my mind to the possibility of remaining where I was for some time.

It began to rain.

The tree gave little shelter, but I didn't particularly mind. The drops spattered through the dying leaves in a soft shower, fresh and interesting on my skin. I'd never been out in the rain before with no clothes on, that I could remember. I lifted my face up, and opened my mouth, and drank what came my way.

After a while the rain stopped, and it grew dark. All night, I thought coldly.

Well. All night, then. Face it. Accept it. It's not so hard.

I was strong and healthy and possessed of a natural inborn stamina which had rarely been tested anywhere near its limits. The restriction to my arms was loose and not unbearable. I could sit there for a long time without suffering. I guessed, in fact, that I would have to.

The greatest discomfort was cold, to which I tried to shut my mind, joined, as the night advanced, by a desire for a nice hot dinner.

I tried on and off to rub the handcuffs vigorously against the tree trunk to see if the friction would do anything spectacularly useful like sawing the wood right through. The result of such labors was a slight roughening of the tree's surface and a more considerable roughening of the skin inside my arms. Small the tree trunk might be, but densely, forbiddingly solid.

I slept, on and off, dozing quite deeply and toppling sideways once, waking later with my nose on the dead leaves and my shoulders stretched and aching. I tried to find a more comfortable way of lying, but everything was compromise: sitting was the best.

Waiting, shivering, for dawn, I began to wonder seriously for the first time whether he intended simply to leave me to the elements until I died.

He hadn't killed me in the hotel. The injection in my thigh which had put me unconscious could just as easily have been fatal, if death had been what he intended. A body in a rug could have been carried out of a hotel as boldly dead as unconscious. If he'd simply wanted me out of his life, why was I still in it?

If he'd wanted revenge . . . that was something else.

I'd told Kent Wagner confidently that Giuseppe-Peter wouldn't kill by inches . . . and perhaps I'd been wrong.

Well, I told myself astringently, you'll just have to wait and see.

Daylight came. A gray day, the clouds lower, scurrying, full of unhappy promise.

Where's the Verdi? I thought. I wouldn't mind an orchestral earful. Verdi . . . Giuseppe Verdi.

Oh, well. Giuseppe . . . It made sense.

Peter was his own name—Pietro—in English.

Coffee wouldn't be bad, I thought. Ring room service to bring it.

The first twenty-four hours were the worst for a kidnap victim: chapter one, Liberty Market training manual. From my own intimate viewpoint, I now doubted it.

At what would have been full daylight except for the clouds, he came to see me.

I didn't hear him approach, but he was suddenly there, half behind me, stepping round one of the laurels; Giuseppe-Peter-Pietro Goldoni, dressed in his brown leather jacket with the gold buckles at the cuffs.

I felt as if I had known him forever, yet he was totally alien. There was some quality of implacability in his approach, a sort of mute violence in the way he walked, a subtle arrogance in his carriage. His satisfaction at having brought me to this pass was plain to see, and the hairs rose involuntarily all up my spine.

He stopped in front of me and looked down.

"Your name is Andrew Douglas," he said in English. His accent was pronounced, and like all Italians he had difficulty with the unfamiliar Scots syllables, but his meaning was clear.

I looked back at him flatly and didn't reply.

Without excitement but with concentration he returned me look for look, and I began to sense in him the same feeling about me as I had about him. Professional curiosity, on both sides.

"You will make a tape recording for me," he said finally.

"All right."

The ready agreement lifted his eyebrows: not what he'd expected.

"You do not ask . . . who I am."

I said, "You're the man who abducted me from the hotel."

"What is my name?" he asked.

"I don't know," I said.

"It is Peter." A very positive assertion.

"Peter." I inclined my head, acknowledging the introduction. "Why am I here?"

"To make a tape recording."

He looked at me somberly and went away, his head round and dark against the sky, all his features long familiar because of the picture. I'd nearly got him right, I thought. Maybe in the line of the eyebrows I'd been wrong: his were straighter at the outer edge.

He was gone for a period I would have guessed at as an hour, and he returned with a brown traveling bag slung from one shoulder. The bag looked like fine leather, with gold buckles. All of a piece.

From his jacket he produced a large sheet of paper which he unfolded and held for me to read.

"This is what you will say," he said.

I read the message, which had been written in laborious block capitals by an American, not by Giuseppe-Peter himself.

It said:

I AM ANDREW DOUGLAS, UNDERCOVER COP. YOU IN THE FUCKING JOCKEY CLUB, LISTEN GOOD. YOU'VE GOT TO SEND THE TEN MILLION ENGLISH POUNDS, AS WAS SAID. THE CERTIFIED CHECK'S

GOT TO BE READY TUESDAY. SEND IT TO ACCOUNT NUMBER ZL237/42806, CREDIT HELVETIA, ZURICH, SWITZERLAND. WHEN THE CHECK IS CLEARED, YOU GET FREEMANTLE BACK, NO FINGERS MISSING. THEN SIT TIGHT. IF THE COPS COME IN, I WON'T BE MAKING IT. IF EVERYTHING IS ON THE LEVEL AND THE BREAD IS SATISFACTORY, YOU'LL BE TOLD WHERE TO FIND ME. IF ANYONE TRIES TO BLOCK THE DEAL AFTER FREEMANTLE GOES LOOSE, I'LL BE KILLED.

He tucked the paper inside the front of his jacket and began to pull a tape recorder from the leather bag.

"I'm not reading that," I said neutrally.

He stopped in mid-movement. "You have no choice. If you do not read it, I will kill you."

I said nothing, simply looked at him without challenge; trying to show no worry.

"I will kill you," he said again: and I thought yes, perhaps, but not for that.

"It's bad English," I said. "You could have written it better yourself."

He let the tape recorder's weight fall back into the bag. "Are you telling me," he asked with incredulity, "that you are not reading this because of the style literary?"

"Literary style," I said. "Yes."

He turned his back on me while he thought, and after a while turned back.

"I will change the words," he said. "But you will read only what I say. Understand? No . . ." He searched for the words but said finally in Italian, "No code words. No secret signals."

I thought that if I kept him speaking English it might fractionally reduce my disadvantage, so I said, "What did you say? I don't understand."

He narrowed his eyes slightly. "You speak Spanish. The maid at the hotel said you were a Spanish gentleman. I think you also speak Italian."

"Very little."

He pulled the paper from his jacket and found a pen, and, turning the sheet over, began to write a new version for me, supporting it on the bag. When he'd finished, he showed it to me, holding it so that I could read.

In elegant handwriting the note now said:

I AM ANDREW DOUGLAS. JOCKEY CLUB, COL-
LECT TEN MILLION ENGLISH POUNDS. TUESDAY,
SEND CERTIFIED BANKER'S DRAFT TO ACCOUNT
NUMBER ZL237/42806, CREDIT HELVETIA,
ZURICH, SWITZERLAND. WHEN THE BANK CLEARS
THE DRAFT, MORGAN FREEMANTLE RETURNS.
AFTER THAT, WAIT. POLICE MUST NOT INVESTI-
GATE. WHEN ALL IS PEACE, I WILL BE FREE. IF
THE MONEY IS NOT ABLE TO BE TAKEN OUT OF THE
SWISS BANK, I WILL BE KILLED.

"Well," I said. "It's much better."

He reached again for the tape recorder.

"They won't pay ten million," I said.

His hand paused again. "I know that."

"Yes, I'm sure you do." I wished I could rub an itch on my nose. "In the normal course of events you would expect a letter to be sent to your Swiss account number from the Jockey Club, making a more realistic proposal.''

He listened impassively, sorting the words into Italian, understanding. "Yes," he said.

"They might suggest paying a ransom of one hundred thousand pounds," I said.

"That is ridiculous."

"Perhaps fifty thousand more, to cover your expenses."

"Still ridiculous."

We looked at each other assessingly. In the normal course of events negotiation of a ransom price was not conducted like this. On the other hand, what was there to prevent it?

"Five million," he said.

I said nothing.

"It must be five," he said.

"The Jockey Club has no money. The Jockey Club is just a social club, made up of people. They aren't all rich people. They cannot pay five million. They do not have five million."

He shook his head without anger. "They are rich. They have five million, certainly. I know."

"How do you know?" I asked.

His eyelids flickered slightly, but all he said again was, "Five million."

"Two hundred thousand. Positively no more."

"Ridiculous."

He stalked away and disappeared between the laurel bushes, and I guessed he wanted to think and not have me watch him at it.

The Swiss bank account was fascinating, I thought: and clearly he intended to move the money more or less at once from ZL237/42806 to another account number, another bank even, and wanted to be sure the Jockey Club hadn't thought of a way of stopping him or tracing him, or laying a trap. As some of England's top banking brains could be found either in or advising the Jockey Club, his precautions made excellent sense.

One victim in return for the ransom itself.

One victim to return when the ransom had disappeared into further anonymity.

Morgan Freemantle for money, Andrew Douglas for time.

No drops to be ambushed by hepped-up carabinieri: no stacks of tatty—and photographed—notes: just numbers, stored electronically, sophisticated and safe. Subtract the numbers from the gentlemen of the Jockey Club, add the total, telex it to Switzerland.

With his money in Zurich, Giuseppe-Peter could lose himself in South America and not be affected by its endemic inflation. Swiss francs would ride any storm.

Alessia's ransom, at a guess, had gone to Switzerland the day it had been paid, changed into francs, perhaps, by a laundryman. Same for the racecourse owner, earlier. Even with the Dominic operation showing a heavy loss, Giuseppe-Peter must already have amassed an English million. I wondered if he had set a target at which he would stop, and I wondered also whether once a kidnapper, always a kidnapper, addicted: in his case, for ever and ever.

I found I still thought of him as Giuseppe-Peter, from long habit. Pietro Goldoni seemed a stranger.

He came back eventually and stood in front of me, looking down.

''I am a businessman,'' he said.

''Yes.''

''Stand up when you talk to me.''

I thrust away the first overwhelming instinct to refuse. Never antagonize your kidnapper: victim lesson number two. Make him pleased with you; make him like you; he will be less ready to kill.

Sod the training manual, I thought mordantly: and stood up.

''That's better,'' he said. ''Every time I am here, stand up.''

''All right.''

''You will make the recording. You understand what I wish to say. You will say it.'' He paused briefly. ''If I do not like what you say, we will start again.''

I nodded.

He pulled the black tape recorder from the leather bag and switched it on. Then he plucked the sheet of instructions from his jacket pocket, shook it open, and held it, with his own version towards me, for me to read. He gestured to me to start, and I cleared my voice and said as unemotionally as I could manage:

''This is Andrew Douglas. The ransom demand for Morgan Freemantle is now reduced to five million pounds . . .''

Giuseppe-Peter switched off the machine.

''I did not tell you to say that,'' he said intensely.

"No," I agreed mildly. "But it might save time."

He pursed his lips, considered, told me to start again, and pressed the record buttons.

"This is Andrew Douglas. The ransom demand for Morgan Freemantle is now reduced to five million pounds. This money is to be sent by certified banker's draft to the Credit Helvetia, Zurich, Switzerland, to be lodged in account number ZL237/42806. When that account has been credited with the money, Morgan Freemantle will be returned. After that there are to be no police investigations. If there are no investigations, and if the money in the Swiss bank has been paid clear of all restrictions and may be moved to other accounts without stoppage, I will be freed."

I halted. He pressed the stop buttons and said, "You have not finished."

I looked at him.

"You will say that unless these things happen, you will be killed."

His dark eyes looked straight at mine; level, at my own height. I saw only certainty. He pressed the start buttons again and waited.

"I am told," I said in a dry voice, "that unless these conditions are met, I will be killed."

He nodded sharply and switched off.

I thought: he will kill me anyway. He put his tape recorder into one section of his bag and began feeling into another section for something else. I had the most dreadful lurch of fear in my gut and tried with the severest physical will to control it. But it wasn't a gun or a knife that he brought out of the bag: it was a cola bottle containing a milky-looking liquid.

The reaction was almost as bad. In spite of the chilly air, I was sweating.

He appeared not to have noticed. He was unscrewing the cap and looking in the bag for what proved to be a fat, plastic, gaily-striped drinking straw.

"Soup," he said. He put the straw into the bottle and offered it to my mouth.

I sucked. It was chicken soup, cold, fairly thick. I drank all of it quite fast, afraid he would snatch it away.

He watched without comment. When I'd finished he threw the straw on the ground, screwed the top on the bottle and replaced it in the bag. Then he gave me another long, considering, concentrated stare, and abruptly went away.

I sat down regrettably weakly on the loamy ground.

God dammit, I thought. God dammit to hell.

It is in myself, I thought, as in every victim; the hopeless feeling of indignity, the sickening guilt of having been snatched.

A prisoner, naked, alone, afraid, dependent on one's enemy for food . . . all the classic ingredients of victim breakdown syndrome. The training manual come to life. Knowing so well what it was like from other people's accounts didn't sufficiently shield one from the shock of the reality.

In the future I would understand what I was told

not just in the head but with every remembered pulse.

If there were a future.

Nineteen

Rain came again, at first in big heavy individual drops, splashing with sharp taps on the dead leaves, and then quite soon in a downpour. I stood up and let the rain act as a shower, soaking my hair, running down my body, cold and oddly pleasant.

I drank some of it again, getting quite good at swallowing without choking. How really extraordinary I must look, I thought, standing there in the clearing getting wet.

My long-ago Scottish ancestors had gone naked into battle, whooping and roaring down the heather hillsides with sword and shield alone and frightening the souls out of the enemy. If those distant clansmen, Highland born in long-gone centuries, could choose to fight as nature made them, then so should I settle for the same sternness of spirit in this day.

I wondered if the Highlanders had been fortified before they set off by distillations of barley. It would give one more courage, I thought, than chicken soup.

It went on raining for hours, heavily and without pause. Only when it again began to get dark did it ease off, and by then the ground round the tree was so wet that sitting on it was near to a mud bath. Still, having stood all day, I sat. If it rained the next day, I thought wryly, the mud would wash off.

The night was again long and cold, but not to the point of hypothermia. My skin dried when the rain stopped. Eventually, against all the odds, I again went to sleep.

I spent the damp dawn and an hour or two after it feeling grindingly hungry and drearily wondering whether Giuseppe-Peter would ever come back: but he did. He came as before, stepping quietly, confidently, through the laurel screen, wearing the same jacket, carrying the same bag.

I stood up at his approach. He made no comment; merely noted it. There was a fuzz of moisture on his sleek hair, a matter of a hundred percent humidity rather than actual drizzle, and he walked carefully, picking his way between puddles.

It was Tuesday, I thought.

He had brought another bottle of soup, warm this time, reddish-brown, tasting vaguely of beef. I drank it more slowly than the day before, moderately trusting this time that he wouldn't snatch it away. He waited until I'd finished, threw away the straw, screwed the cap on the bottle, as before.

"You are outside," he said unexpectedly, "while I make a place inside. One more day. Or two."

After a stunned moment I said, "Clothes . . ."

He shook his head. "No." Then, glancing at the clouds, he said, "Rain is clean."

I almost nodded, an infinitesimal movement, which he saw.

"In England," he said, "you defeated me. Here, I defeat you."

I said nothing.

"I have been told it was you, in England. You who found the boy." He shrugged suddenly, frustratedly, and I guessed he still didn't know how we'd done it. "To take people back from kidnap, it is your job. I did not know it was a job, except for the police."

"Yes," I said neutrally.

"You will never defeat me again," he said seriously.

He put a hand into the bag and brought out a much creased, much traveled copy of the picture of himself, which, as he unfolded it, I saw to be one of the original printing, from way back in Bologna.

"It was you, who drew this," he said. "Because of this, I had to leave Italy. I went to England. In England, again this picture. Everywhere. Because of this I came to America. This picture is here now, is it not?"

I didn't answer.

"You hunted me. I caught you. That is the difference."

He was immensely pleased with what he was saying.

"Soon, I will look different. I will change. When I have the ransom I will disappear. And this time you will not send the police to arrest my men. This time I will stop you."

I didn't ask how. There was no point.

"You are like me," he said.

"No."

"Yes . . . but between us, I will win."

There could always be a moment, I supposed, in which enemies came to acknowledge an unwilling respect for each other, even though the enmity between them remained unchanged and deep. There was such a moment then: on his side at least.

"You are strong," he said, "like me."

There seemed to be no possible answer.

"It is good to defeat a strong man."

It was the sort of buzz I would have been glad not to give him.

"For me," I said, "are you asking a ransom?"

He looked at me levelly and said, "No."

"Why not?" I asked; and I thought, why ask, you don't want to know the answer.

"For Freemantle," he said merely, "I will get five million pounds."

"The Jockey Club won't pay five million pounds," I said.

"They will."

"Morgan Freemantle isn't much loved," I said. "The members of the Jockey Club will resent every penny screwed out of them. They will hold off, they'll argue, they'll take weeks deciding whether each member should contribute an equal amount, or whether the rich should give more. They will keep you waiting . . . and every day you have to wait, you risk the American police finding you. The Americans are brilliant at finding kidnappers . . . I expect you know."

"If you want food you will not talk like this."

I fell silent.

After a pause he said, "I expect they will not pay

exactly five million. But there are many members. About one hundred. They can pay thirty thousand pounds each, of that I am sure. That is three million pounds. Tomorrow you will make another tape. You will tell them that is the final reduction. For that, I let Freemantle go. If they will not pay, I will kill him, and you also, and bury you here in this ground." He pointed briefly to the earth under our feet. "Tomorrow you will say this on the tape."

"Yes," I said.

"And believe me," he said soberly. "I do not intend to spend all my life in prison. If I am in danger of it, I will kill, to prevent it."

I did believe him. I could see the truth of it in his face.

After a moment I said, "You have courage. You will wait. The Jockey Club will pay when the amount is not too much. When they can pay what their conscience . . . their guilt . . . tells them they must. When they can shrug and grit their teeth, and complain . . . but pay . . . that's what the amount will be. A total of about one quarter of one million pounds, maximum, I would expect."

"More," he said positively, shaking his head.

"If you should kill Freemantle, the Jockey Club would regret it, but in their hearts many members wouldn't grieve. If you demand too much, they will refuse . . . and you may end with nothing . . . just the risk of prison . . . for murder." I spoke without emphasis, without persuasion: simply as if reciting moderately unexciting facts.

"It was you," he said bitterly. "You made me wait six weeks for the ransom for Alessia Cenci. If I did not wait, did not reduce the ransom . . . I would have nothing. A dead girl is no use . . . I understand now what you do." He paused. "This time, I defeat you."

I didn't answer. I knew I had him firmly hooked again into the kidnapper's basic dilemma: whether to settle for what he could get, or risk holding out for what he wanted. I was guessing that the Jockey Club would grumble but finally pay half a million pounds, which meant five thousand pounds per member, if he was right about their numbers. At Liberty Market we would, I thought, have advised agreeing to that sort of sum; five percent of the original demand. The expenses of this kidnap would be high: trying too hard to beat the profit down to zero would be dangerous to the victim.

With luck, I thought, Giuseppe-Peter and I would in the end negotiate a reasonable price for Morgan Freemantle, and the senior steward would return safely home: and that, I supposed, was what I had basically come to America to achieve. After that . . . for myself . . . it depended on how certain Giuseppe-Peter was that he could vanish . . . and on how he felt about me . . . and on whether he considered me a danger to him for life.

Which I would be. I would be.

I didn't see how he could possibly set me free. I wouldn't have done, if I had been he.

I thrust the starkly unbearable thought away. While Morgan Freemantle lived in captivity, so would I . . . probably.

"Tomorrow," Giuseppe-Peter said, "when I come, you will say on the tape that one of Freemantle's fingers will be cut off next week on Wednesday, if three million pounds are not paid before then."

He gave me another long calculating stare as if he would read my beliefs, my weaknesses, my fears, my knowledge; and I looked straight back at him, seeing the obverse of myself, seeing the demon born in every human.

It was true that we were alike, I supposed, in many ways, not just in age, in build, in physical strength. We organized, we plotted, and we each in our way sought battle. The same battle . . . different sides. The same primary weapons . . . lies, threats, and fear.

But what he stole, I strove to restore. Where he wantonly laid waste, I tried to rebuild. He crumbled his victims, I worked to make them whole. His satisfaction lay in taking them, mine in seeing them free. The obverse of me . . .

As before he turned away abruptly and departed, and I was left with an urge to call after him, to beg him to stay, just to talk. I didn't want him to go. I wanted his company, enemy or not.

I was infinitely tired of that clearing, that tree, that mud, that cold, those handcuffs. Twenty-four empty hours stretched ahead, a barren landscape of loneliness and discomfort and inevitable hunger. It began raining again, hard slanting stuff driven now by a rising wind, and I twisted my hands to grip the tree, hating it, trying to shake it, to hurt it, furiously venting on it a surge of raw unmanageable despair.

That wouldn't do, I thought coldly, stopping almost at once. If I went that way, I would crack into pieces. I let my hands fall away. I put my face blindly to the sky, eyes shut, and concentrated merely on drinking.

A leaf fell into my mouth. I spat it out. Another

fell on my forehead. I opened my eyes and saw that most of the rest of the dead leaves had come down.

The wind, I thought. But I took hold of the tree again more gently and shook it, and saw a tremor run up through it to the twigs. Three more leaves fell off, fluttering down wetly.

Two days ago the tree had immovably resisted the same treatment. Instead of shaking it again I bumped my back against it several times, giving it shocks. I could feel movement in the trunk that had definitely not been there before: and under my feet, under the earth, something moved.

I scraped wildly at the place with my toes and then circled the tree and sat down with a rush, rubbing with my fingers until I could feel a hard surface come clear. Then I stood round where I'd been before, and bumped hard against the trunk, and looked down and saw what I'd uncovered.

A root.

One has to be pretty desperate to try to dig up a tree with one's fingernails, and desperate would be a fair description of Andrew Douglas that rainy November morning.

Let it pour, I thought. Let this sodden soaking glorious rain go on and on turning my prison into a swamp. Let this nice glorious fantastic loamy mud turn liquid . . . let this stubborn little tree not have a taproot its own height.

It rained. I hardly felt it. I cleared the mud from the root until I could get my fingers right around it, to grasp. I could feel it stretching away sideways, tugging against my tug.

Standing up I could put my foot under it; a

knobbly dark sinew as thick as a thumb, tensing and relaxing when I leaned my weight against the tree trunk.

I've got all day, I thought, and all night.

I have no other chance.

It did take all day, but not all night.

Hour by hour it went on raining, and hour by hour I scraped away at the roots with toes and fingers, baring more of them, burrowing deeper. The movement I could make in the trunk slowly grew from a tremble to a protesting shudder, and from a shudder to a sway.

I tested my strength against the tree's own each time in a sort of agony, for fear Giuseppe-Peter would somehow see the branches moving above the laurels and arrive with fearsome ways to stop me. I scraped and dug and heaved in something very near frenzy, and the longer it went on the more excruciatingly anxious I became. Given time I would do it. Given time . . . Oh, God, give me time.

Some of the roots tore free easily, some were heartbreakingly stubborn. Water filled the hole as I dug, blocking what I could see, hindering and helping at the same time. When I felt one particularly thick and knotty root give up the contest the tree above me lurched as if in mortal protest, and I stood up and hauled at it with every possible muscle, pushing and pulling, wrenching, thudding, lying heavily against the trunk, digging in with my heels, feeling the thrust through calves and thighs; then yanking the tree this way and that, sideways, like a pendulum.

A bunch of beleaguered roots gave way all together and the whole tree suddenly toppled, taking me down with it in rough embrace, its branches crashing in the rain onto a bed of its own brown leaves, leaving me breathless and exultant . . . and still . . . still . . . fastened.

Every single root had to be severed before I could get my arms out from under them, but I doubt if barbed wire would have stopped me at that point. Scratching and tugging, hands down in water, kneeling and straining, I fought for that escape as I'd never thought to fight in my life; and finally I felt the whole root mass shift freely, a tangled clump of blackly sprouting woody tentacles, their grip on the earth all gone. Kneeling and jerking I got them up between my arms, up to my shoulders . . . and rolled free into a puddle, ecstatic.

It took not so very much longer to thread myself through my own arms, so to speak, bottom first then one leg at a time, so that I ended with my hands in front, not behind my back; an unbelievable improvement.

It was still raining and also, I realized, beginning to get dark. I went shakily over to the laurels on the opposite side of the clearing from where Giuseppe-Peter had appeared, and edged slowly, cautiously, between two of the glossy green bushes.

No people.

I took a deep breath, trying to steady myself, trying to make my knees work efficiently instead of wanting to buckle. I felt strained and weak and in no shape for barefoot country rambles, but none of it mattered. Nothing mattered at all beside the fact of being free.

I could hear only wind and rain. I went on and

came shortly to a sketchy fence made of strands of wire strung between posts. I climbed through and walked on and suddenly reached the top of an incline, the wood sloping away in front: and down there, through the trees, there were lights.

I went down towards them. I'd been naked so long that I'd stopped thinking about it, which was somewhat of a mistake. I was concerned only to get away from Giuseppe-Peter, feeling that he still might find me gone and chase after. I was thinking only, as I approached what turned out to be a very substantial house, that I'd better make sure it wasn't where Giuseppe-Peter was actually staying before I rang the doorbell.

I didn't get as far as ringing the bell. An outside light was suddenly switched on, and the door itself opened on a chain. A pale indistinguishable face inspected me and a sharp, frightened female voice said, ''Get away. Get away from here.''

I started to say ''Wait,'' but the door closed with a slam, and while I hovered indecisively it opened again to reveal the business end of a pistol.

''Go away,'' she said. ''Get away from here, or I'll shoot.''

I thought she might. I looked at myself and didn't altogether blame her. I was streaked with mud and handcuffed and bare: hardly a riot as a visitor on a darkening November evening.

I backed away, looking as unaggressive as I could, and presently felt it safe to slide away again into the trees and reconsider my whole boring plight.

Clearly I needed some sort of covering, but all that was to hand easily were branches of evergreen laurel. Back to Adam and Eve, and all that. Then I'd got to get a householder—a different one—to talk to me without shooting first. It might not have been too difficult in the Garden of Eden, but in twentieth-century suburban Washington, D.C., a proper poser.

Further down the hill there were more lights. Feeling slightly foolish I picked a twig of laurel and held it, and walked down towards the lights, feeling my way as it grew darker, stubbing my toes on unseen stones. This time, I thought, I would go more carefully and look for something to wrap round me before I tackled the door: a sack, a trash bag . . . absolutely anything.

Again events overtook me. I was slithering in darkness under a sheltering canopy-roof past double garage doors when a car came unexpectedly round a hidden driveway, catching me in its lights. The car braked sharply to a stop and I took a step backwards, cravenly ready to bolt.

"Stop right there," a voice said, and a man stepped out of the car, again bearing a pistol. Did they all, I thought despairingly, shoot strangers? Dirty naked unshaven handcuffed strangers . . . probably, yes.

This native wasn't frightened, just masterful. Before he could say anything else I opened my mouth and said loudly, "Please get the police."

"What?" He came three paces nearer, looking me up and down. "What did you say?"

"Please get the police. I escaped. I want . . . er . . . to turn myself in."

"Who are you?" he demanded.

"Look," I said. "I'm freezing cold and very

tired, and if you telephone a Captain Wagner he'll come and get me.''

"You're not American," he said accusingly.

"No. British."

He came nearer to me, still warily holding the gun. I saw that he was of middle age with graying hair, a worthy citizen with money, used to decision. A businessman come home.

I told him Wagner's telephone number. "Please," I said. "Please . . . call him."

He considered, then he said, "Walk along there to that door. No tricks."

I walked in front of him along a short path to his impressive front door, the rain stopping now, the air damp.

"Stand still," he said. I wouldn't have dreamed of doing anything else.

Three orange pumpkin faces rested on the steps, grinning up at me evilly. There was the sound of keys clinking and the lock being turned. The door swung inward, spilling out light.

"Turn around. Come in here."

I turned. He was standing inside his door, waiting for me, ready with the gun.

"Come inside and shut the door."

I did that.

"Stand there," he said, pointing to a spot on a marble-tiled hallway, in front of a wall. "Stand still . . . wait."

He took his eyes off me for a few seconds while he stretched a hand through a nearby doorway; and what it reappeared holding was a towel.

"Here." He threw it to me; a dry fluffy hand towel, pale green with pink initials. I caught it, but couldn't do much with it, short of laying it on the ground and rolling.

He made an impatient movement of his head.

"I can't . . ." I said, and stopped. It was all too damn bloody much.

He parked the pistol, came towards me, wrapped the towel round my waist and tucked the ends in, like a sarong.

"Thank you," I said.

He put the pistol near an adjacent telephone and told me to repeat the number of the police.

Kent Wagner, to my everlasting gratitude, was in his headquarters half an hour after he should have gone off duty.

My unwilling host said to him, "There's a man here says he escaped . . ."

"Andrew Douglas," I interrupted.

"Says his name is Andrew Douglas." He held the receiver suddenly away from his ear as if the noise had hurt the drum. "What? He says he wants to give himself up. He's here, in handcuffs." He listened for a few seconds and then with a frown came to put the receiver into my hands. "He wants to talk to you," he said.

Kent's voice said into my ear, "Who is this?"

"Andrew."

"Jee—sus . . ." His breath came out wheezing. "Where are you?"

"I don't know. Wait." I asked my host where I was. He took the receiver temporarily back and gave his address, with directions. Three miles up Massachusetts Avenue from Dupont Circle, take a right onto Forty-sixth Street, make a right again onto Davenport Street, a quarter mile down there, in the woods.'' He listened, and gave me back the receiver.

"Kent," I said, "bring some men and come very quietly. Our friend is near here."

"Got it," he said.

"And Kent . . . bring some trousers."

"What?"

"Pants," I said tersely. "And a shirt. And some shoes, size ten English."

He said disbelievingly, "You're not . . . ?"

"Yeah. Bloody funny. And a key for some handcuffs."

My host, looking increasingly puzzled, took the receiver back and said to Kent Wagner, "Is this man dangerous?"

What Kent swore afterwards that he said was "Take good care of him," meaning just that, but my host interpreted the phrase as "beware of him" and kept me standing there at gunpoint despite my protestations that I was not only harmless but positively benign.

"Don't lean against the wall," he said. "My wife would be furious to find blood on it."

"Blood?"

"You're covered in scratches." He was astonished. "Didn't you know?"

"No."

"What did you escape from?"

I shook my head wearily and didn't explain, and waited what seemed an age before Kent Wagner rang the doorbell. He came into the hall half grinning in anticipation, the grin widening as he saw the pretty towel but then suddenly dying to grimness.

"How're you doing?" he said flatly.

"O.K."

He nodded, went outside, and presently returned with clothes, shoes, and impressive metal cutters which got rid of the handcuffs with a couple of clips. "These aren't police-issue handcuffs," he explained. "We've no keys to fit."

My host loaned me his cloakroom to dress in, and when I came out I thanked him, handing over the towel.

"Guess I should have given you a drink," he said vaguely; but I'd just seen myself in a looking glass, and I reckoned he'd dealt with me kindly.

Twenty

"You're not doing that," Kent said.

"Yes I am."

He gave me a sidelong look. "You're in no shape . . ."

"I'm fine." A bit tattered as to fingers and toes, but never mind.

He shrugged, giving in. We were out in the road by the police cars, silent as to sirens and lit only by parking lights, where I'd been telling him briefly what had happened.

"We'll go back the way I came," I said. "What else?"

He told his men, shadowy in the cars, to stay where they were and await orders, and he and I went up through the woods, up past the house I'd waited in, and up past the one with the frightened lady: up to the top of the slope, over onto flat ground and through the wire fence.

We were both quiet, our feet softly scuffling on the sodden leaves. The rain had stopped. Behind broken clouds the moon sailed serene. The light was enough to see by, once we were used to it.

"Somewhere here," I said, half whispering. "Not far."

We went from laurel clump to laurel clump and found the familiar clearing. "He came from that way," I said, pointing.

Kent Wagner looked at the uprooted tree for a frozen moment but without discernible expression, and then delicately, cautiously, we passed out of the laurel ring, merging with the shadows, a couple of cats stalking.

He wasn't as good as Tony Vine, but few were. I was conscious just that he would be a good companion in a dark alley, and that I wouldn't have gone back up there without him. He, for his part, had explained that his job was chiefly indoors now, in his office, and he was pleased for once to be outside with the action.

He was carrying a gun like a natural extension of his right hand. We went forward slowly, testing every step, aware of the chance of trip-alarms. There were a good many laurels here among a whole bunch of younger trees and we could get no distant view, but approximately fifty paces from the clearing we caught a glimpse of a light.

Kent pointed to it with the gun. I nodded. We inched in that direction, very careful now, conscious of risk.

We saw no lookouts, which didn't mean there weren't any. We saw the front of a modern split-level house looking perfectly harmless and ordinary, with lights on downstairs and curtains half drawn.

We went no closer. We retreated into the first line

of trees and followed the line of the driveway from the house to the road. At the roadside there was a mailbox on a post, the mailbox bearing the number 5270. Kent pointed to it and I nodded, and we walked along the road in what he confidently assured me was the direction of the city. As we went he said, "I heard the tape you made. Your company relayed it to us from London this morning. Seems the Jockey Club had got it by express courier."

"My company," I said wryly, "were no doubt displeased with me."

"I talked with some guy called Gerry Clayton. All he said was that while you were alive and negotiating it was O.K."

"Nice."

"They did seem to want you back; can't think why."

We walked on, not hurrying.

"I talked to the Goldonis," he said. "Parents."

"Poor people."

I felt him shrug. "He was furious. She was all broken up. Seems she did see her son, did tell him about you. But no use to us. She met him by the Potomac, they walked a ways, then went to some quiet restaurant for lunch. He'd telephoned her in their hotel to fix it . . . never told her where he was staying, himself."

"It figured."

"Yeah."

A step or two further on he stopped, parked the gun in his belt and unclipped a hand radio instead.

"Turn around," he said to his men in the police cars. "Go back to Forty-fifth Street, make a left, make another left into Cherrytree, and crawl along there until you reach me. No sirens . . . No, repeat, no noise. Understood?''

The policemen answered in regulation jargon and Kent pushed down the telescopic aerial of his radio and stuck the black box on his belt.

We stood waiting. He watched me calmly in the moonlight, a hard man offering parity. I felt at ease with him, and grateful.

''Your girlfriend,'' he said casually, ''will be one happy lady to have you back.''

''Alessia?''

''The jockey,'' he said. ''White face, huge eyes, hardly could speak for crying.''

''Well,'' I said, ''she knows what it's like to be kidnapped.''

''Yeah, so I heard. I was talking to her this afternoon. In addition she said she didn't know she loved you that way. Does that make sense? She said something about regretting saying no.''

''Did she?''

He glanced with interest at my face. ''Good news, is it?''

''You might say so.''

''Something about prisoners coming home impotent from Vietnam.''

''Mm,'' I said, smiling. ''I told her that.''

''Glad it makes sense to you.''

''Thanks,'' I said.

''She's still at the Regency Hotel,'' Kent said. ''She said she wasn't leaving until you were free.''

I made no immediate reply, and after a pause he said, ''I didn't tell her you wouldn't make it. That if you did, it would be a miracle.''

''They happen,'' I said; and he nodded.

"Once in a while."

We looked back along the road to where I'd escaped from.

"The house back there is three and a half miles in
a pretty direct route from the Ritz Carlton," he said.
"And . . . did you notice? No pumpkins." He was
smiling in the semidarkness, his teeth gleaming like
Halloween.

He checked things pretty thoroughly, however,
when his cars came, climbing into the back of one of
them, with me beside him, and flicking through
sheets and sheets of computer print-out. The print-
out, I discovered, was of properties offered for
rental, or rented, during the past eight weeks, not
only in the District of Columbia itself but in adjacent
Arlington and parts of Maryland and Virginia. It
seemed to me to have entailed a prodigious amount
of work: and again, like Eagler's efforts, it produced
results.

Kent growled a deep syllable of satisfaction and
showed me one particular sheet, pointing to the
lines:

> # 5270 Cherrytree Street, 20016,
> Rented October 16,
> period 26 weeks, full rental prepaid.

He picked up a map already folded to the right
page and showed me where we were.

"There's the house you called from, on Davenport Street. We walked a block up diagonally
through the woods to Cherrytree, which is parallel
with Davenport. The woods are part of American
University Park."

I nodded.

He heaved himself out of the car to talk to his men, and presently we were riding back in the direction of 5270, driving slowly with side lights only.

Kent and Lieutenant Stavoski, who'd come in the second car, were in full agreement with each other that a sudden all-out raid was best, but a raid on their own well-prepared terms. They sent two policemen through the woods to approach from the rear but stay out of sight, and positioned the cars also out of sight of the house, but ready.

"You stay out here," Kent said to me. "You keep out, understand?"

"No," I said. "I'll find Freemantle."

He opened his mouth and closed it again, and I knew that like all policemen he'd been concentrating almost exclusively on capturing the villains. He looked assessingly at me for a moment and I said, "I'm going in, don't argue."

He shook his head in resignation and didn't try any further to stop me, and it was he and I, as before, who made the first approach, quiet as cobwebs, to the house with no pumpkins.

In the shadow of a laurel I touched his arm and pointed, and he stiffened when he saw what I was showing him: a man standing in an upstairs unlit window, smoking a cigarette.

We stayed quiet, watching. So did the man, unalarmed.

"Shit," Kent said.

"There's always the back."

Behind bushes we slithered our way. The windows facing rearwards to the woodland looked merely blank.

"What do you think?" I asked.

"Got to be done." The gun was back in his hand, and there was both apprehension and resolution in his voice. "Ready?"

"Yes."

Ready, if that included a noisy heart and difficulty in breathing.

We left the shelter of the bushes at the nearest point to the house and crept from shadow to shadow to what was evidently the kitchen door. The door was double; an outer screen against insects, an inner door made half of glass. Kent put his hand on the screen door latch and pulled it open, and tried the handle of the main door beneath.

Unsurprisingly, locked.

Kent pulled the radio from his belt, extended the aerial, and said one single word, "Go."

Before he'd finished returning the radio to his belt there was a sudden skin-crawling crescendo of sirens from in front of the house, and even at the rear one could see the reflections of the revolving lights racing forwards. Then there were searchlights flooding and voices shouting incomprehensibly through megaphones: and by that time Kent had smashed the glass panel of the door and put a hand inside to undo the lock.

There was pandemonium in the house as well as out. Kent and I with the two rear patrolmen on our heels raced through the kitchen and made straight for the stairs, sensing as much as seeing two men pulling guns to oppose the invasion. Stavoski's men seemed to have shot the lock off the front door: in a half glimpse after the staccato racket I saw the blue uniforms coming into the hall and then I was round the bend of the stairs, heading for the upper level.

Still quiet up there, comparatively. All doors except one were open. I made for it, running, and Kent behind me cried agonizedly, "Andrew, don't do that."

I looked back for him. He came, stood out of the line of fire of the door for a second, then leaped at it, giving it a heavy kick. The door crashed open, and Kent with gun ready jumped through and to one side, with me following.

The light inside was dim, like a child's nightlight, shadowy after the bright passage outside. There was a tent in the room, grayish-white, guy ropes tied to pieces of furniture: and standing by the tent, hurrying to unfasten the entrance, to go for his hostage, stood Giuseppe-Peter.

He whirled round as we went in.

He too held a gun.

He aimed straight in our direction, and fired twice. I felt a fierce sharp sting as one bullet seared across the skin high on my left arm, and heard the second one fizz past my ear . . . . and Kent without hesitation shot him.

He fell flat on his back from the force of it, and I went over to him, dropping to my knees.

It was Kent who opened the tent and went in for Morgan Freemantle. I heard the senior steward's slow sleepy voice, and Kent coming and saying the victim was doped to the eyeballs and totally unclothed, but otherwise unharmed.

I was trying with no success at all to wad a handful of folded tent against my enemy's neck, to stop the scarlet fountain spurting there. The bullet had torn too much away; left nothing to be done.

His eyes were open, but unfocused.

He said in Italian, "Is it you?"

"Yes," I said, in his tongue.

The pupils slowly sharpened, the gaze steadying on my face.

"I couldn't know," he said, "how could I have known . . . what you were . . ."

I knelt there trying to save his life.

He said, "I should have killed you then . . . in Bologna . . . when you saw me . . . I should have put my knife . . . into . . . that Spanish . . . chauffeur."

"Yes," I said again, "you should."

He gave me a last dark look, not admitting defeat, not giving an inch. I watched him with unexpected regret. Watched him until the consciousness went out of his eyes, and they were simply open but seeing nothing.

ABOUT THE AUTHOR

Dick Francis is a former champion steeplechase jockey who rode for some years for Queen Elizabeth, the Queen Mother. When age and injury grounded him at thirty-six, he was asked to write a weekly racing column for the London *Sunday Express*. From this experience he branched out into fiction, using the inside world of horses as the background for his novels. Dick Francis is married, lives in Oxfordshire, England, and still rides whenever he can.